The Old Mill

The Old Mill

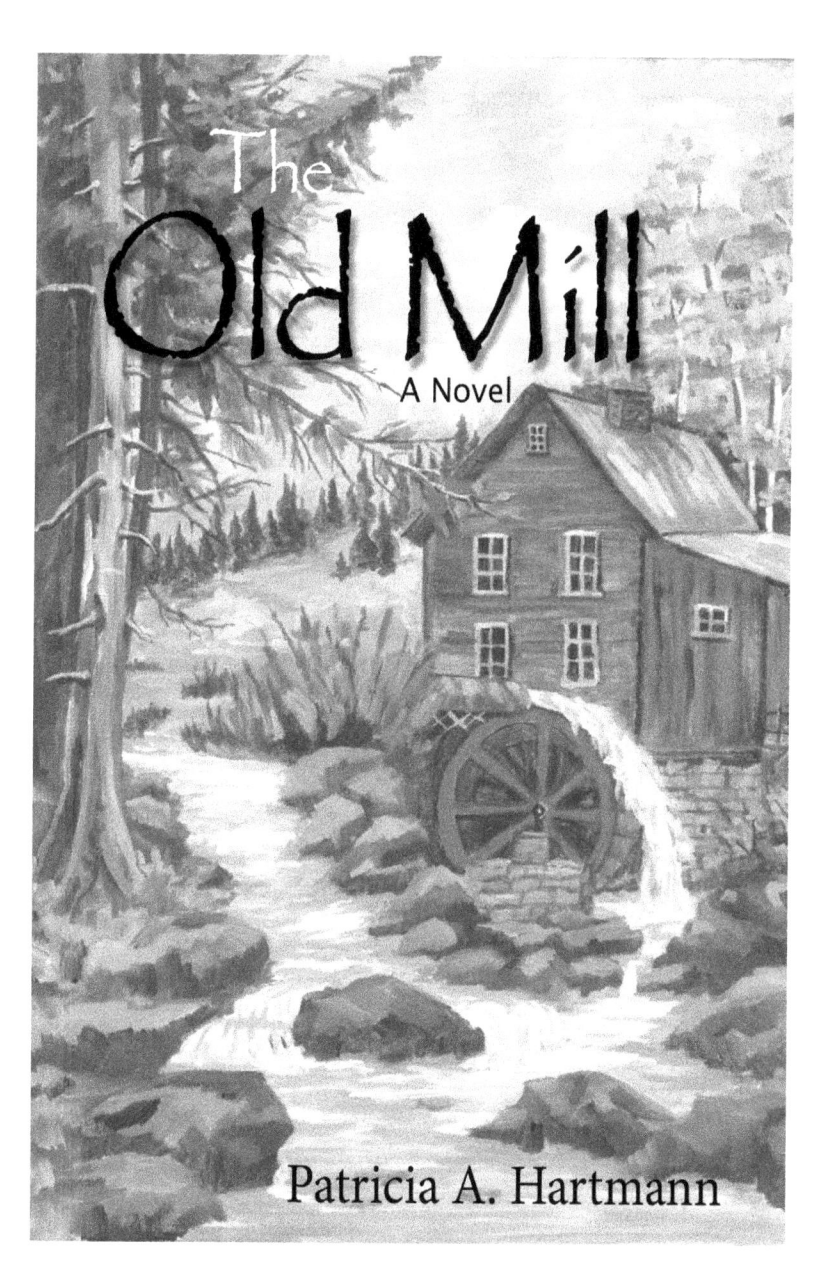

A Novel

Patricia A. Hartmann

XULON PRESS

Xulon Press
2301 Lucien Way #415
Maitland, FL 32751
407.339.4217
www.xulonpress.com

xulon PRESS

© 2021 by Patricia A. Hartmann

All rights reserved solely by the author. The author guarantees all contents are original and do not infringe upon the legal rights of any other person or work. No part of this book may be reproduced in any form without the permission of the author. The views expressed in this book are not necessarily those of the publisher.

Due to the changing nature of the Internet, if there are any web addresses, links, or URLs included in this manuscript, these may have been altered and may no longer be accessible. The views and opinions shared in this book belong solely to the author and do not necessarily reflect those of the publisher. The publisher therefore disclaims responsibility for the views or opinions expressed within the work.

Unless otherwise indicated, Scripture quotations taken from the Holy Bible, New International Version (NIV). Copyright © 1973, 1978, 1984, 2011 by Biblica, Inc.™. Used by permission. All rights reserved.

Paperback ISBN-13: 978-1-6628-3158-4
Ebook ISBN-13: 978-1-6628-3159-1

Patricia Hartmann's
"Buttermilk Falls" Series:

1. Lonesome Mountain
2. Lost Lake
3. The Old Mill

Dedication

To my beloved husband, Larry.
You will always have my heart—
just as I hold yours.

Chapter 1

Away

*Where can I go to escape your Spirit?
I could ask the darkness to hide me...
but to you night shines as bright as day.*
Psalm 139:7-12

The *clacketty-clack, clacketty-clack* of the railway car beat an annoying cadence in Kyle Anderson's ears. Like someone tapping aimlessly on a computer keyboard, typing nonsense. The noise drummed through his skull, his disjointed thoughts as tangled as his life.

He was just a guy on a train—a guy on the run. Not from the law...but from all that his life had become.

The destination didn't really matter. As long as it was *away*.

Kyle ran a hand through his thick thatch of dark hair, neatly styled in the latest cut. Out the train window, the changing landscape sped past. As each mile clicked by, his gut unclenched a little bit more. He threw off his jacket and willed the tension in his throat to relax. Still, he found himself beating a tempo with his fingers on the denim of his jeans. He was only twenty-two, but felt much older. Bit by bit his once youthful idealism had been stripped away, like oozing pine bark scraped raw by a bear itching its back.

The crowded railway car was stifling, sunlight glinting in rhythmic flashes through the closed windows. Each passenger sat, stony-faced, eyes downcast, ears wired to their phones, as a deliberate barrier to any attempt at casual conversation.

Kyle's tumultuous thoughts pounded louder than the music droning through his own ear-buds. A drumbeat of despair. The world, according to his sociology professor, Dr. Karl Lichenstein, was fatally tainted. Dirty politics, global warming, detrimental trade wars...nothing but corruption and greed. From what he'd seen, Kyle was inclined to agree. Here he sat...with a worthless UCLA Bachelor of Arts degree in English Literature jammed in his backpack. Lot of good that would do him.

His exhaustion ran deep. And hopelessness had dug a profound well of sadness in his spirit. Four years of studying and reading the works dead poets. Four years marked by partying, drunken hook-ups and living the insular life of a student.

Kyle regretted much of it now. The women he'd bedded and shedded when they grew too demanding. He tried to forget the names of the girls he'd hurt. The wounded look in their eyes when he broke another promise.

Kyle rubbed at the headache throbbing in his skull. Who had he become? He'd been raised to see value in each human being. Looking back, he saw that he'd lost something fundamental along the way. He'd grown cynical after four years of having his beliefs questioned, his faith mocked and his certainty in anything good shredded by his agnostic professors.

What good was any of it? What good was he?

He massaged his temples...trying not to think at all.

At last, the train left the over-crowded cities and congested freeways behind. High rises gave way to tract homes and then to farmsteads, half-hidden by tall fields of corn. As the tracks began weaving through patches of trees, the air freshened. He cracked open his window and drew in a renewing breath of pine-scented air. The smell revived memories of a simpler time spent on his grandparents' small farm. A time gone forever.

"Chico… Next stop Chico," intoned the conductor over the PA system.

Kyle nervously fingered his backpack. Chico might be as good a place as any to get off. He folded the railway schedule and stuffed it in his pocket, eager to escape the claustrophobic railway car. When the train slowed, he stood, hefted his backpack and exited the coach. He stood alone on the platform as the train rumbled away, his body still swaying from the pulse of the engine.

Mountains rose in the distance. He'd head up there. *Away.*

In downtown Chico, Kyle found a used car lot, where he eyed a brand new, fully-loaded Dodge RAM 1500.

"Lookin' for a truck?" asked a middle-aged salesman wearing a cheap suit, sunglasses and a fake smile.

"Might be…"

"This one's a beauty." The man patted a shiny black fender. "We can arrange financing."

Kyle glanced at the sticker price and raised an eyebrow. Who was he kidding? He only had a modest amount in his checking account, no job, and no prospects. "I need something more reasonable," he admitted. "Like *way* more reasonable."

The salesman's hopes faltered, along with his smile. "This way." He wandered over to the used car section.

An hour later, pretenses gone, Kyle drove off as the proud owner of a white, six-year-old, only slightly dented, Ford 150 pickup truck. He liked the vehicle. Decided to name it Frosty, after his favorite poet.

Next, Kyle drove to a nearby Walmart where he bought a tent, sleeping bag, camp stove, camping chairs and a lantern. He wrangled an ice-chest, skillet, utensils, a few pots and food items into a second cart. After checking out, Kyle unloaded his purchases into the truck bed, and stashed some sacks of groceries in the back seat. He hadn't felt this adventurous in a long time. He ripped open a bag of sour-cream flavored chips, crammed some into his mouth and pointed his white truck north...toward the mountains.

It was the first time in years he'd headed out without a goal or even a plan. Maybe it was better this way. So far...his life hadn't gone at all like he'd imagined it would.

After his folks had been killed unexpectedly during a mission trip in Africa, he'd gone to live with Nana and Papa, his father's parents, for his high school years. On their small farm, they each coped with the devastating loss in their own way. Nana baked. Papa built things. Kyle pitched in with farm chores, tending the livestock. He studied hard at school and played football, where he enjoyed crushing his opponents.

Even back then, Kyle didn't fit in with the other kids. He didn't laugh as easily or joke around. Grief had hollowed him out inside. Made him more somber. More aware of how everything could change in an instant. How nothing good lasts forever.

He was grateful for the farm and the seasonal patterns of crops and weather. Hefting a bale of hay or feeding livestock kept him grounded. He'd been nurtured by his grandparents' love. In the stillness of cool, country nights—he sought solace, looking up at the lovely and lonely stars set in an ebony sky.

After high school, they'd sent him off to college, expressing high hopes for his future. His frugal grandparents had squirreled away their hard-earned money for his school tuition. So, unlike most of his classmates who were mired in student loan debt, Kyle's expenses were covered. With part-time jobs on weekends, he'd only made it home a time or two during breaks. Something he felt guilty about now. At the time, it seemed easier to stay away. Easier to work at a restaurant or coffee bar for spending money, instead of slinging hay and feeding stock. It seemed pretty selfish now.

Kyle had buried both of his elderly grandparents during the fall of his senior year of college, one just a few months after the other. The two solemn services in the town's black-iron fenced cemetery merged in his mind, closely linked by loss and grief. The wind scuttled dry leaves across their grave sites as Kyle had stood alone in the misting rain. Their church's young pastor intoned some timeworn *ashes to ashes…dust to dust* scriptures. New to the parish, the minister hadn't really known his grandparents. But, to Kyle, they'd been a lot more than dust.

Nana and Papa hadn't lived to attend his graduation or witness the liquor-laced sendoff after, at a local bar. In a way, he was relieved they hadn't been there to see how hardened he'd become. How alone he'd felt crossing the stage to receive his diploma, with no one to take note but a few buddies he'd likely never see again.

His grandparents had taught Kyle to use the gifts God had given him to bless others. And for a while he had…helping out when he could, encouraging others who were in a rough patch. But, in the end, Kyle had been no different from his college peers. Doing what he wanted. Rationalizing every sin.

Living only for himself had proved strangely empty. Now, driving through the mountains with the windows open and the warm scent of pine spicing in the air, a faint hope arose. Kyle longed to stir himself to do something worthy. If only he knew what that might be.

These days, Kyle's faith was as shaky as the moldering planks of the old bridge spanning the creek at Papa and Nana's farm. Not to be trusted. He wondered if it was only his grandparents' faith he'd lost? A childlike religion borrowed, but never really believed—roots too shallow to take hold.

As he drove the winding road higher into the mountains, Kyle's mind swayed on the unstable suspension bridge of all his doubts—thoughts jumbled, hands tensing on the wheel.

His stomach rumbled. He hadn't eaten since a hurried breakfast this morning between train stops. With only enough money left in his account to keep him afloat for a few more weeks, Kyle needed to find a way to survive. Later, he'd figure out what the heck to do with the rest of his life.

Kyle read the sign. Buttermilk Falls. *You've got to be kidding.* Someone actually gave a place such a lame name? A tall, imposing mountain loomed over the town. Lonesome Mountain, another road sign announced. *Perfect.* No one was more lonesome than a depressed guy, alone with his thoughts.

He was starved. Kyle parked in front of a well-lit restaurant called "Maggie's Diner." A place right out of the fifties, it seemed. Not a retro reboot, but an actual old place with faded red-leather seats, Formica table tops and a linoleum floor, worn smooth in front of the register.

He ordered a burger and fries from a plump, cheerful woman whose name tag identified her as Maggie. The owner, no doubt. Except for the welcoming smile, she looked about as old and worn out as the restaurant.

"New to town?" she asked.

"Uh huh."

"Plan on staying long?"

"Depends."

"On what?" She clearly wasn't taking the hint.

"Look. I just want to eat, not tell my life story." Kyle whipped out his phone and looked down, flipping through a few apps to deflect any more questions.

"Your burger's coming right up." Maggie patted him on the arm. "You've got the look of someone a bit down in the dumps, but you've ended up in the right place."

Either the burger was really good or he actually was starving after several days trapped on that horrible train. Juicy meat, toasted bun, home-grown tomato, red onions, topped with real cheddar cheese and spicy dill pickles. He wolfed it down and licked the salt of the crispy fries from his fingers. Then guzzled his glass of ice water and ordered a chocolate milkshake to wash it all down.

Kyle fished for his wallet in his front pocket as Maggie came by to clear the table.

"It's on the house," she said, whisking away his empty plate. "Milkshake, too. Newcomer's special."

"What?!" Kyle tried to figure her angle.

"No worries. Just a howdy and welcome to Buttermilk Falls."

"You're kidding..."

"Nope. Looks like you were hungry."

"Hungry as a bear," Kyle admitted. "It was a great burger." With her cheerful expression, Maggie looked less care-worn than he'd first thought. "Thanks," he said, remembering his manners. "I appreciate it." He pulled out money for a tip. "Is there a campground around here?"

Maggie grinned. "Sure... You might want to try Singing Springs. Nice little place." She wiped down the table. "Turnoff's about three miles on down the highway and then another half mile of gravel road from there. You should be able to get there before dark."

"Singing Springs?" His words came out with a more sarcastic tone than he'd intended. "That's a real place?"

"Yep. Go see for yourself." She smiled and bustled off to wait on other customers filling the diner.

A few hours later, his tent was set up in a nice spot beside a gently flowing river. Kyle sat in his camp chair, poking the logs of his campfire, sending sparks flying up into the dark sky. There was something elemental about the soft rush of water and the crackling of the fire. Dark silhouettes of pine trees framed a sprinkling of stars he'd not noticed in years, obscured as they'd been by the bright lights of L.A.

Kyle drew in a deep breath. A man could feel small in a place like this. Or was it only properly cut down to size by the Maker of so vast a universe? Somehow, he didn't feel the need to apologize for God out here. The wilderness itself spoke its creator's name.

He was bone tired. With no night life to juice things up, Kyle doused the fire, crawled into his sleeping bag and was dead to the world by half past eight.

Next morning, Kyle rustled up a breakfast of eggs, crisp strips of bacon, and buttered sourdough bread. For dessert, he plucked a few wild blackberries from a nearby tangle of vines and popped them in his mouth. *Sweet*.

The setting reminded Kyle of the many backpacking excursions he'd taken growing up. Cooking over a campfire or a camp stove was second nature. He enjoyed being self-sufficient and out in nature. After cleaning up camp, Kyle headed out on a trail which promised a look at Singing Springs—3.6 miles away.

It felt good to stretch his legs and feel the soft padding of pine needles beneath his tennis shoes, instead of the hard slap of asphalt. His footfalls were muffled and he took a certain pride in moving quietly enough to be scolded by a stellar jay and the chattering tree squirrel he surprised along the way. The trail paralleled the creek, then tucked back into a ravine at the base of Lonesome Mountain. Shaded by alders and sycamore trees, the track was laced with dappled sunlight.

He heard the spring before he saw it. A melodic sound—part water, part joy. Not the forced gaiety of a cement fountain, but the uninhibited freedom of water bubbling up from the raw earth, tumbling over wet rock, and cascading into a glittering pool. He could have sworn the spring was singing.

He moved his hand through the cool water, then splashed some on his face. As it dripped down his chin and onto his t-shirt, Kyle tried to remember what his life song sounded like…the soul melody he'd once called his own. Sighing, he lay back on the slope of the rock embankment, letting the sunlight warm the cold places inside.

Charlotte Long surprised herself by loving high school. Especially her American Lit class. She found herself enamored by the sound of words. Poems and stories. Verse and rhyme.

When no one was watching, she pulled out a dog-eared notebook and scribbled down a few verses of her own. Nothing all that great. Just observations of things she noticed here at Lost Lake. Today, on a quiet Saturday afternoon, she sat in a rocker on the front porch of Manzanita cabin—the place she was learning to call home. She opened her notebook and read what she'd written a few days ago:

Ponderosa

*The Ponderosa Pine's bark
is jagged—
a jig-saw puzzle
neatly fused together,
linked piece by piece
around its massive trunk.
While above,
scented green pine needles flourish,
holding sap-sticky cones.
All arranged in perfect symmetry—
unlike me.
I'm still
unsure and unformed,
not yet knowing who I'll be.
Or how the scrambled jig-saw pieces
of my life will fit together.
I'm
Trouble tumbled
Mistake fumbled
But maybe…one day
Whole.*

Charlotte tossed a fall of tangled, red hair back over her shoulder. Her green eyes studied the still waters of the lake. When her pup, Bonfire, licked her fingers, she rubbed him behind his ears, just the way he liked it.

At sixteen, Charlotte was still recovering from a childhood marred by an alcoholic mom and a missing dad. Distrustful of others, she could be impulsive and dark tempered. Her inebriated mom had died after ramming their car into a tree, just over a year ago. So, she'd come to live with her father, Rowdy Long, here on the shores of Lost Lake. She'd arrived wounded—her arm broken in the accident…her spirit injured from years of neglect.

She and her dad, Rowdy, a former rodeo cowboy, were still mending fences. Trying to find a way to let the hurts go and the love in.

The poems helped. Got the thoughts out of her head…let the painful emotions find voice and allowed a fragile thread of hope to emerge.

The cabins that Rowdy managed for his son Wyatt, Charlotte's half-brother, were quiet today. Caught between the summer tourist season and the arrival of the first seasonal deer hunters. Charlotte set down her notebook and walked to the sandy shoreline. Bonfire trotted eagerly alongside. She threw a few sticks for the dog to fetch, glad to no longer be encumbered by that old pink cast on her left arm. The arm was tan now, dotted with freckles, the pallor and weakness beneath the cast erased by sunlight and swimming—a skill her brother, Wyatt, had taught her over the summer. She felt healthy and strong. Adventurous. Who knew where that would lead…

Sunlight sparkled atop the rippled blue water of Lost Lake. *Lost Lake?* Had the lake been considered lost before it was first discovered? Or was it just a tranquil and healing place for lost souls to be found? Either way, she was starting to feel at home here, beneath the pine trees and a sky so blue you could almost reach out and use a marker to write poems on its open canvas. Charlotte lifted her arms and twirled in a circle. Bonfire gave a joyous *yap*.

The sky and the quiet lake filled her heart—as fresh and dizzying as all of the impossible possibilities spread out before her.

※

Three days in, Kyle liked the place well enough to considerer hanging out in the area for a while. That meant he'd have to find some work. A paying job to cover groceries and gas money. Plus, with snow due in a few months, camping out wouldn't work for much longer.

His college buddies would have laughed at such a provincial town with its overly-friendly shopkeepers and blatant ignorance of a world going to hell. Instead of debating global issues, he'd overheard the townsfolk gathered at Maggie's Diner chattering about the price of alfalfa, the road-paving project down the highway, or the record-breaking litter of 15 piglets some farmer's sow had farrowed down in Greenville.

Didn't they know what was going on in the world? Had they even considered the dangers of climate change or ways to reduce their carbon footprint? Although, he had to admit they seemed pretty tight with nature. No one was jetting across the country or driving a Hummer down the winding dirt roads. Some farmers came to town trailing the smell of manure, with straw clinging to their overalls and mud caked on their work boots. The cows dotting the fields were sleek and well cared for. He had to admit that he liked these folks. Liked their honesty and lack of pretense.

Kyle headed out in his truck, Frosty, wondering if the local paper had a help-wanted section. Probably not much of an opportunity here for a guy with an American Lit degree, but no teaching credential.

He passed a truck with a flat tire pulled off to the side of the road. *Not my problem.* He caught a glimpse of some guy pulling a tire iron from the back. For some reason, he slowed. *Are you crazy?* he thought. *You don't know who that guy is, could be a psycho or a mugger.* But in Buttermilk Falls?

Before he could stop himself, Kyle pulled off, turned around and came up behind the vehicle. "Need some help?" he asked, suddenly aware of the week's growth of dark beard hiding his face. He hadn't bothered shaving since boarding the train.

The man grinned. "Wouldn't turn down the offer," he said. "Want to unbolt the spare from under the truck bed?" He handed off a wrench.

Was the guy messing with him? "Sure." Kyle was up for the challenge of crawling though gravel, even though he hadn't changed a tire since he left his grandparents' farm.

"I'm Gabe. Gabriel Reed. On my way to a construction job." The man held out his hand.

"Kyle Anderson. Nice to meet you." The two shook hands. Firm and solid, noticed Kyle. But thankfully, not a grinding vice-grip…testing either one's manhood.

They worked together, getting the flat tire off and the spare secured.

"Just passing through?" asked Gabe.

"I was," admitted Kyle. "But lately I'm thinking of staying on for a while. Nice little town."

"It is."

Gabe didn't seem like a hick, Kyle noted. Sounded educated… "You wouldn't know of any job openings around here, would you?" he ventured.

"What did you have in mind?"

"I'd take most anything. Worked on my grandparents' farm, growing up. Then in coffee bars and restaurants through school." He gave a little shrug. "I'm fresh out of college with a useless degree in American Lit."

"My wife's a teacher here in town." Gabe tightened a lug nut. "She might know of something."

"Thanks," said Kyle. "But right now, a classroom's the last place I want to be."

Gabe knew the feeling. He remembered Charlie taking him under his wing when he was a high school rip-up. "You know your way around a construction site?"

"Not really," Kyle admitted. "But I helped my grandpa build a barn and we put up our fair share of outbuildings."

"Willing to learn?" asked Gabe, as he put away the tire iron and hefted the flat tire into his truck bed. He wiped his hands on an old towel and handed it off for Kyle to use.

"I am." After so many years stuck behind a school desk and a computer, working with his hands actually sounded appealing.

"Follow me." Gabe climbed into his truck.

Kyle tailed him to a construction site at the edge of town where a remodel of an old recreation center building was in progress.

The two got out of their trucks and Kyle filled out the necessary paperwork. Then Gabe handed him a hard hat, safety glasses and gloves. "You okay with doing some grunt tear-down work for a few days, while I process your workman's comp and employment papers?" He lifted out a long-handled sledgehammer.

"Sure." Kyle didn't even care much about the wages. The idea of taking a sledgehammer to a wall seemed just the outlet he needed—all primal sweat and burning muscles.

"That whole wall has to come down to the framing," directed Gabe. "Trash goes in that dumpster." He nodded toward the bin. "The old electrical has already been disconnected. So, all the old wiring comes out, too." Gabe fished a set of wire-cutters from his truck and handed them over. "Think you can handle it without damaging the studs?"

"Yes, sir."

"You'll start at minimum wage, with a chance to earn more if you stay on and your skills improve."

"I'm good with that."

"I'll leave you to it, then."

Kyle ran a hand along the wall as he noted the placement of the studs. Then he eased back the sledgehammer and swung, bashing a sizeable hole in the drywall. He swung again and again, blasting away the old material, prying chunks of sheet-rock free with the crowbar. *Nice.*

If only the layers of hopelessness inside could be torn down as easily.

He hefted the sledgehammer and swung again. Take that, Professor Lichenstein! *Bam!* And that, you smug enemies of joy! *Bam! Bam!* Take that, you entitled undergrads! *Bam!* Get out of my head, you glib mockers of God and everything good! *Bam! Bam! Bam!*

He was sweating now. Honest sweat. It felt good.

Chapter 2

Weary

*Come to me
all who are weary and burdened
and I will give you rest.*
Matthew 11:28

Lizzy was in trouble. Her husband, Gabe, could see the deep exhaustion in the smudges beneath her eyes and in the guarded look in their depths.

He'd asked too much of her. She'd gamely taken on two step-children in less than a year. And now she was pregnant with their child. Even as strong and spirited as Lizzy was, she'd been pushed too far. Asked to handle too much. What had he expected?

In addition to the children, her teaching job would be starting again in September, less than a month away. And the busy harvest season was just around the corner for the apple orchard and Christmas trees at their home at Sweet Apple Farm. Crazy making. No one could be expected to handle it all and stay sane. Gabe had pitched in as much as he could, but he had his own full-time work as a builder.

With his hip braced against the front porch railing, he raked his fingers through his dark hair, took in a lungful of the crisp morning air, and considered their options. He looked over at the rows of mature apple trees, heavy with fruit. Nothing more rewarding than a bountiful crop—the literal fruit of their labor. The drone of a tractor in the distance told him that their farm manager, Harley, was already at work.

There was a natural rhythm to the seasons out here. Planting and harvest, sowing and reaping, summer and winter. Fall was the in-between time—the earth gone fallow and expectant. Leaves turning gold and tumbling to the ground. A time of letting go.

Gabe went inside. Sitting across from his wife at their farmhouse table, he watched Lizzy toy with the scrambled eggs on her plate. Her other hand lay protectively over her belly, sheltering a womb stretched taut in the fifth month of her first pregnancy. A December baby. Another bout of morning sickness had taken its toll, and he noticed his wife's usual robust appetite had dwindled.

On this day in mid-August, beneath clear blue skies, the temperature outside was quickly rising. Warm gusts from the open window lifted the gauzy curtains. Gabe got up to shut it.

At the breakfast table, Chloe and Max squabbled over the last piece of bacon, which ended up in Chloe's grip.

"It's mine," said Chloe, stuffing the crispy strip in her mouth with a smirk. She gestured to the door. "Go out and get the eggs, Max. I did it yesterday." At six, she was already learning how to boss around her older, more mellow brother.

"No, you didn't," corrected nine-year-old Max. "I found that double-yolker that Miss Lizzy used in the pancakes. Remember?" He scowled when she stuck out her bottom lip and kicked him under the table.

"No kicking," Gabe reminded his daughter. "Chloe...you go out and fetch the eggs...right now."

She frowned. "But I..."

"I'll go do it, if you want," said Max. "I don't mind."

With his legal adoption into the family still pending, Max was being extra careful not to make any waves. Too careful. Gabe had begun noticing how quick his daughter was in taking advantage of the boy's vulnerability.

He rose and put a hand on Chloe's shoulder, shifting the young girl out of her chair. "Thanks, Max, but it's Chloe's turn and she'll do it."

"But, it's getting hot outside..." She shook her dark curls and speared Gabe with a flash of angry, violet eyes.

Gabe handed her the egg basket and pointed her toward the door. "Any more arguing and you'll be doing the breakfast dishes, as well. We all pitch in with chores around here."

Chloe banged the door shut on her way out.

Lizzy, he noticed, was unusually quiet, absent-mindedly pushing blueberries around on her plate, tuning out the kids squabbling in her kitchen.

Max sprang up, eager to help clear the dishes, his sun-streaked blond hair sticking up like spines on a porcupine. The boy, Gabe noted, was still trying to prove himself—determined to earn his keep. Max's abusive, alcoholic father had really done a number on the poor lad over the years. Until the fateful night the man drove drunk once again, wrapping his car around a tree and leaving the boy an orphan. Unable to undo the damage, Gabe balled his hands into fists.

In spite of his troubles, Max was still good-hearted and eager to please. Gabe understood why Lizzy had developed a soft spot for him as his teacher last year. But becoming a happy family, he was finding out, was easier wished for than done.

He needed to get to work, but first, Gabe pulled his wife aside into the relative privacy of the living room. Almost two years ago he'd helped restore this farmhouse for a newly arrived Lizzy, who'd inherited the farm from her great-aunt Daffy.

He looked at their family motto, which he'd painstakingly carved into the thick oak of the fireplace mantle:

Live Simply, Love Deeply

If only it were as simple as the words. He was losing his wife in the midst of the chaos.

He settled her into her favorite recliner, and got her feet up. "What can I do to help?"

"Maybe a soda cracker," she said, through dry lips.

"Feeling nauseous?"

She nodded. "Kind of queasy, today. I thought, this far along, the morning sickness would let up." Lizzy closed her eyes and leaned her head back, tucking a copper-colored curl behind an ear.

Gabe returned with a ginger-ale and a waxed sleeve of soda crackers. He pulled a chair next to hers while she took a bite of cracker. "I've been thinking..." He leaned toward her. "Maybe you shouldn't be teaching this fall."

Her eyes flew open. "What!"

"I know you love teaching," he said. "And you're great at it. But with two kids to raise and a baby on the way... Maybe it's too much."

"I'll take a leave after the baby comes...like I planned."

"You're exhausted already," he gently reminded. "And you'd only have three months of teaching before your leave, anyway."

"I promised I'd be there at Pine Ridge Elementary to start off the school year." She jutted out her chin.

"Only to leave a few months later? Wouldn't that be disruptive for the kids?"

"But I..." Lizzy lost her train of thought. "They...they need me at the school."

"Max and Chloe need you here. You're good with them. And good for them." He ran his fingers along her soft cheek. "You won't want to leave our new baby with a sitter, Lizzy. I know you." His hand cupped her chin. "Things change, love. A teaching job will always be there later on, but our kids are only little once."

"True, but..." Lizzy glanced at the kitchen, where Max earnestly scrubbed the egg pan.

"Think about it," Gabe suggested. "I've got some steady construction jobs lined up. We can cut back here and there." He reached for her hand. "We'll make it work."

Lizzy took a sip of ginger-ale. "It's just that I've been so sick lately. I'll bounce back soon."

Gabe kissed her on the forehead. "You're not Superwoman, Lizzy. Maybe we should hire someone to help out," he offered.

"No. Absolutely not." She tried to sit up straighter. "I can handle things around here."

He brushed the hair back from her temples. "Not saying you can't. But you shouldn't have to do everything. There's a lot on your plate right now."

Lizzy sighed. "Lately all I want to do is sleep."

"Then that's what you should do." He stood. "Listen... I talked with Doris a few days ago. Turns out she's cutting back on her hours at Java Junction and is looking for some other part-time work. If you'd want, she could come by a few afternoons a week to help out. You like Doris, don't you?"

"How can we afford that?"

"We'll figure it out," said Gabe. "I'll just pick up another side job or something. And the money from the apple harvest will be coming in soon."

Lizzy thought about protesting. Gabe was throwing her a life preserver and she knew it. Deep down, she felt relieved. She'd been drowning for a while now...but was just too stubborn to admit it.

"I do like Doris." She remembered how the older woman had shown up on her doorstep when Lizzy first came to Buttermilk Falls, and had become her trusted housekeeper and friend. Truth be told, if she wasn't so bone tired, she'd do a happy dance and kiss the woman's feet. The older woman reminded her of the mother she'd lost. And she hoped her friend's quiet efficiency and enduring love would right the dizzying whirl of responsibilities sucking Lizzy down the drain.

"How'd you know?" she asked, taking Gabe's hand.

"Because I know you," he said. "Because I love you."

"Could she be here by lunchtime?"

Gabe gave a little bow. "Your wish is my command, my lady."

Doris hung her apron on a hook near the back door of the Java Junction kitchen. A smile edged her lips. Gabe's phone call had made her day. Of course, she'd come. She'd missed Lizzy and the farm. Baking here at the shop was fine, but it wasn't family...or as close as she'd come to family since her daughter-in-law made it clear she wasn't wanted at their place.

Her pre-dawn shift in the bakery didn't allow for much social interaction. Gabe had mentioned that Lizzy needed help with the children. With no grandkids to dote on, Doris hungered for the energy and chatter of little ones. How had God known the unspoken needs of her heart? If she hurried, she'd have time to stop at the store to pick up ingredients for chocolate-chip cookies, and arrive with the fixings for lunch.

The farmstead had changed some since she'd moved out. A few toys and a child's trike were scattered in the yard. A rope swing hung from a sturdy branch of the old oak tree. A floppy rag doll lay on the wood plank seat. Chickens clucked in the coop. Doris smiled.

A young boy raced by, Buddy close at his heels, the dog's plumed tail waving. The boy, dressed in cut-off Levi shorts and a faded red t-shirt, stopped and studied her.

"You must be Max," Doris said. "You like chocolate-chip cookies?"

"Yes, ma'am." Max's bright blue eyes were curious and half-hidden beneath his unruly thatch of blond hair.

"I'm Doris," she said, handing the boy a sack of groceries from the trunk of her car. "I'm here to help out. We can bake some cookies right after lunch, if you'd like."

Chloe flew out the front screen door and ran down the front steps. "Doris! You're back." She hugged Doris's knees. "Can we bake some cookies?"

Doris smiled. "If you and Max help."

Chloe let go and arrowed her hands on her hips. "Boys don't make cookies."

So that's the way of it. Doris recognized the territorial claim, one she couldn't allow. She took Chloe's hand. "They do around here. Some of the finest chefs are men. Of course, Max might need you to show him the ropes...if he's new to the finer points of a kitchen."

Max hugged the grocery bag to his chest, eyeing Chloe. "I don't have to help make cookies," he said agreeably. "I can find lots of other stuff to do."

"I'd like your help." Doris ruffled his hair. "We'll do it together." She winked at Max. "And the ones who bake the cookies are the first ones to eat 'em."

"All of 'em?" asked Max.

"Don't let him gobble them all up, Doris," protested Chloe.

"We'll bake plenty for everyone." She handed a second grocery bag to Chloe. "But first, let's eat."

Chloe peered into the bag. "What's for lunch?"

"Peanut butter sandwiches and chips. Bought some nice seedless grapes, too." The little entourage headed up the steps.

At the door, Lizzy enveloped Doris in a belly bumping hug, laughing. "Oh, Doris...you came."

"Of course, I came. Not to live in, this time, mind you... But I'd love to help out a few afternoons a week."

"You're an angel," said Lizzy.

"A pudgy one, then." Doris slapped her hands on her ample hips. "Working as a baker at Java Junction just gives me more sweets to snack on...not more will power." She cupped Lizzy's cheek. "Truth is, I've missed you. And being here at the farm." Doris studied the young woman she'd come to know and love. "You're looking a bit pale, child. Morning sickness?"

"The worst," admitted Lizzy. "It's left me pretty wrung out. I can't seem to get past it."

"I've got just the thing." Doris led the children into the kitchen and rummaged through the shopping bags. She pulled out a package of peppermint tea. "Sit," she instructed Lizzy. In no time at all, she had Lizzy sitting down in the living room with her feet up, sipping soothing peppermint tea, while the children ate grapes and peanut butter sandwiches.

"Thank you." Lizzy closed her eyes and breathed in the tea's warm aroma.

"I'm guessing you could do with a nap," said Doris. "The kids and I will be busy baking cookies. So, you head on upstairs now. Take your cup of tea with you. Let me know when you're hungry, and I'll make you a snack."

"A nap does sound good." Lizzy hesitated. "You sure you're okay watching the kids?"

"Raised two of my own," she said. "Nice to have youngin's around to lick the beaters."

"We get to lick the beaters?" asked Chloe, clapping her hands.

"What's a beater?" questioned Max.

"You'll see." Doris shooed Lizzy from the kitchen toward the stairs. Then she fetched a big package of chocolate chips from a grocery sack. She opened the bag and poured a trail of chocolate bits on each of the kids' plates. "Let the cookie fest begin."

Sheriff Buck Buchanan cruised his SUV through the campground at Singing Springs. The last of the late summer campers had drifted in, and Buck liked to keep an eye out for firearms or any suspicious activity on this part of his route. Hunting season was nearly over, so he expected mostly hikers, fly fishermen and families enjoying a mountain getaway. The campground had no sewer or water hookups, and no electricity, so there were only a few RVs roughing it. Mostly tent campers.

Buck eyed a brand new two-man tent pitched near the river. The Coleman stove, lantern, and ice chest looked new as well. An older, white pick-up truck was parked in the space, the temporary paper registration taped in the window. No one appeared to be in the campsite. A newbie camper or a guy on the run?

Flipping open his laptop, Sheriff Buck ran the plates. Kyle Anderson. Last residence, Los Angeles. Truck purchased three weeks ago in Chico. No outstanding citations or warrants. He got out and looked in the truck windows. No sign of a gun. Just tools and some empty paper coffee cups from Java Junction. The truck bed was empty. Next to the fire pit, a partially carved walking stick leaned against a folding camping chair, the top carved in the rudimentary shape of an eagle's head. Nothing to alert him to any trouble here.

Sheriff Buck got back into his patrol car and rolled farther into the campground, stopping to wave at a group of kids playing by the water faucet. A bunch of yellow jackets, called meat bees, edged the puddle. The pesky wasps liked mud for their nests, and come suppertime, would be drawn to any raw or cooked meat sitting out, including steaks fresh from the grill. The bees were armed with a painful sting that could be inflicted repeatedly — one of the minor perils of outdoor living.

As he rounded the loop, a campsite at the back corner caught his attention. He noted a pile of empty beer cans next to the fire pit. A rusty axe jammed in a green wood log. An opened sack of corn chips tempting wild critters, including bears, to move in and plunder. No vehicle in camp. Buck would check back later. See what people came with the site.

Kyle hefted the last slab of lath and plaster into the dumpster, stepping away to dodge the layer of dust that wafted up. He shoved his safety goggles atop his head and wiped a bandana across his dirty face. After two weeks on the job, he'd grown to appreciate the physicality and purposefulness of the work. Taking a wall down. Removing the wires. Cutting holes through the exterior for a new door and windows. Here, progress was measured in linear feet, not by the perused pages of a book or the carefully composed words of an essay. Kyle enjoyed getting out of his head and into the physical world of lumber and nails. Building something solid and real.

Now, he was learning to hang drywall. How to measure and cut. The best spots for the screws. Taping the seams and applying the drywall mud. With each new task, Gabe walked Kyle through the steps, told him what he wanted, then stepped away and left him to it.

At lunchtime, they'd ended up going to Giovanni's to grab some pizza. They sat outside at a shaded table, drinking soft drinks while they waited for their order.

"You've been a big help on the job," mentioned Gabe. "A fast learner."

"Thanks. I'm enjoying the work."

"How long you planning on staying?"

Kyle hesitated and paused while their pizza was delivered. "Not sure. Suits me okay for now. Don't know if this work is my life's calling."

Gabe took a bite of his pepperoni-cheese slice. "It's not for everyone, but construction's a good skill to know in any case."

"I see that. Most guys want to build something."

Gabe wiped tomato sauce from his fingers. "Yep. Men love their tools."

"Thing is... I'm not ready to settle down." Kyle took a swig of his soda, chewing on the ice. "I want to travel some. See what's out there."

Gabe nodded. "Sure. It's a big world."

"But I need to save some money first. Maybe hit the road when the weather turns cold. Can't very well sleep in a tent come winter."

"True. These mountains are a whole different place when it snows." Gabe rubbed the back of his neck and looked at Kyle. "As far as the money goes...you're due a raise. I could swing it if you'd commit to see this recreation building project through."

"How long would that be?"

"With you on board, I figure we'll wrap up in three to four more weeks...by early September. We're pushing so it's available for the district's after-school programs in the fall.

"I guess I could do that." Kyle reached for another slice. "I appreciate the work."

"Cuts both ways," said Gabe. "Your help frees up some time for me. I'm needing to find a side job or two for some extra income. We just hired on a part-time housekeeper to help out at home."

"I haven't even thought to ask," Kyle remarked. "You have a family?"

"Yep. Wife and two kids. A baby on the way." Gabe was surprised at how settled and ordinary it all sounded, put into words. The reality...not nearly so settled. But he wasn't getting into any of that with Kyle, just yet.

"How about you?" he asked.

"No family," said Kyle. "My folks died on the mission field. I lived with my grandparents after that. They finished raising me. But they passed away a few months back."

"I'm sorry," Gabe said. "That's rough."

"I got through it okay."

But the quick glance away and the slight slump of Kyle's shoulders said otherwise. The gesture reminded Gabe of Max—another orphan boy trying to find his footing. *Guess there's plenty of hurt to go around*, thought Gabe.

"Why don't you come by the house for supper tonight," Gabe suggested, wishing a moment later he could withdraw the invitation. Lizzy wouldn't appreciate company right now.

"You sure?"

"Of course." Gabe put down some bills to cover his half of the tab. As soon as they were back on the job, he'd ring the house, praying that Doris would still be there, willing to pinch-hit for the family and throw something together for supper. Doris was a crackerjack cook. He wouldn't mind some of her famous lasagna.

Gabe winged up a little prayer for one of those side jobs he'd mentioned, scanning the buildings on their return route for the possibility of needed repairs. He really couldn't afford to give Kyle that raise, but the kid reminded Gabe of how he'd been rescued by his mentor, Charlie, at about Kyle's age. Charlie had given him the gift of work, guidance and love...stepping in as a father figure when he'd needed one most.

He looked over at the boy, whose young, earnest face was shadowed by his new beard. There was pain in those eyes, Gabe noticed. Pain and sadness. Kyle deserved a hand up...even if he was going to take off before the first snowfall.

Chapter 3

Vision

Where there is no vision, the people perish, but he who keeps God's law is blessed..
Proverbs 29:18

Gabe ushered Kyle through the back door into the kitchen. He was glad to see that some color had returned to his wife's cheeks and he kissed her lightly before making the introductions.

"Everybody... This is Kyle. Kyle Anderson, my new apprentice carpenter."

Kyle flushed a bit under his dark beard, but managed a smile. "Hello."

Gabe slipped his arm around his wife's waist. "My wife, Lizzy." He motioned toward the children who were setting plates on the table. "My daughter, Chloe and son, Max." He nodded at Doris who was waving a slotted spoon like a magic wand. "And this is Doris, our..."

"...friend and housekeeper," Doris supplied, with a wicked grin.

Gabe might have added *life-saver* and *answer to prayer*, but Doris took charge. "Sit down everybody. The lasagna's ready." In minutes, she had the bubbling pan on the table—tender lasagna noodles layered with cheese and a rich, fragrant meat sauce. She pulled browned garlic bread from the oven, while Lizzy retrieved a green salad from the fridge. The garlicky smells filling the kitchen were heavenly.

Folding his hands, Gabe offered a prayer of thanksgiving for the meal and a silent prayer of gratitude for the changes at home. Lizzy looked rested, her eyes sparkling. The children dug into the meal without squabbling. Was that a plate of chocolate chip cookies on the counter?

"You new to town?" asked Doris as she passed the bread to Kyle, her radar for wounded souls on high alert.

"Yes. I am," said Kyle. "Just graduated from UCLA. Trying to figure out what's next."

Lizzy smiled across at him. "I hear you helped my husband with a flat tire and he took you to work with him."

"Something like that..." Kyle took a big bite of his garlic bread.

"You on summer vacation?" asked Chloe, loudly sucking in a piece of lasagna noodle.

"Not exactly."

"Are you in trouble?" asked Max, risking a shy glance. "Gabe is good at helping."

Kyle stopped chewing.

Doris intervened. "Just finding his way, Max. Like the rest of us." She ruffled the boy's unruly hair and gave Kyle a sympathetic smile.

The meal was beyond delicious, and conversation flowed freely. Lizzy took a second helping of lasagna. The kids sprouted smudges of Italian red sauce around their lips.

As dinner drew to a close, Doris announced, "Hey...we've got chocolate chip cookies for dessert. Who wants one?"

"Me...me..." chorused the children, who'd already eaten nearly half of a baking sheet of warm chocolaty treats before supper.

Doris brought the cookie platter to the table. "There aren't too many ills that fresh baked cookies and hot coffee can't soothe." She filled three mugs. "Welcome to Buttermilk Falls, Kyle."

"And welcome to our home...such as it is," added Gabe. He looked around at impish Chloe, somber Max, and a very pregnant Lizzy, the love of his life, who stretched to ease a kink in her back. He winked at Doris, their rescuer, who'd most likely spent the afternoon bringing order to the house, plying his kids with sugar, and pulling off this scrumptious meal on such short notice. Buddy, their Aussie, snuck under the table and licked the last bit of tomato sauce from Chloe's proffered plate.

"Thanks." Kyle devoured another cookie. "Can't remember my last home cooked meal."

"Well, don't be a stranger," said Lizzy. "You're welcome here any time." She grinned at Doris. "Especially if Doris is cooking."

A few days later, after the kids were tucked in bed for the night, Lizzy joined Gabe on the front porch swing. "You're right," she said.

"Music to my ears. About what?"

"I can't go back to teaching school. Not now. Not for a long while." She laid a hand on her bulging belly. "Don't know what I was thinking."

"Maybe that you love teaching." Gabe laced his fingers with hers on the warm shelf of her baby bump. "You know that moms are teachers, too. Every day's a new lesson."

"I know." She looked up at him. "I went by the school today... handed in my resignation. I think they were relieved."

"Only because they'd rather have someone not going out so soon on maternity leave."

"Yeah. One teacher for the whole year will be much better for the kids."

"And a full-time mom will be better for Max and Chloe." He squeezed her fingers. "Thanks for doing this."

She brought a hand to his face. "Thanks for bringing me to my senses, Honey. Once Doris came on board and I actually took a real nap, my brain fog cleared. Or maybe it was the peppermint tea."

"I'm sorry, Lizzy. I should have said something earlier when I saw how exhausted you'd become."

"I'm going to need your help. Especially with Chloe. She's becoming a little tyrant."

"I've noticed."

"What should we do about it?"

"Not sure..." Gabe stretched out his legs. "For such a long time she was scared of everything—the dark, thunder, strangers, dogs, even your chickens... Who's afraid of chickens?"

"I remember."

"You made all the difference." He kissed her cheek. "I was so happy to see her coming out of her shell that I let too much bad behavior go. But now that Max is here, I see her acting like a little, violet-eyed, spoiled princess."

Lizzy sighed. "She's got Max scared half to death."

"I see that," said Gabe. "He's had some tough breaks. Max needs to know he's part of our family now."

"Yes." Lizzy nodded. "Because he is."

"We may have to be tough on Chloe for a while...reel her back in."

She raised an expressive eyebrow. "While reassuring her we have love enough for both of them. I don't want Chloe to resent Max...just to play fair."

Gabe nodded. "Together, we'll figure it out."

"How?" she asked. "With the baby coming, there will be even more reason for jealousy and insecurity."

"The way we always have." He kissed her pouting lips. *"Live simply, love deeply."*

The start of school brought a new rhythm to the town of Buttermilk Falls. The long idyll of summer was snatched away, amid the rumble of yellow-orange school busses and a flurry of colorful, dry leaves skittering across the roads.

Since the bus didn't come as far out as the cabins, Rowdy took it upon himself to drop Charlotte at Lonesome Mountain High School each school day. His daughter might be okay with a bowl of cold cereal at the cabin, but he had other plans. Since he was already in town, Rowdy treated himself a few days a week to the much heartier breakfast special at Maggie's Diner—scrambled eggs, bacon, and a syrup drenched short stack of buttered hotcakes, washed down with a bracing cup of hot coffee. Gave him a chance to meet with the guys and catch up on the local gossip. He was still figuring out what to do with his time, now that his son, Wyatt, had married and the Lost Lake Lodge project was done. He felt as restless as a stabled horse—full of oats and short on exercise. In the past, he'd have cut and run. But not this time. He had his kids back and some long-overdue fathering left to tend to.

On one of those aimless fall mornings, Rowdy Long followed the road signs to Singing Springs. The short hike had become part of his early morning ritual. He always paused for a few minutes at the springs...listening to the joy bubbling up from the clear, cool water. Whatever his troubles, the sound reminded him to be thankful. It was a pilgrimage of sorts...a morning prayer walk.

After a lifetime of inhaling dust and sweat on the rodeo circuit, he relished the pure pleasure of breathing in fresh mountain air.

Now, in early September, the cooler air hinted of fall. Here and there, leaves had already turned, fluttering in the sunlight like handfuls of spilled gold coins. Sap rested, still and silent, in dormant trunks and twigs and leaves.

Rowdy followed his dog, Scout, down the trail loop beyond the springs. They crossed an abandoned gravel road before the dirt track plunged back into the woods again. Ahead, his yellow lab sniffed the foundation of the old Walker Sawmill and Foundry. Long abandoned, the wooden building stood on the edge of Coyote Creek, a mile or so past the springs. Rowdy admired the weathered barn-wood siding, wavy glass windows, and sturdy oak support posts—the size of railroad ties. The old water wheel, which had once powered the sawmill, stood lifeless, its broken wooden paddles suspended in the air, casting dark shadows in the swiftly moving water below.

Rowdy paused to admire the neglected structure. The mill was built like a low-slung barn, only with a long, covered porch on the creek side. At the far end, the massive paddle wheel stood over 15 feet tall. Rowdy fancied that the wheel stood suspended in time, longing to shiver off its layer of gray-green moss and plow into the swift current once again.

The wood shake roof of the mill was littered with a layer of pine needles, as was the front decking. *Thump!* A golden-hued sugar pine cone landed close by. Startled, Rowdy's heart beat a bit faster. He looked up at a scolding tree squirrel, who'd gnawed it loose. The varmint flicked his tail and chattered, annoyed at the intrusion. The reddish-hued rodent raced off as Scout gave chase. Rowdy wasn't overly worried about the fate of the squirrel. His dog was a good hunter, but couldn't climb a tree past the first notch.

Stepping up onto the porch of the building, Rowdy rubbed a clear spot in the dirt-encrusted window and held his hands to either side of his face to peer inside. Some of the old equipment was still there—a massive saw blade, workbenches, metal barrels, saw-horses, and the sturdy brick foundry furnace in the back corner.

Somehow the space spoke to him. Called to him. Like some strange, yet comforting dream. Rowdy pictured the place as a simple, lakeside eatery. Saw himself serving up burgers, fries and juicy steaks, smothered in onions, to folks relaxing at tables scattered on the deck.

The crazy idea had first come to him a few weeks ago, in the twilight sleep of a weekday dawn, before he was fully awake. The idea was so ludicrous that he had jumped out of bed in his skivvies, and had run outside barefooted. He splashed his face with the half-frozen water of the rain barrel to clear his brain of any such fool notion.

He stepped away from the window and shook his head again. What was he thinking? He was no chef, and no businessman either. It'd take a lot of money—money he didn't have—to turn this abandoned, cobweb-shrouded building into any sort of a restaurant.

Scout returned from his squirrel chase and pawed at the side door, whining.

"It's no use, Scout," said Rowdy. "I'm loony as a steer grazin' on loco weed to even want it."

Still, with the end of hunting season in just a few weeks, their vacation cabins would be closed for the winter. Closed and quiet. A man could only walk the shore of Lost Lake so many times.

The old latch rattled as Scout pawed the door again. Rowdy noticed that the padlock had almost rusted away, hanging by only a thin strip of metal. It would likely come right off in his hand. As if to save him the trouble, the pitiful lock fell away, and hit the stoop, where it shattered into a pile of rusty metal flakes. The door creaked open and the dog nosed through the opening.

Rowdy set aside any fear of trespass and stepped inside, too. The muted light from the windows fell across the wide floorboards, casting shadows from the sturdy 8x8 rafter support beams. His steps left boot prints in the dust as he moved to the brick furnace in the back corner. It begged a fire, if not one hot enough to smelt metal, then one at least warm enough to welcome guests. His daydream put him in mind of a rock-circled fire pit at roundup, heating branding irons to a red glow. Or maybe a campfire beneath a bubbling cast iron kettle full of molasses-laced beans, hungry cowpokes sniffing the air.

The place had the feel of a stagecoach stop for weary travelers. A rustic haven from the elements, with a nice view of rushing Coyote Creek out the windows and the smell of old sawdust in its joints.

His gaze swung to the far wall. *Shoot! Why in hell did Gloria have to show me those pictures on her computer?* The ones of a long, polished walnut countertop belonging to an old-fashioned soda fountain salvaged from a torn-down drugstore two states away. The one that would fit perfectly on that east wall...like it had always been there.

He'd gone to Gloria's shop, Sparkles, last week to pick up a refurbished nightstand for one of the cabins. He recalled it as clear as Lost Lake's still water at dawn.

"Anybody here?" Rowdy hollered when the jangling bells tied to the door of Sparkles failed to produce the owner.

"Back here...in my office," Gloria called out.

Rowdy walked to the back of the shop and stepped into her office. "Just came by to get that nightstand for Osprey cabin."

"It's ready." Gloria's long fuchsia-colored nails clicked on the keyboard. "Come take a gander at this." She motioned to her computer screen.

Rowdy leaned in to look. He was immediately transported back to the drugstore soda fountain of his youth in Long Bend, South Dakota. He could almost taste the sugary sweetness of the root beer floats, black 'n' whites, and piled high banana splits of his youth. His mouth fell open as Gloria scrolled through photos of the gorgeous soda fountain counter. It was flanked by round red-leather stool tops mounted on chrome bases. Reflected in the wide, mirrored backdrop was an ice cream bay with period lighting. Accessories included three vintage blenders, a collection of dessert glasses in various sizes, sterling cups made to hold paper cones of water, and an array of long-handled silver spoons.

"Don't see many real soda fountains anymore." Rowdy wondered if his kids had ever had a real soda fountain experience. "That brings back some good memories."

"It does," said Gloria. "And guess what? This one's for sale. Wish I had a client for it." She drummed her nails on the desktop. "Wouldn't it be great to have a vintage soda-fountain like this one in Buttermilk Falls." She squinted at the screen. "Don't suppose Wyatt would want it for the lodge, do you?"

"Not really the right place for it. Too far out in the woods." Rowdy couldn't take his eyes from the screen. "It's a beauty."

Now, Rowdy stood in the old sawmill building, picturing the soda fountain nestled against the east wall. The leather stools crowded with families. The jovial banter encouraged by scoops of ice cream topped with whipped cream, diced nuts, and maraschino cherries. His mouth began to water.

"Don't be an idiot," he muttered to himself. A restaurant and soda fountain here? No way. He'd best stick to wishing for possible things. God had already given him more than he deserved.

The back of his neck tingled. Someone was watching him. Rowdy glanced around. Scout scampered to a corner, a growl low in his throat. Rowdy didn't see the beady black eyes peering at him from the rafters. Or hear the little snort of derision. But he felt spooked, nonetheless.

Rowdy hightailed it out the door, calling Scout to heel, and fastened the clasp shut with a stick. He headed toward Singing Springs and his truck, his long strides eating up the ground… not looking back.

His unease was likely just the melancholy of autumn—the shift of seasons from rich summer bounty to the bare and fallow fields of winter. Rowdy didn't much care for the feeling.

He needed something to put his hands to. Some meaningful work to do. For now, though, he'd just head home to Manzanita cabin and sweep pine needles from his own front porch.

Kyle stared into the flickering flames of his campfire. Another Friday night with nothing much to do. He grabbed his walking stick and whittled at the figure on top, chips flying into the fire. He moved his fingers along the rough-hewn shape of an eagle's head and sighed. Right now, his own life seemed as tentative and unformed as his carving. A month in, he was no closer to figuring out his future than he'd been when he first got here. He hadn't slaved through four years of college as a literary scholar to be a carpenter, had he?

What had Robert Frost said? He spoke the verse aloud from memory:

> *Two roads diverged in a yellow wood*
> *And sorry I could not travel both*
> *And be one traveler, long I stood*
> *And looked down one as far as I could*
> *To where it bent in the undergrowth...*

That's where he was now, lost in the undergrowth. All weeds and spiky manzanita. No clear view in sight. For him, nights like this one were the worst. Sitting alone beside a campfire was as quiet and solitary as a dorm room over Christmas break. After the bustling social life of college, he wasn't prepared for this...this mind-numbing quiet.

Laughter erupted from a nearby campsite, the free-wheeling mirth fueled by a few drinks and some bawdy jokes. He missed his drinking buddies. Just having someone to tease and banter with. He'd told himself he didn't need a drink to be happy, but his mouth grew dry, thinking of a cold brew.

"Hey, buddy," said a guy returning from the outhouse. "Come join us." He gestured with his flashlight. "Want a beer?"

That was just what Kyle wanted. "Sure. Thanks." Kyle followed the guy, about his age, to the campsite where two other fellows lounged in camp chairs by the fire.

"I'm Ned." Kyle's new friend, stuck out a hand. "This here's Butch and Tater."

The guys nodded as Ned opened the cooler and handed him a beer.

Kyle nodded back. "Name's Kyle." He popped the top and took a slug, the liquid cool and bracing. "Much obliged."

"What brings you to our neck of the woods?" Ned motioned Kyle to take an empty folding chair.

Kyle paused with the beer can half-way to his lips. These guys weren't his usual crowd. A little too redneck, maybe. The word *college* just might spook them or make him appear uppity. "Workin' in town," he said instead. "Doin' some carpentry." Since when had he started dropping his g's just to fit in? Still, his words were the truth, if only by half.

"Grunt wages?" Butch stirred up some sparks from the fire.

"Pretty much." Kyle's answer betrayed Gabe's generosity, but hey...it was just talk. "What about you guys?" he deflected, looking at the ruddy, flame-lit faces around the fire pit.

Tater laughed, his grin revealing a silver-capped front tooth that sparkled in the firelight. "Trade goods," he said. "Ain't that right, boys?"

"Sure," said Ned. "Buyin' and sellin'. You in the market for a good gun, Kyle?"

Kyle drained his beer and reached for another. A gun did sound pretty good. Around here a fellow should be armed. "What kind are you sellin'?"

"Got a few good rifles in stock. A 22 if'n you're wantin' to plink rabbits. Or maybe a nice, scoped Winchester 30-06 to go after a deer or even a bear."

Kyle's grandpa had owned a rifle of that same make and caliber. Great gun. He'd let Kyle use it from time to time on the farm. "You seen any bears 'round here?" Kyle searched the shadows.

"Sure," drawled Tater. "This place is crawlin' with bears. Bears and stump-stupid farmers."

His buddies laughed at his joke.

"Most don't bother lockin' their barns or nothin'." Butch pulled a Bowie knife from his boot and used it to scratch his back. He hacked off a hunk of dark hair that was hanging into his eyes. "They's dumb as rocks."

Whoa...be careful, Kyle thought, eyeing the blade.

Ned went to his Suburban and brought out a good-looking scoped rifle. Not new, but well cared for.

Kyle liked it. "How much?" He kept an eye on the big knife Butch was polishing on his pant leg.

"Depends," said Ned. "How much can you afford?"

By the time Kyle stumbled back to his campsite an hour later, he was the proud owner of a nice 30-06 hunting rifle, the stock smooth and polished, even if it had set him back a week's wages. He crawled into his tent. Kyle tugged off a boot, basking in the boisterous camaraderie of his new friends.

He burrowed into his warm sleeping bag. A troublesome thought niggled. But Kyle was too numb and too tired to care. "Two roads diverged..." he muttered. "And I... I took the one..." He closed his eyes...and didn't think at all.

Chapter 4

Trouble

In this world you will have trouble.
But take heart!
I have overcome the world.
John 16:33

The yellow school bus hissed to a stop. A choking cloud of dust rose in its wake. It mingled with exhaust fumes as Max stepped off, Chloe tagging close behind.

In the dry heat of early September, the fields were as tangled and brown as an abandoned bird's nest. Max eyed the undulating dirt road leading to the farm, a quarter mile away. He spied a scurrying black and white object in the distance. As the animal drew closer, it came into focus as their dog, Buddy. It was only the second day of school, but the Aussie had already learned the new bus routine. He greeted them with doggy kisses and a wagging plumed tail.

"Hey, Buddy…" Max knelt, putting an arm around the excited animal and stroking his soft fur. "I missed you, too."

"Let's go," snapped Chloe. "I'm hot!"

Max stood and dusted off his knees. For a six-year-old, Chloe could be mighty bossy. They trudged down the road, weighed down by their new backpacks and the lingering tedium of a whole day imprisoned behind a desk. At school, Max had let his mind wander back to the left-behind explorations of a nine-year-old boy in summer—frogs in the pond, red crawdads crouched under creek-bottom boulders, and chicken eggs still warm beneath the brooding hens. He recalled the softness of the pinto mare's lips as she nuzzled apple slices from his fingers, warm sunshine on his shoulders, and the maze of deer tracks wandering through the apple orchard.

Max was happy to be heading home for an afternoon snack. And there was still enough time before supper to explore outside. Chloe skipped ahead, then suddenly cut off onto a faint dirt track. The dog caught up with her, nosing bushes along the trail.

What the heck had lured Chloe off the road? Maybe that panel of shiny metal off to the side, flashing sunlight. Tired and hungry, Max reluctantly tagged after them. This was no shortcut. And, right about now, his mouth was watering for a bite of cookie. The path meandered to an old cabin, half-hidden in an abandoned pumpkin field.

"Chloe!" Max called out. "We're supposed to go straight home."

That crazy girl paid him no never mind. Her dark curls bounced as she raced ahead and vanished inside the structure.

Max forced himself into a trot, his cumbersome backpack lifting with each step, then slamming back down onto this shoulder blades. Miss Lizzy and Gabe, his new mom and dad, had trusted him to walk Chloe home from the bus stop and he didn't want to disappoint.

As he neared the cabin, he saw that it was falling down. Pieces of the weathered board siding were missing, leaving jagged holes behind. The back edge of the capsized metal roof rested on a lichen-covered boulder. Max reached out a hand. In the afternoon heat, the corrugated metal was hot to the touch.

He rounded to the front. The door was lopsided, hanging on by only a single rusty hinge. Max ducked into the dark interior of the cabin and collided with a low hanging board. "Ouch!" He rubbed the scrape on his forehead. Buddy licked his hand.

Max squinted at Chloe, who was heading farther inside. "Hey... What'cha doin' in here?" He stood taller and looked around, excited by the prospect of exploring an old, abandoned cabin. Who knew what they might find?

Chloe grinned at Max and crouched beneath a section of collapsed roof. She brushed some dirt from a trap door set in the plank floor. "Look at this!" She tossed aside some sticks and leaves. "Let's open it!"

Buddy sniffed the gap, a low growl in his throat.

"I dunno," Max said, as the roofing timbers moaned above their heads. "This place is falling down. Dangerous. We might get in trouble."

"Big fat chicken." Chloe frowned. "You scared?"

"Not really," Max said. Anyway, who could resist a closed trap door? He tugged on the metal ring attached to the wood plank lid, testing its weight against his strength. He was lean, but strong. After a hard tug, the lid moved and he hefted it open with a grunt, the rusty brackets squealing. "Got it!" The released air held a peculiar smell. He bent to peer down into the space below. Wooden steps disappeared into the darkness.

Chloe clapped her little hands. "Oh, look!" She pointed at the dark hole. "It's an enchanted castle dungeon."

"More like a root cellar, if you ask me." Max brushed a thatch of blond hair from his eyes.

"Let's go down," she said. "We might find a magic spinning wheel or a troll's treasure."

Max swatted at a cobweb. "Rats, more likely."

Chloe recoiled slightly, then her violet eyes narrowed. "I'm going down there. But if I get hurt, it'll be your fault."

"My fault? Why?"

"Who opened the trap door?"

Max snorted. "We're s'posed to be headed home, not explorin' some smelly cellar." But curiosity got the best of him. Max already had one foot on the top step and moved Chloe aside. "You stay here 'til I give the all clear."

He probed the stairs, one careful footfall at a time and ducked his head into the dark space, wishing he had a lantern. Something skittered across the floor. "Keep Buddy up there with you," he called out.

Max breathed in the scent of damp earth, tainted with the stench of rat poop and decay. A dim ray of light oozed through a broken board along the top wall, illuminating multi-colored rows of old glass jars, filled with who-knew-what—maybe some moldy green beans, soured pickled cucumbers or vile bottles of moon-shiner's brew. A few old apple crates were stacked against one wall. It was a root cellar, all right. Either that, or a witch's lair.

Stepping closer, his shoe crunched on something hard. It rolled beneath his foot, before shifting away with a dry clatter. He leaned down to inspect the pile of pale sticks…then recoiled in horror.

Bones.

❦

Lizzie pulled the curtains back from the living room window, looking down the long drive, in hopes of catching a glimpse of the kids. She checked her watch again. It was getting pretty late. How long could it take for them to walk the quarter mile home from the bus stop?

She began second guessing their decision to allow Chloe to walk home with Max. Surely a nine and six-year-old were safe in a place like Buttermilk Falls. But the remnant city girl in her recalled the headlines of kidnapping, murder...and worse.

She rubbed the soft swell of her belly and paced back into the kitchen again, eyeing the platter of raisin oatmeal cookies on the counter. Doris had been by this morning to do some light cleaning and her usual baking. The kids must be hungry for their after-school snack.

Unable to stand it any longer, Lizzie finally grabbed her keys and hurried out the door. Normally she would have walked the short distance to the bus stop, but given her sense of urgency, she'd taken the car.

Where was Buddy? The dog usually stuck close to her heels whenever she went outside. A fizzle of anxiety crept up her spine. Something was wrong.

Lizzy scanned as she drove. But the dirt road was empty all the way to the bus stop at the intersection with the highway. Nothing out of place. Just a few crows perched on the fence posts along the way and a wild rabbit darting into the underbrush.

She got out and looked both ways down the highway. Only a few passing cars and big lumber trucks carrying stacks of freshly-cut logs. *Where in heaven's name were they?* She dug out her cell phone and dialed the school. The bus had left on time. No breakdown. Another call to the bus driver confirmed that Max and Chloe had gotten off at their stop...nearly an hour ago.

Lizzy swallowed the panic rising in her chest. She got into her SUV and headed back down the dirt drive, a plume of dust rising like a gray storm cloud behind her.

"Lord," she pleaded. "Please let them be all right."

Max scurried away from the heap of dry bones, jerking upright as his heel struck something round and hard. He glanced down. *Hell fire!!* He'd kicked the head clean off the skeleton! It rolled away, like a tipsy soccer ball, coming to a halt in the corner. A bleached-white human skull grimaced up at him—empty eye sockets mocking.

Yikes!! For a moment, he froze in place, his breath hitching in his throat and his mouth gone dry. Max clenched his teeth against the queasy churning of his stomach, trying not to scream.

He fled—bolting up the steps. Max grabbed Chloe by the arm as he hefted himself up through the trap door and raced across the cabin. He barely noticed when he broke the outer door off its lone hinge on his way out. They stomped across its splintering wood as they ran. Buddy raced after them, the ruff on his neck raised. The dog looked back, nose to the wind, and barked twice in warning.

"Let go of me!" shrieked Chloe, tugging against Max's iron grip. "Stop it!!" Planting her feet, she tried to halt him, but she was no match for her brother's terrorized sprint away from the cabin.

He hauled her small, resisting body along with him, like a guard dog plucking a lamb from the jaws of a wolf. He'd been wrong to let Chloe go into that old cabin. Gabe and Miss Lizzy would have his hide for sure. They'd trusted him to watch over the girl and he'd messed up big time.

A part of him wanted to drop Chloe in the nearest bush and hightail it out of there. Away from the terror and away from his failure. His pa was right. He was a good for nothing boy... More trouble than he was worth.

A dark specter glided above him, its shadow moving along the ground as he ran. *Thief...thief...* a raspy voice cackled. Max looked up. *Hells bells!* A black crow. The spook had found him again.

Lizzy heard a noise and slammed on the brakes. Her ears strained as she cut the motor. *Aarff! Aarff!* Then, another bark. Buddy?

She sprinted toward the sound, heedless of her purse left behind and the car door flung wide open. "Max! Chloe!" A rock-strewn trail wove through the underbrush. Adrenaline pushed her along, ready to do battle with the devil himself, if he threatened her kids.

What she found instead was a burr-matted dog and two sweaty, stick-scratched children—Chloe crying and Max howling.

"Are you all right?" She hugged them close.

"He's gone crazy," cried Chloe, breathing hard.

Max's eyes were as big as pie plates. She hadn't seen such pain and dread in their depths since the night he ran away from his old home...and from his pa. "Talk to me, Max. What is it?"

"Back there...in the cabin..." Max swallowed and fell to his knees in the dirt. He choked out a sob.

She knelt next to him, hand on his shoulder, her face close to his. "Tell me."

He looked up at her, then over at Chloe. Max bent closer to whisper in Lizzy's ear. "At the cabin... D-d-down in the root cellar... I...I stepped on some bones... Bones from a person...and... and... a skull."

"What?!"

He squeezed his eyes shut, as if to block out the memory. "A real skull... White teeth... grinnin' up at me. And h-holes where the eyes should be."

Beneath her fingers, Lizzy felt a shudder run through him.

His grip on her hands tightened. "Please don't send me away, Miss Lizzy. We were just havin' a look see at the ol' place."

"No one's sending you away, Max." Lizzy hugged the boy to her. "Not now. Not ever."

"I... I didn't want Chloe to come down into the cellar... To see..." Max swallowed. "So... I hauled her out o' there."

Caw! Caw! Caw! A big black crow flew toward them, cawing loudly as he passed overhead.

Max's head jerked up, his blue eyes widening in terror. "The spook. Am I goin' straight to hell?"

Sheriff Buck answered the radio call from a turnout on the far side of Lost Lake.

"Got a live one for you," said Carol, the police department radio dispatcher, with a hitch of excitement in her voice. "Oops. Not live exactly... Just out of the ordinary."

"What's up?"

"A skeleton. Discovered in an old abandoned cabin off of the dirt road to Lizzy Reed's place."

"Who called it in?"

"Lizzy did. Her boy, Max, found it... In a root cellar."

Hell. Buck ran a hand across his face. "Call the coroner," he said. "Have him meet me there in twenty minutes."

"Got it."

"Anyone securing the location?"

"Gabe's on his way now," said Carol. "Lizzy said she'd stay put until he gets there and show him the trail leading to the cabin. Then she wants to take the kids home."

"Are they okay?"

"I guess Max is pretty rattled. Lizzy wants to know if you can interview the boy later, at the house?"

"Sure," said Buck. "Best take him home."

When he got back to the main highway, the sheriff turned on lights and siren. Not that it was a matter of life or death. The person was already dead, so a few minutes more or less wouldn't matter much. But anyone's death deserved the full attention and respect of law enforcement. On the hurried drive through Main Street, his speed and wailing siren garnered stares and parted the sparse traffic like Moses at the Red Sea. Buck pondered who the skeleton might belong to...any missing persons or folks unaccounted for.

When Buck arrived, Gabe's truck was parked on the shoulder of the road, a short distance from the main highway. He pulled in behind it. The coroner's van arrived a few minutes later. The three men greeted one another with a handshake and got down to business.

Buck led the way down the overgrown pathway, beckoned by the reflected glare from a tumbled tin roof.

The door to the cabin lay on the ground, trampled into the dirt. The intact part of the cabin's sloping roof allowed entry, if they stooped under the low door beam. A musty smell of decay met them as they entered.

"Here," said Percy, the coroner. He handed out some latex gloves and put on his own. The others followed suit. They had to go to their knees at the trap door to avoid the sagging roof.

Buck descended the stairs first, careful not to disturb anything on his way down. He shone his flashlight along the jars of canned goods on a shelf, the broken seals allowing the contents to molder.

The skeleton lay on the floor—bones long ago stripped clean. A few wisps of rotted fabric were the only remnants of clothing. The skull was disconnected and misplaced. It lay a few feet from the body, eye sockets empty...teeth locked in a horrible grimace. A rat scurried behind a crate in the corner.

The sheriff stepped aside to give the coroner access. He set an electric lantern on the window ledge to light up the space. Percy knelt beside the remains, writing observations in his notebook. He reached out to examine a gem encrusted ring on a bony finger.

Gabe stood on the bottom stair, taking in the ghoulish scene. "A rough thing for a young boy to see…"

Buck looked over at him, catching the pain in his eyes. "Was Chloe down here, too?"

"No… Thank God." Gabe raked a hand through his hair. "Max yanked her away before she came down."

Percy stood and took a few photos. "It's a woman," he said. "Well past eighty when she died."

"How long ago?" asked Buck.

"I'd say two…maybe three years."

"Just before Lizzy came to the farm," said Gabe. "And nobody reported a woman missing…in all this time?"

Buck jotted down some notes of his own. "I'll look into it."

"She might not be from around here," said Percy. "Could be someone just passing through."

"Nice jewelry for a vagrant," noted Buck, gesturing to the ring Percy had taken from the body and bagged in a zip-lock.

Gabe swallowed hard. "It's so darned close to home…"

"You ever been in this cabin before?" asked Buck.

"No. I didn't even know it was here…tucked way off the road like this." Gabe shrugged. "What do you think happened?"

"That's what I aim to find out," said Buck. "We'll treat it as a crime scene until we know better. I'll bring in some detectives to try to identify the remains and start an investigation."

"Let's get out of here." Gabe turned away from the remains. "I need to get home to my family."

They climbed the stairs, only too happy to get out of the cellar and away from the fetid air.

Gabe took in a cleansing breath. "Do you have to interview Max right away, sheriff?"

The Old Mill

"I'd like to. Best to get it over with and written down while it's still fresh in the boy's mind." The sheriff began stringing yellow caution tape around the cabin. He put a comforting hand on Gabe's shoulder. "It really can't be helped."

"That's where you're wrong, sheriff," Gabe cautioned. "I aim to help Max through this any way I can. Protect him. I won't let you run roughshod over my boy. He's been through enough."

"What are you saying, Gabe?"

At the road, Gabe headed to his truck. "I need to talk with him first, feel out how hard this has hit him. He's already thinking we're ready to send him away. It's important to handle this right."

"Meaning?"

"He's a minor...in my custody," reminded Gabe.

"Has he been to this cabin before today?"

"I doubt it," said Gabe. "Let me sort through it first...as his dad. And then you'll have to get past Lizzy. Right now, she's a mama bear, protecting her cub."

"You've got twenty-four hours."

Kyle woke on Saturday with a dry mouth, a hangover, and a niggling sense that his world had somehow tilted on its axis. At college, he'd have driven to the nearest McDonald's for black coffee and a short stack of pancakes, drenched with syrup. But here, in such a small town, his bloodshot eyes and unruly hair might raise eyebrows or unwanted questions at Maggie's Diner. So, he settled for a strong cup of instant black coffee and a stale donut.

He glanced around. No signs of life from the neighboring campsite.

Later, when his stomach had settled, Kyle handled the rifle. The Winchester 30-06 was an older model, with some wear on the wood stock…but it was a beauty, all the same. Freshly oiled and carefully maintained. He didn't want to consider where it might have come from before his neighbors got their hands on it.

Collecting a sack of empty soda cans, he slung the rifle strap over his shoulder, pocketed the box of shells that had come with the gun, and headed down the trail, intent on doing some target practice. He hadn't shot a rifle since leaving the farm.

Kyle trudged past the springs which bubbled up, entirely too cheerfully for so early in the day. His booted footfalls seemed unusually loud as they pounded along the rocky ground. Needing to get a fair distance away from the campground, he hiked into unfamiliar territory and crossed an old logging road.

He stumbled upon a large vacant building alongside Coyote Creek. Tucking his hands in his pockets, Kyle studied the place. Shingled roof, a sprawling covered front porch and, best of all, a fifteen-foot-tall water wheel—its broken paddles suspended mid-air above the rambling creek. *What is this place?*

He climbed the porch steps and squinted at the peeling paint of the sign near the front door. Walker Sawmill and Foundry. He peered in a dirty window. The place looked pretty much abandoned and forgotten. A bit like himself.

Kyle held a reverence for old buildings…maybe because he'd grown up in his grandparents' 1910 farmhouse. He was glad he'd come alone. He suspected that his new pals—Ned, Butch and Tater—would've enjoyed shooting out the old wavy-glass windows, just for fun. The motley gang in the next campsite might be good for a few laughs, but he determined to not breathe even a whisper about this sweet sawmill to them.

He walked back to the logging road and away from the sawmill. It was peaceful out here. Quiet.

A quarter mile farther out, he left the road and set his cans up in front of a dirt embankment. He paced back about ten yards and knelt, bracing his new rifle against a tree stump. Kyle sighted down the scope and squeezed off the first round. *Bang!* A pouf of dirt rose above the first can—a near miss. Adjusting his aim, he fired again. *Bang!* A soda can jumped into the air. This was a great gun! Scope already sighted in...the rifling true.

Kyle plinked at his target cans for another twenty minutes, then decided to save his ammo for some real game. Ever the dutiful environmentalist, like his hero Thoreau, he picked up the demolished cans and spent shell casings to haul back out.

He went back the way he'd come, pausing to look again at the abandoned sawmill. If he had any money, it would be tempting to do something with it. A chance to use his new carpentry skills. In the city, it would be a great space for an artist studio or even a brew pub. No sense even going there, though...he was flat broke, with only a rifle to show for all his hard work pounding nails with Gabe.

Even so, the day was softly sunlit, the forest cool and primeval. Kyle whistled as he made his way back to camp.

Chapter 5

In the Shadow of the Almighty

*Those who live
in the shelter of the Most High
will find rest
in the shadow of the Almighty.
Psalm 91:1*

Sheriff Buck waited a full day before he drove out to Lizzy's farm to interview Max. He assumed she'd kept the kids home from school after yesterday's trauma. He'd phoned ahead to confirm their afternoon meeting, and Gabe said he'd arrange to be there as well. Circling the wagons. Now, if he could just keep Lizzy from going all mama bear on him.

Harley, her farm manager, met him in the yard. "I'd like a word with you when you're done."

"Okay," Buck replied. "I'll check in with you before I leave." On a case like this one, he was all for casting a wide net.

Inside the farmhouse, the air bristled with tension. Buck sat at the kitchen table with Gabe, Lizzy and Max. Lizzy had hired a baby sitter to take Chloe to the creek to play, where she'd be out of earshot.

He accepted the cup of coffee placed in front of him, along with the pile of sugar packets Lizzy set next to it. Buck ripped several sweeteners open and added them to the steaming brew. He pondered what to say as all eyes turned his way. Openers were crucial. They set the tone and eased others into the conversation.

Max trembled. The last time he'd seen the sheriff, he found out his pa was dead. Learned Pa had smashed his car into a tree... drunk again. That's when Max had come to live here with the Reeds—nice folks, who wanted to adopt him. At least they did before yesterday. Before he let Chloe lead him off the road and into danger. Before he stumbled upon that creepy skeleton. Would they send him away now?

He really wanted it to work out. He had fewer worries, living here with the Reeds. Not going hungry, for one. He liked being part of a real family, where nobody yelled or got punched. He even had his own room upstairs. So what if it was smaller than Chloe's? At least it was his.

But the truth was...he hadn't done a good job looking after her. What if she'd been the one to go down into the cellar first? Then she'd be the one frightened by nightmares every night—scared near to death by those haints. No... Better it had been him.

Poor kid looks like he's seen a ghost, though Buck. Pale face stricken. Small, lean body rigid with fear. Well...maybe, in a way, he had.

Lizzy didn't look much better. Her grip tightened on the coffee cup, holding it close for whatever warmth it offered. "Please be careful with your line of questioning," she said, by way of preamble. "He's just a young boy...who's had a bad scare."

"Of course," Buck reassured, looking at Max. "First off... nobody here has done anything wrong. No one is suspected of a crime. It was an unfortunate discovery...that's all. Someone was bound to find the body, sooner or later."

"But an innocent child did," reminded Lizzy, darting him a look.

Sheriff Buck turned to Max with what he hoped was a friendly expression. "I'm just going to ask you a few questions, Max. And you tell me what happened. Is that okay?"

Max nodded, but shifted nervously in his chair, looking ready to bolt.

Lizzy laid a protective hand on his arm. "The truth can't hurt you." She glanced at Buck.

"Have you ever been to that old cabin before?" Buck asked.

"No, sir. I didn't even know it was there."

"So how did you find it yesterday?"

"Chloe saw the trail and left the road. I went after her." Max looked down, his small shoulders sagging. "I was s'posed to watch over her on the way home from the bus stop."

"It's okay," reassured Lizzy. "You didn't know where she was going."

"Not at first," admitted Max. "But, once I got inside the cabin, I wanted to see what was down in that ol' cellar, same as she did." He swallowed. "Chloe thought we'd find a spinnin' wheel turnin' straw into gold down there, or some other silly fairy tale stuff. I was hopin' for somethin' way better... Gold and silver coins, maybe. Or a chest full of real pirate's treasure." He sniffed. "Not some ol' skeleton."

Max closed his eyes, trying to erase the image. "I should'a got her outta there right away. Not lifted the trap door and gone down those steps."

Gabe put a hand on Max's knee. "Listen. Any boy worth his salt would have gone down to explore that cellar. I know I would've. It took real courage, Max."

"It did?"

"Yes. You're the bravest boy I know." Gabe smiled at his son.

Lizzy's expression was far darker. Gabe could tell she wasn't condoning any more dangerous exploits—not that Lizzy or Gabe had a raindrop in a river's chance of keeping their son safe from adventure. Max was a curious boy, who needed to explore his world.

Buck took in a breath and continued his interrogation. "Was the trap door closed when you first got there?"

"Yeah. But I tugged it open."

"Was anything on top of it? Something holding it down...like a heavy box? A rock? A table?"

"No, sir. Just some dirt and old leaves. Chloe brushed 'em off."

"Notice any footprints in the dirt?"

"Nope. But I wasn't lookin' for any. I just saw the big metal ring. Next thing I knew, I was pullin' it up."

Sheriff Buck asked a few more questions, and Max answered, unwinding a bit...now that he wasn't so scared. Buck scribbled down a few more notes. He'd determined that Chloe likely hadn't seen enough to warrant the trauma of questioning. "That's it, then," Buck said, closing his notebook. "Thanks for your cooperation. I'll be in touch as soon as I know anything more."

"Thanks, sheriff." Gabe, stood. "Thanks for everything." He pulled his son into a fierce hug. "I'm proud of you, Max."

"Why?"

"Because you saved your sister. Made sure she didn't go down into that creepy cellar."

"Only because I was scared spitless."

"But you still got her the heck out of there," Gabe said.

"I guess I did," Max conceded, eyes shining.

"Yes, you did," Lizzy added, giving the sheriff a quick nod of approval. "You're our brave boy."

"You're not mad?"

"Nope," said Gabe.

"But I left the road. Went to the cabin."

"As I see it, you went after Chloe to help her." Gabe lifted Max's chin. "Didn't you tell her to come on out and head home with you?"

"Yeah...but..."

"But she didn't listen..."

"Nope."

Lizzy set a plate of oatmeal raisin cookies down in front of Max. "Maybe next time she will."

Buck suspected they'd already talked to Chloe about her part in their misadventure.

"Have a cookie, Max." Lizzy smiled for the first time." She planted a kiss on the top of her boy's head as he grabbed one. She pushed the plate toward Buck. "Help yourself, sheriff."

He tucked his notebook away and took a cookie. He liked oatmeal raisin. "Got any more coffee?" he asked. "Mine's gone cold."

Harley was waiting when Buck came down the front steps. They settled in the barn, sitting on some scattered hay bales. The sheriff decided to ask his questions first.

"You know anything about that old cabin?" Buck asked.

"Sure," Harley said. "It's an old claim-staker's cabin. Dates way back to the 1880's. It's been abandoned and rottin' away since the main farmhouse was built."

"So, nobody's lived there recently?"

"Not for a long time. Lizzy's Aunt Daffodil let a drifter stay there for a spell. You know how that fool woman was always takin' in strays."

The Old Mill

"So, who was he...this drifter?"

"Not a he. A woman. Fifty or so. Went by the name, Birdie." Harley lifted his straw hat to scratch his thatch of white hair. "A gypsy type. Long hair, colorful skirts, lots of flowin' scarves. Bangles clankin' on her arms. That woman reeked of stinkin' pachouli oil, I can tell you...which might be why Miss Daffodil didn't let her bunk at the main house."

"When was that?"

"I'd say about two to three years ago." Harley rolled his ever-present toothpick from one side of his mouth to the other. "Just before Miss Daffodil started losing her wits and went into that rest home."

"What do you know about this Birdie?"

"Not much." Harley clamped down on his toothpick. "Always thought that drifter took advantage of Miss Daffodil...comin' by to mooch food, clothes, even beddin' for her cot in the old cabin. Always makin' off with jars of home-canned stuff, food and clothes...most anythin' not nailed down. Never liftin' a finger, even though she was way younger than Miss Daffodil. Seemed able enough to me."

"So... What happened to her?"

"Beats me. Disappeared after Miss Daffodil went into the old folk's home. No more free handouts, I guess." Harley put a hand to his chin. "I do miss her stories, though. That woman was a born story-teller. She spun some tall tales...that's for sure."

"Like what?"

"Like that old cabin havin' a hidden tunnel. One leadin' to a long-lost gold mine. And talk of all the crusty ol' miners who disappeared searchin' for it."

"Any truth to that tale?"

"Doubtful."

"So, Harley. You think it could be Birdie's body in the cellar?"

"Reckon so..."

After another hard day of construction work, Kyle was in no particular hurry to return to the solitude of the campground. A guy could only whittle by a campfire for so long. Truth was...he was missing wi-fi, the internet, social media sites, and an electrical outlet to charge his cell phone. A campground with no electrical hookups pretty much sucked. And he could sure use a shower. Spit-baths with water warmed over a campfire left something to be desired. He'd made a few treks to the laundromat in town to wash his clothes, and used their pay showers to clean up and wash his hair. But roughing it had its limits.

His pals in the neighboring campsite had been making themselves scarce lately. Gone for days at a time. Just as well. His friendship with Ned, Butch and Tater wasn't wearing well. Butch's casual attitude toward carving stuff up with his impressive Bowie knife was unnerving. And Tater's faulty grammar had begun to grate on him. He was constantly jarred by the misspoken words spewing from Tater's loud, profanity-prone mouth, his oafish smile dominated by that silver-capped front tooth. Who was his dentist anyway? Rocky?

At quitting time, after loading up his tools, Kyle headed out of town, following the road signs that promised a glimpse of a place called Lost Lake. The paved road quickly gave way to gravel and then to dirt. He bumped along through the pines into true wilderness, feeling the tension ease as he drove in deeper.

A deer bounded across the road, startling him. The graceful doe stopped at the edge of the timber and eyed him, ears twitching, before vanishing into the trees. Kyle glanced back to where his new rife lay on the rear seat. It was deer season now, so he'd best

The Old Mill

keep a lookout for a nice four-point buck. He'd secured his deer tag a few days ago at Jeb's Ag Supply. So, he was ready for his first buck of the season. Kyle had done his fair share of hunting back on the farm, where a nice rack of venison was always welcomed. He'd have to talk with the locals at Maggie's Diner about the best hunting spots in the area.

Eventually, the dirt road ended at the edge of a clear, sparkling lake. After the shaded cover of the trees, the water seemed to stretch out forever, its shimmering blue fingers reaching into a series of sheltered coves. A few cabins lined the shore and a small dock nearby tethered an old fishing boat and a few kayaks. Farther on, a striking glass-fronted lodge faced the water. He got out of his truck and stretched. A young, wiggly black lab scurried over to greet him. Kyle was partial to labs. He gave the pup a good rub behind the ears.

"You lost?"

Kyle looked up. A teenaged girl lounged in a rocker on the porch of one of the cabins, her curly mane of red hair aflame against the dark logs.

"Not sure. Is this Lost Lake?" The conversation was like a bad pun.

"Yeah. This is it." The girl set aside her book, stood and leaned against the porch railing. "You wanting to rent a cabin? They're cheaper now, in the off season."

Kyle glanced down the line of cabins, and spied the electrical lines strung from a telephone pole to each building. "Maybe. Do you get internet way out here?"

"Sure do," the girl said. "Good hunting in the area this time of year, too. You here after a deer?"

Seemed like she was rolling out all kinds of possibilities. A warm place to stay as the weather cooled. Electrical hookups. Hot, running water. Access to the internet. A little hunting on the side.

He'd obviously been camped out in the woods far too long. He walked closer. "I'm Kyle," he said. "Kyle Anderson."

She nodded, "Charlotte Long. My brother, Wyatt, owns these cabins."

A lanky cowboy stepped out on the porch behind her, placing a protective hand on her shoulder. "I'm her dad, Rowdy Long." His eyes were sharp in the shadow of his black Stetson.

"Nice to meet both of you." Kyle stood straighter under the man's scrutiny, wishing he'd trimmed his bushy beard. He wanted to blurt out that he was way too old for the man's daughter and was just here to check out the lake. The girl was a looker all right, with those green eyes, flaming hair and spunky attitude. But she was just a kid and likely still in high school, way off limits for a college grad like himself.

"I'm a recent graduate of UCLA," he said, to make up for the beard. "I'm in the area working for Gabe Reed."

Rowdy's shoulders relaxed a notch. "Gabe's a good man. What brings you all the way out here?"

"I'm still exploring the area. Wanted to see the lake...so I followed the signs here. I hope I'm not intruding."

"Of course not." Charlotte tucked a curl behind her ear. "Everyone wants to check out the lake." She shrugged. "And the dogs seem to like you."

A yellow lab had joined the black pup, who was tugging on Kyle's shoelaces. "What're their names?"

"Black one's Bonfire, Charlotte's mutt," said Rowdy. "The yellow lab's my dog, Scout."

"Nice dogs." Kyle reached down to pet Scout. "I'd be interested in hearing more about the cabins."

A half hour later, Kyle had been given a tour of the cabins as well as the lodge and had signed a six month's lease on a snug

The Old Mill

little cabin called Lupine. It looked like he'd be staying in the area after all. He couldn't wait to break camp and settle in, here on the shores of Lost Lake.

On the way back through town, he stopped at Jake's Barber Shop and got a trim and a haircut to celebrate his return to semi-civilization. But he'd had the barber leave his hair longer in back, brushing his collar, just the way he liked it. A cabin was a big step up from his campsite. And his buddies in the campground weren't as entertaining as he'd thought—when first viewed through the haze of a few brews.

He was happy to break camp and head out to his new digs on the shores of Lost Lake.

Three weeks later, Kyle and Charlotte had settled comfortably into the friend zone. He'd convinced Rowdy that he was hardworking and harmless, leaving early for his job and keeping mostly to himself after returning home to his cabin. Charlotte's dad had chaperoned them at first, hanging around whenever they talked, but gradually he'd seen that their five-year age difference made for more of a sister and older brother kind of relationship. Charlotte pumped him about college life and told him the latest gossip about everyone in Buttermilk Falls.

Seems she'd only recently come to live with Rowdy, who used to be on the rodeo circuit. Bronc and bull riding. The whole bit. A part of Kyle envied him for that. The testosterone-laden world of horsehide and leather. The closest Kyle had come to it was riding a horse on his grandparents' farm.

It didn't take long to discover their shared interest in literature. From time to time, Kyle and Charlotte got together to talk about their favorite authors.

One chilly fall afternoon, they met at the lodge and lit a fire. Kyle brought his stainless steel mug of coffee, Charlotte toted a can of soda and a bag of chips. They sat on the comfy green-leather sofa in front of the crackling fire.

Kyle took a sip of hot coffee. "Do you like Thoreau?"

"Sure. We just studied him in school." She crunched on a potato chip. "Thoreau knows exactly what living in the woods is like—that connection with nature." Charlotte sighed dramatically, before quoting, *I want to live deep and suck out all the marrow of life*... "What's not to like about a guy who lived like that?"

At last, a kindred spirit. Kyle laughed, and quoted a few lines himself:

> *I went to the woods*
> *because I wanted to live deliberately*
> *to front only the essential facts of life*
> *and see if I could not learn what it had to teach*
> *and not, when I came to die,*
> *discover that I had not lived.*

"From *Walden Pond*," gushed Charlotte. "Thoreau gets it. He really gets it!" She snapped open the pop top of her soda can. "Don't you agree? Isn't that how you want to live?"

He arched an eyebrow. "I've been camping for two months, Charlotte. Wilderness living might be a bit overrated. And isolating. It's people—and maybe even God—who have the most to teach us."

"You believe in God?"

"I used to."

"What happened?"

He shook his head and turned away, not wanting to get into it.

Charlotte wanted to hear more. Her pa's faith was a real thing, woven into whatever he did. Shaping who he was. But for her, she was just starting to open up to the possibility that there was a God who loved her. She could feel the Almighty here at the lake. See his hand in the beauty and hear his voice in the wind. She wondered what Kyle felt.

"But wouldn't it be wonderful to live tucked away on Walden Pond?" she asked.

Kyle opened his arms to Lost Lake—the water shining just outside the windows. "This **is** Walden Pond!"

And to Kyle it was. As the weeks unfolded, he felt restored by long walks along padded forest trails. Nights looking up at the stars. Ears attuned to the rhythmic lapping of waves on the shore and the whisper of wind toying with the tops of the pines…listening to the haunting call of a loon.

Even with electricity and access to the internet, he found that social media sites didn't interest him, as they once had. So many of the posted comments seemed pompous, trivial, or even downright petty. And how many selfies did some girls need to post anyway?

Away from the pressures of his college peers, he was changing. Getting out of his head and becoming more attuned to simple everyday things. The tactile feel of a hammer handle as he pounded in a nail. The woodsy smell of sawdust from a freshly-cut board. The pattern of leaf shadows on a path. A spider's web catching jewels of dew in the morning light.

That still, small voice—once drowned out by noise—began to speak to his soul.

One simple word… *Peace*.

Rowdy paced the shoreline of Lost Lake, Scout close at his heels. Counting his blessings. He had a lot to be grateful for. After years of running from God, he'd finally laid his sins at the foot of the cross and asked for forgiveness. No homecoming was sweeter.

After repentance had come restoration. He'd reunited with his kids. Mended fences with them as best he could. Tried to live an honest life. These days, he had plenty of lake trout to eat and the solid roof of a cabin over his head. He lived with his daughter beside a nice, quiet lake. So why this nagging restlessness in his soul?

He wasn't a rodeo cowboy anymore. The work on the cabins was done. The Lost Lake Lodge was finished, nestled on the point, as if it had always been there. He wondered what came next. A man needed a purpose and something to occupy his hands. He envied young Kyle that—the satisfying work of a steady job he enjoyed. Even if the boy had seemingly gone to college for nothing, he'd landed on his feet with no complaints.

He saw that Kyle was home from work. His truck was parked in front of Lupine and a light was on in the cabin. Rowdy decided to stop by for a few minutes and say, howdy.

As he passed the boy's truck, his gaze fell on the rifle lying on the back seat—a nice Winchester 30-06. The gun had a glossy, uniquely-patterned, walnut stock, and a special-order scope he recognized. It was well-used, with a small dent in the butt plate, and worn bluing on the barrel.

He opened the cab door and lifted out the rifle, allowing himself a loving caress of the smooth stock. Rowdy clenched his jaw and marched, rifle in hand, up the three steps of Kyle's cabin. He didn't bother knocking.

Rowdy banged the door open, noted Kyle's alarmed expression, and snarled, "What the hell are you doin' with my rifle?!"

Chapter 6

Sovereign Over Us

*I declare the end from the beginning
and from ancient times
things not yet done.
Isaiah 46:10*

Kyle looked up in surprise as Rowdy stormed into the cabin. The boy caught a glimpse of a rifle and the searing rage heating Rowdy's face. He raised his hands in a gesture of surrender. "What's wrong?"

"How could you be such a low-down cuss, stealin' my best rifle?!" Rowdy thundered. He slammed his fist on the table—mad enough to spit nails.

Kyle jolted back in his chair, sending his open copy of *Walden* thudding to the floor.

"You've got a lot of nerve," bellowed Rowdy. "Livin' here right under my nose in one of my cabins! Didn't peg you as a common thief."

Rowdy had recognized his beloved Winchester 30-06 immediately—the gun he'd carried throughout his rodeo days. Stolen nearly a month ago from his truck. And to think he'd trusted Kyle.

His blood thundered in his ears as Rowdy tried and failed to reign in his red-hot anger. He spat out, "Stealin' a man's gun ranks right up there with horse theft—a hangin' offense."

Kyle sucked in a breath. "I didn't steal that rifle."

"Yeah, right." Rowdy didn't believe a word of it.

"I bought it…I swear." Kyle stood and took a step back, hoping to calm the situation.

Rowdy lifted the rifle, punching the air with it. "This is *my* gun! Where'd you get it?"

"Bought it from some guys in the campground," Kyle stammered. "I had no idea it was yours."

"What guys?" Rowdy demanded. "Ever think it might be stolen?"

Of course, he'd thought it… That thought had niggled his conscience at the time, and brought a boat-load of guilt crashing down now. Wanting to overlook the possibility, Kyle had bought the gun anyway…even if it might be stolen. No excuse, really. He'd been trying to fit in with the neighboring campers. Acting like their drinking buddy. Posing as a big spender—a guy with a wad of cash in his pocket. Now look where it'd gotten him.

"I'm sorry," he said. "It was a dumb thing to do."

"Got that right."

Kyle's face heated with shame and embarrassment. He'd been taught better. He didn't so much mind being out the money. What hurt most was that he'd crossed someone like Rowdy. Someone whose opinion mattered. "I suspected it might be stolen," he admitted, "but bought it anyway." Kyle looked away. "Not my finest hour."

THE OLD MILL

Rowdy nodded, his rage cooling down a tick. "You drinkin' at the time, son?"

"Yes. But that's no excuse. I knew better." Kyle lifted his head and met Rowdy's eyes. "For what it's worth... I really am sorry."

"That's it?"

Kyle shook his head. "It's a big mistake. I'll be packed and out of here in an hour."

Rowdy laid the rifle down on the table. "So...you're just going to tuck your tail between your legs and sulk away?"

"What do you want, then?"

What the heck did he want? Rowdy asked himself. He'd jumped to the wrong conclusion, accusing the boy of stealing his rifle. Worse yet, he'd let his temper get the best of him. Weren't people more important than a favorite gun? *What now?*

Kyle reminded Rowdy of his own son, Wyatt, the child he'd abandoned as a kid. This boy had that same look that pleaded for acceptance, and maybe even for love. Rowdy wasn't fooled by Kyle's dark growth of beard. The outward badge of manhood hid the insecurities of a youth still finding his way. Could he be here for Kyle in ways he hadn't been for Wyatt? The thought pleased him. He knew Kyle had lost his parents and, more recently, both of his grandparents. As a college graduate who loved books, but was working in the trades, he likely had a few tangles in his tail.

Rowdy admired the way the boy had come clean about the rifle. And he could see why Kyle had liked the gun and wanted it. It was a good, honest gun, without pretense.

"You got any strong coffee 'round here?" he asked.

"I can make some," Kyle said.

"Good. I think we'd best sit and talk for a spell."

While the coffee brewed, they sat at the kitchen table and stared across the rifle at each other.

Rowdy clenched and unclenched his fist. "For starters…I'd like the names of the fellas who stole my gun."

Kyle nodded, splaying his hands on the table. "Ned's the leader. His buddies are Butch and Tater."

"Made up names?"

"Don't think so. They aren't the sharpest tools in the shed." Kyle got up and poured two mugs of steaming coffee. "Sugar…creamer?"

'Black's fine." Rowdy took a bracing gulp. "Got any last names?"

"Afraid not."

"They have any other guns for sale?"

"Yes. But I only saw this one."

"Other stolen goods?"

"More than likely." Kyle clutched his mug, warming his hands. "Don't know why I hung around with them. They went on and on about stump-stupid farmers who don't bother to lock their doors." He stared into the dark liquid. "That should've been my first clue," he admitted. "Guess I only saw what I wanted to see."

"A gang like that could explain the rash of thefts in the area lately." Rowdy frowned. "But they might have underestimated folks 'round here."

Kyle's fingers tensed on his mug. "You're not going after them, are you?"

"Probably not. I'll let the sheriff handle it." Rowdy took another gulp of coffee. "Over the years, I've learned to never approach a bull from the front, a horse from the rear or a fool from any direction."

Kyle nodded, a pained look on his face. "I guess that fool would be me." He studied his hands. "Thing is… I was willing to overlook all of it. Only one place I drew a line… I just wanted to keep them from finding out about the old sawmill. Didn't want them shooting out the old windows."

Rowdy straightened in his seat. "You know 'bout the sawmill?"

"Yeah…sure. I stumbled upon it the day I took my…*your* rifle into the woods for target practice." Kyle eyed Rowdy's 30-06. "That's one nice gun and scope, by the way. Shot straight as a plumb line...every time."

A smile lifted Rowdy's lips. "I've had that rifle for well over twenty years. Mighty glad to have it back." He fingered the smooth, glossy stock. "Maybe I should thank you."

"What for?"

"If they'd sold it to someone else, I might never have seen it again."

"Well…there's that." Kyle attempted a smile. "Does this mean I can stay on here?"

Rowdy drummed his fingers on the table top. "You buy anything else from them yahoos?"

"No, sir."

The silence stretched.

At last, Rowdy spoke up. "I guess I'll allow you to stay, then. I'm a big believer in second chances."

"Thanks, Rowdy." Kyle bowed his head, shoulders sagging in relief. "I really do like it here."

"Lost Lake is a good spot for lost souls," said Rowdy. "…If you pay attention."

"Well, you certainly got my attention when you busted through the door." Kyle picked up his copy of *Walden* from the floor. "Any idea who owns that old sawmill?"

"Not really. Why'd you want to know?"

"Oh… No reason." Kyle set the book on the table. "There's just something about that abandoned building that I'm drawn to. It'd make a great artist studio."

"Or a nice steak and burger joint," blurted Rowdy.

"Wait…" You want to start a business there?"

"Just pie in the sky," said Rowdy. "Don't have the money to do it."

"Me, neither," admitted Kyle. "If wishes were horses..."

Rowdy nodded, "...beggars would ride."

Sunset was Sheriff Buck's favorite time of day. He parked in the vista turnout on the main highway and got out to have a look. He never tired of seeing the red ball of sun tuck itself behind Lonesome Mountain in a blaze of glory. Its afterglow pinned the pines against a vivid canvas of bronze, purple and gold.

The only rival to the evening spectacle was Gloria Gilbert, owner of Sparkles, a local repurposed art and furniture store. Gloria's sparkling personality, colorful hair and outlandish clothing still left Buck gob-smacked. The woman drove him crazy. How could someone so obviously *not his type* turn his thoughts into a mush of irritation and longing. And why the heck was he thinking about her now, recalling her glittering blue eyes and the clatter of bangle bracelets sliding down her arms...jangling loud enough to wake the dead?

No way was he going down that bumpy road. Buck brought his attention back to the view. One thing he knew for sure, the quiet glory of a mountain sunset was way less complicated.

Buck got back into his patrol car. He still had work to do. In the gathering twilight, he pulled off at a turnout near the entrance of Singing Springs Campground. He intended to walk in on foot, coming up behind that last campsite, where he could watch it unobserved.

Keeping to the pine-needle strewn edges, Buck stepped carefully, moving as quiet as a ghost. He settled on a downed log, hidden in the woods, and used his night vision binoculars to scan the campsite. Three rough looking guys in their twenties. An acrid-smelling campfire fed with logs way too green. Plenty of beers to go around. A battered four-man tent, poorly pegged. No cook stove, or even a lantern. Junk food wrappers strewn around.

Turning his binoculars toward the edge of the camp, he glassed the cargo compartment of their dirty, dinged-up Suburban. Lots of boxes piled inside, along with some tarp-covered goods. He'd bet dollars to donuts they had at least one weapon in the car, and likely no license to carry. Call it a lawman's instinct.

Buck jotted down the license plate number. Days earlier he'd checked the campsite registration. The older, tan SUV supposedly belonged to Ned Nichols with an address in Sacramento. He'd reserved the site for 5 days, and this was the last night of their scheduled stay. Buck had meant to get out here sooner, but the investigation of the skeleton found out at Lizzy's had kept him from following up.

He was a bit too far away to make out much of the profanity-laced conversation, but Buck doubted these guys were here for the scenery. He'd need to get a search warrant for the car and campsite. See if there was any connection to the series of petty thefts being reported from the outlying farms. But he'd likely missed his chance, if they'd be packing up tomorrow.

Leaving as quietly as he'd come, Buck got back in his patrol car and pulled out his laptop to run Ned Nichols through the system. But before he could type in the name, his cell rang.

"Buck. It's Percy."

He'd been half expecting this call from the coroner. "What did you find?"

"We've ID'd the remains in the cabin from dental records." Percy cleared his throat. "And you're not going to believe who it is..."

Kyle stopped off at the post office on his way home from work. His box was full—mostly catalogues, missives from graduate schools and junk mail. An official looking envelope with a return address of the law firm of Burke, Butterfield, and Waite caught his eye. He stiffened. What business did a law firm have with him? He thought back to a few unpaid parking citations. Or had Rowdy changed his mind about the stolen rife? Was he in trouble?

He went outside, sat on a bench and ripped open the envelope with trembling fingers, pulling out the single sheet of white paper. He read quickly:

> *Mr. Kyle Anderson,*
> *Your grandparents, Bert L. Anderson and Bethany S. Anderson retained our services for drawing up and executing the provisions of their revocable Anderson Family Trust. You are the sole beneficiary of this trust. Please contact our office at your earliest convenience so that we can discuss the trust provisions with you.*
>   *John Waite*
>   *Attorney at Law*
>   *Burke, Butterfield, and Waite Law Firm*

His grandparents had a trust? He'd thought they were dirt-poor hay farmers, barely scraping by. And he suspected their land had been heavily mortgaged to pay for his college education. Surely the law firm didn't expect him to take on the mortgage payments? He'd have to sell the place for sure. Since their funerals, he left the farm in his rear-view mirror, trying not to think about it at all. The fields lay fallow, the farmhouse tightly locked. Kyle hadn't

THE OLD MILL

wanted to return to the place bereft of his beloved nana and papa. His grief was still too raw.

Kyle waited until he got back to his cabin to make the call. He sat in a rocker on the porch, and drew in a deep breath while the phone rang in the law office. He checked his watch. After hours. No one was likely to pick up.

"John Waite speaking. How can I help you?"

From the man's voice, Kyle pegged him as over 60, smart, efficient and helpful. "This is Kyle Anderson calling," he said. "I understand you're handling my grandparents' trust."

"Ah...Kyle. My condolences for your loss. Your grandparents were nice folks. Thought the world of you."

A lump constricted Kyle's throat. "Thank you," he managed to choke out. "I didn't know they had a trust. Do they owe back taxes...an unpaid mortgage?" Kyle asked. "Thing is...I don't have much right now."

John Waite chuckled. "No. Nothing like that. Your grandparents had a great investment portfolio. It's grown steadily over the years to a tidy sum, as they never touched the principle."

"What?"

"You have an inheritance, Kyle. A sizable one," he said. "In addition to the farm, they left you a nice bundle of stocks, bonds, and other investments."

"What are you saying?"

The attorney cleared his throat. "It means that if you don't get greedy—and manage it well—you'll have a nice little income on the side for the foreseeable future. A nest egg. Or money to invest as you see fit."

"I always thought my grandparents were poor."

"Hardly. They just chose to live frugally."

"But the farm..."

"Your grandpa loved that farm. Loved working the land. You coming back to it?"

Kyle shrugged. "Hadn't planned to," he admitted. "I'm not really a farmer."

"Well..." said Mr. Waite. "You could always sell it. Or lease it for a while in case things change."

After he thanked the attorney and hung up, Kyle kneaded the tension knotting the back of his neck. He rocked back in his chair and looked out at the shimmering surface of Lost Lake. The phone call could change everything. He had an inheritance. A bit of land and some money. But did he want to pull up his new roots here and move back to the farm?

Lonesome Mountain rose in the distance—an imposing, yet benign, guardian. Kyle hadn't even climbed to the top yet. Hadn't kayaked on the lake or stepped out on Goose Island. So many places yet to explore...including his own soul—the rough, interior terrain he was just getting to know. He wanted to be better than the floundering, young man the gun incident had exposed. There was something for him here. Some inner demons to cast out. Some perspective to find. He wasn't ready to leave. Not yet.

Sheriff Buck pressed the phone tighter to his ear, straining to hear the coroner on the other end. "So, whose body is it?" he asked.

Percy sucked in a breath. "It's Daffodil. Daffodil DuPonte."

"How's that possible? Wasn't she buried years ago?"

"The town buried what we assumed were her remains."

"What do you mean?"

"Must have happened just before you came to work here," said Percy. "You don't recall the fire at Sweet Apple Farm?"

"What fire?"

Percy sighed. "Long story. And it's been an even longer day. How about we meet up at your office first thing tomorrow. We'll sort it all out then."

※

Early Friday morning, Carol ushered the coroner back to Sheriff Buck's office. She left the door slightly ajar.

Buck shook Percy's hand and shut the door. No need for Carol to be listening in. News like this would get around town soon enough—seeds of gossip scattered like dandelion fluff in a wayward wind.

Percy waved off Buck's offer of freshly brewed coffee and stretched out his lanky frame in an office chair, feet crossed at the ankles. "This is a strange one," he said. "A body missing all this time and no one even knowing."

Buck raked his fingers through his hair. "You suspect foul play?"

"Can't say for sure."

"Cause of death?"

"Damage to the vertebrae indicates she fell down the stairs and broke her neck." Percy leaned forward. "Went real quick."

"The trap door was shut," Buck said. "Seems unlikely she'd have closed it behind her. Think she was pushed?"

"Hard to say. I didn't find any defensive nicks on the bones." Percy paused. "And Daffodil didn't have any enemies. Everyone thought the world of her."

Buck frowned. "So how could a mix-up like this have happened?"

"Well... Daffodil DuPonte had increasing dementia and had been placed in the local rest home. She snuck out one night just a few weeks later. Folks said she wanted to get back to the farm to help some drifter who'd been hanging out around her place," said Percy. "A woman." Percy rocked back in his chair. "By the time they discovered Miss Daffodil was missing and launched a search party that night, the fire department got called to a blaze on her property. An outlying shed was fully engulfed in flames. The old wood structure went up like a pile of kindling. Investigators determined someone had lit a kerosene lantern that night and most likely dropped it, starting the fire. Add to that, the fact that some gas cans had been stored in the shed, made for a mighty hot blaze. Afterwards, they found what they presumed to be Miss Daffodil DuPonte's cremated remains inside. Not enough left for a positive ID. And since Daffodil was never found, it was just assumed that she'd burned to death in the shed. An unfortunate accident—given her poor mental state and all..."

"I see." Buck brought a hand to his chin. "So...the misidentified body from the fire? Whose was it?"

"Don't know for sure. But I'm guessing it was the drifter," Percy said. "Nobody saw her after the fire, either. Folks just assumed she'd moved on."

"Did the drifter have a name?"

"Called herself Birdie."

"That's what Harley told me." Buck added to his notes. "So, why would Miss Daffodil have gone to the old cabin?"

"She'd let Birdie stay there for a while and was worried about her, so it made sense that's where she'd go looking."

Buck huffed out a breath, thinking about the mix-up. *Poor Miss Daffodil... Down in the cellar all these years. And a stranger in her grave.*

Chapter 7

Choices

*I have set before you life and death.
Blessings and curses.
Choose life that it may be well with you...*
Deuteronomy 30:19

*K*yle hadn't slept much. His mind was whirling in a mixed state of both excitement and panic. He remembered from his studies that the Chinese character for *crisis* was a combination of the words *danger* and *opportunity*. Now he understood why. He'd need wisdom to decide how best to use his unexpected inheritance.

At work the next day, he pulled Gabe aside during break. He trusted the man's values and hoped for some sound advice. The rich, earthy scent of freshly sawn wood surrounded them as they settled on a stack of lumber.

"What would you do?" Kyle asked, after sharing the news about his sudden windfall.

"I don't know," pondered Gabe. "Easy money can be a blessing or a curse, depending on how you use it."

"I get that," said Kyle. "The kid in me wants to go hog wild on a ridiculous spending spree. But then I see it as an opportunity—seed money for my dreams."

"So, what are your dreams, Kyle?"

"That's the thing. I'm not sure. I'm more drawn to business, not farming. My grandparents loved the farm life—planting a crop, watching it grow, bringing in the harvest. I'm more social. I like people. Conversations. Getting together. Sharing ideas. Making things happen."

"What about construction? You're good at it."

"That's the thing." Kyle shrugged. "I enjoy the process. Building something lasting. Learning practical skills. But it really isn't me."

Gabe bent to tie a lace on his work boot. "So, what are you passionate about?"

"Not sure. I really like it out at Lost Lake," Kyle said. "The quiet. The raw beauty. And then there's this old mill just out of town. The building is really something. It could be a great gathering spot for artists to display their work, and for people to hang out. Maybe have something to eat. But I'd be too scared to do it on my own." He rubbed his neck. "And it's hard to make money representing artists. Could turn into a real money pit."

Gabe straightened. "Funny you should mention the old sawmill. Rowdy likes the place, too."

"I know. We talked about it a few days ago. Way different visions. He thinks it could be a great burger joint."

"So... Why not a burger joint with some local art on the walls?" Gabe grinned. "A good mix of both visions."

"An interesting idea…" Kyle ran a hand over his bearded chin. "But, like I said, I'm no carpenter."

"Did you know Rowdy restored all those old cabins at the lake?"

"He did?"

The Old Mill

"Yes. He's got great carpentry skills. Knows what to change up and what to leave alone in an older place. He worked on the Lost Lake Lodge as well. That building, overlooking the lake, fits in like it's always been there."

Kyle's eyes lit up. He knew he'd need some major help and expertise if he took on a project like this. But the idea of it excited him. He felt like a kid launching a crude stick boat who'd suddenly been asked to build a cruise ship. He had no idea how to even begin.

The idea of partnering with Rowdy was even crazier. It was an idea only God could have come up with. Especially after the whole rifle incident. "A partnership? Could that even work?"

"You tell me." Gabe stood. "Break's over. So, unless you're quitting today, let's get back to it."

Kyle buckled on his tool belt. His head spun with possibilities.

Bonfire bounded along the lakeshore, a stick in his mouth. Kyle hefted his backpack over a shoulder and smiled at the sight. The pup scampered up the steps to the back deck of the lodge and Kyle followed. There, paintbrush in hand, Charlotte was standing beside a canvas mounted on a three-legged easel.

He walked up beside her quietly, not wanting to break the spell. Charlotte's mouth was pursed in concentration, her hand moving the brush fluidly as she applied strokes of deep blue acrylic to a lakeside scene. It was a striking painting. Majestic pines reflected in still water, capturing the quiet beauty of Lost Lake. The girl had some serious talent.

Sensing his presence, she paused, brush in mid-air, a streak of blue paint on her cheek. "Don't look too closely. It's not done yet."

He looked anyway.

Charlotte frowned and took a step back, assessing her work. "You like it?"

"I do." Kyle looked from the image on canvas to the lake spreading out before them. "I'm no art critic, but you've really captured the beauty of the lake…even a bit of mystery in the deep shadows."

"Thanks, Kyle. I'm loving my art class, even if Mr. Starkweather is tough. I'm just learning how to do reflections on water." She looked up expectantly. "What do you think?"

"You've got a gift," he said. "Actually, if your painting is up for sale, I'd love to buy it." She didn't need to know that after four years as a starving student, it would be his first art purchase.

"Really?" Her face lit up.

"It would look great in my cabin," Kyle said, meaning it. Pleasure lit Charlotte's face. Maybe, with his newly hatched plan, he could help promote other local talent, too. "Consider me a patron of the arts."

"What's a patron?"

She really was young, thought Kyle. "A patron's a supporter of talented artists."

"Oh."

Kyle gave Bonfire a rub behind the ears. "Any idea where your dad is?"

"Last I saw, he was out on the dock, fixing a boat cleat."

"Thanks." Kyle headed to the docks. A week had passed since his talk with Gabe and now he needed to have a serious discussion with Rowdy.

"Hey, Rowdy." Kyle stepped up on the dock. "Need any help?"

"Nope. I'm just about done here." Rowdy finished tightening a cleat screw and straightened.

One weighty matter still stood between them. Kyle decided to clear the air before making his proposal. "Ever talk to the sheriff about those gun thieves?" Kyle ducked his head. The memory of his misstep still stung.

Rowdy folded his arms. "Sure you want to go there?"

"Not really, but I need to know if we can get past it."

"Why's that?"

"Lots of reasons. Mostly, I'd like a chance to earn back your trust."

"All right, then. You learn anythin' from it?"

'I hope so…" Kyle drew in a breath. "Saw a side of myself I wasn't too proud of. I aim to do better in the future."

"That's a start."

"I know my excuse falls short, but I really am sorry…"

"Apology accepted."

Kyle looked up. "Just like that?"

"Son, forgiveness isn't a piecemeal thing. You either choose to give it or you decide to withhold it. God forgave me for a whole lot worse, so I'm just returnin' the favor."

"Thanks, Rowdy." Kyle's face flushed. "It means a lot."

Rowdy nodded.

Kyle drew in a breath. "So, did the sheriff catch the gun thieves?"

"Not yet."

"Oh… I'd hate to see them get away with it."

"Well…what goes 'round comes 'round." Rowdy lifted a shoulder in a philosophical shrug. "It'll catch up with 'em sooner or later."

Kyle hoped so. In the whole rifle debacle, he had one other thing he owed Rowdy for. The cowboy had kept quiet about Kyle's part in it. No small thing. Not many folks would have been as kind.

Maybe it was pushing things to even suggest they partner up. Why would Rowdy want to work with a green kid like him, anyway?

A light breeze blew across the dock, bobbing it softly up and down on the undulating surface of the water. Kyle braced his feet to steady himself. The sun began to set, burnishing the sky and the lake in shimmering reds and golds. As the temperature dropped, the air freshened around them.

Kyle toyed with the slack end of a dock rope, slapping it against his palm. "Thing is... I've had some news."

"Nothin' bad, I hope." Rowdy looked up.

"No. Just the opposite. If wishes were horses, this beggar now *can* ride."

"What?"

"My grandparents left me some money. Enough to dream a little."

"You gonna buy a horse?"

"No. I'm going to buy the old Walker Sawmill and Foundry."

"You're kiddin'."

"Nope. Dead serious."

"You have money for somethin' like that?"

"I'm still pinching myself, but I do," said Kyle.

"Shoot. You gonna turn it into some fancy pants artist studio?" Rowdy grimaced.

"Not quite. I was thinking more along the lines of a restaurant."

"Hold your horses, son. Is the place even for sale?"

"It is. I've already put in an offer."

Rowdy's jaw fell open. "How'd that happen?"

"Easier than you'd think," said Kyle. "I went on the internet last week and researched the property title. Turned up the name of the lawyer who's handling the trust for the sawmill owner's estate. Apparently, William Walker died over a decade ago. His lawyer was only too happy to hear from someone with an interest

The Old Mill

in the long-abandoned property. Seems the out-of-state heirs don't want it."

Rowdy leaned against a dock support. "That's a piece of good news."

"It gets better," said Kyle. "The lawyer threw out a number that was in the ballpark and I jumped to put in an offer. It was just accepted."

"Congratulations, Kyle. That's amazin'." Rowdy had to admit to a stab of jealousy. If his life had played out differently, he might be the one buying the place.

"There's more," said Kyle. "Can we sit down somewhere for a few minutes?"

"Sure." Rowdy ducked beneath the shady canopy of a pontoon boat moored at the dock. He sank down on one of the cushions and motioned Kyle on board.

Kyle stepped into the boat and sat across from him. "Thing is... I'm looking for someone to head up the renovation and help me run a nice, mid-priced restaurant—everything from steaks to burgers. I'm thinking you'd be the perfect partner to bring on board."

Rowdy quirked an eyebrow. "A partner? Why me?"

Kyle glanced upslope. "I hear you remodeled these cabins."

"Yep. I did."

"Well, I'm living in one of them and I really like it," said Kyle. "It's got all the modern conveniences inside, yet still feels authentic. That's what I'd want for the sawmill...a full renovation, while retaining the feel of the old building." Kyle gestured to the point. "And then there's Lost Lake Lodge. I hear you had a big hand in building it as well. Look how great it turned out." He met Rowdy's eyes. "Truth is, I need someone like you, with the skills and experience to head up the job."

"You've no idea what you're askin'," said Rowdy. "Do you have the faintest notion of just how much money and work it'd take to pull it off?"

"Not a clue," admitted Kyle. "But I know we're both drawn to the place for a reason. It's begging to be saved and I'm thinking we're the ones to do it."

Rowdy could sense God's handprints all over it. Something too crazy for either of them to have come up with on their own. Still, he frowned. "You know I ain't got two nickels to rub together. What's the catch?"

"No catch," said Kyle. "I think we can come to terms. They're eager to unload the run-down place at a reasonable price. Thanks to my grandparents, I've got some unexpected money to invest. You've got the expertise to head up a remodel. We'd be business partners in the truest sense of the word. It might even be fun meshing our ideas together. See what we can come up with. I'd like to work alongside you…learn as I go."

Rowdy raked a hand across his mouth. "So…I'd be actin' as general contractor. Workin' full time. Drawin' up plans. Orderin' materials. Doin' most of the grunt work." Rowdy hid his grin. Exactly the sort of thing he loved to do. But no sense spilling those beans just yet. So, he threw in, "All without any guarantee that the place will even succeed?"

"I know it's a risk." Kyle straightened his back. "I may be young, but I'm not stupid. Most of my inheritance would be riding on the business making it…so it's a gamble for both of us."

Kyle started to sweat, his confidence wavering. He'd been counting on Rowdy coming on board when he'd made the offer on the place. Now what?

The pontoon boat rocked with an incoming wave from a jet skier out on the lake.

Rowdy folded his hands, wondering how different their expectations actually were. "What about your art studio idea?" he asked. "You givin' up on that?"

"Not exactly," said Kyle. "We'll need art on the walls, won't we? I was thinking of having a rotating display of local art. Give the restaurant a touch of class. And what better spot for artists to gather than a trendy place along the river?" He hesitated. "Our place."

Rowdy brow wrinkled. "Partners? I'd have to think on it." He rubbed his chin. "How'd you feel about an old-fashioned soda fountain?"

"What?"

"You know... One of those ice cream soda counters with tall stools and a big mirror."

"I've seen one. Why?"

Rowdy braced his hands on his knees. " 'Cause I've got my eye on one. It'd be perfect along that back wall."

Kyle rubbed a hand along the coarse hair of his beard. "Could work, I guess."

Rowdy's smile vanished. "Turning it down would be a deal-breaker."

"Okay, then. I'm on board," said Kyle. "Definitely."

"Good."

"So, would you consider partnering with me?"

Rowdy leaned forward. "I would."

"Okay, then... Let's talk specifics." Kyle braced his hands on his knees. "What kind of partnership do we want?"

The two spent the next hour pulling together a workable plan of shares and compensation, duties and dreams. Kyle tugged a notebook from his backpack and wrote up a tentative agreement. They talked about food items and floorplans, renovations and responsibilities...their ideas meshing surprisingly well.

"This may be an unlikely partnership," said Kyle. "But I think we'll work well together. I've got a lot of crazy ideas, and you've got the practical experience to keep us grounded."

"The cowboy and the college grad." Rowdy laughed. "You know this plan is totally nuts."

"Maybe. Maybe not." Kyle felt the rightness of it in his gut.

"You don't expect me to cook, do you?" Rowdy asked.

"Only if you want to."

Rowdy pushed up the brim of his black Stetson. "I never imagined a chance at somethin' like this."

"Me neither," said Kyle.

Rowdy scanned the still waters of Lost Lake, his mind on an old mill and foundry ten miles upstream.

"So… You in?" Kyle, stuck out his hand.

Rowdy clasped Kyle's hand in his work-roughened grasp. "I'm in."

※

Charlotte had gone all out on this one. The assigned art project required painting a building or cityscape, using two-point perspective. She'd tried a daring bird's eye view depiction of the Lost Lake cabins, imagining what they'd look like from an eagle's viewpoint—with sloping roofs and unfurling green treetops spearing the sky. Something was off a bit with the perspective, but she hoped her art teacher, Mr. Starkweather, could give her some pointers on how to make it work.

In his first year of teaching, he was an accomplished artist with several degrees and some impressive work. Not to mention being young, still in his twenties, and good looking. A strand of his tousled dark hair curled over his forehead, half hiding the piercing brown eyes set beneath thick expressive brows…just like Picasso or Matisse. The girls in class, including Charlotte, were half in love with the man.

Passing her painting to the front with the others, Charlotte leaned forward, eager for the group critiquing session. Mr. Starkweather lined up the paintings on the whiteboard tray and stood back to study them. "Two-point perspective," he reminded. "Let's see how you did."

"Well...isn't this something," he said, plucking up her painting. He held it up for the scrutiny of the class.

Charlotte's heart beat faster.

The instructor cleared his throat and gave a little *tsk tsk* sound with his tongue. "Here's a great example...of what *not* to do."

Her face flamed with embarrassment.

Mr. Starkweather turned her picture over, looking for the name on back. "Ah... Miss Charlotte Long. Is this your painting?"

"Yes," she squeaked out.

His eyes raked the painting with distain. "Overambitious, failed perspective, poor technique all around. I must say, Charlotte... You don't have the experience to attempt something like this, yet."

A loud roar filled Charlotte's ears. For a moment she thought she was going to be sick.

The class grew deadly quiet, while he moved on to the next painting. "Now this piece at least has the perspective right..."

Charlotte lurched to her feet, grabbed her offending picture from the ledge, and ran blindly out the door.

※

Kyle hammered a board in place and stopped to grab another nail from his tool pouch. A misplaced sound caught his attention — something between a sob and a stifled wail. He listened again. It was coming from somewhere behind the Java Junction addition.

Backing down the ladder, Kyle went outside. He peeked around the trunk of the big oak tree. What was Charlotte doing here? Wasn't she supposed to be in school?

Kyle came over and knelt beside her. "Charlotte... What's wrong?"

She looked up, eyes wet, face full of misery. Her cheeks were splotched with tears. "I'll never paint again," she blurted. "Never!"

A ruined art canvas lay next to her. It had been punched in, stomped on, and pretty much destroyed. "What happened?"

"I'm worthless as an artist," she wailed. "Worthless... all around."

Kyle touched her shoulder. "Why would you say that?"

The whole sad story of the disastrous art critique came tumbling out. Kyle felt his own anger rising. Recalling the pointed insults that Dr. Karl Lichenstein—his sociology professor—had hurled his way in college, he understood how an arrogant teacher could rattle Charlotte's confidence. It must have been devastating...especially in front of the whole class. The man had no right. No right to use his position to put down a young woman who *did* have talent. Charlotte needed approval, not distain. Kyle fisted his hands. He'd like nothing better than to charge over to the high school and throttle the guy.

He forced himself to draw in a calming breath, instead. "It's not true. Not a word of it. You're a good artist already, and still finding your way. One painting might not work out, but so what? You'll learn something from your mistakes." Wasn't that what Rowdy had told him? What he'd been telling himself about the whole rifle fiasco?

"No," Charlotte disagreed. She wiped her runny nose on her sleeve. "I'm just fooling myself to even think I can paint."

"Hey..." Kyle leaned toward her. "I have a great Lost Lake landscape painting on my cabin wall that says different. You're gifted."

"But Mr. Starkweather said..."

"Mr. Starkweather is a jerk," Kyle insisted. "A good teacher would have shown you how to make the painting better, not berate your talent. His talent as a teacher is what's lacking."

"Have you seen the painting?" She wiped her eyes.

He picked up the tattered canvas. "This it?"

She nodded, avoiding his eyes.

Kyle straightened the rumpled picture, tugging a few torn pieces back into place.

The artwork in his hands was so ridiculously off kilter that Charlotte suddenly found it funny. A giggle rose in her throat, forcing its way past her lips in a nearly hysterical guffaw. "It's terrible," she admitted. "Even before I stomped it to death."

Lifting an eyebrow, Kyle held the bedraggled canvas an arm's length away. "Terrible might be a bit harsh. How about *interesting*?"

Charlotte doubled over with a howl of laughter. "A modern art masterpiece."

"Impressionism," grinned Kyle. "With perhaps a touch of cubism." He brushed away some mud and an oak leaf. "Oh, forgive me..." he intoned, in his best professorial voice. "Was it multi-media?" He laughed along with her.

Charlotte tugged some tangled curls behind her ear and sobered. "Oh, Kyle... I'm really in trouble now."

"How's that?"

"I left campus without permission. Pa will kill me."

"He's more likely to go after Mr. Starkweather when he finds out what happened," suggested Kyle.

"What do you mean?"

"Rowdy's a real grizzly when it comes to safeguarding what's his."

"What makes you think that?"

Kyle's mind replayed Rowdy's rage when he burst into the cabin, his stolen rifle in hand.

But, he'd rather Charlotte didn't find out about that embarrassing incident. He deftly switched gears. "He's very protective of you. As any father would be."

Charlotte set the ruined painting aside. "Please don't tell Rowdy about this whole episode. He'd just overreact."

"He won't hear it from me."

"Thanks."

Kyle extended a hand to help her to her feet. "I do have some big news, though… concerning your pa."

"What news?"

"Rowdy and I are going to be business partners." He could hardly believe it himself.

"Really? What kind of business?"

"A restaurant and art galley… Out at the old mill."

"That dusty old place?"

"The very same… It has a ton of potential. Rowdy wants to put in a soda fountain."

"That'd be cool."

"I think so, too." Somehow, just talking about the restaurant made it seem more real. An eating place for folks to hang out. Somewhere for local artists and young talent, like Charlotte, to display their work and gain confidence. Food for body and soul.

Charlotte gathered up her things.

"You okay?" Kyle turned to go.

"Yes. Much better now." Charlotte dusted off her jeans and slung her backpack over a shoulder. "In any case… I'm destroying the evidence." She grabbed the mangled canvas and tossed it in the nearby dumpster.

"Multi-media," she mused, wiping the smudged mascara from under her eyes. "I just might give it a try."

"See you later..." Kyle headed back to work. He pounded another stud into place for the coffee shop addition. Soon, he'd be placing studs in his own space, hammering in nails to secure his future livelihood. He was a little scared and a lot excited. The old mill property was already in escrow. There was no going back now.

His favorite lines from a Frost poem, "The Road not Taken," ran through his head:

> *I shall be telling this with a sigh*
> *somewhere ages and ages hence:*
> *Two roads diverged in a yellow wood, and I—*
> *I took the one less traveled by,*
> *and that has made all the difference.*

He felt both incredibly young and impossibly old...standing at this crossroad in his life. His motivation was no longer to get away—the impulse that had first brought him here—but to stride eagerly toward a new, nearly impossible, dream.

Like Charlotte, he had to try his wings. And hoped to soar.

Chapter 8

Spiritual Wickedness

*For we wrestle not against
flesh and blood enemies,
but against principalities, against powers,
against the rulers of the darkness
of this world,
and against spiritual wickedness
in high places.
Ephesians 6:12*

Long past his bedtime, Max sat up, ramrod straight…willing himself to stay alert. He was supposed to be asleep, but he sat alone in the dark instead, a blanket flung across his thin shoulders for warmth.

Maybe if he didn't close his eyes—if he stayed awake—the night terrors wouldn't come.

From his second story window he could see a gazillion stars sprinkled across the sky like glitter glued on black construction paper. Max wondered if God was up there somewhere, looking down.

Since coming to live at the Reed's, he'd gone to church each Sunday at Good Shepherd Chapel.

"God loves you," his Sunday school teacher said. "He watches over you and cares for you with a father's love."

Max couldn't wrap his mind around that. Did God keep a belt at the ready to whip him if he stepped out of line, like Pa used to do? Was God a mean drunk with a temper? Or maybe God was more like his new dad, Gabriel Reed, who found a way to be proud of him, even when he messed up.

Max was afraid to pray, unsure which God might show up. So, he tried a little practice prayer in his head. *God...are you up there? Can you see me down here through this window, lookin' up? Them bones scared me spitless. I didn't want to find nothin' like that. Please don't let the haints get me. Don't send me straight to hell.* He squeezed his eyes shut and whispered. "Amen."

When he opened his eyes, the sky was as black as ever. A few stars twinkled above. But Max still felt alone. And tired. So very tired. His head nodded a few times, but he forced himself awake, leaning a shoulder against the corner post of the headboard. His eyelids grew heavy as wet mud...

He was back in the cellar. His hand groped along the cold wall as he felt his way down the wooden stairs. They creaked under his weight, and he shushed his own footsteps, bringing a finger to his mouth in warning. "Shhh... You'll wake the dead."

But it was too late. The bleached white skeleton in the corner jolted up and rose from the floor with a clatter of old bones. The skull swiveled toward him, skewering him with an accusatory stare from shadowed, empty eye sockets. Lipless teeth grinned up at him. "So, you're back."

"It was an accident... I swear," Max stuttered. His knees shook and he felt as cold as death. "Didn't mean to bother you none. Didn't even see you there, 'til..."

"Shush! Who told you to talk? You sneakin' down here to steal my bones? Or maybe it's treasure you're after?" The skeleton jerked an arm up, pointing a bony finger at Max's chest. "You bad little boys are all alike. Bunch of thieves. Taking what don't belong to you."

"I'm not after your treasure..."

"Liar! You think I wouldn't find you out?" The skeleton's toothy mouth opened in a wicked grimace, sending chills clean through him.

Max tried to escape, but his feet were stuck in a black, sucking goop that held him fast. He bolted right out of his shoes and fled up the stairs and out the door. He raced barefoot down the rocky trail, limping across jagged rocks and losing his way in the prickling undergrowth. A black specter flapped above him on whipping wings. The skeleton's eerie chortle followed the crow. "My dark minion will pluck your eyeballs out, you little thief. You can run, but you'll never get away from me... From meee..." she cackled.

The evil black crow swooped closer, its sharpened talons stretched out, cruel beak clicking.

Max covered his head with his arms. "Help!" he shrieked. "Somebody help me!!"

A light flipped on. The darkness fled. Gabe stood in the doorway, backlit by the soft glow of the hallway lamp. He scooped Max up in his arms and held the trembling boy in his lap. "Another nightmare?"

Max nodded, embarrassed to be such a baby. He looked over to make sure the evil crow wasn't roosting on the headboard of his bed.

The Old Mill

"The skeleton?"

Another nod. "It...it called me a little thief. Out to steal its bones. Then my feet got stuck in some suckin' muck, and the black crow came after me to...to scratch my eyes out." Max's voice quavered, his words sputtering to a halt.

"You're not a thief," Gabe reassured. "You're a good boy and a fine son."

"But I stepped... I stepped on it...thet ol' skeleton. Knocked the head clean off."

"Not on purpose." Gabe rubbed Max's back until he felt some of the tension leave the boy's shoulders.

Max ran a knuckle across his cheek, brushing away the tears. "Am I goin' straight to hell?" he asked.

"Certainly not! Where'd you get that idea?"

"Pa said I was the devil's spawn."

"That's a lie!" A fierce furrow formed between Gabe's eyebrows. He took in a deep breath. "We found out something about that skeleton today. Something you should know."

Max shivered. "What?"

"It belonged to a really sweet lady named Daffodil DuPonte, Lizzy's great aunt. This used to be her home."

Max's eyes widened and he clung even tighter to Gabe. "Is she hauntin' us here right now?"

"No way," said Gabe. "She was a wonderful person. Always helping others. She was so nice that she gave this house to Lizzy so she could have a farm of her own. So that we could all live here one day and be happy." He pulled an old photo from his pocket. "This is her."

Max stared at the photo. The woman was smiling. She had curly hair like Lizzy's and lively blue eyes. She looked more like a real person than a ghost—like somebody ready to have some fun. Someone like Doris, who might bake a batch of cookies or put marshmallows in the hot chocolate.

Gabe pointed to the floppy hat Aunt Daffodil wore in the picture. "See. That's the same gardening hat our Lizzy wears, the one with all the yellow daffodils around the brim."

"That's the skeleton lady's hat?"

"Yes, it is. It suited her." Gabe squeezed his shoulder. "Lizzy affectionately called her Aunt Daffy."

"Cuz of the daffodils?"

"Exactly. And you know what else?"

Max shook his head, just now getting some air back into his lungs.

"Aunt Daffy wants to thank you."

"For what?"

"For finding her body down in that cellar. For letting us know where she was all this time, so that we could give her a proper burial and remember her for the fine, giving woman she was." Gabe grinned. "You gave her that, and you didn't even know her."

Max looked at the photo. At the sunny smile and the eyes looking straight at him. "She doesn't look too scary."

"She's not. Aunt Daffy would have loved knowing you." He ruffled Max's hair. "Now, in a way, you do know each other. You helped bring her home to her family."

Max nodded. "Never thought 'bout it like that." He rubbed his eyes and stifled a yawn.

"Think you can sleep now?"

"Maybe so."

Gabe switched on a nightlight near the door. "Let's leave this on tonight." He helped Max get into bed and tucked the covers tightly around him. "Tomorrow we'll find some more photos of Aunt Daffy. Maybe Lizzy can share stories of the summer she spent with her here as a girl. She loves to talk about all the fun things they did together."

"Did they bake cookies?"

"Pretty sure they did."

Max thought of chocolate chip cookies, fresh from the oven, and hot chocolate with half-melted marshmallows floating on top. He pictured Lizzy in that floppy gardening hat, blooming with daffodils.

Gabe patted Max's shoulder. "Night, Son."

"Night, Gabe." Max squished his eyes shut and listened as Gabe's footfalls faded.

Max wished and hoped that God was a dad like Gabe. Someone who cared deep down inside about a naughty boy like him—a boy who Pa said was bound for mischief. Had God heard his whispered prayer after all?

Gabe left the door open. Before heading downstairs, he lowered himself to the top step and sat, resting his head in his hands. "Oh, God," he pleaded. "Have mercy on our little boy."

Max reminded Gabe of himself at that age, only without his simmering anger. With no father in his life, Gabe remembered the rage that drove him as a kid. He sassed his poor mother, mad at the world. Hunger for a father had left a deep void within.

Max had been dealt a different hand—first losing his mother to cancer, then ducking the fists and the accusations of a drunken father. Both Gabe and Max bore painful wounds. Wounds only God could heal.

He'd been a hot-headed, rebellious sixteen-year-old, with little to recommend him, when Charlie Martin had taken him under his wing. Gabe had begrudgingly showed up under a court order to work with Charlie. It was either that, or jail time for petty theft, after his mother finally kicked him out. Learning carpentry skills under Charlie's watchful eye had gradually sanded away the resentful chip on his shoulder.

Gabe sighed. What would have become of him without someone like Charlie to believe in him, when he didn't believe in himself? Charlie was gone now. Passed away at age 89 last winter.

And now Gabe was going to be Max's step dad. The one to believe in him. The one charged with showing him how to be a man.

There was a sweetness about Max. A desire to please that Gabe hadn't possessed as a child. Max had it in spades. Somehow the boy still trusted that things would get better. He still dared to hope.

Funny how Aunt Daffy had touched all three of them—two in life, one in death. Like many an aimless boy, Gabe had found his way to Miss Daffodil's table on occasion. There, good food and good council had buoyed his spirits. And Lizzy's summer with Aunt Daffy had changed her, too...in ways she was just now discovering. He and Lizzy hoped to do the same for Max—provide him with a good stable home and with love.

Now he wondered if that would be enough. Like a cheerful mockingbird, arising each day before dawn, singing its heart out, Max had always bounced back. Until the discovery in the cabin. Until the nightmares began.

Gabe prayed that God would show him how to help their boy. How did you make a skeleton human? Aunt Daffy's picture had seemed to help. Putting a face to the bones. But Gabe's words seemed so inadequate.

He felt a hand on his knee. Lizzy. She'd just gotten home from her book club meeting.

"You okay?" she asked.

"I'm not sure how to help him," he admitted.

"Another nightmare?"

The Old Mill

"Yeah. Spooked the heck out of him."

"Our brave boy has a superstitious streak."

"Of course, he does. His old man specialized in family curses." Gabe raked his hands through his hair. "Uttering threats of what the devil would do to a *bad boy* like Max."

"Words can carry curses." Lizzy squeezed his hand. "Or blessings." She went into Max's room and found him fast asleep. She brushed a strand of blond hair away from his face, flushed with slumber. Dark lashes smudged his cheeks. She planted a kiss on Max's forehead and lingered in the doorway.

Gabe got up and stood beside her, watching over their boy, so sweet and innocent as he slept. "Finding the skeleton really freaked him out."

"It would bother anyone. Can you believe that poor Aunt Daffy was down there all this time, and nobody knew?" Lizzy sighed. "I always thought she died in a fire."

"Everyone thought so."

"She gave me the best summer ever."

"Let's build on that," Gabe led her downstairs to the kitchen. "We need to make *that* Aunt Daffy real to Max. Put flesh on those bones so they don't keep haunting him." He cupped her cheek. "Think we can do that?"

"We can," said Lizzy. "I'll dig out the old photos and dust off the memories. Maybe Max, Chloe and I can do some of the things Aunt Daffy and I did that summer...in her honor."

"Great idea."

"And Gabe..."

He looked up.

"You're all the father he needs."

A call from dispatch pinged on Buck's phone. "Sheriff Buchanan."

"Hey, Buck," said Carol. "The security alarm's been set off at Sparkles, that boutique in the old Rafferty building. You want to go check it out?"

"Gloria's place?" Bucks heart rate accelerated. "She installed an alarm...here in Buttermilk Falls?"

"Yes and yes."

"I'm on my way." Buck drove quickly toward town.

No lights were on in the building when he pulled up, but he could hear raised voices coming from inside. Buck sprinted across the empty gravel parking lot. He stepped over an abandoned crowbar on the ground, likely the tool used to bust in the lock on the open back door. He pulled out his flashlight and entered. A muffled shout hurried him toward Gloria's office in the back.

"Don't move...or I'll be forced to stab you," said a high-pitched voice.

"You're crazy, lady. I could squash you like a bug," a man retorted.

Buck flattened himself beside the office doorway and leaned in for a look.

There stood Tater—the dumb, heavy-set guy from the campground. He clutched a fistful of bills from the cashbox, and held his other hand out to ward off his attacker.

"Get 'em up!" demanded Gloria, jabbing him with a pitchfork. The farm implement was decorated with a cluster of daisies, secured to the handle by a big floppy bow.

"What the hell?" yelped Tater, his silver-capped front tooth flashing in the moonlight. "You gone plum loco?" Reluctantly, he raised both hands above his head in a gesture of surrender. In seconds, Tater was backed against a filing cabinet, the sharp tines of Gloria's pitchfork pressing against his belly.

"Don't move," she said.

"Best listen to the lady." Buck entered the doorway with his service revolver drawn. "I'm going to turn on this lamp. I've got a gun, so nobody get jumpy."

The room flooded with light.

"Don't shoot," Tater pleaded, hands still raised. "Get this crazy woman the hell away from me."

Gloria looked over, still grasping the pitchfork. "About time you showed up, sheriff." She blew a wayward strand of pink hair out of her eyes with a huff of breath. "Thought I might have to hogtie the scoundrel myself."

Buck had to admire her spunk. She looked fantastic, even in her flowered PJ's, wielding a pitchfork…face flushed and fire in her eyes.

He brought out the handcuffs. Slapped them on Tater's wrists in one smooth motion. "Where are your buddies?" He looked into the dark recesses of the store.

"Wouldn't you like to know?" Tater sniped.

"This way." Buck escorted both Tater and Gloria out to his patrol car. He settled the thief in the back seat of the police cruiser, shutting the door tightly and locking it.

"Stay here," he instructed Gloria "…while I clear the building."

Going back inside, Buck flicked on the overhead lights and made a thorough search of the premises. It was empty, except for Gloria's resurrected treasures. Nothing else seemed to have been disturbed. Looked to be a one-man job, limited to the office. Buck wondered if the other two missing campers had set out in the car on their own crime spree in town. He'd know soon enough.

Buck holstered his weapon and hurried back to Gloria. She stood just where he'd left her, pitchfork still in hand. She cast a wary look through the car window at a disgruntled Tater, who was cursing under his breath. *Thank God he hadn't hurt her.*

After checking that the criminal was still secure inside the cruiser, Buck led Gloria back inside the store and had her look around. "Anything taken?"

"Don't see anything missing," she said. "Except the money from the cash box." Gloria lowered her weapon, and stood uncertainly in the middle of her office, staring at the tens and twenties, strewn across the floor.

"You okay?" he asked.

"Fine and dandy."

He noticed her hands were shaking. Ushering her out of the ransacked office, Buck led her to a newly upholstered, red sofa in the showroom and sat beside her. "What happened?"

"I heard a noise," she said. "Then the alarm went off. So, I came in from my living quarters to check things out."

"You didn't think to call the police?"

"Well, sure. But what if it was a false alarm?"

"And what if it wasn't? Like tonight?" Buck raked a hand through his hair. "You might have been hurt...or worse."

"I can take care of myself." She sat up straighter.

"With a gussied-up pitchfork?"

"It did the job."

"What if he'd had a gun?" His concern edged toward anger at her foolishness.

"Maybe then I would've grabbed a bulletproof trashcan lid."

"Glitter isn't bulletproof, Gloria."

"It is on some decor."

"Really?!" Buck, not amused, huffed out a breath. "You should have called me, Gloria. You could have been killed."

"Not on your watch." She grinned up at him.

"I don't have ESP."

"And yet, here you are…" She leaned in for a kiss.

The Old Mill

Buck wanted to lecture her. Wanted to warn her not to repeat such foolhardiness. But, as it turned out, he wanted the kiss even more.

Their lips touched with a sizzle. Buck pulled her close—where she belonged.

You're on duty, you idiot, said a niggling voice in his head. He broke off the kiss and stood.

"I swear, Gloria. You'll be the death of me yet."

"One can only hope."

Buck saw her safely back to her quarters, insisting she leave the crime scene intact for now. He secured the back door of Sparkles and got behind the wheel of his patrol car.

"This is police brutality," whined Tater from the back seat. "Leaving me sitting out here all this time in the dark and cold. And these cuffs hurt."

"I'd shut up if I were you," said Buck, clenching his jaw. "Neither this patrol car nor the slammer are meant to be Club Med." He started the car and pulled out. "You're just darned lucky you didn't hurt the owner."

"Hurt *her*?" Tater grumbled. "She stabbed me with a pitchfork."

"You were robbing her store," reminded Sheriff Buck. He began to cruise the back streets of town, looking for the beat-up, tan Suburban. *Where were they?*

Maybe if he needled Tater a bit, the captured crook might spill something. "So, they left you all on your own, huh, Tater. Guess that didn't work out so well for you." Buck turned a corner way too fast, throwing the crook hard against the side door.

"Are you nuts!?" shrieked Tater. "You're drivin' like a maniac!"

"Just want to make sure you remember the ride." Buck slowed only slightly for the next curve. "Since you're not talking…guess you're the only one going to jail tonight."

"I asked for the mercantile job..." Tater mumbled.
"What'd you say?"
"Nothin'."

Chapter 9

Ancient Ruins

*They will rebuild the ancient ruins
and restore the places long deserted.*
Isaiah 61:4

Sheriff Buck cruised the alley behind Lucille's mercantile. No sign of the tan Suburban. But, in the glare of his headlight beams, glass shards glittered in the weeds. The store's rear door stood ajar and the back window was shattered.

Buck parked, drew his revolver and entered the building. Too late. The gun safe, tucked against the wall, was splintered…ransacked and empty. The nearby ammo display had been cleaned out, as well. Who knew what else might be missing? He did a sweep of the store, assuring himself no one was still lurking around. The cash register drawer stood open and bare. Buck hoped that was the way Lucille left it at night, after depositing the day's receipts.

Buck mulled over the day's events as he headed back to his patrol car. The perps must have decided to pull a few robberies on the way out of town. Or maybe they'd holed up somewhere nearby.

After booking Tater into jail, Buck planned to call the local motels to see if any of the suspects had checked in.

He slid behind the wheel. Tater, still handcuffed in the back seat, was agitated, muttering oaths. How far would loyalty to his buddies extend? Or their allegiance to him? Would they cut and run, when they found out their pal had been arrested? Or would they try something even more stupid, like trying to break Tater out of jail? Buck almost wished they'd be dumb enough to try. Most folks underestimated rural law enforcement, thinking they were bumbling Mayberry types. It angered him that they'd targeted Gloria's store, and now the mercantile—businesses close to his heart.

A whiff of Gloria's flowery perfume lingered on his jacket. Too bad this rash of break-ins would keep him tied up for a while. He'd sure like to follow up on that kiss.

Mid-morning, Kyle and Rowdy stood shoulder to shoulder in front of the old Walker Sawmill and Foundry. The college grad and the cowboy. Two kids in a candy shop.

Now that the place was in escrow, Kyle felt free to go inside to explore.

"Won't need a key," Rowdy had assured him. "The lock's plumb rusted away."

They considered the lines of the old building for a few minutes, admiring the motionless water wheel, its broken paddles hovering just above the swift-moving water of Coyote Creek.

"It'll be a real beauty, once it's back in motion," Rowdy said.

"Looks pretty far gone to me," Kyle countered. "Think it's even fixable?"

"I'd sure like to try."

The Old Mill

They tromped up the steps to the door. Only a stick in the latch held the entry closed. Kyle pulled out the twig and tugged the door open, with a reverent pause before stepping inside.

Dust motes floated in the air. Kyle noticed the massive, steel saw blade first…leaning against the side wall. Six-feet in diameter. Three-inch-deep notched points raking out like shark's teeth along the rounded outer edge. When mounted on a wall, it would be a stunner—the centerpiece of their newly named Old Mill Restaurant. He looked around. He'd salvage those metal-banded wooden barrels for atmosphere, as well as some of the vintage workbenches to use for a salad bar or beverage station. The wide floorboards and hefty support beams added a lot of character. And with a lit fire, the sturdy brick foundry furnace tucked in the far corner would add both warmth and charm. Kyle was already mentally hanging artwork on the walls and arranging tables in cozy groupings. The place could be like his favorite LA restaurants, only with a country authenticity those places lacked.

Rowdy was thumping boards for soundness and checking the mortar between the furnace bricks.

"Well?" Kyle, tried not to look too eager.

"Have we died and gone to heaven?" Rowdy ran a hand across a cracked brick. "This place is amazin'…even better than I remembered. Needs a lot of work, though."

"How much work?"

"A few months, at least," said Rowdy. "I'm hopin' it's mostly cosmetic. Structurally, the place seems sound. Just a few spots of dry rot here and there, that I can see." Rowdy pulled out his Swiss army knife and probed between the foundry furnace bricks. "This fireplace could use some fresh mortar." He stomped on the floor in a sagging spot. "And a few foundation joists likely need replacin'."

"What about the roof?" Kyle looked up.

Rowdy stared up past the open roof beams. "The old tin might need a repair or two, but in my earlier checks, I didn't see any signs of a leak."

Kyle sobered. "How much will those repairs set us back?"

Rowdy shrugged and named a price twice what Kyle had expected. "But, if we do most of the work ourselves, we can save a lot on labor." Rowdy resettled his Stetson on his head. "Then our main expenses will just be in materials—lumber, drywall, commercial kitchen equipment, tables and chairs...nuts and bolts stuff. I'll spring for the soda fountain myself."

"You know where to find one of those?"

"Just happens I do." Rowdy let his eyes rove over the empty space. "Like I mentioned earlier, it'd be perfect along that back wall. Long beveled mirror. A lit marquee. Beautiful, polished walnut counter. Chrome stools, with red-leather seats. Can't you just see it?"

Funny thing was...Kyle could see it. All of it. Like walking into a half-remembered dream. He'd sat at a soda fountain like that once as a kid in a small town in Denver. One of the best times of his life. He could almost taste it. Vanilla ice cream piled high in a big glass bowl. He'd been fascinated, watching the soda jerks ladle on chocolate syrup and squirt a spray of whipped cream, before placing a single bright red cherry atop his very own sundae. Adding a sprinkle of nuts. He remembered washing all that sugary deliciousness down with sips of water from a white paper funnel cup, nestled in a silver holder. Seeing his own reflection in the mirror...grinning.

"I can." Kyle blinked. "You're a genius." Rowdy's soda fountain would add another layer of charm to the place. Rekindling fond memories for some, and making new ones for others. He could practically taste the restaurant fare. Ice cream sundaes and chocolate malts cold enough to give you a brain freeze. Juicy

The Old Mill

hamburgers and French fries dipped in ketchup. Grilled steaks smothered in onions. A gathering spot for friends and family.

A smile parted Kyle's dark beard, his eyes shining. He stretched out his arms in the dust-covered space. "Our very own restaurant. Right here."

"It's somethin', all right," agreed Rowdy. "Folk'll want to come and hang out here...just for the feel of the place."

A skittering sound came from the rafters. The men glanced up, but saw only a moving shadow.

"Guess we'll have to chase off some varmints," said Rowdy.

"Rats?"

"Most likely."

A pair of beady eyes locked on the strangers. What are they doing here? Poking around. Trying to uncover my secret hiding spots? *Well, I was here first*, the creature reasoned. *And I can make plenty of trouble.*

The bells tied to the door of Sparkles jangled as Rowdy came in. He went back to the office. "Whoa...what happened?"

Gloria looked up from the scattered cash, overturned chairs and jumbled file cabinets in her usually tidy office. "I was robbed. The investigators just now left, so I can finally clean up."

"Any idea who did it?"

"Well... Buck arrested some idiot named Tater." Gloria picked up a few scattered greenbacks, stacking them into neat piles.

Tater? The name rankled. He was one of the guys who'd stolen Rowdy's rifle. "So, how come he didn't take off with the cash?"

"Didn't get a chance to. I surprised him in the act. We had a standoff, eyeball to eyeball."

"What?"

"My security alarm went off and I caught him red-handed with my money."

"You stopped that creep all by yourself? You totin' a gun?"

"Nope." She pointed to the beribboned tool. "I armed myself with that pitchfork." Gloria bent to pick up some scattered invoices from the floor.

Rowdy grunted. "The sheriff know 'bout this?"

"Of course. He took the guy to jail."

"I'm guessin' he's none too happy about you playin' hero."

"Like I told him, I'm not helpless." She scowled. "So, what brings you to Sparkles, Rowdy? Or did you just come by to give me a hard time?"

"Hey..." He held his hands out in a placating gesture. "I'm here on business."

"Redecorating your cabin?"

"Nope." Rowdy tucked his hands in his back pockets. "But I'll likely need your help down the road with that kind of stuff. We aim to keep a country feel to our restaurant."

"Restaurant? What restaurant?"

"The Old Mill Restaurant. The one Kyle and I are fixin' to make out of the old Walker Sawmill and Foundry along Coyote Creek."

"Really?" She raised an eyebrow. "You and Kyle?"

"An unlikely pairin', I'll admit." Rowdy shrugged. "But so far it's workin'."

Gloria straightened her computer monitor and righted the keyboard. "Renovating that old mill... Sounds like something I would enjoy. So, what's on your mind this morning?"

"For starters, I'd like to take another gander at the ol' soda fountain you showed me on the internet."

"For the mill?"

"Yep."

Gloria efficiently bundled the loose cash, stashing it in the open cashbox, then tucked it in a drawer. "Let's see if I can find it." She sat at her computer.

Rowdy righted the rest of the office chairs, then stood behind her.

In a few minutes, she had an image of the vintage soda fountain up on the screen.

It looked even better than he'd remembered... Wooden countertop. Cushioned chrome barstools, begging a body to sit and sip a soda or down a decadent banana split.

Gloria pointed to the screen and laughed. "Beautiful, don't you think?"

"Perfect."

"You want to get it?"

"I do. But I've no idea in hell how to buy it from a computer."

"No problem. I can do it for you." Gloria clicked a few keys. "Got a credit card?"

"Yep." He handed it over.

In minutes, she was printing out his receipt. "It's yours now." Gloria handed him a printed sheet of paper. "It'll be delivered to the mill site whenever you call and set it up."

"That's it?"

"All done."

Rowdy bent closer to look at the screen one more time. "I can hardly wait."

Buck stood in the doorway. *What the heck was going on?* He didn't like the way Rowdy was leaning over Gloria's shoulder... heads close together. A leaden feeling stole into his chest, making it hard to breathe. His cheeks grew hot and his hands clenched into fists. If he didn't know better, he'd think he was jealous.

"They don't make 'em like this anymore," gushed Rowdy.

Buck tamped down his runaway emotions. After all, they were just looking at something on the computer screen. "So, what's happening?" He stepped into the room.

Gloria looked up. "Hey, Buck. Did you know that Rowdy and Kyle are going to turn the old mill and foundry into a restaurant?"

"Really? That's great." Buck was always interested in a new eating spot. He looked over her shoulder at the screen. "You putting in a soda fountain?"

"Yep." Rowdy folded the receipt and tucked it in his pocket. "It's a beauty, ain't it?"

"Sure is," said Buck, relieved that Rowdy was here on business.

Rowdy turned to go. "I heard about the robbery. What a shame."

"Yeah." Sheriff Buck shook his head. "They hit the mercantile, too. Made off with a bunch of rifles." He straightened up. "Looks like the same bunch that stole your gun."

"That's what I heard. Think you can catch 'em?"

Well, we've already got one of 'em locked up. That gives us a better shot at tracking the others down. But, so far, he's not talking."

"Lucky I got my gun back, then." Rowdy squared his shoulders. "It's my favorite rifle."

Gloria yawned. "Think I'll be closing up now, boys. Last night's excitement is definitely catching up with me. I really need a nap."

"And I've got lots of orderin' to do." Rowdy, headed out. "Thanks, Gloria."

Buck lingered for a few minutes, making sure that the repaired door was set to lock when he left. "Be careful," he reminded Gloria.

"If I was being careful, I wouldn't be flirting with you."

"You're flirting?" Buck hadn't noticed any batting eyelashes or coy looks.

"Well...not right this minute," she admitted.

"I can stay...if you'd like to work up to it," he teased.

"You'd best move along, sheriff. A girl needs her beauty rest." A smile played at the corners of Gloria's expressive mouth. "Or do I have to get my pitchfork?"

※

Sunlight streamed through the kitchen window as Lizzy finished cleaning up after breakfast. "Let's do a fun Thanksgiving craft," she said to the children. "We can make some dried apple strings...like the ones in this photo." She pointed to the old picture of herself on the farm as a young girl, holding up a chain of dried apples...grinning.

"What do you do with apple strings?" asked Chloe.

"They look pretty, smell good, and make people happy." Lizzy waved the photo. Aunt Daffy was smiling in the background, toting a bushel basket full of Macintoshes. Her floppy daffodil hat capped her flyaway mass of blond curls. "Aunt Daffy and I made lots of apple chains when I was here for the summer. I loved doing crafts with her." She didn't add that she hoped the project might humanize Aunt Daffy for Max and let him see her as a fun person.

"They'll look sweet and homey in a country kitchen, like ours." She pointed to the picture. "Later on, we'll add bows and cinnamon sticks between the apple slices, like in this photo, so they'll make a room smell really nice."

"Can I give an apple string to Doris when they're ready?" asked Max. "She always cooks stuff that smells good."

"Of course." Her sweet boy was back. Lizzy prayed it would last.

Max shrugged. "Won't them apples draw flies?"

"That's why we have to cut them into thin slices and dry them first." Lizzy laughed. "But, for starters, we have to go out and gather some apples. Let's get enough to make a pie, while we're at it."

"I love apple pie," said Max.

"Me, too," chimed in Chloe.

She and the children headed to the apple orchard to pick up windfall apples scattered on the ground. Hampered by her pregnancy girth, Lizzy let the children do most of the bending over.

Soon they were back in the kitchen, busy cutting up apples. Chloe helped by laying the slices on drying trays to set on a table out in the sun. It would be close to a week before the apples were dry enough to string. When the trays were full, Lizzy peeled apples for a pie. She let the kids help roll the dough out on a floured breadboard and shape it for the two crusts. Before long, the sweet smell of baking apples and cinnamon filled the kitchen.

Lucille finished sweeping up the mess inside the mercantile, dumping the wood and glass splinters from the broken gun safe into the trash. "Law' o' mercy," she muttered. "What's this world comin' to?"

She looked up as a woman entered. A stranger. "Can I help you?" she asked.

"Oh...well...I...I'm just looking around," said the woman.

Shifty eyes, thought Lucille. But she was itching to tell someone about the robbery. "Guess you heard about the break-in..."

"No... I'm new to town." The woman squinted up at her. "What happened?"

"Some crooks broke in and stole our whole stock of huntin' rifles last night." Lucille sniffed. "And right at the start of huntin' season, too. I'm just cleanin' up the mess now."

Lucille wiped off the counter as she sized up her customer. Middle aged. Shoulder length, mousy, brown hair. Cheap, rhinestone-studded glasses perched on a sharp, pointy nose. The woman stuffed her hands in the pockets of a shabby corduroy jacket, worn over faded blue slacks. The poor thing looked a little down on her luck. Scuffed leather shoes. A defeated slump to her shoulders.

Lucille's innate sympathy overcame her initial harsh judgment. "But don't let it scare you off. A robbery is pretty unusual for a nice, quiet place like Buttermilk Falls." She gave a reassuring smile. "My name's Lucille and I've worked here nigh onto forever. If I can help you find somethin', just let me know."

The woman shuffled closer. "Thanks. I'm sorry about the break-in." She stepped up to the counter. "I'm Wilma. Wilma Watts." Her pinched mouth lifted in a brief smile. "Maybe you can help me. I'm looking for my brother's place. His name's Rod…Rod Radding. Passed away a few months back. Did you know him?"

"You're Rod's sister? Well…ain't that somethin'." Lucille leaned her elbows on the worktop, keen for any tidbit of fresh gossip. "I'm real sorry for your loss," she added, remembering her manners.

"Thank you," the woman said.

"Such a sad accident," Lucille added. "Drinkin' and drivin'. A real bad mix."

Wilma nodded. "Yes. Very sad. Rod was my only sibling. My big brother."

Lucille had never heard of Rod having a sister. She wondered why he hadn't called on Wilma to help out when his poor wife was so sick, or after she passed and he had Max to raise on his own. Why hadn't Wilma stepped up then?

Lucille pondered that for a moment. Wilma was in for a big let-down if she thought Rod had left her any inheritance. "You should know," informed Lucille, "…his place was sold at auction… for back taxes."

Wilma's brown eyes widened behind the lenses of her dark-framed glasses. The rhinestones at the corners glittered in the light as she shook her head in disbelief. "Sold? The whole farm?"

"Yep. 'Fraid so." Lucille leaned closer. "Did you come for the boy?"

"Rod has a kid?!" Wilma's thin eyebrows rose in alarm before she remembered to school her features.

"You didn't know about your own nephew?" Lucille's mouth dropped open. "How could that be?"

"Rod and I lost touch over the years," Wilma said. "You know how that goes."

Lucille nodded, but did some mental calculations. Max was nine. And Wilma didn't even know Rod had a son? That was some estrangement.

"So, now that you know about the child, I'm guessin' you'll want to take him under your wing," prodded Lucille. "Since, he's an orphan."

"No. I don't think so," said Wilma. She twisted her fingers together in a nervous gesture. "I... I don't have the means to care for a child."

"Well, little Max does have some inheritance," volunteered Lucille.

"Oh? What'd he get?"

"Not sure," admitted Lucille. "Heard rumors 'bout some nice jewelry."

"Jewelry, you say?" Wilma took off her glasses and wiped the lenses with the tail of her shirt. Rod must have done well at one time, if he could afford to give his wife real jewelry. Or maybe she'd inherited it from her side. "How old is the poor child?"

"Nine," said Lucille. "And a very sweet boy."

"Where is this...this... Max, did you say?" Wilma asked.

The Old Mill

"Yes. Max." Lucille hesitated, a stab of concern stirring. Max was just getting settled in with Gabe and Lizzy. They were about to adopt him. Maybe she'd said too much. Lucille searched her brain for something, anything, that might scare Wilma off.

She cleared her throat as an idea formed. "Of course, little Max has been pretty upset lately, after stumbling upon that dead body in the cellar."

"What?"

"More just a skeleton, really. After all this time 'n' all." Lucille pulled out her rag and resumed wiping down the already spotless counter, forcing Wilma to take a step back.

The mercantile door opened, and Rowdy Long entered.

Lucille was glad for the distraction. Not to mention having someone else to tell about the most excitement to be had at the mercantile in over 30 years. "Hey, Rowdy." She moved out from behind the counter. "You hear about the break-in?"

As she left the store, Wilma kicked herself for letting on that she didn't even know Rod had a son. A dumb mistake. In her mind, her brother was still eighteen with a surly twist to his lips, walking out the door with a battered suitcase...leaving her behind.

She stopped at a nearby bakery and ordered a cinnamon roll and some coffee, needing a chance to get her wits about her. Wilma licked sticky sweet icing from her fingers. So, Rod had a son. That was a serious wrinkle. And a drinking problem. No big surprise there. She let out a frustrated sigh. She'd just have to play the cards she'd been dealt. With the farm already sold, the kid's inheritance was all she had left to go after. Nobody ever called Wilma Watts a quitter.

Lucille's stall tactic, Wilma soon discovered, had only delayed the inevitable. Buttermilk Falls was, after all, a town full of folks who prided themselves on being helpful. A half hour after her informative stop at the bakery, Wilma pulled her old tan sedan up in front of the main house at a place called Sweet Apple Farm.

Lizzy answered the knock at her door. "Hello," she said to the stranger. "Can I help you?"

"You must be Lizzy Reed," the woman said.

"Yes, I am."

"Is Max here?"

Lizzy hesitated. "And what business do you have with him?"

"I'm his aunt," she said. "His blood. I've come to take him back to the city with me...just like my brother, Rod, would've wanted."

Lizzy felt the color drain from her face. She stepped outside, shutting the door behind her. "You have any proof of that?"

"Of course. It's all right here in my satchel." She lifted up a worn leather case and pulled out a manila envelope. "I'm Wilma. Wilma Radding Watts. I've got copies of everything. Birth certificate. Family tree. Tax statements. The works." Wilma handed the documents to Lizzy. "Look these over. The proof's right here." She gave a half smile. "When can I see the boy?"

"Rod never mentioned having a sister." Lizzy rook step back. "And he died a few months back. Where have you been all this time?"

"Sadly, we lost touch over the years." Wilma squared her shoulders. "But I'm here now. And I've come to fetch my nephew."

"You can't just show up out of the blue and take a child like he's a loaf of bread." Lizzy scowled, hands on her hips. "We love Max. We're in the process of adopting him."

"So you say…" Wilma waved a hand in dismissal. "I've got the better claim. To Max and to any assets he's got."

"Assets? He's just a little boy."

"And Rodney's legal heir."

"Rod died broke and in debt."

"I heard there was an inheritance—some jewelry, perhaps." Wilma gave Lizzy a cold stare. "I'll need those assets to care for the boy properly."

Good Lord, thought Lizzy. *Is that what she's after?* Apparently, the woman didn't know that the jewelry came from Mildred—a local widow recently passed away—not from Rodney.

"I need to talk with my husband about this." Lizzy moved Wilma back as she stepped toward her. "And most likely, the sheriff."

"The sheriff? What for?"

"To check on the legalities. Right now, you need to leave. I'm not handing Max over to a complete stranger. And just so you know…" She looked Wilma squarely in the eyes. "We'll fight for him with everything we've got."

Wilma fumed on her way back to the run-down motel at the edge of town. Maybe she'd overplayed her hand of being Max's blood kin in her encounter with that hoity-toity Reed woman. Going for the sympathy angle might have worked better—a grieving sister, coming to save her poor orphaned nephew. Pa always said she didn't use her head. But she hadn't had much time to fine-tune her spur-of-the-moment plan.

Just her luck. First, she'd found out that her brother had died flat broke. And now, she was being blocked from taking the kid, along with the inherited jewelry that'd finally give her a decent life.

She couldn't catch a break. Their parents had lost themselves in a whiskey bottle, ending up barely scraping by. They all lived in a ramshackle trailer in a run-down park. Then Rod took off as soon as he turned eighteen, leaving her behind. She'd never forgive him for that. Pa finally drank himself to death. But not before he beat Wilma black and blue every chance he got. With kin like that, no wonder she was a mess.

Wilma had been left alone to tend to her ma. The unhappy woman made life miserable. She cursed Wilma out for every little thing. Like not getting a meal on the table fast enough. Or blaming Wilma when the liquor and cigarettes ran out. Ma's monthly social security check, on which she regularly forged her mother's signature, barely stretched to cover the lease on the ticky-tacky trailer and a few groceries. And Ma had no idea how hard it was for an underage girl to steal booze and smokes, time after time, from the same local Wal Mart or the only liquor store in the area without security cameras.

Wilma let herself into her motel room and flopped on the orange-flowered bedspread, looking up at the cracks and water stains on the ceiling. She'd seen way too many rooms like this one after her mama finally died and she'd drifted from job to job and man to man.

She flipped on the TV and scanned through the channels. She watched a soap opera for a while, but all the drama and arguing was too much like her own life...only without the perks of servants, mansions and glamorous gowns. Wilma switched it off. Reaching into her battered handbag, she thumbed through her wallet, counting the thick wad of ones. Couldn't a customer tip her with a twenty or even a five once in a while? Fifty-three bucks and a handful of change wouldn't last long...not if she wanted to eat. And her credit card was already maxed out by the motel charges. She'd held her breath at check in, pulse racing, hoping the card wouldn't be refused. Wilma had been light-headed with relief when it went through, grabbing the motel key and scurrying upstairs to this dismal room.

She lay back down on the bed, covering her eyes with an outstretched arm. A headache threatened. Probably all that sugar from the sticky buns. How had she ended up here in another flea-bag motel?

Her one brief marriage had ended in disaster when Willie Watts gambled away their rent money and skipped town, taking their only car and every penny of her meager savings with him.

Wilma rubbed her temples. She sure had bad taste in men. Over and over, she'd get her hopes up that the latest guy was the one to save her from the daily drudgery of being a waitress at the local diner. But then he'd turn out to be a jerk...just like all the others. Her latest lowlife boyfriend had left just a few months ago. While she was busy at work, he took off with her TV and DVD player...along with her jar of tip money.

No. Life had not been kind to Wilma Watts. She still lived in that same run-down trailer on the outskirts of Chico—her dream of renting a decent house or owning a condo one day seemed as impossible as ever.

At least until a customer at the diner mentioned he'd seen her brother's obituary in the Plumas County News Press. Said that Rodney's wife was dead, too. At the news, Wilma's emotions quickly swung from shocked to scheming. After all, her brother owed her for abandoning her to that hell hole of a life with their parents. As his only sibling, she'd be his next of kin. Heard he had a farm up in some podunk town called Buttermilk Falls.

She sighed. Wilma hadn't counted on a kid. She hated kids. Never had any of her own. They were whiney and demanding at the diner, mashing French fries and crayons on the carpet beneath their booth...more clean-up work for her.

But if the kid came with an inheritance, maybe she could buy herself a nice condo and just plop him down in front of the TV.

Odd how that angry pregnant lady, Lizzy, seemed to actually want the boy. Max. How could she play this one? She drummed her fingers on the thin bedspread. Wilma knew she could be charming when she set her mind to it. Her false front had earned her plenty of tips. Just chat 'em up, fawn over folks and give 'em a big old smile. A little touching didn't hurt either. A hand on the arm. A little pat on the shoulder. People liked that—hungry for human contact.

Wilma knew all about that kind of hunger—the kind a burger and fries couldn't satisfy. She'd bet anything Max had a hunger like that deep inside. She could use a weakness like that to her advantage. After all, wasn't she his dear old Aunt Wilma, so delighted to find him after all these years?

Chapter 10

Desolate

*God sets the lonely in families...
but the rebellious live in a sun-scorched land.*
Psalm 68:6

"What are we going to do?" asked Lizzy, in a low voice. "She can't just waltz in here and take Max."

"Not without a fight, she can't." Gabe rubbed the back of his neck. "Rod's hand-written will didn't make any mention of a sister. And the adoption agency hasn't heard of her. So, first we have to find out if she really is Max's aunt."

"Do you think these are legitimate?" Lizzy gestured to the documents from Wilma that Gabe held.

"They seem to be," he said. "But we'll need to have a lawyer check them out."

"She's never even seen the boy, Gabe. How could she care about Max?" Lizzy leaned a hip against a fence post near the barn, where they'd come to talk in private. "I think she's just after his inheritance."

"Did she mention it?"

"Yes. How would she know about Mildred's jewelry?"

"Something doesn't add up," said Gabe. "We need to pray about this." He took her hand and the two of them stormed heaven for God's best for their boy.

Max sensed a change in the air. He was good at reading folks. The whispered talk lately between Lizzy and Gabe was a bad sign. Maybe they were still upset at him for bringing bad luck on the family by finding that old skeleton and all. His nerves got all jumpy inside...wondering what was up.

He tended to his chores—feeding a flake of alfalfa to the horse and mucking out the stall. He gave Gypsy a good once over with the curry comb for good measure, until the mare's coat shone. He even used a pick to clean packed manure from the mare's hoofs.

Since Chloe had a tummy ache this morning and was drinking weak tea in the kitchen, he tackled her chores as well—collecting eggs, filling the waterers and feed troughs, and raking up the chicken poop...all without complaint. Max didn't want to slip up and have them wonder if he was worth his keep.

Still, it might not be enough. Surely, he'd stirred up some really bad mojo. Max scratched his head, trying to think what he could do about it now.

Living with Pa, he'd learned a lot about staying on the good side of evil spirits. Pa knew all the tricks. He forbade Max from washing off the muddy handprint he'd left by the back door after coming in out of a rain storm. "A kid's muddy handprint guards the place from haints," Pa had said. An hour later, he chided Max for opening his umbrella indoors. "Don't you know that'll make bad luck fall on you like rain?" When he gave Max his first pocket knife on his seventh birthday, Pa handed over a penny at the same time. Otherwise, he warned, the father/son bond would be cut by the blade.

Ma had been just as superstitious. Some mornings, she shushed the lively song Max started to warble out. She was quick to remind, "Sing before breakfast...you'll cry before night."

In the Radding family, superstitions rang as true as God's own gospel. Bite your tongue while eating and it was a sure sign you'd just told a big, fat lie. Sure enough, Max had likely spit out some whopper, trying to avoid Pa's fists that day, or when making excuses to get away from the house at the earliest opportunity.

Spooks were everywhere, just waiting to slip in. If you left a rocking chair a'rocking when you got up, it sure as shooting invited spirits to come sit for a spell.

Max tired real hard to avoid all the things bringing on evil. He made sure to never tie one shoe before putting on the other one, or he'd be doomed to being mad as a wet hen all day. Maybe that's what put Pa in such a foul mood most times—tying his first shoe too soon.

A penny rubbed on a wart was supposed to make it go away, but that never worked for Max. The wart on his thumb was still there.

But then, hadn't he heard three quick owl hoots the night before Pa died—a sure warning of death?

Max pondered what spooks he might have stirred up by stepping on a skeleton and knocking its head clean off. He could still see it rolling lopsidedly into the corner...grimacing up at him. If only he'd stayed away from that darned cellar.

The nightmare overtook Max as soon as his eyes drooped shut. He was sneaking out the front door of his old home when he heard the creak of a rocking chair on the porch. He froze.

The squeak of wood on wood was joined by another and another, until the whole front porch, lit by moonlight, was lined with rockers. In each chair sat a boney, white skeleton. Eye sockets vacant. The haints rocked back and forth in a bumpy, out-of-sync rhythm. Rocking and rocking. Max pressed his hand over his ears to muffle the horrid sound.

When he took a step to try to escape, the rocking stopped. The skeletons turned and stared at him, dry bones rattling as they moved. For a moment, an unearthly quiet fell, like the stillness of chirping crickets silenced by a stray, prowling cat.

Then, with a low moaning sound, the spirits rose as one and turned toward him, their horrible skeletal fingers reaching out, grabbing at his clothing...

Max bolted upright in bed. He muffled a scream by stuffing a fist in his mouth. *Lordy, I mustn't wake anyone!* They'd get shed of him, for sure.

But before he could stifle a sob, Lizzy was there, her arms around him. "It's all right, Max. You're safe here with us."

Sheriff Buck thumbed through his case file. Nothing but a bunch of dead ends. No leads on the homeless woman called Birdie. Nobody knew her real name or where she'd gone. Had she died in the shed fire, as the coroner suggested?

Buck sighed. He hadn't made much progress on the robberies, either. A stolen license plate on the SUV. Zero sightings of Ned, Butch or the tan Suburban. No fingerprints lifted at the mercantile. Looked like Tater had been left high and dry by his pals...and he wasn't talking.

These days, Buck was just chasing his tail.

The Old Mill

On a whim, he invited Gloria out to breakfast at Maggie's Diner. Maybe she'd remember some detail from the robbery that might help.

Sitting across from her in the red-leather booth, Buck felt lighter than he had in weeks. She had on a sparkly lavender top and earrings that looked like little clusters of grapes. Something about Gloria's smile restored hope in a world suddenly gone crazy.

"So, how are you holding up?" he asked. Buck sprinkled a third sweetener packet into his coffee.

"Okay," she said. "Not sleeping too well, though."

"Not surprising. Confronting a bad guy would rattle anyone."

"Yeah. Maybe I didn't look as scary as I thought in my pink flowered pajamas...even with the pitchfork." She took a bite of her strawberry covered crepes. "I must have been on an adrenaline high...angry that someone would try to steal money I've worked so hard for."

"Well...it was dangerous. If something like that happens again, I hope you'll call the police first." Buck gestured at the gold badge pinned to his uniform.

"Very funny," said Gloria. "But thanks for coming to my rescue."

He squeezed her hand before letting go. "Anytime, Darlin'." Buck poured syrup on his tall stack of pancakes, then looked up with a frown. "Seriously, though. You could have been hurt."

"That part's just starting to sink in," she said. "Guess I can be pretty impulsive sometimes."

Buck raised his eyebrows. "Sometimes?"

"You might want to throw a few more packets of sugar into your coffee, Buck. Sweeten up your disposition."

He scowled.

"But look on the bright side," she added. "I'm here with you at eight in the morning, aren't I? You barely gave me enough time to pull my look—hair and makeup and this gorgeous outfit—together." She twirled her blond curls, which were swept back in a silver clip.

Buck studied her across the table. Hair and makeup? He took in the dark eyelashes, ruby lips and soft glow of her skin. Somehow, he'd just assumed she got up looking this fabulous.

"Darn." Gloria grinned. "Now I've gone and ruined my feminine mystique."

"Hardly," he said. "You're as mysterious as ever."

The waitress came by and refilled his coffee. Buck sweetened it up and leaned in a bit. Best get to the reason he'd invited her to breakfast. "Did Tater say anything that might help with the case against him?"

"Not that I recall." She took another bite of her crepe, leaving a smudge of whipped cream on her upper lip.

She licked it off before he could move in to brush it away with his finger. If she got any cuter, he'd have to lean in for another kiss.

Gloria gestured with her fork, color rising in her cheeks. "He complained that my place didn't have anything worth stealing. *Just a bunch of flash and trash*, he said." She tucked that vibrant pink strand of hair behind her ear. "What an insult! I nearly poked him…standing there in my office with a fistful of cash in one hand and my laptop in the other."

"Pretty nervy. Anything else?"

Gloria frowned. "Well…when I berated him for being such an inept crook, he did boast about some stash of stolen guns and a prison town. Talked about *sellin' 'em cheap enough to get some schlep to part with his weekend beer money*." She shrugged. "I guess when you steal something, you don't plan on getting top dollar."

"He mentioned a prison town?"

"I think so…"

"Susanville is the nearest town with a prison. Four of 'em, in fact." Sheriff Buck checked his watch. He was on duty in twenty minutes. "Ready to go?" he asked, paying the tab and leaving a generous tip.

She nodded. "The nerve of him," Gloria muttered as they left the diner. "Calling my shop flash and trash..."

Raising herself as a child in a dysfunctional home had made Wilma pretty resourceful. So, it didn't take her long to find a lawyer in the yellow pages who'd take her case for a piece of that jewelry money. Better to lose a bit of the cream on top than not get any milk at all.

Within a week, her lawyer had managed to arrange a supervised visit with the kid. Now she just needed to figure out the best angle to win the boy over. How to pretend she cared about her long-lost nephew. She planned to lean on the idea of them being blood kin—like a debt he owned her. She'd figure out the tender places of the boy's insecurities and root around there. As the orphaned son of an alcoholic, he was sure to have plenty of those.

"A supervised visit? Can't we stop it?" Lizzy's heart hammered in her chest as she took the phone call. How could a complete stranger have access to their son, even if she was his long- lost aunt? She felt nauseated. Max had been through enough. An abusive childhood. Losing both parents and his elderly friend, Mildred. Finding the skeleton. The nightmares. And now this. How could she tell Max they might lose him?

"I'm sorry," said Sheriff Buck. "Wilma Watts has a court order. She wants to meet him, and as his only surviving relative, she's within her rights. It seems Wilma really is his aunt."

"So, where's she been for the past nine years?" asked Lizzy. "Doesn't that matter?"

Buck braced his elbows on his desk and gripped the phone tighter. "Of course, it matters," he said. "And you can fight that out in court." He sighed. "But, Lizzy...you need to prepare the boy. Give him time to process the news and get his feet under him before the supervised visit. Then, stand back a bit and give Max a chance to get to know her. Maybe she's not the wicked witch you think she is. Maybe she really just wants a chance to meet her only nephew."

"You didn't hear her, Buck," said Lizzy. "She asked right away about Max's inheritance. Not about Max. How can she care about a child she's never met?"

"That's exactly what her lawyer's asking for. A chance for them to meet. You can't stop this visit, Lizzy," he said. "But you can stop Max from being blindsided by it."

※

Max swallowed. Something was up. Gabe and Lizzy had asked him to walk to the barn with them while Doris and Chloe cleaned up after breakfast.

They sat on a few scattered hay bales by Gypsy's stall and he offered the mare some tufts of grass plucked from the ground by the doorway.

"We want to talk to you about something important," said Gabe.

Max sat, his hands dangling between his knees. "Did I do somethin' wrong?" he asked. The rough straw poked him in the back of his knees, through his jeans.

"No," said Lizzy, her eyes shining. "You're a good boy, and we both love you very much."

"The thing is..." said Gabe. "It turns out that your pa has a sister named Wilma. She lives in Chico and wants to meet you. She would be your Aunt Wilma. Although you've never met, she'd like a chance to get to know you."

"Oh... What's she like?"

Gabe and Lizzy exchanged a look.

"Best you meet her and decide for yourself," said Gabe.

"Is she taking me away?"

Lizzy jumped up. "No! Never!"

Gabe put a hand on her arm. "We don't want that to happen," he said. "You're part of our family now."

"And forever," said Lizzy.

"So, what's wrong?" He was getting a worry lump in his throat again.

"Nothing's wrong," reassured Gabe. "There will just be a short meeting between you and your Aunt Wilma. A visit with her in a conference room at the library." Gabe's eyebrows drew together like they did when he was thinking real hard. "We'll be right in the next room if you need us."

"When's this meetin'?"

"Tuesday...right after school."

"What if I don't wanna go?" he asked. But Max already knew the answer.

Too many haints were afoot, rocking on the porch now. And no matter how many lucky pennies he found on the ground, bad luck followed him like a storm shadow.

He suspected it was about to rain.

Wilma sucked in a breath when Max came into the library conference room. He looked just like her brother Rod as a boy. This was going to be harder than she thought. A flood of memories overwhelmed her. All the times they'd gone frogging down at the creek, bringing home plump, black pollywogs in a jar. Drying supper dishes while standing on a stool next to him at the sink. Snitching cookies when Ma wasn't watching. Rod holding her sweaty hand tightly, as he walked her to the neighborhood park.

How had she forgotten those moments? How had she let the good times become overshadowed by the bad?

She shoved the memories aside and cleared her throat. "Hi, Max. I'm your Aunt Wilma." She patted a spot next to her on the sofa.

"Hello, ma'am." Max sat in a chair across from her instead, his gaze not quite meeting her eyes.

Wilma glanced over at the social worker, sitting unobtrusively in the opposite corner. The woman gave her an encouraging nod.

"So...Max. I'm so happy to finally get to meet you." She pasted on her best smile. "I hope you and I can be friends."

He looked up at her with Rod's blue eyes. "Yes, ma'am."

"I brought you something." Now, she wasn't so sure that a nerf gun was the best choice. Who would he have a mock shooting war with? But Lucille at the mercantile had insisted that all nine-year-olds loved them. She held the gift bag out to him.

"Thank you." Max's eyes lit up when he lifted the tissue paper away from the gun. "A nerf gun! Thanks."

"You're welcome." She didn't know enough about the boy to move the conversation along, so she reached out and placed a hand on his arm. "You look just like my brother, Rod, did as a boy." She gave him a little pat. "It makes me so happy, just to look at you."

"Why didn't you ever come to see us?"

Shoot. He would have to ask that. The kid was no fool. But then, neither was Wilma. She'd try playing the victim card. See how that went.

"I wanted to, Max. I really did. But you know how your pa was... Never wanting anyone in his business. He always had some excuse about why it wasn't a good time for a visit." She managed to dredge up a few alligator tears and blotted her eyes with a tissue. "It about broke my heart when you were born and he wouldn't even let me see you—my only nephew." The kid didn't need to know that she'd only learned about him a few weeks ago. "That's why it means so much to me now. A chance to get to know you and all..." Wilma let her breath hitch a bit. "It's like having my own dear brother, Rodney, back with me again."

Max glanced up...compassion etched on his face. And in that moment, he really did look like Rodney, big blue eyes shadowed in concern. She realized that Rod had been just a kid when all of the misery started. He'd looked at her that same way, wanting to help. Wanting to protect her. She saw, perhaps for the first time, that's why he'd taken her to play at the stream and to the park...to get her away from the madness.

Wilma swallowed, honest emotions shimmering to the surface, like sunlight dancing on a summer pond. "He used to take me frogging," she revealed. "We'd bring home glass jars of mossy water holding big fat pollywogs and watch 'em grow legs and lose their tails—all the while changing into big, fat bullfrogs."

"Pa took me froggin', too," said Max. "We always took them bullfrogs back to the pond when they was growed. Let 'em go to have a happy life."

A happy life? Wilma hadn't thought too much about what kind of life Max would have with her. A dumpy trailer in Chico, versus living on a real nice farm in the country. But no... With Max's inheritance they'd buy a fancy condo. Maybe even one with a pool. Live high on the hog. She could finally afford to quit her job. Pay to have her hair and nails done. Buy some nice clothes. *And then what?*

Wilma shook her head. She'd figure all that out later. *Keep your eyes on the prize. Win the boy over, first.*

All too soon, the social worker stood, pointing to her watch. "Time's up," she said.

A few days later, the five involved adults met in the conference room at the Plumas County Court House in the town of Quincy, an hour's drive east of Buttermilk Falls. Sheriff Buck sat at one end of the long table. His big uniformed frame and ram-rod straight posture radiated authority. On one side of the conference table, Lizzy held fast to Gabe's hand, worry creasing her brow. On the other, Wilma pushed her glasses up on her long nose and attempted a smile. The social worker, a no-nonsense woman named Marsha Miller, sat at the head of the table. She slid a thick folder from her briefcase and laid it on the table.

Marsha cleared her throat, opened the folder and began the meeting. "Thank you all for coming. We're here today to gather facts and hear from both sides in a disputed custody case involving a minor. My recommendations, coming out of this meeting, and from any additional input, will be presented to a judge at a later date, when this matter is heard in court."

She nodded at Wilma. "Wilma Radding Watts, your identity has been verified and documented. As Rodney Radding's sister and next of kin, it appears you have some claim on your nephew, Max Radding."

Wilma sat up straighter. "Yes, I do."

Lizzy drew in a tortured breath and placed a protective hand on her pregnancy-swollen belly.

"However," Marsha said, looking at the couple, "Gabriel and Elizabeth Reed were appointed as his legal guardians, after the death of Max's father, Rodney Radding. At that time, you did not come forward. Max has been living with them for five months. And they are in the middle of adoption proceedings to legally make the boy a part of their family."

Marsha removed her readers and addressed Wilma. "Until a few weeks ago, Mrs. Watts, your existence was unknown. And Rodney made no mention of you in his will or other legal papers. How do you explain that?"

Wilma squirmed in her chair, and ran moist hands down the slacks of her best pantsuit. Pale lilac, with a complementing, white and purple, flowered blouse, the outfit made her look soft and vulnerable. Her light brown hair was freshly washed and pulled into a clip at the back of her neck. At 32, she was trim, if a bit thin. The dash of red lipstick was calculated to give her a take-charge look — the one she used on her most demanding restaurant customers.

She had her story ready. "Rodney and I had a difficult childhood," she said. "After he left home at 18, I cared for our aging parents until their deaths. Over the years we lost touch. I only recently learned of his death and that of his wife, a few months earlier. I had to come. I had to make sure Max was safe."

Marsha turned to the Reeds. "What do you two have to say?"

"We know Max and we love him," said Gabe. "He'll have a stable home with us. An intact family with a mom and a dad. A step-sister who's 6." He squeezed Lizzy's hand. "And a new baby brother or sister on the way. We very much want to adopt Max. The process is almost completed. And Max would continue to live in the small town he knows and loves. He can attend the same school and live on a farm in the country. He loves being in Buttermilk Falls. Don't take all that away from him."

"And you?" Marsha nodded at Lizzy.

"Max is part of my heart," she said. "I was Max's fourth grade teacher all of last year. And we're very close. In the past five months, since he's been living with us, we've become a family." Lizzy drew in a breath. "Max has already had a lot of trauma in his short life, losing both parents. We've helped him heal and adapt. He has school friends, chores, a routine and a community that cares about him." She looked over at Wilma, meeting her stony eyes behind the dark framed glasses. The rhinestones at the corners twinkled dully, like the fake diamonds they were.

Lizzy turned her attention back to Mrs. Miller. "It's not right to send him away with a total stranger—someone who never even met him until a few weeks ago. Someone who never had children. Wilma would be a single parent with the responsibility of shaping a young life. He'd be an only child, alone and lonely, with no father figure."

Lizzy paused. She still had one valid point to make. Was now the time to use it? Or would it be unfair to Wilma? The tussle with her conscience lasted only until she recalled Wilma's fixation with the jewelry. The woman didn't want Max. Not really. She'd come for an inheritance and found there was none. So, she'd latched onto what she could. But Wilma had no right to Max's inheritance from Mildred…something to be revealed at a more strategic time. For now, Lizzy played another card, one that might move the social worker. A Radding family secret. She prayed God would understand…

Lizzy cleared her throat and turned toward the social worker. "You should know that Max already has emotional scars from abuse at the hands his father, Rodney Radding."

The Old Mill

"What abuse?" Wilma screeched, her eyes wide behind her glasses.

"As a teacher, Max's teacher, I was a mandated reporter," said Lizzy. "Sheriff Buck will attest to the reports I filed. The bruises, the black eyes. The lack of food and proper clothing. Shaming Max. Telling the boy he was worthless."

"Is this true, sheriff?" Marsha asked.

Buck nodded. "All true. I brought copies of my files for you." The sheriff handed them over. "The poor boy was beaten, half-starved and a runaway the night his pa drove drunk and died in a car wreck." He wiped a hand across his eyes, as if to rub out the memory. "Max has a good home with the Reeds. It'd be a shame, and perhaps even dangerous to his well-being, to put him through any more trauma."

"Are you a psychologist, sheriff?" asked Marsha, one eyebrow tilting higher.

Buck didn't back down. "No ma'am. Just a lawman who's seen it all."

"Well, sheriff," said Wilma, with a smirk. "Then surely you must be aware of the recent trauma the Reeds themselves inflicted on my poor nephew, Max."

"What trauma?" Buck asked.

"You think it's okay to let a child wander into the cellar of an old cabin all by himself?" Her eyes bored into Lizzy's. "And what did he find down there? The skeleton of a dead person, that's what. I hear tell he even stepped on the bones."

Marsha Miller paused in her note-taking, tapping her pen nervously against the tabletop.

Lizzy brought a hand to hip. "No one knew about the body," she said. "Or even the cabin."

"And who was supposed to be supervising him?" Wilma asked.

"He and Chloe were walking home from the school bus stop," said Lizzy.

"Alone?" The word spat from Wilma's thin, painted lips.

"This is Buttermilk Falls," Lizzy retorted.

"Exactly," said Wilma.

"Why do you think he'd be better off with you?" asked Mrs. Miller, turning toward Max's Aunt Wilma.

"Blood is thicker than water," insisted Wilma. "Max is my only blood relative. All I have left. He belongs with family. He belongs with me."

Chapter 11

Good for Evil

*You meant evil against me,
but God meant it for good.*
Genesis 50:20

Lizzy half rose from her chair. "Maybe you should tell Mrs. Miller how you plan on supporting Max. Do you have room for him in your little trailer?"

"Not to worry. I'll be looking for a new place." Wilma squared her shoulders.

"On your waitress salary?"

"I won't need to waitress. Max's inheritance should help out."

"It's not your inheritance to spend," insisted Lizzy, glancing at Buck for reassurance.

"Of course, it is." Wilma laced her fingers together on the table top. "I'll cash in the jewelry from Rod's estate. He wouldn't want his boy living in a trailer park."

"You think Rod's wife or her kin had expensive jewelry?" Lizzy asked.

"I heard she did."

"You heard wrong," said Sheriff Buck. "The jewelry belonged to an elderly widow named Mildred Stein. She gave it to Max, so it's not from Rod's family. It's held in trust for his college education someday. You can't lay hands on it."

"But I... I thought..."

Lizzy laid a gentle hand on Wilma's across the table. "It's time to think about Max. You've met him. You know what a sweet boy he is. He deserves our best. Surely you see that."

"You're messing with me," said Wilma angrily, jerking her hand away. "You two are the ones after the money." She looked at Lizzy's swollen belly. "When the baby comes, you won't even have time for Max."

"And who'll watch him while you're at work?" Lizzy asked.

"Well, I...I..." Wilma stuttered.

"I'm guessing there's a lot you haven't thought through, since you've never raised a child," said Lizzy. "Is this what you really want?"

"I want my nephew."

Lizzy took a deep breath and extended an olive branch. "You could come to visit. See him from time to time. Get to know Max. Enjoy being his aunt. Then decide what's best for him...and you."

"I think I've heard enough for now," said Marsha Miller, standing. "Let's recess for the lunch hour."

Sheriff Buck figured it was worth a trip to Susanville to follow up on Gloria's lead about a prison town. He drove east through the high country, enjoying the sights of meandering streams and split-log rail fencing in the meadows. On the steep climb down the backside of the Sierras, the landscape gave way to scrub pine and then to desert sage. The tentacles of the arid high desert clawed

The Old Mill

up the rocky incline, where everything lush dried up, becoming dull and brittle.

Buck suspected the dreams of lots of folks had met a dead end here, as well. The small town of Susanville was home to a Wal Mart, a Dollar Store and five prisons. The sprawling high desert, without much else to recommend it, made an ideal location for penal lock-ups. They provided high-paying jobs for prison workers, and reasonable rents for families of the incarcerated. As sheriff in a neighboring community, he'd dealt with each detention facility at one time or another.

Lethal loops of concertina wire topped the chain link fencing of the closest prison, tucked into the far edge of town. High Desert State Prison was a high security, Level IV prison. The worst offenders in the state, murders and rapists, with little hope of parole, were housed here. Same for the nearby Antelope Conservation Camp # 25—also high security. Farther out were two minimum security facilities, the California Correctional Center and Lassen County Juvenile Hall. The proximity of so many prisons clouded the air with an almost palpable aura of defeat. Off in the distance, the pink block buildings of the Lassen County Adult Detention Facility housed the county jail where Buck would book any suspects he arrested today…an optimistic viewpoint, he realized, in a pessimistic town.

Susanville had a dispirited, down-on-its-luck feel to the place. The town attracted tumbleweeds blown about by the hot desert wind and an assortment of folks biding their time, or reduced to scrub farming.

The only local highlights breaking up the monotony of the setting were last summer's Lassen County Fair and several small-time rodeos that came through.

Buck noted from the banners strung over Main Street that the Lassen College Rodeo was in town this weekend, so there'd likely be a big crowd in the area. He took the left off Main and headed north, toward the fairgrounds. Sheriff Buck cruised the small parking lot, on the lookout for the tan Suburban. He suspected that Ned and Butch weren't the sharpest tools in the shed and might be foolish enough to hang out in the area a while longer.

In the far corner of the lot he spotted it—the SUV with the stolen plates. Sheriff Buck got out and peered in the windows. Blankets covered something in the rear compartment. The stolen rifles? He didn't have a search warrant to check inside.

Stashing his patrol car around the block, the sheriff flashed his badge at the ticket window and got into the fairgrounds. He passed booths hawking western hats, oil on black velvet paintings, and flashy cowboy belt buckles—big as a man's fist. The air smelled of hotdogs, cherry sno-cones, popcorn and cotton candy. Near the stadium, the spicy scent of Indian tacos wafted in the warm breeze.

Buck hadn't worn his uniform. So, his casual dress of jeans, t-shirt, athletic shoes, and billed ball cap allowed him to blend in with the crowd. But he was carrying concealed…just in case.

He hung out near the beer booth and stepped aside for some wranglers who led their haltered horses toward the stables. Collegiate cowboys congregated in small groups, dressed in tight Levi's and shod with the requisite V-toed, slack heeled cowboy boots—some embellished with fancy spurs. Big silver belt buckles and white Stetson hats were the trophies of their trade. Piped in music carried the twang of a country western ballad.

Buck stood in line at the taco stand and walked away with an oversized piece of warm fry bread stuffed with chicken mole', beans, rice and salsa. He sat at a table on the lawn and eavesdropped on the conversations swirling around him—talk of the ladies' breakaway calf roping, barrel racing, and team roping to come. A group of girls in form-hugging Levi's and tank tops giggled when some lanky cowboys strode past.

After finishing his meal, Buck carried his soft drink and prowled the perimeters of the fairgrounds. He checked the shady spots beneath the bleachers and the empty pens in the swine barns. With a relaxed stride, he eyed the guys hunkered down in lawn chairs beneath a clump of cottonwoods and cruised past the bull pens where hunky cattle swatted flies with their tails. At the horse stalls, he peered in the open-top double doors, pausing to rub the soft nose of a curious pinto mare. He didn't see his guys.

There were a thousand and one places in the fairgrounds to hawk a stolen rifle, but only one likely place to hand over the merchandise. So, the sheriff borrowed a lawn chair from a hot dog vender, bought another soft drink, had his hand stamped, and went out the gate.

He settled behind some cars in the shade of a scrub oak, stretched out his long legs, and tugged the bill of his ball cap down over his eyes. He let his head fall forward as if lost in warm afternoon slumber. But even as he relaxed in his out-of-the-way hidey hole, he was alert…his eyes fixed on one particular car across the lot—the tan SUV.

Lizzy had been avoiding this conversation. But her husband wasn't letting it go. They sat on the porch swing after the kids were tucked in bed for the night. Stars winked in the dark sky and a tepid breeze cooled the sticky sweat beneath the hair at the nape of her neck. She tucked a loose strand back into her ponytail.

"We have to talk about it," he said, as she'd known he would. He took her hand in his and caressed the top with his thumb. "It's not going away."

"Maybe Wilma will come to her senses. Give up on the whole idea."

"You said she could get to know him," reminded Gabe. "She's Max's blood kin—his aunt. We owe her that chance."

Lizzy frowned. "A chance for what? To worm herself into his heart with her little sob story?"

"I know it's hard," Gabe reassured. "But we've got to trust that God is in this."

"It's not God who I mistrust." Lizzy shook her head. "Wilma doesn't know a thing about children. She just wants..." Fear thickened her throat. Lizzy bit back the ugly words, her heart aching in her chest.

"If Max is meant to stay with us, God will work it out." Gabe gave her hand a squeeze. "Surely you believe that."

She ran a hand across the curve of her rounded belly. Maternal instinct raged like a sudden fever. She knew she'd protect her unborn child with her life. In the same way, the fierceness of her attachment to Max blinded her to any redeeming qualities Wilma might have.

"She can't have him!" Lizzy insisted.

"I don't want that, either." Gabe put his arm around her. "But we're not in control here. We have to let Max have a say in this."

"But, he's only a little boy." Lizzy leaned into the comfort of his shoulder.

"Max is his own person," he said. "It may be up to the courts to decide who he lives with, but he gets to decide who he chooses to befriend...and even to love. If we rob him of those choices, we rob him of something precious. Remember how you felt when your parents wouldn't let you see Aunt Daffy? Just when you'd gotten to know her..."

"That was different."

"Was it?"

"They were being unreasonable."

"No. They thought they were protecting you."

The Old Mill

"But I *am* protecting Max."

"From what?" He squeezed her shoulder. "Getting to know Wilma?"

Lizzy hated it when Gabe was right...and even more when she knew she sounded like a petulant child.

"I can't bear it," she whimpered, crumbling against the swing pillows, with a sob. "What if she steals him away?"

"What if she doesn't?" Gabe drew her close. "What if this is all part of God's bigger plan for good?"

Lizzy nodded as the tears came. "Okay," she said. "I'll do it. I'll let Wilma join us for a picnic. But I don't have to like it."

Early October. The morning of the picnic was crisp, dew dampening the ground. The air held an unmistakable trace of fall, silently signaling the end of another Indian summer. The aspen leaves had turned, fluttering like gold coins in the stiff breeze. Against the backdrop of deep green pines, maple trees put on showy garments of orange and red.

The shift of seasons filled Lizzy with melancholy. What else would change after today? Once they'd arrived at the creek, Lizzy busied herself setting out a hamper of wrapped sandwiches on a blanket, the same old quilt her beloved Aunt Daffy had once used for their jaunts to the river. Even after last night's earnest prayer of surrender, Lizzy braced herself to be a wary observer.

But Max had other ideas. He and Chloe chased butterflies across the meadow, returning with fistfuls of wildflowers. Max handed his bunch to Wilma, whose eyes glittered in surprise, like sparkling chips of mica in small stones of dark granite.

"No one ever gave me flowers before," she said, looking both stunned and pleased.

Chloe gave her flower bundle to Lizzy. "Mama. For you." The stems were still warm from her grasp.

Gabe and Max threw a Frisbee, laughing when Gabe jumped up for a save. Then Max and Chloe took Aunt Wilma down to the river's edge to show her a patch of flowering lupine. They tossed rocks in the water.

On the way back, Wilma stooped to pick up a penny laying in the dirt. She chanted:

Find a penny, pick it up.
All day long, you'll have good luck.

"My dad used to say that," said Max.

She dusted the coin off and handed it to him. "For luck."

Sitting on the quilt, they ate ham sandwiches and potato chips, washed down with bottled water.

Wilma told them how she used to make peanut butter and banana sandwiches for Rod when she was a kid and how they both loved summer watermelon. "Rod and I would have a contest to see who could spit the seeds the farthest," she said. "Of course, he always won."

The story softened Wilma's features and Lizzy could almost see the little girl she'd once been. Lizzy fetched a plastic container from the wicker hamper. "I've only got apple slices," she offered. "But they're from our own apple orchard." The children grabbed some before heading back to the river's edge to play.

An awkward silence fell among the three adults. Lizzy finally spoke, choosing her words carefully. "How long has it been since you last saw your brother?"

"Over thirty years," Wilma admitted. "I was mad at him for abandoning me. But he had his own troubles, I guess."

"How old were you when he left?"

"Fifteen. He took off as soon as he turned eighteen."

"Pretty young, himself, to take responsibility for a kid sister," suggested Gabe.

"Yeah," said Wilma. "I get that now. All these years, I've been kind of stuck...seeing things from that little girl's eyes." She plucked at some tufts of grass. "I guess I expected too much. Took my anger out on him. In the chaos of our home, it was pretty much every man, or kid, for himself."

"Kind of like it was for Max," said Gabe. "Living with the alcoholic parent Rod became. You have that in common."

Wilma nodded.

"Do you really see yourself raising a child?" Lizzy asked, trying for a calm tone.

Wilma looked up in surprise. "Why not?"

Lizzy gazed over at Max who was floating small leaf boats down the river. "Because this isn't about us. It's about what's best for Max."

Things weren't really turning out like Wilma expected. She hadn't known how sweet children could be. She fingered the bouquet of wildflowers laying on the quilt. A simple gift of love.

There was no inheritance. She was still trying to wrap her head around that bitter disappointment. No financial buffer against her own money woes. The lawyer would drop her now. But today—here with Max—she'd found unexpected joy.

The sun was warm on her shoulders...the air fresh and clean. Max whooped at Chloe's attempt to catch a scampering lizard, and raced to join her. He was a country boy—dirt under his fingernails and a sprinkle of freckles on his nose. Would it be fair to bring Max to her small, dingy trailer? What if he ended up like Rod—just waiting for a chance to bust free?

But she was drawn to the boy. Drawn to the simple goodness of him. He made her want to be better...kinder. She wasn't about to give that up.

Max and Chloe came back to the picnic spot...skipping. In his hand Max held an old mason jar with a two-part screw-on lid—air holes punched in the top. "Brought you somethin'." He handed it to her and twisted off the lid.

The smell of warm, mossy water rose, flooding her with memories...

Grinning Max was young Rod as a boy, and she was a pig-tailed five-year-old again. They'd conspired to carry home the jar of river water—alive with plump, black pollywogs and river moss. The two siblings hid the jar from their pa in a cool corner of the backyard shed and hurried out each morning to check on their only pets. In wonder, they watched the creatures grow legs, absorb tails, change from inky black to moss green, and morph into sleek, young frogs...ready to hop away. Then they made another trip to the river to free the frogs...envying them the liberty of escape.

She and Rod loved the wonder of it...until that last pollywog season. One morning they'd gone to the shed to check on their charges, only to find a mud puddle and shattered glass strewn across the dirt floor. The wizened bodies of the dead tadpoles lay in the wreckage, swarming with flies. A crushed, empty beer can lay nearby.

"No!" cried Wilma, her hand covering her mouth.

"Damn him!" cursed Rod, moving to shield her from the shocking sight. "Why does Pa have to wreck everything?"

They'd never gone tadpole hunting again.

"It's pollywogs," said Max. "Like you had as a kid."

Wilma's eyes filled. "You brought me pollywogs?" Her heart broke.

"I can let 'em go," offered Max, misinterpreting the tears.

She brought the jar closer, eyeing the sluggish black pollywogs. "No. Thank you, Max. I'd like to keep them," she said. "It'll be nice to watch the tadpoles grow up."

Five men marched toward the SUV, gravel crunching beneath their boots. Buck eyed them from beneath the brim of his baseball cap. Ned and Butch led the way. Ned took a look around, then popped the rear door on the Suburban and leaned in. He pulled out a rifle, the rich bluing of the barrel glinting in the sun. Sheriff Buck tensed, but still retained his fake sleep posture. He slouched to the right…hiding the cell phone he brought to his ear.

Buck made a quick phone call. "Move in," he said, alerting his backup. He watched as the money changed hands. Leaning into a crouch, Buck scooted between parked cars, emerging just behind the unsuspecting men. Squatting low, he unholstered his service revolver and clicked off the safety. He stood, gun held in front of him.

"Police! Drop the rifle! Hands up!! All of you!"

It was a bold move, five against one. But he had the element of surprise. And a locked and loaded firearm. The men jerked their arms up, like puppets on a string. The rifle fell to the ground with a dull *thud*.

Even so, Buck wasn't foolish enough to think he could handle them all on his own. He relaxed a bit when the local police roared up, in with a blur of lights and sirens. Good thing, too as Butch was reaching for his knife. The menacing blade joined the rifle on the hot asphalt.

When all of the men were cuffed, Sheriff Buck pulled back the tarp and uncovered the rest of the rifles. Twelve in all. He was pretty sure they'd match the serial numbers of the ones stolen from the mercantile. Lucille would be delighted to have her inventory back, right at the start of hunting season.

The thieves and their buddy, Tater, could have a little reunion in jail. And after the trial, with so many prisons here in Susanville, the boys would feel right at home.

Chapter 12

Hope

*Those who hope in the Lord
will renew their strength.
They will soar on wings like eagles.
They will run and not grow weary;
they will walk and not be faint.
Isaiah 40:31*

After the police investigation, Aunt Daffy's remains were cremated and buried in the local cemetery beneath the grave marker mistakenly used earlier for the stranger's ashes. Lizzy placed a bouquet of garden flowers on the stone and traced the engraved granite words with her finger.

Daffodil DuPonte
A Friend to All

Knowing her...
*My heart with pleasure fills
and dances with the daffodils.*

W. Wordsworth

Whoever had selected the marker's sentiment had chosen well. Never married, with no children of her own, Daffodil DuPonte had embraced the whole town as her family. She'd lived up to her name, as bright and sunny as a swaying field of daffodils. Each spring the daffodil bulbs Aunt Daffy had planted by the front steps bloomed in reminder.

"Aunt Daffodil was a wonderful woman. And so much fun to be with," Lizzy told the children. "I wish you could have known her."

Max frowned. To him, the woman was still just a scary skeleton he'd stumbled upon in the cabin basement.

Lizzy hoped to make the woman more real to the children. Let them see the sunshine that still radiated about the farm, thanks to Aunt Daffy's joyful spirit and sense of adventure. Compared to her great aunt, Lizzy realized, she was a real sick-in-the-mud. She'd have to do better.

Lizzy rested a hand on the cold stone. This day had been a long time coming, she realized with a pang...and way too late. She hadn't come to Aunt Daffy's funeral two years earlier. Hadn't even known her great aunt had died until she was contacted by her lawyers. But today, she and Gabe brought the children here for a brief private memorial. She wanted the kids to know more about the woman who'd gifted the farm to Lizzy, bringing her to Buttermilk Falls. Gabe read a scripture and recounted some of his own memories of Miss Daffodil, whose council and warm meals had helped him get through some rough teen years.

Lizzy welcomed the chance to say a final goodbye to the aunt she'd known so briefly, but remembered so fondly. What she hadn't expected was the surge of emotions that flooded her eyes with tears. Overcome by memories, she couldn't choke out what she'd planned to say.

"I'll take the children for a walk along the river," Gabe volunteered. "Give you some time alone..."

She nodded her thanks. Lizzy sat on the nearby cement bench and let the memories wash over her. Memories of those life-altering summer weeks when she and Aunt Daffy had gone vagabond on the property, wresting fun and adventure from each sunny-side-up day. Canning fruit, collecting eggs, milking the cow, making apple chains, swimming in the creek. Searching for rocks shaped like hearts, and finding crosses in ordinary twigs, afternoon shadows and the undersides of leaves. Nights of reading books aloud, games of checkers, hobo dinners cooked over a campfire. She couldn't have known it then, but the time with Aunt Daffy changed her in deep ways. It primed her for the simple joys of country life...and maybe even for love.

"Thank you, Aunt Daffy," she murmured, blotting her eyes. "Thank you for all of it." She wanted her children to have the same adventures...feel the same bond with family, earth, and God.

She started on that goal that very afternoon when they got home from the cemetery. The windfall apples they'd sliced and laid in the sun a week ago were dry now. At the picnic table outside, she helped the children string alternating tiers of dried apples and cinnamon sticks into hanging chains—the spicy smell sweetly scenting the air. They tied red gingham bows at the top of each string and left a loop for hanging.

Lizzy looked over at Max, his tow-head thatch of hair mussed, a frown of concentration wrinkling his freckled nose as he stabbed an apple with his needle. Fear hitched her breath at the thought of losing him. He was already as much a part of her family as her stepdaughter, Chloe. And even her unborn baby—a child she suspected was a girl. She laid a protective hand on her belly. Secretly, she'd named her child, River Grace — their very own *river of grace*. Max would be a great big brother, just as he already was to Chloe.

"God," she breathed, "Please don't take Max away from us."

The raccoon scrubbed a paw across his whiskers and swiveled his ears toward the sound of footfalls on the warehouse floor. Darn! They were back again...those pesky humans. Didn't they know this was his space? Even worse, they'd brought that big yellow mutt with them. Already the dog was sniffing him out behind the barrels. He twitched his nose, senses alert. What was that yummy smell? Food!

He darted around some crates to lose the dog and scurried up to the canvas sack that held the scent of some tangy vittles. Using his nimble fingers, he easily unlaced the ties and pulled out a paper sack that smelled of meat.

Woof! Woof! The dog was on him like stink on a skunk.

But the wily raccoon was faster. He scurried toward the hole in the corner, tugging his stolen meal with him.

"Coon," Rowdy called out. "Hey! He's makin' off with our lunch." They watched Scout thunder past, knocking over a crate as he chased the big raccoon across the room. The critter gave a quick backward glance, beady dark eyes bright in the black mask on his face. The paper sack firmly gripped in his mouth. Then he disappeared beneath a wallboard, Scout hot on his heels.

"Hey!!" shouted Rowdy. "So, you're the one who's been spyin' on us."

He and Kyle inspected the hole. Nothing but darkness. Their sack lunch was long gone.

The Old Mill

"Darn. I was really lookin' forward to those ham sandwiches," groused Rowdy.

"Not to mention the tub of fresh potato salad," said Kyle.

"Shoot. You brought potato salad, too?"

"Yep. Fresh from the deli." Kyle rifled through the backpack. "You don't think he got the sodas, do you?"

"Let's hope not." Rowdy frowned. "That darn rascal."

"Yeah…Rascal. A good name for him," said Kyle. "I always wanted a pet raccoon.

"You're kiddin'."

"Nope." Kyle grinned, pulling out the sixpack of sodas. "He is kinda cute. And he left the drinks behind."

"Trust me, raccoons are nothin' but trouble." Rowdy reset the Stetson on his head and grabbed a soft drink. "You plan on sharin' these with your new pet, too?"

Kyle shrugged. "Probably not…no opposable thumbs to manage the pop top."

"Very funny…" Rowdy popped the top on a cola, and took a long gulp. "I can't believe that greedy critter is sittin' 'neath this buildin', eatin' our ham sandwiches."

"We'll stop by the deli on our way home," suggested Kyle.

Making do with the sodas, Rowdy pulled out a notebook. The two men canvassed the space, listing the repairs needed and planning the scope of the remodel. "We can frame in a kitchen and bathrooms in that rear corner," he said.

"What? You don't think the old outhouse will do?" Kyle teased, nodding toward the forlorn single-seater set under an oak out back.

"Sanitation might have an issue with that." Rowdy wrinkled his nose. "Not to mention the customers eatin' down wind."

"Okay… Okay." Kyle threw up his hands in mock surrender. "We'll put in a septic tank. Do we need a permit for that?"

"Son," said Rowdy. "For a restaurant, we'll need a permit to spit in the wind."

As they moved through the building, Rowdy saw that Kyle was the dreamer. He was all about open space, rustic beams, art work, hanging the massive saw blade, and creating an inviting atmosphere. Rowdy saw himself as the more practical one, concerned about sealing up any possible points of re-entry from that devil, Rascal. Bringing in a 500-gallon propane tank for cooking and heating. Meeting codes. Upgrading the electrical. And installing a new front door with an actual dead bolt lock. They'd make a good team.

Only on one point did Rowdy let nostalgia reign. The soda fountain was his baby—his tie to an earlier and simpler time, before life took a wrong turn. He wanted young adults to court at that counter over banana splits and ice cream sundaes. He pictured old folks bringing grandkids along or sitting on the red-leather stools to stare in the eyes of a true-love of forty-plus years.

He didn't plan on sharing any of that sentimental nonsense with Kyle, but he'd already ordered the vintage counter. It was warehoused and ready to ship. Rowdy could see it nestled along the far wall, complete with mirrors and polished chrome malt blenders.

A few hours later, they packed up to return home. As Rowdy latched the door with the useless stick, he caught a parting glimpse of Rascal as the critter bolted beneath the outside deck. The raccoon's belly was taut with their lunch. Rowdy shook his head. He sensed nothing but trouble ahead.

The dog started to give chase, but was halted by Rowdy's command to "Leave it." Rowdy looked Scout in the eye and explained that Rascal was part of the place and they'd try to peacefully co-exist. His dog, he allowed, could still chase the pesky squirrels. Scout wagged his tail, as if he understood every word.

Kyle watched the canine lecture, a skeptical look on his face. The business partners walked down the steps together.

Rowdy paused to look up at the towering water wheel—the feature that had drawn him to the old mill in the first place.

"Let's paint 'er red," he said to Kyle. "Put that ol' water wheel front and center."

"Red?"

"Why not?" Rowdy grinned. Maybe he was more of a dreamer that he'd allowed.

Kyle grinned back. "Think we'll need a permit for that?"

Buck found himself drawn back for another look at the old cabin on Lizzy's property. The body had been removed and the site photographed, investigated and cleared. But some inconsistencies still niggled. If Daffodil had fallen down the stairs searching for Birdie, why was the trap door closed? Had she been pushed?

Reviewing the records from the rest home, he determined that Daffodil DuPonte had likely snuck away just before dark and walked to the cabin from there—a journey of nearly a mile. A cold walk, in slippers, wearing only a nightgown and robe. But he'd learned that Lizzy's great aunt, while suffering from dementia, was not a frail woman. She'd kept in shape tending the farm, with the help of her farm manager, Harley.

But, according to his notes, she hadn't taken a flashlight from the care center. It would have been dark by the time she got there. So, it made sense that she would have lit a lantern at the cabin in her search for Birdie—the vagrant she'd taken under her wing. Concern for Birdie's well-being had kept her agitated at the center and probably led her to steal away that fateful night.

He drove to the site and hiked the overgrown path to the cabin. Inside, the partially collapsed roof made access to the trap door dicey. He had to fold his six-foot one-inch frame to crouch next to the open portal. But if Birdie was staying here back then, the roof had likely been intact and the cabin inhabitable. The metal cot in the corner attested to the fact that someone had once slept here.

Buck experimented with the heavy, metal lid, opening and closing it several times, its corroded hinges groaning in protest. The thing likely weighed twenty pounds and only opened to a ninety-degree angle. Max must have really struggled to lift it.

The welded iron ring on top gave a nice handhold for opening the trap door from above. But its heavy weight would make it difficult to heft open from the cellar side. He noticed a round mark on the underside where something had scraped the rusty metal.

Looking for other clues, Buck searched through the leaf litter near the trap door. His fingers found rocks and sticks, then a cold, hard object. He lifted it free. A busted lock. Wait. Not busted, so much as cut. The pin was still inserted in the lock, but had been shorn by some type of bolt cutter—a long time ago, by the oxidation on the cut edge. A welded loop on the door frame provided a place to secure the padlock. So...at one time the cellar had been locked up. Why? Pulling out a zip-lock, he bagged and pocketed his find.

Then Buck opened the 2x2 foot trap door and eased himself through. He'd feel better if he could prop it open from the inside ledge...just in case.

The steep wooden stairs creaked under his weight. His foot struck something on the wall edge of the third step. It rolled loose and clattered down. He found it at the bottom—a half inch round steel bar about two feet long. Buck carried it back up, wedging one end against the worn spot on the door—the other on the ledge

THE OLD MILL

of the opening. A perfect fit. He'd just found the missing prop... something used to ensure the door couldn't slam shut on its own.

But it had been shut when the body was discovered.

He tried to put himself in the shoes of the deceased. Sheriff Buck pictured a disoriented Miss Daffodil coming to the cabin at night from the rest home. Maybe lighting a lantern in the cabin to find her way. She would have been tired and couldn't have lifted the heavy lid by herself. So, it had likely been left open... maybe for a long time, to allow Birdie access to the goods below. Miss Daffodil could easily have started down the stairs, holding a lantern, calling out for Birdie. Maybe in her disoriented state of mind she'd dislodged the prop, allowing the trap door to slam shut behind her.

If she'd been startled, or her slipper caught on a stair, she could have tumbled to the bottom, breaking both the lantern and her neck in her fall. But no lantern pieces had been found in the cellar. Buck checked again, just to be sure, feeling along the bottom edges of the cobwebbed dirt and board cellar walls. *What the heck?* One wooden wall felt chilled—a draft of cold air seeping in from the other side.

Buck switched his flashlight into lantern mode, and set it on the ground. The boards were nailed securely against a wood frame, and he couldn't pry them loose with his fingers. He went back up, searching for some sort of lever. Buck pulled part of the metal frame from the broken-down cot in the corner. Making sure the steel rod prop was still securely in place, he went back down. Grunting with effort, he pried the first board loose. Dank, cool air rushed in from some hidden chamber. He pulled off a second board and then another, directing his flashlight beam into the darkness beyond. Some kind of cave? His light played on the walls. A tunnel hewn from the rock stretched out for a good thirty feet ahead. Birdie's gold mine?

After enlarging the opening, Buck eased through, and was able to stand up in the cold cavern. He panned his flashlight along the rock walls. Green and blue veins sparkled when the light struck them—glowing with luminescence. His college geology course kicked in as he fingered the rock. Pressed inside the granite were bands of malachite and azurite. Strips of copper carbonates. Not gold... Copper!

Harley's gold mine story, told second hand from Birdie, had thrown him off. He'd been researching abandoned gold mines in the area, so he'd only glanced at references to local copper mines. If he wasn't mistaken, this was the old abandoned Pumpkin Hallow Copper Mine—dug beneath what had once been expansive pumpkin fields on the farmstead over one hundred years ago. The fact that someone had built a cabin above with a locked trap door to the mine made sense. An open, abandoned mine in a pumpkin field would be dangerous. So...who had cut the lock off and when? Was it for access to the cellar? Had Miss Daffodil even known about the old mine? Somehow, he doubted it.

Buck dug out a chunk of the rock with his pocket knife to have it analyzed, bagged it, and tucked it in his pocket with the old lock. After a last look around, he left the cavern, climbed the stairs and broke out into the sunlight.

He sat on a stump close by and took out his phone, pulling up the Pumpkin Hallow Copper Mine. Apparently, those green and blue strips of iron rust had yielded only 30% copper ore back in the day, so when prices dropped, the mine closed. Since then, Buck noted, copper prices had come back up.

Back at the station, Buck read over the investigation notes about the cabin discovery. And reports about the burned out shed where another body had been mistaken for Miss Daffodil's. The pieces had to fit together somehow. Two deaths...likely on the same night.

What if Daffodil lit a lantern, but set it at the edge of the trap door while she started down? What if she reached for it, but grabbed the round prop bar instead, dislodging it? It might have fallen to that third step. What if the trap door slammed shut, startling her into that fatal fall?

The key was the lantern. Surely, she'd not tried to navigate the cabin's cellar in the dark. But what happened to it? A lantern had started the shed fire, not fifty yards from the cabin.

How did the old copper mine play into that night? A hidden mine might explain why the cellar had once been locked. What if Birdie had discovered it while staying at the cabin? Kept it a secret from Miss Daffodil? Was that enough of a reason for her to have killed Daffodil?

In the investigative notes from the fire, buckets of copper filings had been found in the burned out shed. Had Birdie mined the ore, hoping to get rich? Had she tried to hide it from whoever might come looking for Daffodil?

Or maybe there was a more innocent explanation. What if Birdie had heard Daffodil calling for her? What if she came to the cabin, saw the burning lantern and the shut trap door? Maybe she tried to lift it, but found it too heavy. Then she panicked and ran for help. Did she stop by the shed first to get something? Hide something?

In her haste, Birdie might have dropped the lantern, accidentally igniting the stored cans of gasoline. She'd been trapped by the ensuing fire and died. Poetic justice or a tragic accident? It was all speculation. Buck ran a hand through his thick hair. They'd likely never know for sure.

The cabin was on Sweet Apple Farm property, so rightfully, the Pumpkin Hallow Copper Mine belonged to Lizzy. With her ongoing troubles over Max's custody, what would she think of this new wrinkle?

Charlotte tried to hold onto what Pa said when she'd finally told him about the devastating art critique. He'd nudged his Stetson up in front and said, "Baby girl… *There never was a horse that couldn't be rode. Never was a cowboy who couldn't be throwed.*"

"What's that supposed to mean?" she'd asked.

He looked her in the eyes. "When you get bucked off, best to get up, dust yourself off and get right back in the saddle. Otherwise, you'll never learn to ride."

"So, you think I should keep on painting?"

"Sure. If you enjoy it."

"But what if he's right and I have no talent for art?" she protested. "No talent at all?"

"I don't know a lot about art," he said. "But I like yours. You like doin' it?"

"Not now."

As a child she drew crayon pictures of big yellow suns, colorful flowers, and trees with red apples. Her simple art had decorated the walls in each of her and her mom's latest dingy apartments.

"God's the best artist." Rowdy pointed toward the lake. "He created all this beauty for us to enjoy. And I reckon he likes to see you try to put a bit of it on canvas, just to say thanks."

Charlotte did feel grateful when she painted. More mindful of all the colors and details of nature…the sheer extravagance of the beauty around her. The bright yellow sun bringing light and life. She wasn't about to let a teacher rob her of that.

"Okay, Pa," she said. "Guess I'd better saddle up."

Sitting in the far back corner of her art class the next day, Charlotte worked quietly on a multimedia piece. She wanted to recapture the joy. But things had changed. She caught Mr.

Starkweather looking her way a few times, an unreadable expression on his face. Charlotte thought back on how he was hard on some students, and made pets of others.

Seems that his own talent as an artist hadn't make him good at helping his students. He'd scoffed at the color wheel pinned to the wall, remarking that any dummy knew that primaries made secondaries and that opposing colors complimented each other. She'd been too intimidated to admit she'd never even seen a color wheel before.

The only thing that made class bearable was her revenge fantasy of Pa and Kyle storming in to defend her. Preferably in the middle of another scathing critique. After a few quick punches, her teacher's smug smile would falter. The wicked thought made her lips quirk up at the corners.

Charlotte turned back to her artwork. She found herself second-guessing her whole project. She held the split half of a pinecone up to her collage, unsure of the right placement.

Her father's sentiments came back to her. *God's the best artist. Look to what he created.* She let her mind wander past the walls of art class to the cool, dark woods beyond their cabin, seeing the play of light and shadow in the pines.

She looked down at her own artwork. Charlotte moved the pinecone a smidge to the left, pressing it into the sweep of her impasto-painted pine bough, bristling with cobalt-green needles. There. Just right. She could almost smell the sap stickiness of it— pine pitch dripping in the warm glow of a yellow sun.

Chapter 13

Love is Kind

*Love is patient. Love is kind.
Love is not jealous or boastful, proud or rude.
It does not demand its own way.*
1 Corinthians 13:4-5

Wilma sighed, twisting her hands in nervousness. Today was the chance for her to make her case...to win Max over. The social worker had arranged an unsupervised one-on-one morning for Wilma and Max. Confined to the local area, she'd opted to take the boy to the river at Buttermilk Falls—a place she'd never seen.

She picked Max up at the farm. He gave her a shy grin and hopped in.

"Kinda a small town, isn't it?" she observed as they drove down Main Street.

"Not to me," said Max. "We've got Maggie's Diner, the mercantile, and Jeb's Ag Supply with feed for the horse and chickens. Everythin' we need."

"Of course." She'd gotten it wrong again. Wilma searched for a safer subject. "Have you been to the falls before?" she asked.

"Sure. Everyone 'round here knows it."

"I hope it's a good spot for us to spend some time together... get to know one another."

He nodded as they drove into the dirt pullout.

The falls were impressive. A big drop from dark tall cliffs with churning water foaming at the base, like real buttermilk...not that she'd ever tried any.

It was pretty noisy by the tumbling water, so Wilma led them farther away to a spot at the edge of the grassy meadow where they could sit at a rustic bench. So...what should she do with a little boy? She couldn't picture herself playing catch with Max, or coloring together. She was a lousy artist. No telling about the boy. They were starting from square one. He looked as nervous as she felt.

Food. That was the ticket. She pulled out some granola bars, a bag of pretzels and two bottles of water from her bag. "Hungry?"

"I guess." Max took a snack bar and peeled back the wrapper.

They ate in silence.

She searched her mind for a game or some other childish diversion. "Rod and I used to play tic-tac-toe," she said. "Think you could find us a couple of sticks to scratch a game in the dirt?"

"Yes, ma'am."

While he foraged for some sticks, Wilma though of other games she'd played with Rod. Hide and seek. Scavenger hunts. Marbles and mumblety-peg. Of course, the latter required a sharp knife to hurl into the dirt and carve up the drawn circle, like slices of pie. The person ending up with the biggest piece won. She wondered if Max had a knife.

When Max brought back a pair of long twigs, he drew a game board on the ground in front of them. They placed X's and O's in random patterns until each developed a strategy. If Max went

Love Is Kind

first, he won every time. On her go, it was a cat's game. He was a clever boy. Soon they both tired of the game.

She leaned back in the bench seat. "Thanks for the pollywogs," she said. "I haven't seen one in a long time."

"Don't you have no streams where you live?"

"Oh, sure," she said. "I've just been busy working."

"Doin' what?"

"I'm a waitress. I work for a diner that serves up breakfast, lunch and dinner. You'd like our biscuits and gravy."

"I like Maggie's Diner," he said. "Pancakes are my favorite."

"Humm." The silence stretched uncomfortably. Wilma fiddled with her stick. "You have a knife, Max?"

"Sure. You need somethin' cut?"

"No. Just thinking of a game." Of course, a country boy would have a knife, even at nine. Rod had one at that age. "Your pa give it to you?"

"Yep." Max pulled it from his pocket and held it out with pride. "For my seventh birthday."

"He give you a penny to go with?" she asked, aware of the old superstition.

Max nodded. "Of course... A penny so's the blade wouldn't cut the father/son ties." He looked down. "Didn't work, though."

Wilma's heart sank. "I'm right sorry about your pa," she said. "Drink is a devil." She lifted his chin, needing the truth. "Your pa ever hurt you, Max?"

His eyes flew to hers. "He...he didn't mean to. If only I hadn't been so bad. That's why the haints are after me. Rockin' and rockin' on the porch."

Wilma cringed. *Lordy.* So, it was true. The family curse had hurt Max, too. Rod heaping on the abuse he'd once lived with. Would the chains never be broken from her family?

She used a stick to draw a circle in the damp soil closer to the river. "Ever play mumblety-peg?" she asked.

"Sure," he said. "My knife throws real good."

"Let's get to it then." She gave Max the first throw.

Wilma had nearly forgotten how to hurl a knife into the dirt. On her turn, the blade bounced off the ground twice, before she stuck the third throw. She'd just started to get the hang of it by the time Max had carved up the circle leaving only a tiny wedge in her territory. She'd tired of the game, which had seemed a lot more fun when she was a girl. "You win," she conceded, knowing she couldn't possibly stick the final throw. "You're good with a knife."

"Thanks," he said, carefully wiping off the blade. He folded the knife and put it in his pocket. "I got a lot of practice back home, alone in the yard, lookin' for somethin' to do."

Wilma was getting a dismal picture of what his life with Rod had been like. "How'd you like to come live with me, Max?" she blurted. At the startled look on his face, she followed her next impulse. A little guilt never hurt. "It's what your pa would've wanted."

Max stiffened. "Do I have to?" He drew a zig-zag line in the dirt, as ragged as his pent-up emotions. "Lizzy and Gabe would be real sad if I left." He looked up, a silent plea darkening his eyes. "I promised Miss Lizzy I'd help out with Chloe and the new baby."

Two could play the sympathy game. "But you like me, don't you? After all, I'm your only blood kin. Your Aunt Wilma."

The pain in his eyes gave her a stab of conscience.

Why had she made her way here anyway? Truth be told, she'd hoped for some mention in Rodney's will. Some nod that he still loved her. And, barring that, she'd have settled for some money. A little payback for him leaving her behind.

But maybe Rod, like herself, had only been trying to survive. Her own stubbornness had kept them apart all these years. Kept them from reconnecting as adults. Kept her from knowing her nephew even existed.

And now here she was, messing with Max's life. After the muddle she'd made of her own, she had no business asking him to choose. She pondered Lizzy's question... *Is this what you really want?* Wilma didn't know the first thing about raising a boy. She didn't even know how to keep him entertained at the river for a few hours. Her cheeks flushed in shame.

"I'm sorry, Max. I shouldn't have asked that of you." She fiddled with the collar of her blouse. "You really like living here, then?"

He nodded. "It's all I know. Where I grew up. My school's here...and all my friends."

"How do you feel about staying with the Reeds?" she asked.

Max's expression brightened. "Can I?" He poked the dirt with his stick, snapping it in two. He tossed the broken twig aside and raked a hand through the spikes of his blond hair. His jaw worked as he tried to come up with something more. Wilma had already discovered he wasn't much for speech making. A boy of few words...like Rod had been.

"Lizzy was my teacher," he said. "She looked after me. And since I've come to live with them, she's always nice to me, even when I get in trouble. And Gabe...he teaches me stuff 'round the farm. He's not like Pa," Max added, with a furtive look to see how she was reacting. "He never yells or gets mad. And there's plenty of food, so my stomach's not a growlin'."

"I see," said Wilma, seeing more than she wanted to. The poor kid had really had it rough. "So, you feel you belong there?"

Max nodded, his face flushing. "Thing is...I was needin' a real family, what with Ma and Pa gone an' all. I'm hopin' to be 'dopted soon." He scuffed his shoe in the dirt. "I like havin' a sister, and a new baby comin'." He touched her arm, a pleading look in his eyes. "Can you still be my aunt, if I don't come live with you?"

Wilma pulled him close, breathing in the sweaty, little boy smell of him. "Yes, of course, Max. I'll always be your Aunt Wilma."

Rowdy had invited Gloria to come have a look at the Old Mill to see what decorating ideas she might have. They met at the building early Monday morning. She followed him up the steps and across the expansive porch to the front door. As she tried to match his lanky stride, Gloria was relieved that she and Rowdy had settled firmly into the "friend zone." One bull-headed boyfriend, like Buck, was enough to keep her slightly off balance.

Rowdy tugged the wooden peg from the doorlatch of the building and ushered her inside.

"Wowzer," she said, eyeing the expansive, vacant space. She admired the hefty headers soaring above and planks of weathered wood underfoot. Lots of mullioned windows and a brick foundry furnace nestled in the corner. "This is incredible. When can I get my hands on it?" A big, rustic place like this was a designer's dream.

Her mind zinged with decorating ideas—starting with that huge saw blade, which would make an eye-catching wall-hanger, while reflecting the history of the place. Her assessment took in the scattered wooden barrels, vintage tools, and a box of stamped flour sacks peeking from the storeroom. In her head, she was already sewing serving aprons from those *Walker Flour Mill* embossed cotton sacks. She envisioned planting trailing succulents in some of these hefty barrels, artistically displayed on the deck.

"It'll be a while," he admitted. "I'm still shorin' up the foundation, checkin' floor supports, upgradin' electrical...all the borin' stuff." Rowdy rocked back on his boot heels, hands snugged in his pockets. "But all that hidden stuff's important."

Didn't she know it. Her mind flashed back to Buck's kiss the night of the robbery, wondering if it was a foretaste of something more between them than a bristly friendship. Two people as independent and strong-minded as Buck and herself had better shore up some pretty hefty beams beneath their relationship to withstand the regular earthquakes of their colliding temperaments. She grinned. Buck was so adorable when he was riled. Made her want to poke him on purpose. Give him plenty of rope to hang himself... and the time to do it. Next meeting, she might need more than a beribboned pitchfork to do the job.

"...and it'll sit right over here," said Rowdy, gesturing to the far wall.

Feeling a little guilty, Gloria tugged her thoughts away from the Sheriff Buck rabbit trail. She'd missed most of what Rowdy had said. "What?"

"The soda fountain. It'll tuck in right along that wall."

She pictured the vintage setup on her computer screen. Of course. That's why he'd brought her here, to confirm that his splurge was right for the space. "Oh, Rowdy... It'll be perfect. Better than perfect." And it would be. Just right for a small town stuck in a bit of a time warp. For a cowboy, he had a darned good eye. And a surprising touch of nostalgia. "Can I have the first ice cream sundae?"

Rowdy grinned. "Done."

"So...you're partners with that kid, Kyle, on this..." she said. "How's that working out?"

"Well...that's yet to be seen." Rowdy lifted his black Stetson and scratched the back of his head. "Right now, he's got more money than sense. But I think he'll come around."

"He know anything about restoring a place like this?"

"Not really," said Rowdy. "But I do."

"Then this space will make a fine restaurant."

"And art gallery..." added Rowdy.

"Art gallery?" Her eyebrows rose. "Kyle's idea?"

"None other. Scary thing is... I'm startin' to warm to the idea." Rowdy shrugged and smiled. "He's goin' to hang some of Charlotte's pictures in here."

"That's great! She's got some serious talent."

"Thanks. Kyle thinks so, too. And she's over the moon about it."

Gloria twirled around, giving the place another once over. "This space has a ton of potential..."

Rowdy grinned. "...said the spider to the fly."

"Hey... You're the one who showed me this honey hole. Can't blame me for drooling."

"It really needs your touch," said Rowdy. "Like you did for the Lost Lake cabins. You're the perfect one to pull it all together."

"Thanks," said Gloria. "I'm itching to get started."

Something big and furry scurried across the floor. "Yikes!" yelped Gloria, taking a step back. "What the heck was that?"

Scout whined, but sat back on his haunches, licking his lips.

Rowdy grunted. "That's Rascal, our pesky resident raccoon."

"A raccoon? You sure?"

"Sure as shootin'." He pointed to the black-masked face peeking out from behind a barrel. "Have a gander for yourself."

She bent down to look. The critter ran a hand across his black button nose. "He is kinda cute."

"Cute?! He's a menace." Rowdy stomped on the floor, to warn the critter away. "I'm workin' hard to block all his entrance points. You can't have wildlife in a restaurant."

Gloria dug out the remnants of a half-eaten cookie from her oversized handbag, pitching it in Rascal's direction.

"No! Don't feed him," begged Rowdy, frowning.

The coon hesitated for a second then dashed out, snatching up the offering.

"Now you've done it." said Rowdy. "He'll turn into a mooch raccoon, for sure."

"Is that such a bad thing?"

"Not if you don't mind a twenty-pound *rat* scamperin' 'neath the tables."

"Oh…" She clamped her mouth shut, shivering at the image.

Rascal sniffed the soft, flat rock tossed his way. It smelled great—sweet as honey in a hive. He snatched it up with dexterous fingers and headed to the river to wash it off before eating it. Rascal liked these humans. He'd grown used to them hanging around the place and sometimes even setting out food for him.

When the humans first came to the old mill they were a curiosity. Something new to learn about. Best thing was…they smelled of food. He'd learned to get tasty treats by stealth or even by a little begging. At first, the yellow wolf-dog scared him, but the beast just sniffed the scent of the young raccoon and didn't give chase, so Rascal soon relaxed around him.

But he was still wary of the other humans camped farther up the river. Those folks carried big fire-sticks they used to kill squirrels, rabbits and even strong, big-antlered bucks. Their scent was pungent and acrid in the woods, with the smell of fresh blood on their hands. So he stayed away.

Rascal was just a kit when his mother and two brothers had been run over by a box truck—flattened on the road into a pile of blood and guts. As the runt of the litter, he'd been trailing behind when the *whoosh* of the vehicle roared past. He'd hung out at the site along the highway for a few days, mewling for his mama. But hunger finally drove him into the woods in search of something to ease the knot in his belly.

When he'd stumbled upon the old mill, he'd been lost, wet and bedraggled, shivering in the cold downpour of a spring rain. He wiggled through a small opening in the rotting boards. It was dry inside with a few soft places to nestle into. A pile of dried corn spilling from an old sack in a corner had kept him alive through the worst of the storm.

When the storm broke and the sun at last spilled through the windows, Rascal crept back outside in search of roots or insects to eat. Survival instincts deep inside kept the young raccoon going. He hunted mostly at night and returned to the relative safety of the building at dawn. He'd have to be clever to stay alive. Slowly he toughened up. Fattened up. Grew up. And wised up.

Curiosity drove him. He explored the stream...foraging for crafty crawfish, flat-footed frogs, and tasty minnows. The young raccoon became familiar with every inch of a good four-mile stretch of the creek. He snatched grasshoppers from the weeds and voles from their tunnels.

By now, he knew how to survive. If humans could add some sweets to his diet, so much the better. Rascal washed off the honey rock in the racing water and chewed it to bits.

Yummy!

After supper at his cabin, Rowdy thought back on Gloria's comments. He was beyond pleased that she was on board with the soda fountain. And—as he'd known she would be—Gloria couldn't wait to put her Sparkles touch on the place.

But she'd gotten him thinking about his partnership with Kyle. The kid was still wet behind the ears and prone to stupid mistakes, like what happened with his rifle. He'd been darned lucky to get his favorite gun back.

Remembering his recent trials with his own son, Wyatt, he wondered why he'd signed up to go through it again with Kyle. Mentoring without meddling was as tricky as heeling a nervous yearling calf. He'd have to think quickly and talk slowly...not easy for an old cowboy like him. The young man often made decisions without really knowing what he was doing. Like thinking the restrooms would be best on the west side of the building, without realizing all of the plumbing and hook-ups for the kitchen were at the other end. But with Kyle, what was lacking in experience was made up for in bravado. All hat and no cattle. Rowdy sighed as he took his mug of coffee out to the porch.

He thought back to their first real head-butt last Friday, when they'd argued over the water wheel. Not the color. Red appealed to the boy's artistic side. Kyle was opposed to putting money into expensive new gears and bushings—items that wouldn't even show—unless you actually wanted a working paddle wheel. And Rowdy definitely did.

He explained the engineering. A functioning water wheel required more than replacing the worn boards and re-bracing it. The strength of any wheel originated from the central metal hub outward to the spokes and paddles, which took the brunt force of the moving water.

"It's just for looks anyway," protested Kyle. "What does it matter how well it turns?"

"We may not be usin' it for power, like they did for the lumber and flour mill," said Rowdy. "But to have a workin' paddle wheel we've got to do things right."

"It's not like riding a bull," Kyle countered. "Nobody's going to get hurt if the wheel doesn't turn smoothly. For that matter, maybe it doesn't even need to turn at all. It's been dead-stopped in the water for a coon's age."

"There's no shortcut to any place worth goin'," said Rowdy.

"My point exactly." Kyle frowned. "That old paddle wheel doesn't need to turn. It's not going anywhere."

Rowdy sucked in a breath. He tried counting to ten, but only made it to four and a half. "You ever hear the sound of a workin' water wheel?"

"No. What's it like?"

"Like nothin' else. One of your poets could likely do it justice." Rowdy lifted his Stetson to welcome some cool air to his scalp. "It has a song all its own. The rhythmic slap of this paddle wheel will calm even our crankiest customer."

"We'll have music for that," Kyle insisted.

Rowdy eyed the water wheel—its mossy blades silent—yearning to break free and churn, once again, in the swiftly moving river. "Not like this."

Back in her hotel room, Wilma picked up the glass mason jar and peered inside. Already the pollywogs were lightening in color, a hint of green traveling along the plump black bodies. Leg buds sprouted near the tail. Growing up.

She fell back on the bed and replayed her morning with Max. Wilma felt for the boy. She knew what it was like to be berated by a father. To believe the lies. She carried the scars still. Max had a chance to break free. Only, most likely...not with her.

Apparently, Rod hadn't fallen too far from their own tragic family tree. He'd abused his own child...just like he'd been abused as a boy. Under stress, would she do the same? Raise a hand to the boy? Or use words to break him, like Mama had with her?

Why had she filed for custody in the first place? Wilma had never wanted kids of her own. After being Mama's caregiver for so long, she'd wanted freedom—not some snotty-nosed brat to care for. For the first time, she realized that might have been a mistake. The freedom she'd wanted had turned out to be a dead-end, leaving her alone and lonely. She had no one she had to take care of, but no one who cared about her either. She'd messed up—carrying a chip on her shoulder and letting bitterness sour her heart. But at her age, she'd never have a child of her own. Just her nephew, Max.

Wilma sighed and swiped away a tear. She was done with her pity party. Done blaming others for her troubles. Done with feeling sorry for herself. If a fat pollywog could grow into a handsome frog, maybe she could somehow grow into the woman she was meant to be. No more expecting someone else to rescue her.

Max had shown her how. Shown her how a kid could take life's hard knocks and still be happy. He was a sweet boy. But she wasn't the one to raise him. He'd have a fine home here in Buttermilk Falls with Gabe and Lizzy—growing up with a real family. A better life than he'd ever have with her. Wilma determined to set Max free—like she and Rod had done with their pet pollywogs when they'd grown into frogs.

The Reeds had invited her to dinner on Friday. She'd stay in town until then and use the occasion to break the news. Good a time as any, she supposed.

What did she have to give him, really? Only this…

Then why did it hurt so much to let him go?

Lest she be tempted to change her mind between now and then, she pulled out her battered suitcase and started packing.

Chapter 14

Treasures in Heaven

*Store your treasures in heaven,
where moths and rust cannot destroy
and thieves do not break in and steal.
Where your treasure is,
the desires of your heart will also be.
Matthew 6:20-21*

Buck met Lizzy and Gabe at the old cabin, and escorted them down the steep steps to the cellar. He was extra careful to keep the trap door propped open. They stood at one end of the small space, glancing into the cold, dark recesses of the mine.

Buck shone the beam of his heavy-duty flashlight into the cavern. "Welcome to the Pumpkin Hallow Copper Mine," he said. "It's been boarded up and hidden down here for nearly a hundred years." His lantern flashed on some shiny copper carbonate.

Gabe stopped Lizzy when she tried to step over a fallen board to enter the mine. "You're not going in there," he said. "It's not safe for you...or the baby." He glanced down at the rounded mound of her seventh-month pregnancy—their cherished unborn child. "Who knows what kind of bracing is left in there, after all this time."

Lizzy's shoulders sagged in disappointment. "But it's my mine. I want to see it."

"Of course, you do," he acknowledged. "But you'll have to make do with the view from out here."

"You've been inside, haven't you, sheriff?" Lizzy asked.

Now she was putting him in the middle. "Sure," Buck said. "But Gabe's right. It's too risky." Buck had seen the care Gabe had taken helping Lizzy down the stairs. When he'd extended the invitation, Buck had conveniently forgotten about her condition. Lizzy had always been such a fireball of energy. Good thing she had Gabe to watch out for her.

Buck pulled another flashlight from his belt. "Use this." He handed it to her. "You can see a lot from right here at the entrance." *Though not the raw beauty of the rich vein six yards in.* But he wasn't telling her that.

She peered in the entrance. Not much to look at, really. Just a dark tunnel. And cold, too. She shivered.

Buck took out his phone. "How about I take a few photos inside so you can get a look that way?"

"What about your safety?" she asked, only half in jest.

"I'll take my chances," he said. "Best you stay outside, too, Gabe. Make sure your wife stays put." He knew that Gabe, like any testosterone-fueled male, was itching to explore the mine. The least he could do was provide a way to hold Gabe back, without him losing face.

They were probably all fools for being down here checking out a dangerous abandoned mine. *What had he been thinking?* "Why don't you take Lizzy back outside," he suggested. "Out of this dank cabin to a safer area. You can come back down and spot me from here."

"Okay," Gabe agreed. He escorted Lizzy out.

After Gabe returned, Buck trekked inside the mine for several yards. *Here it is,* he thought, as his light hit the rich copper vein. The green/blue streak of malachite and agate held a wedge of gleaming copper.

The first sample he'd taken from the mine, a few weeks before, was at the lab. He wanted Lizzy to be able to handle a piece of the raw ore. So, using his knife, Buck pried loose a chunk the size of a railroad spike and slipped it in his pocket. He snapped some photos of the vein and of another smaller trace at the back of the cave. A gust of wind whispered in the dank cavern. A chill raced up his spine. Buck sensed a malevolent force, closing in. This cave held bad juju. He could feel it.

Maybe it was Miss Daffodil's sudden death in the nearby cellar—with all of the unanswered questions—or some other premonition of evil. He sent a silent plea heavenward as he turned away from the glittering copper vein and edged back out the way he'd come.

Would Gabe and Lizzy be corrupted by this sudden windfall? Would it change who they were? Blind them to the true riches they already had?

Sheriff Buck had seen it happen before. The lure of easy money changed people. Incited a hunger for just a little bit more. Case in point. Sweet Mildred Stein's son, Ethan, had turned on his own ailing mother in her last days, chasing the promise of easy riches. And even Wilma seemed more intent on his inheritance than on little Max.

A small rock slide slithered down the side wall with a clatter, depositing a jumble of stones at his feet. Buck leapt over the rocks and hurried through the wood slats into the cellar. "Let's get out of here," he said to Gabe. "This place gives me the creeps."

Gabe glanced at him. "You a church-going man, Buck?"

Buck halted. Had Gabe sensed his unspoken prayer—the surest defense against such pure evil? "Haven't bowed the knee in over twenty-five years," he admitted.

"Might be time to rethink that," said Gabe, with a quick smile.

What the...? Buck admired Gabe. Maybe even envied him a bit for the family he had, and the one he was creating. But he never took him for a holy roller. "God and I have an understanding," Buck blurted. "One that works for me."

"Things change."

"Not likely," countered Buck, trying to shake off his unease from being in the cave.

"God just might surprise you," said Gabe as they climbed the rickety stairs together.

Lizzy greeted the two of them as they emerged. "What did I miss?"

"Copper," said Sheriff Buck. "A whole wall of it." He tugged the sample from his pocket and handed it to her."

"Pretty." She held the hefty chunk up to the light. "Who knew such riches lay hidden under this old pumpkin field?"

Who, indeed? thought Buck. That was a question worth pondering.

As he closed the trap door, Buck glanced at Gabe. "This is a dangerous place," he said. "Keep it locked up tight and the kids away."

≼ℓℓ

So, she owned a copper mine. The idea didn't sit as well as she expected. For Lizzy, the cabin was the site of Aunt Daffy's death and the source of Max's tormenting dreams. Like Buck, the place gave her the creeps. She looked at the chunk of copper ore Buck had given her. She'd placed it in a small basket on the bedroom bureau where its distinctive green stripe glowed like the eyes of a shifty cat. She threw a hand towel over those discontented eyes, putting off making any decisions about that cursed mine.

Today, she was caught up in final preparations for the annual Sweet Apple Stomp at the farm, starting in just a few hours. This much-anticipated fall event gathered the town teens together for a country themed dance, where they could press apple cider, down warm spicy wedges of apple pie and dip caramel apples. The event was one of Aunt Daffy's legacies, a way of bringing young folks together.

It was a good thing she had Harley to manage the apple trees and the Christmas tree farm. Lizzy had been far too busy and too pregnant to be very hands-on this year. Almost unnoticed—under Harley's expert care—the apple trees had bloomed, set fruit and produced a bumper crop of Granny Smiths, Braeburns, and Honey Crisp apples. Time to celebrate the harvest.

With her growing pregnancy, she'd been forced to enlist the help of family and friends for hosting the event. She'd enjoyed finding just the right task for each volunteer to use their unique talents. The farm was a hub of activity, the way Aunt Daffy had liked it.

Lizzy came awkwardly down the stairs and into the kitchen which was bustling with commotion. A huge pot of spicy chili simmered on the stove and pans of cornbread cooled on the sideboard. Doris and Maggie pulled freshly baked apple pies from the oven, golden juices bubbling at the edges. Chloe wore a dab of flour on her cheek as she rolled out a lopsided pie crust. Her daughter's borrowed apron had been folded several times at the waist, but still hung well past her chubby knees. Pursed lips and violet eyes animated the six-year-old as she stood on a chair and smiled up at Lizzy. "Look, Mommy. I'm rollin' pie."

"Good girl," said Lizzy, touching her cap of dark curls. "You're becoming a great little cook." She smiled at Doris and Maggie. "You women are awesome. And the pies smell heavenly."

She carried a tray of washed Granny Smiths and a box of pointed, caramel apple sticks outside for Max to jab in the fruit—after a thorough hand washing. What boy wouldn't enjoy that task? Except for the hand washing part. Later, they'd melt caramel cubes in a cast iron pan for dipping. Lizzy hoped being busy and feeling needed might help Max settle a bit. She'd made sure to include him in the manly jobs of table moving, pumpkin hauling, band stage building and leaf raking. She'd see that he took his turns on the apple press crank as well.

Charlotte had been recruited to make Sweet Apple Stomp posters to hang around town and collect pinecones and colorful leaves for the tables. Gloria was in charge of decorations. Lizzy could see she'd been busy—arranging mini-pumpkins and pinecones on the tables, swags of fall leaves on the stage, and hanging lanterns in the trees. Off in the corners, Gloria had created fetching displays of plows and cornstalks. On random stacks of hay bales, old watering cans sprouted sunflowers. Was that a scarecrow wearing a baseball cap and sunglasses?

Sheriff Buck arrived at the Sweet Apple Stomp, just as the sun was going down. He was here in a semi-official capacity, his presence calculated to keep a lid on any youthful high jinks. Excited teens swarmed out of cars and pick-ups, like bees on the scent of clover. Music boomed from speakers in the barn and lanterns gave an inviting glow to the yard.

Buck noticed two boys he'd had truck with, Red and Larson. Petty theft at the auto parts store. They'd lifted small items to work on an old Model T in Red's backyard. As a car guy, he could understand the temptation. He hoped the repayment costs and hours of community service had taught them a lesson. Everyone deserved a second chance. He strode into the farmyard near the barn, a bit self-conscious in his uniform.

Harley was cranking up the cider press, his sweat-stained straw hat firmly in place in spite of the oncoming darkness. He grinned at Buck around the toothpick clenched in his teeth. "Howdy, sheriff."

Buck nodded. "Harley. Need any help with that?"

"No thanks." He jerked a thumb at the invading horde of high schoolers. "That's what the young bloods are for. Let 'em earn their supper." Harley soon had two muscled football players turning the crank while another dumped in a carton of windfall apples. Nothing went to waste on a well-run farm.

Buck scanned the area, checking for trouble. *Ah...there she was.* Over at a far picnic table Gloria laughed with ol' Clive, who was carving pumpkins into jack-o-lanterns with a pocket knife—a skill he'd perfected over the last 50 years. Her laugh was music in the air, drawing him to the sound. "Evening, Gloria," he said, giving her an appreciative once over.

"Hi, Buck."

Had her eyes always been so blue? Her blond curls reflected the lamplight, her rounded lips painted a startling shade of red. His breath caught, imagining the taste of them. Reluctantly he turned to the pumpkin carver. "Hello, Clive."

"Howdy, sheriff." He smiled. "I'd shake your hand, but mine's all slimy with pumpkin guts."

A thick, newly cut piece of pumpkin flesh fell away, and the jack-o-lantern gave a wicked grin. "Artists," said Buck. "A temperamental lot."

Gloria tucked her hand into the fold of Buck's arm. "You hungry?"

You've no idea... "Sure," he croaked out. "Want some chili?"

"My mouth's watering." She walked with him to the cast iron kettle banked in the campfire coals. "There's cornbread, too."

They sat at a table eating steaming bowls of chili and wedges of cornbread smothered in honey butter.

"You like the decor?" she asked.

"What decor?" He found himself bedazzled by the sparkly pumpkin design on her t-shirt and the swing of the glittery, star-shaped earrings peeking from beneath the fall of her blond hair. The pink streak had gone purple tonight...or was it the scant lighting?

She pointed to some pinecones and leaves on the table, and nudged a slender shoulder at the plow and cornstalks behind them.

"Oh...very nice," he said.

"Liar. You haven't even noticed."

"I've noticed plenty." He brought a hand to her cheek, nudging a glittery hanging star. "I like your earrings."

Her cheeks colored. "Nice save, sheriff." She pulled back and spooned in more chili with a mischievous grin.

The blaze of warmth lingered where Buck's finger had brushed her cheek. Gloria welcomed the bite of the spicy chili that burned her taste buds. Whatever was between them was as combustible as a stick of dynamite. She let her gaze fall to the dark hair covering his muscled forearm, the sheer maleness of him unsettling. She needed a diversion. "You know how to square dance?"

He looked up, startled. "A big lug like me? I'd crush you on the first do si do."

"Ever tried it?" she pushed. "You'd do a mean roll away to a half sashay."

"We talking dancing here?"

"Sheriff, come quick!" Harley called out, tugging on his arm. "Max is in trouble."

Buck bolted.

The Old Mill

Who knew a dorky event like this Sweet Apple Stomp could be so much fun? Charlotte hadn't, in her craziest dreams, expected to learn how to square dance. But she had...thanks to the mad skills of a fiddling caller who patiently taught the teens, one new step at a time. Goodness...her toes were still tapping as she mentally rehearsed the swings and sways of the square: *Allemande left, do si do, find your corner, promenade, circle left, ladies in...men sashay.* She'd feared being a wall flower at the barn dance, but discovered once you volunteered for a square, you were in...and in for it. You didn't even pair off, like at a regular dance...not really. Partners changed back and forth in the circle as they laughed and moved to the boot-stomping rhythm.

Charlotte found herself to be a popular partner. Guys who barely spoke to her at school took her hand to *swing your girl*, her red curls flying. When she finally sat out...breathless, guys competed to fetch her a glass of fresh pressed apple cider or a slice of homemade apple pie, still warm from the oven.

Somehow, Gabe and Lizzy's farm had been transformed into a fall harvest fairyland. As darkness closed in, twinkle lights glowed in the trees. Lit jack-o-lanterns grinned from atop stacks of hay bales. Farm lanterns cast long languid shadows, like an illustration for the *Legend of Sleepy Hallow*.

She hadn't known the charms of an evening campfire, or how beautiful folks faces looked when cast in its burnished glow. When her pa had first brought her to this small town, she'd expected to be bored and restless. But she'd found plenty of fun things to do. How could such a simple thing as chili warmed in a cast iron kettle and ladled into paper bowls taste so good?

Basking in the whole feel-good vibe of the evening, Charlotte was startled to literally run into Mr. Starkweather at the edge of the crowd. Their shoulders collided with a jolt. What was he doing here? Probably a high school chaperone. Just her luck.

"Oops... Sorry," she mumbled.

"Oh, Charlotte. I'm the one who's sorry."

"Just an accidental bump. No harm done."

"It's not the shoulder bump I meant." Her art teacher pushed his dark-framed glasses nervously up on his nose.

Since when had he worn glasses?

"Could I have a word with you?"

"I guess..." *Why did he have to show up and totally ruin the festive mood?*

He guided her to a hay bale at the edge of the crowd, where they sat down. "Listen, Charlotte. I feel badly about the tough art critique I gave you. The one where you ran out of the room." He looked around to be sure no one overheard. "I was out of line."

She had no idea what to say.

He fiddled with his ill-fitting glasses and finally removed them, jiggling them on his knee. "These darned glasses! My eyesight's going, and they make me look like some old fuddy-duddy professor...but that's beside the point."

Was he trying to apologize? Charlotte looked for some way to escape.

"Listen," Mr. Starkweather said in a strained voice. "I'm making a real mess of this."

Got that right.

"Thing is, that day... I'd received a bit of bad news and took it out on you. I'm sorry."

Charlotte swallowed. "Okay..."

"Got turned down for the master's art program at my alma mater." He shoved his glasses back on. "Guess I was sulking. Upset they didn't think I had the talent for it." Mr. Starkweather sighed. "Thinking…about how, now, I'll be stuck teaching art at Lonesome Mountain High."

"Is that so bad?" asked Charlotte.

"Oh… I didn't mean it like that. Just that I always pictured myself as a college professor." He cleared his throat. "I fell into thinking of teaching here as just a placeholder. But, turns out, I really like it. I enjoy seeing kids, like you, learn to express themselves."

"Well…my painting really wasn't very good."

"Maybe not that one. But most of your artwork is exceptional. You have a lot of talent, Charlotte."

She looked up. "You really think so?"

"Absolutely. A style all your own. With a little guidance, you could do some great work."

"Thanks." Charlotte sobered. "Sorry about that master's program."

"Don't be. Thing is…somewhere along the way, I strove so hard to excel at technique, that I lost the pleasure of it. Your art work reminded me of the simple joy of creating." He gave a self-conscious shrug. "I'd like to be a better teacher. I hope you'll give me another chance."

"Of course," she said. "I've still got a lot to learn."

This close, Mr. Starkweather smelled of cigarettes and the spearmint gum which clicked against his irregular teeth as he spoke. Charlotte allowed her former hero to topple down a peg or two. She noticed the gray hair edging into his dark mop, and the black-framed glasses he'd perched awkwardly back on his long nose.

"Thanks for the apology, Mr. Starkweather." Charlotte stood and faced him. "And the kind words. I appreciate it."

He lifted a hand in farewell.

Charlotte mulled over his comments as she rejoined the crowd of kids huddled by the fire pit. She'd never in a million years have expected Mr. Starkweather to apologize.

Sated on chili and cornbread—and budding friendships—she felt downright mellow. Part of a real community for the first time ever. It felt good. Like cozy covers on a cold night. Like coming home.

Charlotte was startled when a few loud firecrackers popped out in the cornfield. She turned toward the sound.

Buck followed Harley toward the old oak in the front yard, his flashlight illuminating the way. A huddled form lay on the ground, blood oozing from his forehead. "Max? What happened?"

Max opened his terror-filled eyes. "The haint... It came for me."

Sheriff Buck knelt, eased Max to a sitting position, then checked the boy's injury. The wound appeared to be superficial... only a bit of a laceration, but Max was shaking. Buck pulled out a handkerchief and held it to the wound to stop the bleeding. "It's okay now, Max. I've got you."

The hair prickled at the back of her neck. *Something was wrong.* Lizzy turned away from the festivities and sniffed the air. Smoke? A few sizzling pops resounded, almost hidden beneath the loud boot-stomping beat of the music.

She moved toward the sound, in the direction of the cornfield. Flashlight beams played on the tall stalks, like search lights probing the darkness.

Pop! Pop! Pop! Lizzy scurried faster.

The Old Mill

Under the oak tree Buck was joined by Gabe, who pulled the trembling boy into his lap, his arms snugged tightly around him. "You're safe now," Gabe said. "How did your hurt your head?"

"I was runnin' from the ghost."

Gabe and Buck exchanged a look. "What ghost?" asked Gabe.

"The one in the cornfield. The one that tried to grab me."

"What did you see, Max?" Buck asked.

"A skeleton." Max closed his eyes "Like...like the one in the cellar."

Gabe held him closer.

"Gabe..." Max looked up. "The skeleton talked to me."

"What did it say?" Gabe rubbed his boy's back.

"It had a real scary voice," sobbed Max. *"I'll find you..."* Max mimicked in a quivery voice. *"Make you pay..."*

Dear God, thought Gabe. *Can it get any worse?*

"How'd you hurt your head?" he asked, lifting the cloth. The bleeding had stopped.

"I ran away," said Max. "Ducked under this here hoot owl tree to hide 'n' got knocked clean to the ground. Thought they got me for sure."

So... he'd likely cut his head on a low-lying tree branch. *But what had scared him so?* Buck wondered.

"Why were you in the cornfield?" Gabe asked his son.

"Two boys said someone wanted to see me out there. So, I went with 'em." Max looked behind him, checking for ghosts.

Buck straightened. "What boys?"

"Some high school guys I've seen in town. One's called Red. Don't know the other's name." Max shuddered. He looked up at Gabe, eyes wide. "That ghost's still out there...waitin' to get me."

Pop! Pop! Pop! More firecrackers sounded from the corn.

"That's it, now!" Max cried, stiffening in Gabe's arms.

"I'll go check," said Buck. "See who's really making all that racket." He stood. "Gabe, can you stay here with Max?"

"Of course." Gabe pulled his frightened boy closer. "We're fine."

<hr />

The fool kids gave themselves away by the flashlights waving around like beacons in the tall dry stalks of the cornfield. Sheriff Buck actually enjoyed sneaking up on them from behind and grabbing them by the shoulders...one in each of his big hands.

He applied a crushing grip and called out in a high-pitched quavering voice, *"I'll find you... Make you pay..."* The boys yelped, nearly jumping out of their skins. One boy clutched a plastic Halloween skeleton suspended from a broom handle. He let it fall to the ground.

Buck took no small pleasure in flicking on his flashlight, turning them around, and shining it into their startled eyes. He recognized the culprits. "Red. Larson. What kind of idiots scare a little kid half to death?" he asked, his voice a deep and commanding baritone. "And those fireworks are illegal and dangerous. This sorry prank will earn you boys a night in jail."

"But we were just havin' some fun..."

"Save your breath," Buck said, grabbing them by their collars. "You two have some apologizing to do. Bring that skeleton."

Lizzy tumbled through the corn and jerked back at the sight of the skeleton suspended in mid-air. "What's going on?" she demanded.

"Pure meanness," snarled Buck. "Come along. I'll take you to Max."

"What happened?" she asked.

"A sick prank gone wrong." Buck hustled the boys through the dry corn stalks, Lizzy following closely behind.

"Is Max all right?" Lizzy asked, a hand cradling her stomach.

"He will be. He's a strong boy."

Chapter 15

A Spirit of Fear

For God has not given us a spirit of fear;
but of power, and of love,
and a sound mind.
2 Timothy 1:7

Buck planted the two young pranksters in front of Max, a beefy hand on each boy's shoulder. They looked down at their shoes. Even in the scant moonlight, he could see Red's face flush, as brightly colored as his hair. Larson's eyes had grown as round as pumpkins.

Still reeling from his scare, Max jerked back when Sheriff Buck thrust out the plastic skeleton. "This your ghost?" he asked.

"I guess," stammered Max. "It's…it's not real?"

"Nope…just a plastic Halloween prop." He laid it on the ground. "Go ahead…check it out."

Max reached out a shaking hand. *Plastic…not bone.* He looked up at his tormentors. "You fooled me!?" he said. "Why'd you do it?"

"We're real sorry," Red blurted. "We was just havin' some fun."

The Old Mill

Gabe stood. "Fun for who?"

Larson remained silent, chewing his bottom lip.

"Max got hurt because of you!" raged Lizzy, hands on hips. "Get off this property right now! You're not welcome here."

"Whoa... Hold up a minute." Sheriff Buck tightened his restraining grip on the boys' shoulders before they could bolt. "I'm escorting them to jail," he said. "They'll be facing charges of malicious mischief and setting off illegal fireworks. Lucky thing they didn't start a fire in the dry corn. They'll not get off with a warning this time."

Sheriff Buck returned to the farm an hour or so later. All was calm, now that the spook had been laid to rest. He'd try not to let a few bad apples spoil the evening. Maybe Max could get over some of his fears and superstitions now.

He pulled up a crate to sit beside Gloria, mindful of his long absence. "Sorry about that. Police business." *Lame.*

She eyed him. "Some guys will do anything to get out of square dancing."

Was she mad at him? Or was her pretty pout just a tease? "What'd I miss?"

"Two jack-o-lanterns had a duel over a fetching sunflower. Guts all over the place. Maybe you should go investigate that."

He frowned. "You making fun of my job?"

Gloria sighed. "No. Not really. I just missed you, is all." She wouldn't let on how his quick exit had left her feeling downright lonely. As if the shining disk of the full moon overhead had slipped behind a cloud, darkening her spirit. She was a fool to let a man affect her like this. She threaded her hand into the bend of his elbow. "Max okay?"

He placed his hand over hers. "He had a scare and a bump on the head. He'll be all right."

"Good." She tossed back her hair. "And Buck..."

He looked over, his unnerving grey eyes on hers.

"I'm really glad you're back."

He smiled at that. Buck had a great smile.

Still, Gloria wondered about her role in Buck's life. Tonight had highlighted that his job always came first. Sometimes she felt like an afterthought. Someone who was convenient and undemanding. Was she willing to settle for that?

Buttermilk Falls was a family town. She'd made friends with Amy, but since the town vet married Rowdy's son, Wyatt, they hadn't seen much of each other. For a while she'd mentored Rowdy's daughter, Charlotte, but now the teen seemed to be doing fine on her own. Besides Buck, she didn't really have a close friend. As Buck's occasional date, and a single business owner of Sparkles, where did she really fit in?

Behind them, kids dipped skewered apples into a pot of melted caramel. Others moved to the boot-stomping music of fiddlers calling out one final square dance. Those gathered around the last cider press of the night poured fresh apple cider into clear gallon jugs and then into paper cups to wash down slices of warm apple pie. A popcorn machine spewed out bags of fluffy kernels drenched in butter, which some of the guys pitched at young couples spooning in the darker corners. Jack-o-lanterns grinned as adult chaperones chatted about crops and the weather.

Buck watched the evening play out. This was the best of Buttermilk Falls. A throwback to simpler times. Wholesome pleasures, tied to friendships and community. An acknowledgement of the changing seasons and the bounty of fall. Something akin to gratefulness filled his chest.

The Old Mill

He wondered if the nearby hidden copper mine would change everything—destroy the deep sense of community. He glanced over at Gloria. She looked stunning, even sitting on a hay bale. The lamplight sparked gold in her hair...angel hair. Her manicured hand rested on his arm, the warmth of it more satisfying than the spicy chili he'd downed earlier...filling a hunger he'd long tried to deny. Was he headed for trouble?

Lizzy made her rounds, a hand resting unconsciously on her swollen belly. She tousled the hair on Max's head, above the scrape, as he carved a pumpkin under Clive's watchful eye. She smiled at Chloe, who ran through the crowd with a crepe paper streamer, tailed by their dog, Buddy. Gabe came up behind her and drew her close, his hand circling her side.

Buck took it all in. Sometimes people didn't even know what they had.

After the excitement and adrenaline rush of the night, Buck couldn't sleep. He got up and banged around his cabin, brewing a mug of strong coffee. After adding the requisite sugar, Buck sat at his computer. He logged onto a police site, and pulled up records from the burned body in the shed. Female. Five foot five. Age indeterminate, due to the burned state of the bones. Teeth in need of dental work. Signs of poor nutrition. A turquoise ring on her right middle finger, identified as Miss Daffodil's—part of the mistaken identification. Copper bracelet on her left wrist.

Copper? Buck looked up and raked a hand through his uncombed hair. The pink of dawn tinted the windows and eager birds outside began to call out to one another.

He scrolled down the screen to check if the bracelet had been stored in the evidence locker. It had. Curiosity and the drive to tie up loose ends almost sent him straight to police headquarters in town, but the gnawing hunger in his belly stopped him. He rustled up some scrambled eggs and toast, downed another mug of strong coffee and grabbed his keys.

Twenty minutes later, he dropped the copper bracelet from the storage baggie onto his desk. Buck fingered it, turning it over for any markings. Unsigned, the piece was hand forged, pounded from the raw material. Where did Birdie get the copper? He thought he knew. Birdie had her benefactor's ring. Had she stolen it? And the bracelet? Had the copper mine cost Daffodil DuPonte her life?

Max lay awake for a long time. An owl hooted outside. He rubbed the sore spot on his forehead. His heart still raced at the memory of that twitching skeleton and the quavering voice... *I'll find you... Make you pay.*

Gabe and Lizzy had prayed with him before tucking him into bed. They asked God to watch over him, to comfort him and take away his fear. But he was still scared. Maybe the big God in heaven couldn't see a little boy like him.

Pa had always believed in ghosts. But his new dad, Gabe, told him that God was near to protect him from evil. Evil like those two mean boys? They were in jail now. For lighting firecrackers. But what about the haints?

Max squeezed his eyes shut, tossing and turning until morning. After breakfast he went outside, striding past the hay bales still strewn about and the burned-out jack-o-lanterns with sullen, sunken smiles. He headed for the corn.

The dry stalks rustled in the wind. His knees grew weak, his throat dry...his fear as paralyzing as a knock on the funny bone of an elbow. But after last night's scare, he was determined to face it.

Max stepped into the corn.

He chanted a snatch of the prayer Lizzy had taught him, *"God has not given me a spirit of fear. God has not given me..."* A swiftly moving shadow streaked down the row toward him. A ghost? *"...a spirit of fear."*

He closed his eyes as the haint scuttled closer. Something wet touched his hand. His eyes flew open. Buddy sat on his haunches, pink tongue lolling. The Aussie dog nudged Max's hand, his tail wagging. Max plunged his hands into the dog's warm fur. *"...but of power, and of love, and a sound mind."*

As he spoke the words, courage grew. *Power.* Buddy leaned against him and he felt braver. *A sound mind.* His pa had often acted crazy. Crazy and mean...addled by the liquor. He didn't want to be like that. *Love.* He'd found that here. Love that made room for him.

Fear was its own prison, keeping him locked up inside. As the fear fell away like a heavy cloak, he strode down the rows of corn, Buddy at his side—marching to the steady beat of his own courageous heart.

In early November, work began in earnest on the Old Mill Restaurant at the old Walker Sawmill. Rowdy woke early, full of purpose. Kyle had quit his construction job to put all of his efforts into the new project. His youthful energy was contagious. Rowdy allowed that the boy was a fair carpenter...if you laid out the job for him. Support beams, rafters and foundation stones all got a thorough inspection and repairs where needed. The place, nearly one hundred years old, had been built sturdy, with true 4x4s and beams as thick as a man's thigh. Rowdy called Gabe in to assess the best approach for restoring the original pine board flooring.

Splotched with oil stains and worn where work stations had once been, the boards had been laid over the joists without any subfloor.

"These are incredible," exclaimed Gabe as he bent to examine the wood—each six-inch wide board had been milled nearly two-inches thick and secured in place with hand-forged nails. "You can't find planks like this anymore." He glanced over at the giant saw blade leaning against the wall. "Cut with that very blade, no doubt."

"We're hopin' to leave 'em," said Rowdy. "Think they can be brought back to life?"

Gabe knelt. Before Kyle could react, he spit on the floor, rubbing it in with his fingers. The wood darkened, allowing a rich grain to show through the dirt and grime.

"Amazing," said Kyle. "Do we have to polish them with spit?" Kyle wasn't sure if he was joking or not.

Gabe stood, a grin lighting his face. "As much as I'd enjoy seeing that, a light sanding and a nice warm stain should do the trick."

"Thank heavens," breathed Kyle. "I thought I was about to experience a new definition of spit and polish." He toed the floor. "But what about these unsightly oil stains, and those old worn spots?"

"Character," said Gabe. "This was a working mill and foundry. It's all right for the floor to look its age and reflect its history. Desirable in fact." He dusted off his knees. "Some folks purposefully distress new wood to get this look. You got it for free."

"That's what I've been tryin' to tell 'im," said Rowdy. "Like laugh lines that were hard earned—not somethin' to be spurned." He jammed his hands in his back pockets, rocking on the heels of his cowboy boots. "This place has a story to tell. Our job is to let it."

"I agree," said Gabe. "This space will be fantastic. The whole town's already buzzing about it. You letting Gloria get her hands on the decor?"

"Sure thing. Not that we could stop her," said Rowdy, with a grin.

"Looks like you two have your work cut out for you," said Gabe eyeing the large, unfinished space. "Mind if I have a look at the plans?"

"I'd be obliged if you would," said Rowdy. "Make sure we haven't overlooked something crucial."

"I second that," said Kyle, running a hand over his darkly-bearded chin. "Since I left your employ, I've been working myself half to death over here. I'd hate to have to redo anything major."

Rowdy unrolled the sheaf of blueprints on a large sheet of plywood flung atop two sawhorses. The three bent over the plans, eager as hound dogs on a puma scent.

"What are we going to do about that fool mine?" asked Lizzy.

Gabe looked up from reading the Buttermilk Falls Bugle. "What do you want to do with it?"

"I've no idea."

I can see the headlines now," said Gabe, gesturing with his hand. "*Pumpkin Hallow Copper Mine Haunted by Ghosts.*"

I half-believe it is haunted," she said. "Buck sure seemed rattled down there. What's up with him, anyway?"

"Chased by the hound of heaven. The place spooked him."

"The sheriff? Nothing scares him."

"You're wrong there, my darlin'. Gloria scares him."

"Gloria? Why?"

"Because she gets him. And gets to him."

"That's ridiculous."

Gabe smiled. "If you say so…"

"Don't be glib, Gabe. What is it you know that I don't?"

"Truth is…you women are the civilizing influence on us men." He grinned at her. "Buck's just resisting taking the bit in his mouth."

Lizzy put a hand on her hip. "So, you think women are just trying to control you men?"

He brought a hand to her cheek, cradling it tenderly. "My dear Lizzy… You've got it all wrong. Love is what tames us, harnesses us to be useful, satisfies the soul." He kissed her on the nose.

"Well…when you put it like that…" Lizzy said, flushing. "Maybe Buck does need to hitch up with someone like Gloria."

Gabe nodded. "But right now, he's worried about sudden riches from the mine ruining us. And then greed and envy seeping out and destroying the town."

"I worry about that myself," she said. "Greed. Jealousy. Theft." She picked up the piece of copper ore, fingered it, and then set it back down. "Look what's already happened just because Wilma thought Max had a fortune."

"We're still wading through that one," he admitted. "She's angry at losing an inheritance she expected."

"I think she's starting to see that Max is the real inheritance. That worries me, too." Lizzy bit her bottom lip. "And what if Max tries to go back down into that cellar, chasing ghosts?"

"He's under strict orders not to go anywhere near that cabin," said Gabe. "And just in case, I rebuilt the door and put on a secure lock."

"That's good. Thank you." Lizzy sighed. "I keep thinking that an open pit mine would ruin the land. Take away the sheer beauty of this place—a place I've come to love."

Gabe drew another imaginary headline in the air. *"Mine Owners Strike it Rich and Lose their Souls and their Scenery."*

The Old Mill

Lizzy threw a couch pillow at him. "I wish there was no copper mine," she lamented.

Gabe set aside the paper. "Me, too. Things will change once the town finds out. And not for the better." He pulled her in close for a real kiss, laying a hand on her rounded belly. "The only change I want is this sweet little kiddo."

"Yes," she said, tucking his arms around her vanishing waist. "The sooner the better."

Over the next few weeks, Kyle and Rowdy had a few more go-rounds about the *unnecessary* expense of getting the old paddle wheel working.

"It's just for looks, anyway," insisted Kyle.

But Rowdy dug in his boot heels like a rodeo cowboy halting a roped steer. Kyle soon realized that it wasn't a battle he was going to win. Even when he dug in his own heels, clad in nearly new work boots, his hard-headed partner ordered the parts anyway. Rowdy started replacing the damaged paddles with new ones hewn from hand sawn oak. "You'll thank me in the end," he insisted.

In a childish fit of pique, Kyle purposefully avoided the paddle wheel. While Rowdy worked on cogs and gears, unpacking new parts, Kyle stomped around the building, slamming cut board into stacks...hammering nails home with a vengeance. And just generally making his anger known.

Rowdy ignored him. "Keep up the good work," he jabbed over lunch. "You move a heck of a lot faster when you're ticked off."

Kyle let his temper rage on for a few days, but when the red paint came out, his curiosity got the best of him. Some boards had been coated before their installation, but Rowdy had to perch on some sketchy scaffolding to finish the paint job on the towering wheel.

"Be careful up there," Kyle cautioned.

Rowdy grunted.

At the end of the day, Kyle had to admit that the water wheel looked spectacular—the fresh, crimson red a real standout against the old wood siding. "Nice," he allowed.

I think we should celebrate the launch day after tomorrow, when the paint's dry," said Rowdy. "You in?"

Kyle hated to admit the jolt of excitement that swept through him at the prospect. "You mean it's ready to rock and roll?"

"Yep."

"Sounds interesting. Should I bring some champagne for the christening?" he joked.

"Sure... Why not?"

And that's how they came to be standing on the rocks by the flashy paddle wheel two days later. Kyle gripped the neck of a bottle of cheap champagne tucked into a paper bag, feeling slightly foolish.

"Let's christen the whole place while we're at it." Rowdy was grinning like a kid at a birthday party.

"Okay. Want me to do the honors?" Kyle looked over his shoulder, glad that nobody was around to witness the over-the-top event.

"Sure thing. Knock yourself out," said Rowdy.

Kyle was a bit surprised by the lump of pride that swelled in his throat. He swung the bottle, smashing it against the wheel. "I hereby christen you, The Old Mill Restaurant and Gallery."

For some reason, the words of an Irish blessing sprang like a prayer from his lips. "And to all who enter here...

The Old Mill

May the road rise up to meet you.
May the wind be always at your back.
May the sun shine warm upon you...
The rains fall soft upon your fields.
And until we meet again,
May God hold you in the palm of his hand."

"Amen," added Rowdy.

It was a holy moment.

Rowdy moved to set the refurbished wheel in motion. In one surprisingly graceful motion, he pulled out the stop in the central steel cog. The moment felt like releasing a wounded hawk—long caged and newly recovered from a badly broken wing. Would it truly soar again?

Kyle held his breath as the wood slats groaned and shook loose from the confines of their lengthy neglect. The spines of the wheel caught the current and spun free...like a giant pinwheel turning in a freshening breeze.

Oh, the glory of it! Moving...churning...nearly alive! Churning out a rhythmic song of life.

It slapped the water in a cadenced throb—like a steady heart beat—marking time. Rowdy had been right. The water wheel had a song of its own. It dipped into the water, rose, and sent a cascade of white spume cascading back down to froth in the swiftly moving river. A glorious thing!

Rowdy had the grace not to say *I told you so*. The two men just looked at each other...swept up in silence by the sacred.

Kyle lingered at the Old Mill long after Rowdy had headed home. He sat at a table on the deck and watched the sun sink behind the pines, turning the water of Coyote Creek a deep pink—shot through with gold. A pretty sight.

The river water flowed past...timelessly.

He listened to the slap and splash of the towering, red paddle wheel which continued to churn in the water. Funny how it seemed that it had always been in motion—the years of silence, the dream. Kyle rested his chin on his folded hands, listening. His own heart steadied to match the rhythm of the wheel, which tinted deep crimson in the lingering light.

He thought back on the despair that had first brought him here. The long train ride. His impulsive disembarking in Chico. Buying a truck and heading off into the mountains...anywhere to get away.

What had he been running from? Himself, mostly. After today's simple celebration, he realized even more how the cynicism and world-weariness of college had deadened his soul. How he'd let the blows of life numb him to any real hope. His life had been a sad litany of bereavement and failure. The death of his parents and grandparents. His loss of faith. The slow slide into sin. An English Literature major that had led him to settle for living life secondhand through the stories of others, rather than forging one of his own.

He remembered the aching hunger driving him to find something worthy to devote his life to. One thing leading to another. That initial encounter with Gabe...*who just happened* to have a flat tire and a job offer. The man hadn't really needed an apprentice. But Kyle had needed the carpentry training to prepare him for this project.

Had it all been so random? The stolen gun that made him face his own duplicity. The target practice that walked him past the mill. The spontaneous trip to Lost Lake that led to meeting Rowdy, his unlikely new business partner. If he still believed, he'd be tempted to think the hand of the Almighty had orchestrated the whole thing.

Sitting near the river, listening to the song of the water wheel, he let nature soothe his soul, just as Thoreau had at Walden Pond. The author's words rang clear: *Go confidently in the direction of your dreams. Live the life you've imagined.*

Kyle brushed sawdust and dirt from his pants. Was this the life he'd imagined? *Not yet.* His shoulders ached from cutting boards. His elbow throbbed from hours of hammering nails. But it was a stepping stone to what he wanted. His very own restaurant and art gallery.

The building behind him was taking shape. Already he could picture artwork on the walls and imagine the sound of laughter and witty banter inside.

Every town needed a gathering place. Maggie's Diner was fine for the older folks, but Kyle's generation needed more than cracked, leather booths and pancakes smothered in syrup. They needed a welcoming place to discuss art and books, philosophy and the meaning of life. The small, intimate tables, the deck outside and the whole vibe of the place would foster a different type of interaction. Even Rowdy's soda fountain invited intimacy. Teens and young families could gather there for an ice cream treat and sweet connection.

Maybe he was creating what he'd lacked and longed for—a safe place to sort himself out in the company of friends.

His mind drifted, weaving a dreamscape of this place. There was a girl out there somewhere. One he hadn't met yet. Not one of the casual hook-ups he'd discarded in college. A real soul-mate. She'd come in the door, sit on a stool, order an ice cream sundae and smile in his direction. She'd...

Thump. A dark shape scampered onto the deck and grunted, nails scratching wood.

"Hey, Rascal. How was your day?" he asked, knowing this was the only conversation likely tonight.

The raccoon chirped and put a fingered paw on his knee. He and Rascal had reached an understanding. The critter would stay outside, where he belonged, and Kyle would keep some dry cat food handy. He often saved bread crusts from lunch for handouts on the deck.

Kyle fished a fistful of kibble and a piece of sandwich crust from a baggie in his jacket pocket and held it out to the animal.

Rascal was a polite eater, gently snatching one nugget at a time from Kyle's outstretched hand and crunching it down. When the food was gone, he squeaked out a farewell and waddled off toward the creek.

Kyle leaned back and looked out at the river. A lot of things had changed over the past months. Not just to the mill, but inside himself. He had to admit that he'd started out questioning Rowdy's every decision, just to be obstinate. Gradually, they'd fallen into a more workable rhythm. Over time, they'd come to trust and even appreciate each other. Things had shifted again today when the water wheel had come to life. Seems Rowdy knew more than Kyle had given him credit for. Deep things… Things that mattered.

The sun disappeared and darkness descended quickly, like the flame of a candle guttering out. Kyle let it surround him—the darkness and the rhythmic slap and song of the old paddle wheel.

Chapter 16

Orphans

*I will not leave you as orphans.
I will come to you.
John 14:18*

As had become his Friday custom, Kyle once again found himself seated at Gabe and Lizzy's supper table. Even after he'd quit the construction job, his former boss kept up the once-a-week dinner invitations. Maybe Gabe knew how much Kyle savored each home-cooked meal. Or that he needed the uplift of real conversation and a sense of family.

Doris usually cooked on Fridays, and if he was lucky, she'd make one of her famous key-lime cheesecakes for dessert. He pulled up his chair, inhaling the heady aroma of beef stroganoff.

When everyone was settled, Gabe bowed his head to ask a blessing. "Lord, we thank you for everyone gathered here...for friends and family. You promised that you will not leave us orphans, but would send your Holy Spirit to guide us and bind us together as God's family. We are grateful for this food and the hands that prepared it." He nodded at Doris, a small smile on his face. "Amen."

Murmured *Amens* of agreement echoed around the table.

Until Gabe's prayer, Kyle hadn't really thought of himself as an orphan—just a guy setting off on his own after college. Even after his parents had died when he was in high school, he'd still had his grandparents to look out for him. But when they passed a few months back, he was truly alone.

Max eagerly grabbed a slice of warm bread from the basket, and Kyle recalled that the little boy was an orphan, too. In private, Gabe had let it slip that Max's pending adoption was now at risk—embroiled in a heated custody battle between the Reeds and some long-lost aunt. His mentor had tried to downplay the issue, but Kyle had seen the pain in Gabe's eyes at the thought of losing the boy.

Gabe sat at the head of the table, a very pregnant Lizzy on his right. Their hands were intertwined on Gabe's knee. Must be true love. The man had it all...a farm, a thriving business, a wife, two kids and a third on the way. Kyle felt a twinge of envy. Not that he was ready for raising any kids.

Across the table, Chloe sat next to her stepmother, Lizzy. *What happened to the little girl's birth mother?* he wondered. A story there for sure... Sara Beth, Chloe's best friend and another frequent visitor, fidgeted beside her. Harley, the ranch manager, came in and took a seat next to Lizzy. The huge dining room table was quickly filling up.

Soon, Doris carried in a large covered casserole dish, holding the beef stroganoff. She added a bowl of steaming noodles and a platter of asparagus spears. The serving dishes made the rounds among the hodgepodge of dinner guests. Seemed he wasn't the only stray here tonight. A middle-aged woman he didn't know sat beside Max. Where had she come from?

As if reading his mind, Gabe spoke up to make the introduction. He nodded in her direction. "Kyle, I'd like you to meet Wilma Watts, Max's aunt."

The aunt!? The one wanting to take Max away? Kyle frowned. *What was she doing here?* Remembering his manners, Kyle managed a half smile. "Nice to meet you."

He directed a quizzical look at Gabe, who gave a slight shake of his head.

Between bites of food, Wilma tucked a strand of mousy, brown hair behind her ear, and fiddled with the top button of her simple blouse.

As they dug into the meal, conversation flowed. Gabe inquired about the Old Mill and Kyle was happy to fill him in about their progress. The place had been rewired, plumbing upgraded and the pine floors refinished. Things were moving along.

Harley talked about shearing the Christmas trees on the farm last summer and how they'd sprouted out nicely, just in time for the upcoming season. Max shared about how they'd piled the last of the jack-o-lanterns from the Sweet Apple Stomp into a wheelbarrel and hauled them to the compost pile where—according to Max—they'd gleefully *smashed 'em to smithereens.*

Plain country talk. No hint of one-upmanship about status, possessions or smart career moves. Did they know how refreshing it was to talk so openly?

As folks finished eating, Wilma jumped up and started clearing the table, stacking more plates on her arm than he'd thought possible.

"You don't need to do that," said Lizzy. "You're our guest."

"Comes natural," Wilma said. "I've been bussing tables since I was a teen." She scurried into the kitchen.

Kyle noticed that Lizzy had grown quiet. She pushed her food around on her plate, a small frown marring her brow.

Wilma returned, carrying the steaming coffee pot. "Coffee anyone?"

"You're not a waitress here," barked Lizzy. "Please sit down."

The smile vanished from Wilma's face as she stumbled back to her chair. "I was just trying to help."

"Haven't you done enough already?" sniped Lizzy.

Gabe touched her shoulder in warning.

"Maybe I should go," said Wilma, her eyes glistening. "I'm not here to cause trouble."

"Please stay," said Gabe. "We're glad that you could come to the farm today to visit Max...and stay for supper. Gives you and the boy a chance to learn more about each other."

"And another chance to try to steal him away." Lizzy's face was set in stone.

Kyle sat in stunned silence. He'd never seen this side of Lizzy—such blatant rudeness. But he also saw the raw fear on her face. The stress of an all-out tug-o-war for poor Max, who sat wide-eyed in the strained tick of silence. The boy shifted uncomfortably in his chair. Things seemed likely to implode at any moment.

Gabe took charge. "Max, could you please take the girls outside for a bit. We'll have dessert later."

Max cast a sideways glance at Wilma. Then, obediently got up and led Chloe and Sara Beth out the back door.

Harley excused himself as well. "Got chores to do." He left quickly.

Kyle stood, about to do the same, when Wilma held up a hand. "Wait. Please. I've something to say." She looked at Kyle and Doris. "You might as well hear it, too."

Lizzy started to comment, but a quelling look from Gabe silenced her.

"What is it?" he asked.

"Something I should've made clear when I first arrived this afternoon." She looked over at Gabe and Lizzy. "I was waiting for the right time." She glanced at all of the long faces. "Now look what I've done." She shook her head.

Wilma tugged at her blouse collar. "I'm dropping the custody suit," she said. "I've come to see that Max will have a good life here on the farm. Something I can't offer him in my little trailer with my crazy work schedule." Unshed tears shimmered in her eyes. "He's better off with you."

"You sure about this?" Gabe questioned.

Wilma nodded, looking down at her lap. "It's not easy, giving him up. He's such a sweet boy. My only living relative." She glanced up at Lizzy. "But here he'd have siblings, get to grow up in the country. Be surrounded by love." She blinked. "Such love..."

Lizzy heaved herself out of her chair and came over to wrap Wilma in her arms. "Oh, Wilma. Please forgive me. I'd no right to treat you so shamefully." She blotted her eyes with a tissue. "I... I just couldn't bear the thought of losing Max."

Wilma gave a lopsided grin. "Believe me, I know the feeling. It's had me tossing and turning for days now."

"But now you're willing to step aside?" Lizzy's eyebrows rose in question.

"Yes." Wilma's shoulders slumped. "He deserves better than me."

"Don't say that, Wilma," said Gabe. "It takes an unselfish person to place the boy's welfare first. We'll do our best to honor your trust."

Wilma stood, shaking herself loose from Lizzy's hold. "Just one thing..."

Kyle held his breath. Could this get any crazier? *Don't ruin it, Wilma,* he silently pleaded. He and Doris exchanged an uncertain glance.

"I want visitation rights," said Wilma. "A chance to be a real aunt to Max."

"What kind of visitation?" asked Gabe.

Wilma placed a hand on the back of her chair. "I'll not interfere in the raising of the boy," she said. "But I want the occasional day with him." She straightened the black-rimmed glasses on her nose. "Maybe once a month. Either here on the farm or for some nearby outing."

"No," Lizzy said.

Wilma's face fell. "No?!"

"We can do better than that," Lizzy suggested. "Every boy needs a doting aunt. We'd want you here for holidays, birthdays, and family dinners. You have a standing invitation to be part of it all...whenever you want to come."

Wilma's expression brightened, but she looked to Gabe for confirmation. "You'd be open to something like that?"

"Of course," said Gabe. "You're Max's only blood kin. And Chloe and the baby could use an honorary aunt as well...if you're willing." He grinned.

"I'm speechless," said Wilma. "I never expected... Never thought..." She blotted her tears.

"Hooray!!" called out Doris, clapping her hands in glee. "This calls for a celebration."

In the emotion of the moment, Kyle felt like clapping, too. Gabe slapped him on the back.

Lizzy and Wilma were hugging it out.

Kyle tried to make sense of the unfolding drama of such imperfect perfection. All he knew was that he and Max might both be orphans...but today, they'd been saved by grace.

Doris went into the kitchen and returned carrying two luscious key-lime cheesecakes. "Wilma?" she said, a twinkle lighting her eyes. "Would you be so kind as to fetch the children? We've a family milestone to celebrate, and dessert to eat."

"My pleasure." Wilma grinned and headed toward the door.

"Just one thing..." Doris said.

Wilma hesitated, one hand on the door knob.

"I could use a hand with cleanup tonight. You in?"

A megawatt smile lit Wilma's face, erasing years. "Wash or dry?" she asked.

Felling a few trees to make room for the new parking lot at the Old Mill appealed to Kyle's macho side. Nothing said *manly* like the rumble of chainsaws and the cry of *timber* preceding the loud crack and crash of a falling pine. Not that he'd attempt it himself. Buttermilk Falls had plenty of seasoned lumberjacks to do the job.

The crew had arrived just after sunrise—a time of day Rowdy called *O-dark-thirty*. But Kyle didn't mind getting up early. He was excited to watch the trees come down and help stack the freshly cut wood for later use in the foundry fireplace.

"Just one thing..." Kyle joked as the woodsmen unloaded their gear. "Try not to land a tree on that old outhouse." He pointed to the small wood structure at the edge of the back lot. The mossy, shingled roof and crookedly-hung, hinged door spoke of its advanced age. "We're still using it."

With the trees out of the way, they could finally dig a hole for the septic tank they'd need to hook up to the new bathrooms in the building. Then, once the lot was graded and graveled, they could take delivery of the kitchen equipment.

The head logger, a strapping guy named Axel, crushed out his morning cigarette, blew out a plume of blue smoke and pierced

Kyle with a look. "We know what we're doing." He hefted a monster chainsaw with a muscled arm, as easily as if it were a toothpick. The man wore an official-looking, yellow vest trimmed with silver reflective tape. His long, gray hair, tied back into a ponytail by a series of rubber bands, was topped by a metal hard hat. "You got the trees marked?"

"Yeah." Kyle stepped out of his way. "We're taking down those six trees banded with blue tape.

Kyle glanced over at the building, wondering where Rowdy was. The rugged cowboy wasn't one to miss out on this kind of action.

The roar of a chainsaw split the quiet mountain air. The machine whined as it bit into the trunk of the nearest tree, shooting out yellow shards of shredded wood.

Over the noise, Kyle faintly registered the familiar squeal of the rusty outhouse door hinges. Rowdy emerged, buttoning his fly, just as Axel hollered, "Timber!"

He'd never seen Rowdy sprint before. The man held up his britches with one hand and high-tailed it in the prancing gallop of a wrangler shod in cowboy boots. Kyle snorted as Rowdy raced by. But in a blink, he made his own heart-pounding dash to safety as the tall tree splintered and twisted in their direction. He pulled up next to the building, turning back just in time to see the heavy pine come crashing down, landing squarely on the shingled roof of the outhouse. In a pouf of dust, the hapless one-seater crumbled, like a beer can crushed under a man's work boot. The tip of the pine landed with a *whoosh* and a lift of dust just a few yards from where Kyle and Rowdy stood, openmouthed. Their legs trembled in the waning adrenaline rush of the mad dash that had barely spared their lives.

The Old Mill

Rowdy calmly buckled his belt and resettled his black Stetson on his head, the brim casting a deep shadow across his weathered face. "You might'a warned me," he said.

Kyle eased down the wall to sit on the ground.

Axle rounded the still-quivering tree at a run. "You guys okay?" he asked, panting—face flushed beneath his silver hard hat.

"What the hell happened?" Kyle yelped. "You nearly killed us!"

"Sorry 'bout that," Axle said. "I didn't peg that tree as a widow-maker." He ran a hand across his whiskered face. "The darned thing twisted on me as it fell...but, no real harm done."

"You flattened my outhouse!" protested Kyle.

"With me almost still in it," added Rowdy, with a growl.

"That old thing..." said Axel, looking disdainfully over his shoulder at the crumbled remains, nearly hidden beneath the fallen tree branches. "Not worth much."

"It is when you need one." Rowdy rocked on his heels, hands in his back pockets. "Just be darned careful not to take out the Old Mill buildin' next. Got big plans for it."

Axel spat on the ground. "We know what we're doing."

"So, you said," reminded Kyle.

"You want these trees felled or not?"

Kyle shrugged. "Guess so..."

Axel beckoned his men over to start limbing and bucking the tree. They progressed expertly along the trunk, reducing the once grand tree into thick rounds of wood. A worker fired up the splitter to turn them into smaller chunks of firewood.

The other trees came down in an orderly fashion—one after the other—plummeting down into the clearing with a resounding *craaack*. The fallen pines lay on the unfamiliar ground—limbs splayed against the earth, as if trying to catch themselves. Bare sky intruded where they'd so recently stood. The lot looked a bit forlorn without its tall trees, but there were still plenty of pines around to make a nice backdrop, Kyle reasoned. He began to stack the split logs neatly inside the woodshed by the back door. It was hard to wrap his mind around the fact that each tree had been a living thing just an hour earlier. Beneath his fingers, the wood was still warm.

The loss of the outhouse spurred Kyle and Rowdy into quickly having a septic tank installed. The company dug leech lines far out into the woods. Now they could hook up the His and Hers bathrooms they'd built inside. Kyle had come up with a list of possible names for the johns—Hens and Roosters, Dudes and Darlin's, Beauties and Buckaroos, Ladies and Gents.

"How about this?" said Rowdy, pointing to generic white on blue, Men and Women, placards in a catalogue. "Folks shouldn't have to guess which door to open," he added. "Save cutsie for the menu items."

"I see your point," said Kyle. "Especially after they've had a few beers."

"Good. I'll order these then."

Kyle smacked his fist into his forehead. "Menu items... Who the heck will we get for a cook?"

"I've been thinkin' on it," said Rowdy. "We want basic stuff: steaks, burgers, fries, chili, biscuits... right?"

"Yes," Kyle agreed. "But..."

Rowdy jumped in. "This guy I know ran chuck wagon for cattle roundup. Great cook. He could whip up steak 'n' taters 'n' sourdough biscuits in a skillet over a cow chip campfire in the time it took to swat a skeeter. Coffee so stiff and black you could tar a barrel with it."

"We're not feeding cowboys here, Rowdy."

His partner shifted his ever-present black Stetson lower on his eyes. "Who are we feedin'?"

The Old Mill

"Farmers, townsfolk, yuppies from Chico and Reno up for the day. Couples looking for a romantic date. Old marrieds wanting a special night out. Poets and art lovers needing a little inspiration with their meal."

"What kind of food are you talkin' 'bout, then?"

"Not just the basics, like some run-of-the-mill burger joint," said Kyle. "We'll offer sides like sweet potato fries and spicy coleslaw to go with the steaks and burgers. Maybe have some upscale items like smoked chicken and salmon filets served with asparagus and twice-baked potatoes. And feature some nice, fresh salads on the menu with artichoke hearts, pinion nuts or grated zucchini. And in cold weather, we'll have hearty soups with homemade rolls... We need items you won't find on the blue-plate special at the diner."

Kyle gestured to the coffee bar. "And specialty coffees. Fair traded blends from around the world."

Rowdy whacked his hat on his jeans. "Guess my guy's out then."

"Afraid so..." Kyle thought back to the restaurant chefs in places where he'd eaten while still in college. He'd love to nab some young upstart from a culinary school with some fresh ideas and a down-to-earth attitude. Kyle itched to get online and see what he could find. Of course, then he'd have to talk that person into coming to a backwater town like Buttermilk Falls. Not exactly the kind of place a culinary grad, hoping to make a splash, was looking for. He hadn't considered that bump in the road.

Kyle had felt the same when he came here just over five months ago. Had it really been only such a short time? Back then, he'd been looking for a mountain town to lose himself in. He'd found himself instead.

But how could he ever explain that kind of small-town magic to the cook he so desperately needed?

Chapter 17

Dream Again

"In the last days," God says,
"I will pour out my spirit...
young men will see visions,
old men will dream dreams."
Acts 2:17

For Rowdy, taking delivery of the vintage soda fountain ranked right up there with staying atop the rank bull Cyclone for the full eight seconds. He took a crowbar to the packing crates and pulled out the disassembled pieces, as excited as a kid at Christmas.

It took him five days to sort out all of the pieces and reassemble his baby: the long counter, the raised step supporting eight bar stools, both the front and the back work bays and the mirrored back wall. He screwed in the last bulb lighting the stained-glass marquee and flipped the switch.

Light glowed from the backlit "Soda Fountain" sign, throwing warmth on the polished wood countertop. *Awesome.* He ran a hand across one of the red-leather seats of the chrome stools lined up in front, daring to dream again.

For a few minutes, he was that ten-year-old kid with a buzz cut, sitting next to his mama, wearing cutoffs and a lopsided smile... waiting for the magic of a fountain treat. The future was bright. All was right with the world. His eyes focused on the soda jerk with the white cap who was putting together his ice cream sundae: scooping out the ice cream, ladling on the warm chocolate sauce, shooting on whipped cream, sprinkling a spoonful of chopped nuts, and at last—when his patience had stretched to the breaking point—adding a bright red maraschino cherry, with a stem, on top. Perfection. Handed across the counter at last, the production of the mouth-watering sundae was half the joy of the eating. What could go wrong in a world where you could spoon in such delight?

Rowdy blinked. A whole lot had gone wrong over the years. His parents' divorce, his own rebellious teenage years. Marrying too young. Getting caught up in the drinking and carousing of the rodeo circuit. Abandoning his own children—Wyatt and Charlotte.

After his *come to Jesus* conversion, Rowdy had done his best to mend fences. To ask for forgiveness. To start over.

Charlotte now lived with him in his place at the lake. Wyatt and his new wife, Amy, had their own cabin a few miles away. But the scars of his mistakes would always be there—frayed rope ends of pain woven into their lives.

The soda fountain. It felt like a way of turning back the clock. A way to give others the same blissful experience of his boyhood—a scoop or two of pure joy.

He patted the countertop like an old friend and set to unpacking the boxes holding stainless steel ice cream and condiment bins...

blenders, glassware, straw holders, and long handled spoons. One additional box, from a printing company, held flour sack aprons and black caps emblazoned with their newly designed logo—items that Gloria had ordered for him. He ran a hand across the raised rendering of the waterwheel beside stylized red lettering announcing The Old Mill. Rowdy took off his cowboy hat, resting it on the counter. He snapped open an apron, slipped it over his head and tied it around his waist. In a decisive movement, Rowdy doffed the black, red-lettered hat, adjusting the bill to shade his eyes.

"I want one of those," said Charlotte, ambling through the door. Her eyes fell on the soda fountain—awash in bright light. "Cool," she said. "I thought you were just hyping it, Pa...but this really is something."

"You like it?"

"I love it!" she said, grinning. Charlotte plucked an apron and cap from the box and scurried around the cabinet, putting them on as she went. She stood behind the counter, red curls unfurling from beneath the cap, and raised an imaginary order pad and pen. "Welcome to the Old Mill Soda Fountain," she chirped in a bright voice. "What can I get for you?"

A slug of pure happiness slammed into Rowdy's chest. "I've already got everythin' I need," he said, realizing it was true. "Right here. Right now." He brushed away the moisture leaking from the corners of his eyes. "And by the way...you're hired." Rowdy pulled out a glass bowl. "Let's get some fixin's in place so you can practice whippin' up ice cream sundaes."

Rascal sniffed the night air, his sensitive nose wriggling. What was that smell? Some kind of nut, for sure… A cunning raccoon like him didn't live on crawfish alone.

His hiding place beneath the deck had been way too noisy lately. People coming and going. Dragging in bags and boxes. Stomping on the wood floors above his head. Banging on the walls. How was he supposed to sleep?

Rascal yawned and scurried onto the deck, snuffling at the door. The aroma of nuts from inside made him drool. Lately, the human called Kyle had been too busy to give him his usual treats. So, the raccoon was extra hungry tonight.

Only problem was…they'd blocked off all of his favorite access points. He prowled the perimeter, searching for a way in. At the back corner, he clawed at a chink in the rock foundation. When the stone gave way, Rascal burrowed in deeper. At last, he squeezed through the hole and stuck his snout through to the other side, coming out just below the fire cave. A little sideways sashay and he was in.

Waddling across the floor, Rascal followed his nose to the new, short wall running along the back. It was an easy jump from one of the tall red mushrooms up to the countertop. His mouth-watering snack was hidden just under a covered hole in the workspace below. Rascal jumped down and lifted the lid with deft fingers. *Oh boy!!* He sampled bits of some new kind of nut. *Yummy!* He was starved.

Kyle shifted the stack of framed paintings under his arm as he unlocked the door of the Old Mill. He set them on a table top and scanned the walls for the best places to hang the first of their rotating art exhibit.

He'd talked Charlotte into letting him display some of her best lake and landscape paintings. She'd promised to bring them by today. And Mr. Starkweather, the high school art teacher, was on board with submitting student art in lots of different genres. It had been easy to contact the town art club, and independent local artists, keen to offer their art work for sale. A win/win for everybody. He'd hang a few of the larger paintings today.

With Gloria's help, they'd already displayed a few artifacts: old hunting traps, carpentry tools, oil lamps, and, of course, the massive saw blade. She'd found industrial tables and vintage work benches to serve as group seating. The smaller tables, from an old winery, boasted solid oak tops and thick iron supports. Metal-legged chairs with wooden backs and comfortable padded seats flanked the tables. Gloria had found several hand-hewn cabinets with just the right look for their hostess and serving stations. At Rowdy's suggestion, she had repurposed four large iron wagon wheels into hanging light fixtures, suspended by rusty chains. Big, overflowing planters of small trees and ferns gave privacy to seating areas of the outside dining porches. Later, Gloria would bring in potted succulents for each of the tables, and add some colorful flowers to the salvaged barrels flanking the door.

Kyle grabbed a hammer and an impressive landscape painting and strode toward the nearest bare wall.

"What the hell!?" groused Rowdy, as he entered from the kitchen, slipping on something on the floor. He slid to a halt near the soda fountain, mouth agape, and lifted a booted foot covered in whipped cream and chopped peanuts. "Who's been messin' with my stuff?"

Rowdy skirted behind the counter. Banana peels lay scattered about. Chopped nuts littered a meandering trail of whipped cream and chocolate sauce that dripped from the stainless steel serving bay he'd so lovingly polished just yesterday.

THE OLD MILL

Kyle set the painting aside and hurried over. He had to hide a grin at the outraged expression distorting Rowdy's face—mouth hanging open, eyes wide, dark eyebrows shooting up to hide beneath the brim of his black Stetson. Rowdy's cowboy boots were covered in whipped cream and chocolate. But Kyle knew better than to laugh.

"Who'd break in and make a mess like this?" Rowdy fumed. "Wait'll I get my hands on 'em." Yesterday, he and Charlotte had been experimenting with soda fountain items. Now, the waist high, half-fridge door stood open, cans of whipped cream scattered about—white goop puddling on the floor. Luckily the ice cream freezer's sliding top was still closed. But the lids were off both the chocolate syrup and chopped peanut containers which were recessed in the workstation. The lids from the caramel and maraschino cherry tubs were off, too…evidenced by the swirls of tan caramel and red cherry stems strewn in the mix on the floor. What a disaster! He hadn't expected this kind malicious vandalism. Not here.

Why was Kyle trying not to laugh? "You think this is funny? A break-in. Vandals messing up my soda fountain?"

"More critter than hooligan, I'd guess." Kyle gestured to the sets of baby handprints in the goop. Then pointed to the tell-tale track of paw prints parading across the polished wood floor, vanishing at the foundry furnace wall.

"A raccoon?" yelped Rowdy. "Rascal? Why…that low down varmint. I'll have his hide!"

"It's partly my fault," argued Kyle. "I've been so busy…I forgot to give him his evening kibble."

"You're feedin' 'im?"

Kyle's face reddened. "We made sort of a deal. After blocking him out, I gave him a few treats to make up for it."

"A coon's a wild animal, Kyle…not a pet."

"If you say so..."

"If I..." Rowdy clamped his mouth shut before he said something he'd regret. After all, the Good Lord had reformed his language...if not his raging thoughts. "Better fix that hole you missed," he said, pointing to where Rascal's tracks ended by the furnace. "If it happens again, you're on cleanup duty."

"Yes, sir," Kyle said. "By the way... There's a bag of kibble in the kitchen pantry..."

"What for?"

"For Rascal, when he finally wins you over."

"When hell freezes over," muttered Rowdy, as he swiped at a gooey puddle of chocolate.

"Yeah...then." said Kyle.

Chloe was at it again...wanderin' off on her own. Max caught sight of her in the distance as the six-year-old skipped down the drive and disappeared around the bend. *Darn that girl! She was s'posed to stay in the yard.* Max grabbed his bike from the barn, hopped on and gave chase.

By the time Max spied her again, his mouth had run plum dry of spit. Quick as a wink, Chloe disappeared in the weeds at the turnoff to the abandoned cabin. Buddy tagged her like a shadow, plunging into the brush right behind her...but what could the animal do? He was only a dog.

Max stood up on the pedals to go faster. That old cabin was no place for little girl. He'd learned that the hard way.

When he reached the cutoff, sweating and out of breath, Max ditched his bike and hurried down the overgrown trail. "Chloe!" he yelled. "Come back!"

The Old Mill

Off in the distance, Buddy gave his two-bark warning. The hair rose on the back of Max's neck. He sprinted toward the sound, his breath hitching as his lungs burned.

Max froze at the front of the cabin. He'd never wanted to be back here again...let alone go back inside. And Gabe had told him to never, ever come back here. "Chloe?!" he yelped.

Only Buddy's bark answered from inside.

Max's heart thudded. His jaw clenched, remembering the roll of bones beneath his feet and the ghastly grimace of that smirking skull. The skeleton, he knew, was gone now and buried. But what about the haints? It was bad luck coming back here, for sure.

A new padlock latched the repaired cabin door, so Chloe had likely gotten in some other way. "Chloe?" he called again, as if she might magically open the door and come out.

"Max! Down here," Chloe cried out in a muffled voice.

"How'd you get in?" he asked.

"There's a broken board 'round back."

Max skirted the cabin and spied a splintered plank in the back wall. He tugged at the rotted board, breaking it off to widen the opening, and crawled through. The cabin was dimly lit—sunlight slanting in from the broken windows. The trap door was propped open—the stairway to hell gaping like a hungry mouth.

"Help me, Max!" Chloe's voice quavered from below. "I'm trapped."

Max rubbed his arms against the sudden chill. He'd found his courage in the cornfield, remembering words from the Bible. He said them aloud now. "The Lord has not given me a spirit of fear..."

"Help, Max! Help!!"

Max sucked in a lungful of air. "Jesus help me," he said as he dropped through the trap door and skittered down the stairs. Buddy met him at the bottom, gave a tail wag and disappeared into an opening in the far wall. *What's this?* Max followed the dog into a cave, the rough-hewn walls glittering with something like embedded stacks of copper pennies.

Chloe stood behind a tumbled wall of fallen rock, only her face visible above the rubble. The barrier was too close to the ceiling for her to climb over.

"Are you hurt?" he asked.

"Not really..." Chloe brushed away a trail of tears. "The rocks came down right behind me," she said. "I... I can't get back out."

At his side, Buddy barked. A small piece of ore clattered to the floor.

Max tried to think. He could go for help. But by the time others got here, the whole tunnel might collapse, right on top of Chloe. He couldn't leave her. Max looked around. A well used shovel leaned against the other wall. He grabbed it and began to dig away the pile of rocks that blocked Chloe's exit. *Ka-chunk. Ka-chunk.* It was slow going...shoveling and tugging away larger rocks with his bare hands. He hardly noticed they were bleeding.

Finally, the pile of debris had been shoveled low enough in one area for her to get out. "Try now," he said, reaching for Chloe's hand.

She grasped his arms as he lifted her up and over the rubble, tugging her to his side.

"Wait," she said. "Susie's still in there!" She jerked free of his hold and leaned back over the cleft in the wall.

"No!" Max hollered. He jerked when a smattering of stones let loose from the ceiling. The debris landed with a *clatter* just behind him, rocks rolling to a stop at his feet. "We need to get out. Now!" Max grabbed Chloe by the arm. Despite her protests, he hauled her up the rickety stairs and back through the trap door, Buddy close behind. A low *rumble* sounded. A pouf of dirt chased after them, as more of the cavern collapsed.

Max burst through the padlocked door, like a wild man, ripping it from the hinges. When they were safely outside the cabin, he fell to the ground, panting.

When he could breathe again, he stood up and gave Chloe a little shake. "What were you thinkin'...reachin' back into the cave like that?"

She raised a skinny arm, holding aloft her favorite dolly. "I had to save Susie," she said. The doll had a nasty scrape across her painted face. A bow was missing from one tangled pigtail, and a dark stain of dirt was smeared across her ruffled pink dress.

Max huffed out a breath. "You almost got us killed! Over a stupid doll?"

Chloe hugged the dolly to her chest. "Susie's not stupid." Her bottom lip protruded in a pout.

"Why'd you come back to this old cabin anyway?"

She looked away. "I dunno... I wanted to see what treasure was down there. But guess what?"

Max wiped his bloodied hands on his jeans. "What?"

"I found a bunch of gold. Just like Rapunzel." She stretched out her tiny fingers. "I reached up to get a handful and it...it all fell down."

Max closed his eyes. He'd seen the shiny stuff in the mine tunnel—more copper than gold. Maybe it was an enchanted place, after all. But it still gave him the creeps. "I ain't never comin' back here for nothin'," he muttered.

He looked down at Chloe, his hands firmly on her shoulders. "I don't care about any gold. If'n you ever...**ever** come back to this cabin again, I'll let the haints get you!"

Her eyes widened. "What's a haint?"

"A ghost," he said. "The worst kind."

Max helped his little sister to her feet and walked her back to the road where his bike waited. He mounted up, settling Chloe on the saddle in front of him. She held the rescued doll close to her chest. Max's bruised hands were sore and his mouth painfully dry. He pushed off and pedaled toward home.

"Do we have to tell Mom and Dad?" Chloe asked.

"Of course, we do."

"Why?" she questioned. "We might get in trouble."

"'Cause that's the best kind of trouble."

"What's the worst kind?" Chloe hung onto the handle bar with one hand, clutching her dolly in the other.

Max leaned into the pedals, pushing hard against the steepness of the climb. "The kind where nobody cares at all..."

Chapter 18

Father to the Fatherless

*His name is the Lord—
father to the fatherless.
God places the lonely in families.*
Psalm 68:4-6

The sight of Wilma with Max sent Lizzy's emotions churning. How could she not love the joy on her boy's face as they peered at the mossy jar of pollywogs Max kept in the barn? And yet, how could she *not* mistrust and resent the woman who almost stole him away?

Lizzy rubbed her temples. Aunt Daffy had often said, *Confusion is the dust stirred up by the feet of the devil, blinding you to the good God has planned.* So, was this God's plan all along?

She'd promised Wilma access to her nephew—a promise she was now regretting. But didn't Max deserve to know his only blood kin? And shouldn't Wilma have the same chance to form loving bonds with him?

Still, Lizzy wondered why she'd made the impulsive offer to include Wilma in her family. Max's family.

Because Wilma had let go. That persistent thought held the truth of it. Wilma had set Max free. Free to live with Gabe and Lizzy. Free to be their son.

It was a selfless act. Somehow, Wilma had shifted away from her life-long pattern of grabbing for anything that promised self-preservation. She'd let go of Max and of any money she thought she had coming by gaining custody. She'd held on only to visitation rights—to this last link with her brother Rod, who'd let go too soon.

Wilma had confided that Max looked just like Rod as a child. And Lizzy had seen how the woman's face softened when she was with her nephew. Wilma bent over the mossy jars, grinning at the wiggling pollywogs...laughing with Max. Lizzy guessed that Wilma didn't laugh often. With Max, the woman radiated joy... took on beauty. Wasn't that what love did?

Max gestured her over. "Look, Lizzy. They got legs."

Wilma reached up and squeezed her hand. "Isn't it wonderful! Legs. Halfway to being real frogs."

"It is wonderful," Lizzy concurred, squeezing back. Against all odds, God was transforming them all. Giving them legs to walk this new, untrodden path.

At last, the final adoption papers had arrived. After a brief ceremony in front of the judge next week, it would be official...Max would be theirs.

As the sun set, Lizzy and Gabe sat next to each other in the front porch rockers. She reached out and took Gabe's hand, her heart swelling with the knowledge that God was trusting them with this precious boy.

"I'm so thankful Wilma agreed to let us adopt Max," she said.

Gabe nodded. "A court battle would have been hard on all of us… Max, especially."

"Yes…her change of heart is a real answer to prayer." Lizzy noticed her own attitude shift toward Wilma. She'd grown to love the woman. Loved her for her pluck and courage. Lizzy felt empathy for Wilma having survived a difficult childhood, a lot like Max's. She saw the way Wilma tucked Max into her arms like the child she'd never had, and maybe even the one she'd never been allowed to be.

Wilma had blossomed in the last few months. How was it possible for a woman in her fifties to grow more youthful? As she relaxed into the family, her smile was no longer forced. Her eyes brightened, blue and shining behind her glasses. She'd replaced the dated rhinestone-studded ones with a dusty rose frame which brought out color in her cheeks. The overly-plucked brows that once gave Wilma a startled look now arched gracefully above her dark lashes. Even her wardrobe seemed to have been freed from the dark colors she'd once favored into an array of soft pastels. Wilma had come newly alive.

They had a lot to celebrate. "Let's do something to make Max's adoption day extra special," Lizzy said.

"What did you have in mind?" Gabe asked, anticipating that she already had a plan. Which, of course, she did.

"A party," she said. "A really big party. Right here on the farm."

Max could feel his heart thumping in his chest. He'd never seen a real judge before.

The man was scary—black robes flowing out behind him, like crow's wings, as he strode to the big desk up front. Judge

Blackwell shuffled through some papers and peered over his half glasses at Max. "Max Radding?"

"Yes, sir." His voice quavered.

"Please stand."

Max stood.

The judge cleared his throat and spoke directly to him. He pointed to Gabe and Lizzy, standing on either side of Max. "Gabriel and Elizabeth Reed want to adopt you into their family as their own legal son. Do you know what that means?"

"Yes, sir." Max cleared the frog from his throat. "It means I get to live with 'em and be their boy. I get a new family with a sister and a baby comin' soon. I get food to eat and chores to do..." Max's mind stumbled over whether to say he got love there, too. And how he wanted to give some back.

Judge Blackwell started to smile, but put his grim face back on. Max hoped he hadn't heard tell of the skeleton in that spooky old cabin cellar.

"Do you want to be adopted into the Reed family?" he asked.

Max glanced over at Wilma, hoping her feelings wouldn't be hurt. But she'd told him not to worry...that he'd best stay with the Reeds, and she'd still be his Aunt Wilma—no matter what.

Then Max looked up at Gabe, who placed a strong hand on his shoulder, and at Miss Lizzy, on his other side, who looked about to cry. Something fresh and peaceful welled up inside, like a shower of autumn rain falling after a long dry summer. "Yes, sir. I surely do."

"Then that's what will happen here today." The judge smiled for real then. "By the power vested in me as a judge of this court, I hereby decree that from this day forward, you, Max Radding, shall hereafter be named Max Radding Reed and shall be the legal and adopted son of Elizabeth and Gabriel Reed with all the rights, duties and privileges thereof."

Max wiped his eyes. "Thank you, sir," he said, then looked up at Gabe. "Am I 'dopted now?"

Gabe drew him into his arms. "Yes, Son. You are."

Miss Lizzy hugged him so tightly that she near to squeezed out all of his air.

Aunt Wilma had tears dripping from her chin and a huge smile on her face. "Isn't this grand," she said. "I'm so happy for you."

Chloe punched him in the arm. "Hey, big brother..." She grinned at him, then ducked her head.

Harley thumped him on the back and Doris kissed him on the cheek. Even Sheriff Buck had shiny eyes and a big smile. "Congratulations, Max. You couldn't have picked a better family."

Max's heart felt so full...it was near to running over. Tears leaked out of his own eyes. Right there in the courtroom.

His new ma and pa went up front and signed some papers. Then Chloe joined in and the four of them held hands on the short walk through the parking lot. They got in Gabe's truck and headed back to the farm, where they were fixing to hold a big party... just for him.

Already, folks were pulling up with big hampers of food for the potluck. Kids running around and lots of tables set up in the big old barn. *My 'doption party.* He couldn't rightly remember even a birthday party, or any such fuss just for him. Looked like the whole town was showing up for his big day. Max started getting all jittery inside, like a jar of bait crickets ready to bust loose when the lid came off.

As they got out, Gabe tilted Max's chin up with a finger. "Welcome home, Son," he said.

Max swallowed. "Thanks, Gabe." He didn't mean any disrespect. Max's tongue just got all tangled up over what to call his new folks. It seemed disrespectful of his own ma and pa to call his new folks the same. So, for now, he stuck to what he was used to.

"Yes. Welcome home, Max." Lizzy gave him another hug.

Max grinned. "I'll be the best boy ever, Miss Lizzy," he promised.

"You already are," she said. "Don't worry about a thing, today. Just enjoy it."

Max landed his new tennis shoes in the red powdery dirt of Sweet Apple Farm. He tucked in his shirt tail and breathed in the cool air that smelled like hay, horse and apples.

Home.

When they got to the barn, folks came over to tell him how happy they were about his adoption...as if he were part of their family now, too. Max sat at a long table with some of his friends and ate a huge plate of potluck food. Then he sampled most all of the desserts—from Doris's key-lime cheesecake to Lucille's nutty brownies. He would've eaten a slice of Maggie's strawberry pie if his tummy hadn't already been as full as a tick on a hound.

Wilma sat next to Doris, enjoying the gathering...meeting lots of folks from Buttermilk Falls. She could tell Max was flying high, enjoying the attention.

"I hear you're a waitress," said a cowboy type, introducing himself as Rowdy.

"Yep. Going on thirty years now."

"I could use someone with that kind of experience at my restaurant."

"Really? What restaurant is that?"

"The Old Mill." He shifted the black Stetson on his head. "We're fixin' to open just after the new year."

A restaurant job right here in Buttermilk Falls? She'd be a lot closer to Max. Maybe she could become part of the town. Part of a real community. There must have been some reason Rod landed here.

But Wilma's innate skepticism kicked in. The connection sounded a bit too convenient. "How'd you know I was a waitress?" she asked.

"Lizzy told me," he said, without hesitation. "Thought maybe I should talk with you about a job."

"She wants me working here in town?" Wilma asked. "Why?"

Rowdy rocked back in his cowboy boots. "Why not? It's a great place to live."

"I'll get back to you," she said, catching sight of Lizzy. Wilma needed to set a few things straight. She'd been standing on her own two feet for as long as she could remember. It rankled to have someone else calling the shots.

She caught up with Lizzy at the dessert table. "We need to talk."

A look of alarm flashed on Lizzy's face. "What about?"

Wilma led the way outside to a more private spot. "About Rowdy and that waitress job, that's what."

"Oh...that!" Lizzy's shoulders sagged in relief. "I saw Rowdy the other day and thought to mention you. It'd be great to have you right here in town where you could pop in and see Max more often."

Wilma's back stiffened. "You trying to tell me what to do?"

"No. I... I just thought..."

Wilma placed a hand on her hip. "I can run my own life, just fine."

"Of course, you can." Lizzy frowned. "Why are you getting upset? Wouldn't you like a change? Like to live closer to Max?"

"I don't want everybody in my business...thank you very much," Wilma said, in a clipped tone.

Lizzy straightened, placing her own hand on her hip. "This is a small town, Wilma. People knowing your business is part of the charm...because we care about each other." She gestured to the throng of people. "Look how they've all come out to support Max."

"Yes, but..."

"I think you're looking a gift horse in the mouth," Lizzy said. "You can turn down the job if it doesn't suit. But don't turn it down out of sheer stubbornness."

Wilma drew in a breath. Was that what she was doing? Was she fighting it just because...? She shook her head to clear it. "Maybe I am just being stubborn."

"You think?!" Lizzy managed a grin.

"Law' o' mercy," chuckled Wilma. "Old habits die hard."

"Tell me about it," said Lizzy. "Folks gave me a ton of grace when I first came here. They still do."

"This Old Mill Restaurant...what's it like?"

"It's gorgeous—rustic, but welcoming...a dream come true for Rowdy and his business partner, Kyle." Lizzy smiled. "It's going to be great. I think you'd like working there."

"Okay, then..." Wilma patted Lizzy's shoulder. "I've got a cowboy to track down."

Lizzy rubbed her back as she watched Wilma tap Rowdy on the arm to get his attention. From the looks of it, their talk was going well. She had a good feeling about Wilma and the Old Mill.

Scanning the crowded yard, Lizzy spied Max grabbing another brownie and chasing after some of his classmates. The baby kicked and she eased herself down on a hay bale, tucking her swollen ankles beneath her. Hers was a good kind of tired, like a barn cat curling up in the straw in a warm patch of sunlight.

The November air was as crisp as one of her Macintosh apples. The gray clouds overhead bunched and blackened, toying with the idea of winter. In the far end of the barn, a group of fiddlers and a lone guitar played a lively tune. Around the barnyard, folks gathered in companionable groups, like colorful fallen leaves, windswept into the cozy corners. The food table was piled high with sandwiches, side dishes, crock pots of chili and baskets of cornbread muffins...as yellow as ripe ears of corn. The dessert counter held cookies, brownies, cheesecake and an array of pumpkin, strawberry-rhubarb and apple pies. A large coffee urn steamed out the fragrance of Chilean roasted beans.

Given her advanced pregnancy, Lizzy had given in to her husband's insistence that she not even think about doing it herself. Gabe fed the details of Lizzy's party plans to Lucille, who—with her gift for chatter—rallied the troops in record time.

Like the scent of cinnamon wafting from warm apple cider, word of Max's adoption party quickly spread and the whole town pitched in to give Max a day he'd never forget. They'd toted tables, unpacked boxes of table cloths and serving ware and lugged in heavy hampers of home-cooked food.

Warmth filled her. *I love this town,* she thought.

Max washed down the last of his brownie with some apple cider, his belly as stuffed as chipmunk cheeks. He jumped when Gabe clamped a big hand on his shoulder.

"We've got a surprise for you."

"What is it?"

"If I told you, it wouldn't be a surprise," said Gabe, nudging him away from the table. "Come with me."

Max followed him to the far corner of the barn where a bare-limbed tree had been set up in a bucket. Lizzy and Chloe came over and all of the guests gathered around, too.

Gabe cleared his throat. "As part of your adoption celebration, we asked folks to contribute to your very own *tool tree,*" he announced. "We wanted you to have some brand new tools to start off your new life."

Max had never seen anything like it. Tied to the bare branches of the tree, were more shiny tools than he'd ever seen. A hammer and pliers. Screwdrivers and wrenches. A tape measure and a real level with a little air bubble inside the yellow glass. A hand saw and even an electric drill with a box of bits to go with.

Gabe pointed to a big red toolbox resting beside the tree. "Lizzy and I got you this to hold it all."

Max's eyes widened. Tools of his own. Tools to make things. Fix things. Not Pa's old rusted and broken stuff. Real tools. Man tools. As he fingered the cold steel, he felt all grown up.

He swallowed the lump forming in his throat. Since coming to the farm, he'd worked on a few projects with Gabe. They'd even built a bird house together. He'd learned that his new dad was a stickler for taking care of his tools—always wiping them off and putting them away carefully when a job was done.

"I'll take good care of 'em," Max said, ducking his head. "I promise."

"I know you will, Son." Gabe patted his shoulder.

"Just like you do," said Max, looking up. While making the bird house, Gabe had shared that he'd had some of his favorite tools since he was a teen. He listed the brand names with pride: Craftsman, Makita, DeWalt, Black & Decker. As trusted as old friends.

When he'd first worked alongside Gabe, Max hadn't known the difference between a crescent wrench and a pair of pliers. But he'd learned quickly. Now he knew if a job called for a regular screw driver or a Phillips head. There was one of each on the tree. And even one with different sized heads to switch out.

Max gazed at the crowd. He knew most everyone here... Sheriff Buck and Gloria. Kyle and Rowdy. Lucille and Maggie. Charlotte and Chloe. Kids from school. And lots of other folks

The Old Mill

from town. "Thank you, everybody," he said, then looked away, suddenly shy.

Everyone clapped, then moved away to get seconds on the food or just talk with their friends.

"Maybe you'll grow up to be a carpenter, like your new dad," said Harley.

"Wouldn't that be great!" chorused Wilma.

Max grinned at her. Surrounded by friends and family, he felt pretty great already.

Thunder rumbled in the sky and rain fell in big, fat drops, plopping into the dry powdery dirt, like warm tears of happiness, mixed with just a tiny bit of sad. A stray umbrella popped open here and there, but hearty mountain folk weren't overly bothered by a little rain. They just moved to the barn or hunkered under the shelter of trees until the cloudburst passed.

Rain was good for the crops. *Pennies from heaven,* his pa always said. Max wondered if Pa could see him now. What would he think of Max and his new family? Would he be cussin' mad at being left behind, or maybe a tiny bit happy that Max had food in his belly, a room to call his own, and all of these new tools to use?

And what about Aunt Wilma? Would Pa have welcomed her in, or chased her off the place? He tried not to think too hard on it. *Ain't nothin' I can do 'bout any of it now.* He didn't want Gabe or Miss Lizzy to know, but sometimes, like now, his eyes got all stingy and wet from missing both his pa and his ma. Missing the old place—even if he'd sometimes had to sneak out the window to get shed of a whipping.

Max rubbed his eyes with his sleeve and left the barn. The short cloudburst made the yard smell nice...like pine trees, fresh apples, and the clove and cinnamon spices in a pumpkin pie. Maybe there was still some pie left on the long food table. He was mighty hungry.

That night, after being tucked in, Max ran a hand over the smooth top of the tool chest which sat on the floor beside his bed. He opened the lid—quiet as a mouse—and fingered the tools laid carefully inside. Gabe had promised that they'd do a project together this week. Max asked about making a wooden cradle for Chloe's favorite dolly, Susie. With all the fuss about him today, he didn't want her feeling left out.

Gabe's eyes had gotten all shiny when he'd asked. And his new dad had nodded and said "Yes, of course," in a hoarse voice, ending in a cough.

Max didn't feel a bit sleepy. Maybe because his belly was stuffed with too much pie and his head churning with ideas of all he could build with his new tools. He got up and opened the window, slow and silent as an Injun tracking a deer. This time he was sneaking out, not to get away, but to get closer to God. He climbed out on the shingled roof and lay on his back with his face to the dark night sky. He sensed that the big God was up there somewhere. Did God know about the thanks welling up in his heart? About the way he was full, nigh to bursting, with blessings. About the love in his heart, plum spilling over?

For once, Max wasn't afraid of the haints. The rocking chairs on the front porch were empty—as still as statues. The storm had blown through. The left-over clouds eased past like curtains opening for the start of a play. Max put his hands behind his head and looked up at the bright stars poking holes in the sky—letting out tiny bits of the light of heaven.

"I promise I'll be good," he said to the Light behind the stars. "So's my new ma and pa won't never send me away. So's Aunt Wilma can smile and let them bullfrogs go free when they grows up and gets legs. And I'll take good care of my new tools. Keep 'em forever like Gabe did his." He eased the kink out of his neck and back. Max spoke aloud. "Maybe someday I'll be a carpenter, like Gabe. Like Jesus was, too. Does Jesus still have his best hammer up there in heaven? What's he buildin' up there now?"

The damp cold stole into Max's bones, making him shiver. He eased himself up and slid back inside through the window, closing it silently behind him. His bed was soft and warm as he snuggled beneath the covers. He let the tired in his limbs take over. Let starlight swirl behind his closed eyelids. Let himself drift into sleep as he sighed and murmured... "G'night, God. Amen."

Chapter 19

Woman

*She will be called woman,
because she was taken from man.*
Genesis 2:23

Kyle first saw her from across the room at a planning commission meeting—a young woman with straight, chestnut hair falling past her shoulders, a slim build, flawless sun-kissed skin and full rosy lips. It wasn't just her beauty that struck him. It was her eyes—liquid green, sparkling in humor, with something deeply spiritual in their depths.

He couldn't look away.

Rowdy elbowed him in the ribs, bringing his attention back to Mr. Williams, the speaker. The man held court at the long, semi-circular desk up front, alongside the other members of the Community Development Commission, which held the fate of the Old Mill restaurant in their overly-conscientious hands.

"Are we to understand that this project is currently under review by the Environmental Protection Agency?" Williams asked.

The Old Mill

"Yes, sir," stammered Kyle. "We look forward to working with them. We want to protect the Coyote Creek as much as they do."

"Then, I presume you've met Miss Brooke Bowman, their agent." He nodded in the direction of the intriguing woman.

Kyle's mouth went dry. "No… I've not yet had the pleasure." He allowed himself a longer look. A sizeable folder lay open on her lap. *More hoops to jump through?* His eyes locked on hers. Kyle got lost in the deep ocean green of her gaze. He didn't want the two of them to be adversaries. No…not adversaries. And not just friends either. Something more.

Breaking into the silence, Rowdy spoke up for him. "We'd love to meet with Miss Bowman at her earliest convenience."

"This room will be available after we dismiss," said Mr. Williams. "…if that suits."

Brooke Bowman nodded and flashed a shy smile his way. Kyle grabbed onto his chair for support. He felt foolishly light-headed. Maybe he should have trimmed his beard, or worn a better shirt.

"Works for us," said Rowdy.

Kyle lost track of the rest of the proceedings. By Rowdy's jubilant mood, it seemed they'd approved the final plan check and accepted the inspectors' reports.

When the room cleared, Rowdy stood to leave.

"Where are you going?" asked Kyle.

"Home."

"But the meeting with Miss Bowman…"

"I'll let you handle it." Rowdy tipped his Stetson to Brooke on his way out.

Kyle swallowed. All thoughts fled. There was only the tilting room, the open folder, and Brooke's kind eyes…his own reflection swimming in their depths.

He managed to stagger into the chair next to hers.

"Let's start over," she said, holding out her small, perfectly manicured hand. "I'm Brooke. Brooke Bowman."

"Kyle Anderson," he said. As they shook, her dainty hand disappeared in his much larger one. He took care not to crush it.

"Let's talk septic," she said.

"What?"

"I understand you just installed a new septic system at the restaurant," she said in a sweet voice, as if commenting on a flower garden. "Any idea how close to the creek the leech lines extend?"

Their first conversation and they had to talk about sewerage? Kyle rummaged in his folder and pulled out the septic tank specs.

They spent the next half hour bent over plans and blueprints, discussing the destination of black and gray water, the expected traffic impact at the site, and his plans for food sanitation and trash pick-up. She had nit-picks with everything, from the type of soap used in the lavs, to the disposal of food scraps left in the kitchen sink traps. Luckily, the new septic lines were up to code and directed far away from any possible river contamination. Rowdy had seen to that, and had insisted that it all be done according to legal requirements. Kyle was thankful for Rowdy's cut-no-corners stance.

"Why is the EPA involved?" he finally asked.

"All creeks eventually flow to the sea," she said, with a pacifying smile. "Fish and other wildlife rely on clean water. Your proximity to Coyote Creek demands that I make sure that every part of your project meets our high standards."

Fatigue had begun to weigh on Kyle. He'd endured a full day's work. A long, mostly boring, planning meeting. And after that... this grilling by the EPA. He glanced at his watch. 10:45 p.m. Right about now, he wondered what he'd found so fascinating about a woman intent on making his life miserable. The gloss was definitely off.

He scraped a hand across his tired eyelids and closed his folder. "Maybe we could finish up another time," he said, standing. "It's been a long day."

"Yes, of course." Brooke gave an apologetic smile. "How about we meet up for a cup of coffee tomorrow?" She stood as well, gathering up her materials. "I hear the Java Junction makes a nice latte."

"Coffee?" he repeated, sounding like an idiot.

"No more questions or shop talk," she promised. "I'd like a chance to get to know you."

That was supposed to be his line.

She tucked a strand of hair behind her ear. "Your Old Mill Restaurant sounds wonderful. Any chance I could see it while I'm still in town?"

Suddenly, the attraction was back. Had her eyes always been this sea green? Her teeth so straight and white. Her lips so… What the heck was he doing? Walking right into the lion's den…

She put a hand on his arm, the warmth of her touch jolting him back to life.

"Let's meet up at the Old Mill tomorrow," he said. "I'll bring the coffee."

Midmorning the next day, they arrived at the Old Mill. Kyle had taken extra care getting ready. He'd made sure his dark beard was neatly trimmed, his hair freshly cut by the town barber, his teeth brushed, his Levi's and polo shirt clean. He'd decided that polishing his scuffed work boots might be a step too far.

Rowdy was headed to Chico today, picking up supplies and the last of the small appliances they needed for the kitchen, so Kyle and Brooke had the place to themselves.

They settled at a table on the outside deck. Kyle pulled two café mocha lattes and a few pastries from a Java Junction sack. As they sipped their coffees, the morning light cast soft shadows across the forest floor. Below, the creek murmured its way across the rocks and they could hear the red paddle wheel churning in a soothing, syncopated rhythm—water dripping from its rising blades.

"It's lovely here," Brooke said. "A great spot for a restaurant."

"Thanks." Kyle noticed how the muted light accentuated her beauty. Brooke's hair, pulled back into a pony tail, glistened like polished copper. Her eyes sparkled. She'd dressed down today, forsaking last night's dress and jacket for a casual white T-shirt and skinny jeans that showed off her soft curves. She pursed her lips and blew on her coffee to cool it.

Kyle took a sip of his own drink. "Just to be clear," he said. "Is this meeting business or pleasure?"

She held up her empty hands. "No business today. We'll have to see about the other."

Kyle choked on his mouthful of coffee. The attraction spun between them, shimmering like sunlight on water.

She favored him with one of her killer smiles.

"Come see the inside," he said, standing.

They walked past the lush plants and trailing ivy growing in planters outside and through the newly installed French doors, fitted with an actual, working dead bolt.

Brooke stopped in the doorway, taking it all in. "Incredible."

Kyle smiled as he ushered her inside and showed her its finer points: the rock foundry furnace, gleaming soda fountain, and massive original sawblade mounted on the brick wall. He ran a hand across the smooth counter top and adjusted a vintage chalk menu board. The interior was nearly done now, tables and chairs in place. Local artwork hung in small groupings. Gloria's decorating touches were evident in the flourishing plants growing from barrels, the variety of rusted farm implements hung on the walls, and the crystal chandeliers suspended above the more intimate corner booths. Rough-hewn shelves held everything from plump flour sacks, stalks of wheat and wooden utensils, to colorful stacks of Bauer bowls.

"This is wonderful, Kyle!" Brooke turned to take it all in. "You must be so proud. It's authentic, rustic, but fresh and clean at the same time."

"That was the plan."

"When do you open?"

"Just after the new year."

"Pretty exciting." Brooke touched a glittering crystal on one of the hanging chandeliers. "Nice touch," she said. "Unexpected from a couple of guys."

"That's all Gloria," he said.

Brooke's expression shifted. "You have a girlfriend?"

"No," Kyle quickly corrected. "Gloria's my decorator. And old enough to be my mother. She has a good eye for décor, though... don't you think."

"As long as she's not eyeing you."

"No. Not at all." Kyle wondered about the sudden jealous streak.

Brooke moved away from him. "Sorry," she said. "That was totally uncalled for."

Her face fell and Kyle's heart went out to her. "Bad break-up?" he asked.

"How'd you guess?"

"Been there..." He gestured for her to slide into the booth. "How about an ice cream sundae to take the edge off?"

"Now?"

"You look like you could use one."

"This is so embarrassing." Brooke took in a deep, calming breath. "I thought I was way past this."

"I'll be right back." Kyle went to the soda fountain and dished up two chocolate-covered vanilla ice cream sundaes—extra chocolate on hers, with three cherries on top. He set the treats on the table and slid in opposite her, the chandelier casting a subdued amber light.

"I don't want to talk about him," she said, popping a cherry in her mouth.

"Good. Neither do I."

"All I can say is that you don't deserve to be painted with the same brush."

"As your cheating ex?"

"Exactly."

"How long has it been?"

"Long enough," Brooke said. "Over a year now."

"Except that you're still reacting to the old hurt."

"Apparently so..." She spooned in some ice cream, licking chocolate from her spoon.

"Tell you what..." Kyle said, digging into his own sundae. "Why don't we forget about the past for now and get to know each other."

"Okay..."

Darned...he loved her shy smile. The one beneath the formal EPA bravado. The one directed at him.

As their sundaes melted in the pewter bowls, they covered the basics. They were both college grads, single...she, just a year older. She'd majored in environmental studies...he in American Literature. They both loved nature, hiking, and being independent. Brooke lived in the town of Elk Grove, just below Sacramento, a three-hour drive away. She took her work seriously, but also had thoughts of a husband and kids one day. And dreamed of a life in the country someday, away from the harried city vibe.

Here, in a corner booth of his soon-to-be-opened restaurant, it seemed natural to share confidences with Brooke. To let her in a little. She was funny without being silly, bright without being overbearing, sweet without being sugary.

Kyle ran a thumb across her knuckles, giving up on their polite background checks. "How long are you in town?" he asked, his eyes boring hungrily into hers. "Maybe we can have a real date before you have to leave. Go hiking…or something."

"I'll only be in the area on business for a few more days," Brooke said. "It's beautiful country. A hike would be lovely."

"You have any free time tomorrow? We could take a scenic trail up Lonesome Mountain."

"I'd enjoy that," she said, "I could break away by noon."

"Perfect." He wondered how he'd sneak out on all of the work needing his attention at the restaurant. Rowdy didn't take kindly to shirkers. "I'll pack us a lunch."

A skittering sound drew his attention away from Brooke's sweet face. Rascal scampered in through the open front door. *No! Not now!* How many EPA regulations railed against wild animals in a restaurant?

Brooke lifted her head. "Seriously…a raccoon?"

"We must have left the door open." Kyle raked a hand through his hair as the critter wandered over. "Brooke…meet Rascal. He's part of the wildlife along Coyote Creek."

"Hi, Rascal," she said, bending down to greet him. "So, Kyle's an old softie, after all…"

Rascal stood up on his hind legs, placing a paw on Brooke's knee, and looked up expectantly.

"He isn't shy about begging for a handout," Kyle warned, reaching into his pocket for a few pieces of kibble.

The raccoon took the treat and scampered out the door.

"Ahh…so he's got you trained."

"Pretty much… He's supposed to stay outside."

"I'll be sure to put that in my report," she said.

Kyle stiffened. "Hey, I thought this was a no business zone today."

"It is," she said, surprising him with a quick kiss on the lips as she stood to leave. Brooke paused in the doorway, an unreadable expression on her face. "That was purely pleasure."

Rowdy had plenty to say about Kyle taking off at noon on a workday. "So that's the way of it... A pretty gal comes along and you're ready to abandon me like an old bronco rode hard and put away wet?"

"I'm not abandoning you, Rowdy. It's just one afternoon," Kyle reasoned. "And Brooke will only be in town for one more day." He looked at his partner, who stood slightly bow-legged at the sink, up to his elbows in soapy water. "But I'll be sure to remember that *old guy, rode hard and put away wet* image." He grinned. "Must say... It suits you."

"Don't be a jerk," fumed Rowdy. "You might want to benefit from my many years of experience."

"What experience is that?"

Rowdy splashed some dishwater in his direction. "Been divorced once," he said. "And walked away from more 'n' my share of relationships that didn't pan out. When it comes to makin' a woman happy, I know exactly what *not* to do."

"Like what?"

"For starters... Don't drink," Rowdy said. "Not to make her look better in a dark bar or later on...to forget both of your annoyin' shortcomin's."

Kyle snorted. "That's the best you've got?"

The Old Mill

"Don't let all that testosterone do your thinkin' for you." Rowdy scrubbed out a pan. "You can't spend a lifetime in bed. Sooner or later, you gotta eat."

Kyle felt a flush travel beneath his beard. Brooke's kiss had tasted like chocolate. Very sweet chocolate. Attraction was a powerful thing. He'd been thinking about that kiss all night. He grabbed onto the first trite expression to enter his brain... "But doesn't love make the world go 'round?"

Rowdy let out the sink stopper, the water swirling down in a loud gush. "Water down a drain hole goes 'round and 'round, too," he said. "If you're not careful, a pretty gal can suck you right under."

"Are you crazy, old man?" Kyle didn't have time for this. He had to go buy lunch and pick up Brooke at her hotel.

"I'm out of here." Kyle, threw his apron on the counter. "Save your unwanted advice for Charlotte."

Rowdy flinched as the back door slammed. He'd likely overstepped. Kyle was a grown man, after all.

His mind shifted to his daughter, Charlotte. He'd given her plenty of advice over the past year. But just as often, had bitten his tongue instead. She'd arrived with a broken arm, from the accident that killed her mother, and an equally shattered spirit. A lot of it could be laid at his doorstep—for not taking responsibility for his daughter. When her mom, a rodeo groupie he barely knew, turned up pregnant, Rowdy hadn't done the right thing. Instead, he'd pitched a few bucks her way and mostly tried to forget about his child. He had a lot to make up for. He and Charlotte were getting on better now, but for both of them, old patterns were hard to unlearn. And she was her father's daughter, after all.

Now that they'd reunited, the temptation to worry was always there. Charlotte had a few friends he didn't especially like. He'd noticed that she tended to gravitate toward the down-on-their-luck types. The wounded ones, like herself. The ones bound to get in trouble. Just last week he'd caught her sneaking a smoke down at the lake with a girlfriend named Jade. The girl had purple hair and wore sleeveless tops to show off a brazen sleeve tattoo on her left arm. Rowdy toweled off his own tattooed arms. Who was he to judge? Cowboys, college boys, or high-schoolers…no matter. In the end, everyone had to find their own way.

※

The trek with Brooke was a good test of their compatibility. Kyle had picked a moderate hike, leading up the mountain from the trailhead at Buttermilk Falls. Brooke showed up appropriately dressed in Levi's, a warm jacket and a sensible pair of hiking boots. She was an avid hiker, sturdy and not given to complaint. Something about striding along together beneath the pines on a dirt path invited intimate conversation. It seemed natural to hold hands as they walked side by side. They paused to view the valley from the overlook and ate the lunch of sandwiches, apples, granola bars, and water he'd brought along. The sun was already sinking behind the mountain when they headed back, their time together ending all too soon. The goodbye kiss when he dropped her off was sweet, leaving him wanting more. But his own track record with women wasn't great. He didn't want to hurt Brook the way he had so many other girlfriends. She deserved better. Kyle wanted this time to be different…maybe because she was different from all the others.

Alone in his cabin that night, Kyle thought back on Rowdy's unsolicited advice about women. Maybe it wasn't so far off the mark. After all, Kyle had been drinking when he bought Rowdy's stolen rifle from the guys at camp. And drinking had fueled some of his most regrettable college excesses. He didn't want to leap headlong into something he or Brooke weren't ready for. And he hadn't even thought to pray.

Rowdy often said that his credo was *"Stand tall. Live right. Ride hard."* Maybe the old cowboy's advice to always had some validity after all. Kyle stared out his window at the black expanse of the lake. He'd have to find a way to apologize to the man.

After Brooke left for home, Kyle fell into a new pattern. Each night, after work, he went out on the deck to give Rascal some treats and then phoned Brooke. They sometimes talked for over an hour as the moon rose, spilling its golden glow across the river. He and Brooke chatted about her work at the EPA and his progress on the restaurant. About their childhood memories and favorite foods. Best loved songs and movies they'd enjoyed. That evening phone call became the best part of Kyle's day. He'd tuck away bits and pieces of his day to share with her, like a squirrel's stash of nuts. And, he suspected, Brooke did the same.

On weekends, often as not, they found a way to get together. Sometimes meeting halfway at a restaurant or a place to bike or hike. A few times, she came up to Buttermilk Falls to spend time at Lost Lake or hiking the trails of Lonesome Mountain with him.

Kyle ended their latest call reluctantly, the night air suddenly chilly through his jacket. He'd hardly noticed the cold while they were talking. The more he got to know her, the more he fell under the spell of her warm personality, bright mind, and those emerald green eyes. Was Brooke the mysterious woman at the soda fountain he'd dreamt about? That notion didn't seem quite so far-fetched anymore. He tucked his cell into his pocket and watched Rascal scamper along the river bank and disappear.

Kyle looked over at the churning water wheel—its song sweetly sad. The moon rose higher and the water darkened. A few luminescent stars poked out. He sighed, locked up the restaurant, and headed for home.

Chapter 20

Fallout

The enemy comes only to steal, kill and destroy.
I am come that they might have life
and have it to the full.
John 10:10

"Let's do it," said Lizzy.

"Do what?" Gabe hung his coat on the rack behind the kitchen door.

"Blow the darned thing up."

"Whoa... What are we talking about?"

"The copper mine." She brought two mugs to the table. "I don't want the thing. It's dangerous. Look what almost happened to Max and Chloe."

"That was scary, all right," conceded Gabe. "But we could keep it more tightly locked up. Make sure the cabin is secure."

"It's not just that," Lizzy insisted. "I don't want it. It's dangerous...evil."

Gabe pulled out a chair and sat opposite Lizzy at their kitchen table. "What makes you think it's evil?"

"Poor Aunt Daffy already died down there. And think about the trauma Max had, stepping on her bones. Then, rescuing Chloe from the small cave-in."

"True…"

"And that drifter, Birdie… She also died in a fire that had some kind of connection to that same cursed mine."

Gabe took another swallow of his coffee. "Okay…but what about all the copper down there? It's got to be worth a pretty penny…pardon the pun."

"I don't care about the money," she said. "We have all we need right here on the farm." Lizzy sipped her herbal tea, warming her hands against the sides. "What if the mine changes things? What if it changes us?"

"How could that happen?"

"Surely you've heard stories about the gold rush—murders…looting."

"This isn't exactly the wild west." He reached for her hand. "Are you happy, love?"

"Yes, of course." She squeezed his fingers. "With you, always." She drew in a breath. "It's the mine that worries me. I have a bad feeling about it."

"Now you sound like Buck."

"Maybe he's right." said Lizzy.

"So…you really want to destroy the mine?"

Lizzy nodded. "Yes, I do."

"Any coffee left?" he asked, standing up with his empty mug. "I could use another cup before we blow anything up."

Lizzy started to heft her very pregnant self out of the chair, but he motioned her back.

"I'll get it." He placed a protective hand on her belly as he passed by. "You relax." Gabe refilled his mug and returned to the table. "I guess most folks have forgotten about that old mine. No one told you about it when you moved here?"

"Not a soul," Lizzy said. "I had no idea it was even there. And Aunt Daffy never mentioned that old cabin, or what lay hidden beneath it."

"Must have had her reasons."

"Just like I have mine."

"I'm no explosives expert," he said. "But I'm guessing it would take a lot of dynamite to collapse that cavern. Is it even legal to buy explosives?"

"We could ask Buck. He'd know."

Gabe ran a hand through his hair. "Let's sleep on it," he said, taking her hand. "Once done, there's no going back with something like this."

"I know."

A few days later, Gabe got together with Buck to discuss the fate of the mine. In a town with too many listening ears, he didn't want anyone eavesdropping on this particular conversation. So, they met on a back logging road. The two men sat on the tailgate of Gabe's truck, fortified with take-out cups of coffee and a paper sack of pastries. He tossed a handful of sugar packets Buck's way.

"So, what's up?" asked the sheriff, ripping open a sweetener.

"Lizzy's copper mine."

"I have to admit that place creeps me out," said Buck. "Went back to church not long after the investigation."

"Some good came from it, then."

"We'll see…" Buck sweetened his coffee and took a bite of his cheese Danish. "So, what about the mine?" he asked.

"Lizzy wants to blow it to smithereens."

The Old Mill

"What?" Buck stopped chewing for a moment. "Why?"

"She doesn't want a copper mine," said Gabe. "Not this one anyway. Thinks it's evil…"

"Can't say I blame her."

Gabe nodded. "There's even more reason now. Chloe snuck over there a week ago, managed to get past the locked door, and got trapped inside the mine by a small cave in."

"That sounds serious." Buck's eyebrows lifted. "Is she okay?"

"Just a few scratches."

"How'd she get out?"

"Max rescued her," said Gabe. "He saw her take off and went in after her."

"Max went back in that cellar?!" The sheriff shook his head. "That's one brave boy."

"He sure is." Gabe raked an agitated hand through his hair. "He dug her out with an old shovel and his bare hands. Didn't even seem to notice his bloody fingers and scraped knees. Then he rode Chloe and her favorite dolly back home on his bike."

Buck squinted into the sun. "You've got to love that boy."

"We do." Gabe dusted the donut sugar from his hands. "But getting back to the mine…"

"It's a dangerous place. Didn't you lock it up, like I told you to?"

"Of course, I did," retorted Gabe. "I rebuilt the door and put on a new latch and lock the very next day. Apparently, Chloe pried up a loose board 'round back and crawled in."

Buck frowned. "We've got to secure it so nobody else gets hurt. Lock up the trap door as well…"

"Or we could just blow it up," remarked Gabe. "Eliminate the mine altogether and beat satan at his own game."

Buck smiled. "I like the way you think."

"Actually, it was Lizzy's idea."

"She's a spitfire, all right."

Gabe grinned. "You've no idea..."

Buck grew serious. "Blowing up the mine... You sure about this?"

"Sure as Sunday."

"Good." Buck scrubbed a hand across his face. "That mine's cursed for certain. Already cost two lives."

"You see my point."

"Loud and clear. So, where do I come in?"

"Well, first of all...is it even legal for us to blow it up?"

Buck scratched his head. "I'm guessing it's legal to blow up your own mine...with the proper permits. I can check into it."

"Thanks, Buck," said Gabe. "Secondly, do you know a discreet explosives expert? Someone competent to do the deed and keep his mouth shut?"

"I may know a guy." Buck grabbed the last piece of pastry. "But why the secrecy?"

"Thing is... Most folks around here either don't know, or have long forgotten about that abandoned copper mine under Lizzy's pumpkin field. We'd like to keep it that way... Just in case someone decides to go digging for copper one day."

"Makes sense."

Gabe nodded. "But an explosion's bound to be heard."

"Of course..."

"So, is there some way we can do it on the sly?" asked Gabe. "Maybe at night, so no one's the wiser?"

Buck polished off the last of his sweet pastry. "Darkness won't make folks deaf to an explosion, Gabe."

"I know that. But what if we misdirected their concern somehow. Isn't there some blasting happening out on the highway construction site? Makes sense they might do it at night, right? And if we had your help in putting that bug into a few key ears, no suspicion would fall on our farm."

"Very shrewd." Buck shook his head. "Is this your criminal past coming into play?"

Gabe raised his hands in mock surrender. "Heck, no, sheriff… Charlie set me on the straight and narrow when I was still a teen. I'm just trying to please my woman."

"I see…" Buck nodded, understanding dawning.

"So, are you on board?"

"Of course." Buck took a long swallow of his sweetened coffee while he pondered. "Like your wife, I'd like to be shed of that cursed mine." He gave a lopsided grin. "And besides, this could be an interesting caper."

"You up to spreading the distraction rumors?"

"Sure," said Buck. "I've got an idea about that. Leave it to me."

"Thanks, sheriff. I knew I could count on you."

"You'll keep me posted? I'd like to be on duty the night of the fireworks."

'You just want to watch the place go up," teased Gabe.

"Why not?" Buck drained the last of his coffee. "Who doesn't love a good explosion?"

※

It was a quiet evening in Buttermilk Falls. Bedtime stories were read. Children tucked in for the night. Stars winked in the heavens. The Big Dipper took its usual scoop out of the darkness. Then the ground trembled…

The blast rumbled in the deep earth, shooting an eruption of rock and old timber skyward. An eruption of dirt billowed up, nearly invisible in the shadowy night. The flimsy wood frame of the old cabin splintered into fragments, landing in the new grasses along with the clatter of stone shards. In an explosive instant, the

Pumpkin Hallow Copper Mine collapsed, sealing itself tightly... as if it had never been.

"What's that?" A distant rumbling noise stirred Rowdy from his kitchen chair.

Across from him, Charlotte paused in their nightly game of checkers, fingers poised over a red disk.

The earth trembled.

"Earthquake?!" yelped Charlotte, springing to her feet.

They both ran outside and stood in front of their cabin as the arched edge of a full moon peeked over Lonesome Mountain, as if checking to see if the coast was clear. All was still...no more shaking. No sound, but the calling of the loons on the lake.

"Don't worry," said Rowdy, placing a protective arm around Charlotte's shoulders. "I think I know what that was."

"What?"

"Lucille's been yappin' all week 'bout some night blastin' out on Highway 36. The construction crew is settin' explosives to widen the road." Rowdy scratched his head. "Most likely, that's what it was..."

"How would she know about road blasting?"

"How does Lucille know anything?" he countered. "The mercantile is gossip central. She said the sheriff told her."

"Well, in that case...let's get back to our game. I'm about to jump your king." She followed him inside. "I can't wait for the restaurant to open so I can start work at the soda fountain. I've been trying out some different ice cream concoctions. Ever heard of a s'more sundae?"

"Nope," said Rowdy. "Aren't s'mores meant for a campfire?"

"Not this one." Charlotte wasted no time double-jumping two of his kings.

"I was thinkin' we'd just stay with the basics."

"Don't be a stick-in-the-mud, Pa. Folks'll love 'em."

"If you think so..."

"And once we open...what better place to meet all the cute guys."

Rowdy quirked an eyebrow, and admitted defeat.

※

As the earth convulsed, Lizzy's nagging backache shot into the vice-grip of an insistent labor pain. She grabbed onto the door frame and bent over, a soft groan escaping. "Gabe!?"

But her husband was far down the road, watching the mine implode.

"Miss Lizzy?" Max peeked around the corner. "What's wrong?"

A gush of warm liquid ran down Lizzy's legs, pooling on the kitchen floor. She panted as the next pain consumed her. When it eased a bit, she answered Max. "The baby's coming. Can you bring me my phone?"

His eyes widened. "Okay..."

She sank to the floor, as he put the cell phone in her hand.

Gabe answered on the second ring. "Did you hear it, Lizzy? The blast was really something!"

"Come home," she moaned. "My water broke. I'm in hard labor."

"We headed to the hospital?" Gabe asked. "The truck's gassed up and ready."

"No. No time." With only a small clinic in Buttermilk Falls, the closest maternity ward was down the mountain in Susanville. She'd never make it that far tonight. Lizzy gasped as she was consumed by another insistent contraction. She grunted as the pain eased. *I could lose this baby*, she thought in a moment of panic. A home birth? *God, I'm so not ready for this.*

"Hang on, Sweetheart. I'm on my way." Gabe dialed the clinic. He got a recording saying the doctor on call was away on an emergency. Not knowing what else to do, Gabe rang up Doris's number as he raced his truck back to the farmhouse. "Can you get here soon?" he asked. "The baby's coming...fast."

"I'll be there as quick as I can."

When the last of the debris settled back to the ground, Buck came out from behind the cover of a rock outcropping, and removed his ear protection. *That was some explosion!* His ears still rang from the impact. His body vibrated with adrenaline. Sheriff Buck had been the only observer allowed in the vicinity, making sure no one, including Gabe, came close when the blast was detonated remotely. Even Buck was stationed a good twenty yards away.

He strode across the field to the spot where the old cabin and mine had been. The cabin was gone, reduced to a smattering of splintered sticks. The mine had caved in on itself, leaving a one to two-foot-deep depression in the ground in an area about the size of Lizzy's barn. At the edge of the rubble, something sparkled in the moonlight. Buck strode over and bent to pick it up. The twisted shard of metal bore a Coleman logo. The missing lantern?

Suddenly bone tired, Buck sat on a boulder, and tried to slow his breathing by taking in a lungful of cold air and releasing it through his nose. *At least the mine's no longer a danger,* he reasoned. *No one else will die because of it.*

He thought back on Miss Daffodil and the mysterious Birdie. Both gone. Chloe had almost been lost to the mine, as well. He'd always felt the place was evil. A gust of cold wind lifted the edges of Buck's hair. A shiver went up his spine…the sense of a demon spirit skulking past, forced out from his dark, underground lair.

The enemy comes only to steal, kill and destroy.
I am come that they might have life and have it to the full.

Buck looked over his shoulder. Where had that verse come from? He was no Bible scholar. But he'd been cracking the Good Book open lately, curious about what he'd been missing…hungry for something more. The copper mine had promised riches, but had brought death instead. Jesus promised life.

He wanted that life. *Life to the full.* A settled life with a good woman. Maybe even kids one day. Buck suddenly felt weary. He let his head fall into his hands. "God," he whispered. "I'm ready to let go. To let you have your way." He raked his hands though his hair. "I'm sorry for all the running I've done…all the wrong-headed stuff. If you'll have me…I'm yours."

His heart flooded with warmth—with a love he hadn't felt since he was a boy. A sense of coming home…at last.

That's when he heard the cricket—a *chirrp chirrp* rhythm, breaking the heavy silence. Off in the distance, a lone coyote howled…ending in a yap.

After the frightening noise of the explosion, a nature serenade had begun—the field returning to normal, settling in for the night. Buck felt settled as well. Different. Cleansed. Whole.

He looked across the plot of land. Over time, the stony path to the cabin would grow over with mountain sage. Perhaps, someday, pumpkins would once again be planted in the field, their lush vines spreading across the acreage—the neglected space coming back to life. The only hint left of the old mine was the copper ore fragment nestled in the basket in Lizzy's house.

The moon rose, big and full overhead, like a huge, gold coin glistening in the dark sky— payment for man's wayward ways. A token of the immensity of God's great love. Buck wondered why he'd denied love for so long? Avoided it…when he should have given it? He had a few things he needed to say… To Gloria. Right away.

Prenatal classes hadn't fully prepared Lizzy for the way labor took over her body, wracking her frame, leaving her panting. There was nothing but the bed beneath her, Gabe's worried face, Doris's encouraging words and the relentless demands of childbirth.

"Push now, child," said Doris as the next contraction hit. "The head is crowning."

And so it was that River Grace Reed, their very own *river of grace*, was born in her parents' bed in the old farmhouse at Sweet Apple Farm. Lizzy held her daughter, red faced and yowling—the most beautiful child ever. She gathered her close to her breast.

Gabe's grin was part relief and part pride. "Well done," he whispered to Lizzy, brushing damp curls from her forehead. "Look what fine work you did." Their baby girl reached out and wrapped her tiny fingers around his index finger—stealing her daddy's heart.

Doris bustled around, cleaning up, as calm as if she'd just baked a batch of cookies… instead of ushering a new life into the world.

When the kids were allowed in, they gazed, dumb-struck at the tiny bundle in Lizzy's arms. Her rosebud mouth formed a cupid's bow beneath the long lashes of her closed eyes.

"She sure is little," said Chloe.

Max brushed a finger over her wet, dark hair. "I always wanted a baby sister."

Chloe folded her arms, frowning. "Aren't I already your little sister?"

"Sure," said Max, with a shrug. "But you're no baby, are you?"

"No. I'm a big girl," she said, standing pretty tall for a six-year-old.

Gabe put a comforting hand on Max's shoulder. *Well played, buddy,* he thought. He turned to Chloe. "And now you're a big sister to little River." He hugged the two older children. "She'll need both a big brother and a big sister to show her the ropes of farm life."

"I can show her how to go get eggs," Chloe said.

Max grinned. "And I can help her give carrots to Gypsy."

"Perfect," said Lizzy. She looked around the bed at her growing family. "Simply perfect."

Chapter 21

Doubt

Why are you troubled ...
Why do doubts arise in your heart?
Luke 24:38

Charlotte took her responsibilities as an Old Mill soda jerk seriously. Rowdy taught her all the basics: root beer floats, malts, milk shakes, black and whites, and ice cream sundaes. Not to mention gargantuan banana splits with three scoops of ice cream and enough whipped cream to cover a small mountain. She'd learned to make each item quickly and efficiency, practicing on high school kids lured in by the promise of free ice cream.

Now, a few days before the restaurant's soft opening, Charlotte had come in after school to work on a few novelty items she'd devised for soda fountain specials. She said hello to Kyle and pulled out a glass.

The Brown Derby treat started with a cake donut at the bottom, topped with a glorified ice cream sundae and added nuts and sprinkles. The trick, she found, was to mash the ice cream into the donut hole so it would all stick together. Her latest creation was the

S'more Sundae—vanilla ice cream laced with graham crackers, covered in chocolate sauce and topped with marshmallows. She pulled out her mini-blowtorch to roast the marshmallow tops to a golden brown.

As the flame hissed, the front door banged open. Charlotte paused in her marshmallow roasting. Kyle looked up from unpacking supplies.

"Hey, Brooke," said Kyle, smiling. "Nice to see you!"

Brooke didn't smile back. "You can't open as planned."

"Why not?"

"I've found a gross EPA violation. So, I've got to shut you down."

Kyle stood in front of her, arms arrowed, hands on hips. "You're kidding? What violation?"

She held up a glass jar, half full of water. "No joke. The creek water in front of your restaurant is contaminated with sewage... raw sewage. You assured me that the new septic system had been properly installed."

Kyle frowned. "It was. I have the company's paper work to prove compliance."

Brooke waggled the water jar in front of his face. "My tests don't lie. This water is contaminated."

"Hey, cut me a break here," he said. "I thought we were friends. More than friends."

"We are... Were... But I can't stand a liar. Especially someone who despoils the environment."

"Whoa... Back up the trolley." He held up his hands. "I haven't despoiled anything. I'd never dump raw sewage into the creek, especially not right in front on my own restaurant. Do you take me for a total idiot?"

"Then how do you explain this?" She held up the offending jar.

"Don't know, but I'll find out," he growled, pushing past her and out the door.

Brooke dropped her arms to her sides, her shoulders slumping. "I thought he was a good one," she said to no one in particular. "I sure know how to pick 'em."

"He *is* a good guy," piped up Charlotte, from behind the soda fountain counter. "Give him a chance to prove it."

"Oh… I didn't see you there." Brooke glanced over with a nervous smile. "I guess you heard the whole exchange?"

"Hard not to," said Charlotte. "But you've got it wrong. Kyle and Rowdy are sticklers for cleanliness." She pulled her copper-colored ponytail over her shoulder, secure in its netting. "See… Nobody's even here and I'm following protocol. You wouldn't believe how clean this soda fountain is kept. At first, I resented washing everything down between imaginary customers, but I see now that it's become a good habit." Charlotte wiped the counter with a disinfectant. "You won't find any violations here."

"I wish that were true."

Charlotte fired up her blowtorch. "It is… You'll see." She held out the sundae. "Care for a s'more?"

Buck took a few days to digest his experience at the blast site. A few days on his knees. A few days walking the shores of Lost Lake. A few days reading scriptures about love and parables about forgiveness. Had God really forgiven him? He must have. Deep inside he felt the slate of his life wiped clean. His stubbornness and rebellion transforming into something else. Over these past few days, a wall had come down, exposing a new willingness to open up to the possibilities of love.

Unfortunately, Gloria had chosen that very time to make some changes of her own. She seemed a bit distant on the phone.

"Just to let you know," she said. "I'm going away for the Christmas holidays."

"What? Where to?" he asked, as dumb as a dirt clod.

"I've a hankering to see the ocean," she said.

"But I thought…"

"You thought wrong," she said, disconnecting the call.

Buck stared at his phone, the truth sinking in. He'd thought she'd be available to see him over Christmas, whenever he was ready to call or ask her out. But, as usual, he hadn't really asked at all. Hadn't made any definite holiday plans with her. Hadn't yet told her how he felt. Buck raked a hand through his hair. He'd really blown it this time.

Gloria's plan, ill formed as it was, centered around getting in her car and driving down the steep grade and off the mountain. Away from Buttermilk Falls to some place where nobody knew what a pathetic person she really was. Or how, in a family town like Buttermilk Falls, she'd ended up all alone.

Self-reliant. Just the way she wanted it. Right? Suddenly it didn't feel like enough. Gloria had prided herself on her independence since she ran away from home at sixteen. Best not to trust anyone with her heart. That way it wouldn't ever get broken again.

Ironic, she thought, as she threw a suitcase in her trunk and headed out of town. She specialized in taking castoffs and turning them into treasures. Amazing what a sprig of holly could do for a rusty watering can. But remaking herself hadn't been quite so simple.

Something about hearing *I'll be Home for Christmas* shrilling from the speakers at the mercantile yesterday morning had grated on her last nerve. Gloria didn't even have a Christmas tree, except for the extravagantly decorated artificial one in the window of her business.

She'd chosen to stay single. But Christmas was all about family. And she had none. This time of year, she keenly regretted that choice and fought against the crushing loneliness pressing in. She'd hung holly in her shop but not in her heart.

A week before Christmas, and she didn't have any holiday plans…not really. Sure, Buck would probably invite her to tag along somewhere at the last minute. Like a stray dog or a lost puppy. Rowdy had asked her to hostess at the Old Mill Restaurant right after the new year for the soft opening. But that was still two weeks away. A long, weary stretch of false cheer. She'd decorated some homes around town for the season. But her own soul felt barren.

Gloria decided to head to the coast, after all. Maybe the sound of crashing waves would soothe her spirit.

Kyle put in a call to his septic company.

The owner reassured him that the job had been done right. "There's no way sewage is leaking into the creek from your system," he said. "The leech lines are in a low-lying boulder basin a half mile away, with good drainage. And believe me, sewage doesn't run uphill."

"Will you talk to the rep from the EPA?" Kyle asked.

"Of course," he said. "I'll send over our specs today. It's all been signed off."

Kyle ended the call. So why did Brooke's sample show contamination? There had to be some other source. He tucked his phone away and paced toward the creek, sniffing for any tell-tale odor, but smelled nothing. *How could this be?*

What stung most was the idea that Brooke thought him capable of such deceit. Polluting his own stream would be penny wise and pound foolishness. Didn't she know him better than that? Apparently not. And now she was throwing her EPA weight around without even giving him a chance. Kyle felt heartsick about his restaurant being shut down before it had even opened.

He scooped up a handful of water and let it dribble through his fingers. If the water here was contaminated, he'd have to search upstream. Rascal skittered toward him, a candy wrapper clutched in one paw. "Not now, Rascal," he groused. "I'm busy."

The raccoon fingered the candy wrapper and scooted upstream a few yards, then turned back, in a mute plea for him to follow. Kyle grunted. "What? You think you're Lassie or something?" Where had the coon gotten a candy bar, anyway?

Rascal chattered and scrambled a bit farther along the bank before turning around again.

"Heck, why not?" muttered Kyle. "I was headed upstream anyway." He followed the animal as it scurried along the river bank. The masked critter looked back now and then to make sure he was still coming. They kept a lively pace along the riverbank for a good quarter mile, seeing nothing remarkable. He was just starting to feel foolish about following the animal when the raccoon darted off on a side path and up a draw, headed away from the river.

"This is where we part ways, then," he said. "I need to keep to the river."

Rascal wasn't having it. He ran back to Kyle, squeaked something urgent in raccoon, and took off down the side path again. This time, Kyle reluctantly followed, wondering about his sanity as he slapped away overhanging branches and pushed through the thorny brush.

At last, the overgrown path ended in a small clearing, accessible from a back logging road. A dilapidated camper-truck was parked in the unofficial site, gear and trash haphazardly strewn around. Rascal dug through a sack of rubbish and came away with another candy wrapper, which he licked off.

"Great!" grumped Kyle. "You brought me back here for a sack of garbage?" No one seemed to be around. He knocked on the camper door just to be sure. No response. Probably out deer hunting in the surrounding woods. The disorganized look of the camp reminded Kyle of the gang at the Singing Springs Campground. He skirted around the truck.

On the backside of the camper, a sewer hose dripped graywater. *Wait... Was a hose coming from the blackwater tank, as well? In a clearing with no sewer hookups?* He followed the three-inch hose to a small ravine a few feet behind the camper—the smell of raw sewage rank in the air. The careless hunters had been draining their tanks into a ravine that likely fed into the creek—his creek. He'd found the source of the contamination.

Apparently, hell had finally frozen over. Rowdy sat on the front deck of the Old Mill Restaurant, his pocket bulging with dog kibble. When Rascal ambled over, he offered the coon a handful of dry food, plus some treats from the kitchen. "You sure saved our bacon," he said. "So, I guess we're good. You can stay... And welcome." Rowdy watched the animal scratch behind an ear. "As long as you stay outside, away from my kitchen...and my soda fountain," he amended.

Mending fences with Brooke was another matter. And, for Kyle, one far from certain. After the hunters had been cited and the camper truck removed from the area, the water began to restore itself. The restaurant was no longer under suspicion and was cleared to open as planned.

When she came to the Old Mill with his new permit, Kyle took Brooke aside and made his feelings clear. "I know you have a job to do," he said. "But I thought you'd at least give me the benefit of the doubt—not immediately assume the worst." He looked down at the ground. "I'm not sure how we can move forward from here."

Brooke tugged her long chestnut hair back from her face. "I'm sorry," she said, looking down. "You deserved better."

"Damn straight," he said, anger coloring his face. "Don't you trust me at all?"

Rowdy came out on the deck. He lifted his cowboy hat to Brooke and resettled it on his head. "We all make mistakes," he said.

Kyle glared at him, then at Brooke. "Some worse than others."

"Depends on whose thumb is on the scale," said Rowdy. "For you, right now, it's your reputation that matters. For me, a while back, it was my favorite rifle."

Kyle looked down. "I told you I was sorry about the rifle."

"And I reckon Brooke is sorry about what happened here," Rowdy said.

"I truly am sorry," she said, unable to look Kyle in the eyes. "I should have trusted you...believed in you."

"You almost shut us down," he reminded.

Rowdy rocked back on his boot heels. "*Almost...*"

Kyle frowned. "What are you getting at, Rowdy?"

"The way I see it, over the past month or so, you two have found your way into each other's hearts," Rowdy said. "Now you've hit a bump in the road."

"That's for sure," said Kyle.

"So, you plan on throwin' it all away…or find a way to season it with a little grace?" Rowdy tucked his hands in his back pockets. "We're all just sinners saved by grace." He turned and went back in the restaurant.

A plump tear ran down Brooke's cheek.

Kyle reached out and brushed it away with his finger. "Don't cry," he said, shaking his head. "I guess you were just doing your job."

"A little too well," she said. "I jumped to conclusions, when I should have investigated further. Trusted your character."

"Well, my character hasn't been so sterling lately. Just ask Rowdy."

"He's pretty smart for an old rodeo cowboy."

"Sure is."

Kyle pulled her into his arms. "I don't want to lose what we have, do you?"

"No. I don't." She touched his face. "I really messed up. Can you forgive me?"

Kyle nodded. "It was an honest mistake. I see now that you drew the most logical conclusion." He gently kissed her. "I hope you can forgive me for being so self-righteous."

Brooke nodded and gave a watery smile.

Kyle grinned back. "Maybe we can both learn from this. Grow stronger…closer."

"I'd like that." Brooke wrapped her arms tightly about him. "Let's start over…from this place of grace."

They held each other, and listened to the slapping of the red paddle wheel…their future, like its song, shrouded in mist.

Chapter 22

Christmas Comes Softly

Behold, your king is coming to you…
humble, mounted on a donkey.
Zechariah 9:9

Christmas came softly to Sweet Apple Farm.
The rush and bustle of the Christmas tree farm faded away as the last truck carrying a holiday tree disappeared down the road. Harley closed the gate and locked it, satisfied that he'd done his best for another season. A light snow fell as he hung up the CLOSED sign and unplugged the strings of twinkle lights decorating the sales building. He whistled as he strode to his truck, ignoring the annoying hitch in his get-along. Tomorrow night, he'd have Christmas dinner with the Reeds—the highlight of his year. He felt blessed to be a part of it all, especially at his age. He chomped down on his toothpick, then flicked it into the weeds. He could hardly wait to set eyes on that sweet baby girl again. Little River Grace was nearly a month old now and everyone's sweetheart. He wouldn't be talked into holding the wee bit of a

thing, but he'd bend close and take in a whiff of that rarified new baby smell.

In the farmyard, Max gathered a load of split logs into is his arms, stacking it as high as he could carry. He'd sprouted up some since coming to live with the Reeds. His new pa, Gabe, had recently bought him several pairs of jeans at the mercantile, as well as some button up shirts and a new winter coat. He'd chosen a rough-tanned leather jacket, lined with sheepskin, just like the one Gabe wore.

He didn't have it on now, choosing to pull on a castoff sweatshirt instead. Max wasn't about to get any mud or pitch stains on the nicest coat he'd ever owned. Sure, he was a mite cold out here in the yard, with the snow coming down and all. But he'd endured far worse. The work would warm him right up.

Max grinned as he staggered toward the back door with his man-sized load. Light shone from the windows, reflecting on the snow on the ground and the nearby fence posts. It was a cheery sight—light and warmth coming from the farmhouse, and from the folks inside as well. Tromping through the snow with his contribution to the family, he was drawn to the idea of home. Not just shelter from the cold or food to quiet his rumbling belly…but a place where he belonged.

Seemed like he was always grinning these days.

It was the day before Christmas. Gloria sighed as she walked the boardwalk at Morro Bay, glancing in the gaily decorated windows of shops decked out for the holidays. *Holiday*. The word used to mean *holy day*. A day to remember the birth of Jesus. But these days, it was all Santa and snowmen...holly and jingle bells.

She'd left her hotel early, walking the beach as the sun gave a half-hearted attempt to burn off the morning fog. Gloria found a café open for business and ordered an eggs benedict. Did anything scream pathetic like eating alone on Christmas Eve day?

Three cups of tepid coffee and two half-read newspapers later, she returned to her hotel room, dumped sand from her shoes into the trash can, and fell across the bed. She was tired— exhausted in body and spirit. She closed her eyes and slept.

It was dark when she awoke, disoriented. Where was she? *Oh, right... Alone.*

She tried to go back to sleep, but the rumbling in her stomach pulled her out to a local bayside eatery for some fish and chips. She licked grease from her fingers, and nibbled on a French fry dipped in ketchup. Gloria watched the sun set across the bay. Brown pelicans flew by in a Vee formation. Ships creaked at anchor, tugged by the rising tide. Seals barked. Morro Rock, a darkening monolith, stood guard at the edge of the water which tinted orange and then sobered to black.

Gloria left the restaurant patio and walked past a row of giant boat anchors holding rusty chain guardrails, as thick as a man's arm. Headed nowhere in particular, she let a refrain of joyous music draw her up the hill. A nativity scene, lit by spotlights, graced the front lawn of a small, steepled church. She stopped to admire it. Gloria remembered having a creche as a kid. A small set of paper mache' figurines her mother had purchased piece-by-piece from the five and dime. It got lost somewhere after she left home...along with her faith.

Her gaze fell on Baby Jesus in the manger, his hands outstretched. Tears burned behind her eyes. She reached out and touched the small fingers. Unexpected warmth shot through her. The baby's eyes caught hers and held.

Inside the chapel, the singing swelled.

Joy to the world...
The Lord has come.
Let earth receive her King.

She stumbled inside and fell into a back pew. The stained-glass windows were dark, but flickering candles cast the congregation in a soft focus—simple people, like those in Buttermilk Falls. People full of joy.

Let every heart
prepare him room.

Gloria's heart opened, making room...letting grace enter in. Candlelight played with the pink streak in her hair. A woman next to her smiled and squeezed her hand. Tears fell as Gloria came back home. Back home to Jesus. She wasn't alone anymore.

It was the day before Christmas and Kyle was strangely restless. He'd been so busy with the renovation of the Old Mill Restaurant that he'd blocked out any expectations for the coming holidays. But as he scrubbed down the counters in the restaurant kitchen, a sudden melancholy filled him. He remembered Christmas on his grandparents' farm. Nothing fancy. Just a simple meal, a tree hung with tinsel, and a Christmas sing-along beside the old upright piano. Grandma playing the keys with fingers bent from arthritis, her voice clear and resonate as she sang the beloved words to her favorite carols.

He was suddenly homesick. Heartsick that no one was left there to welcome him home. The old farmhouse was rented out now. A closed chapter he could never reread.

Kyle needed to get outside into the woods. To chase the blues away somehow. He locked the door of the Old Mill and headed down the logging road. His boots beat a crunchy staccato on the hard, snow-covered gravel, as loud and discordant as his thoughts. The sound muted when he blindly cut off into the shelter of the trees on a pine-needle strewn path along Coyote Creek. He picked up his pace, until his breathing hitched, and kicked at a pinecone in his way.

At this moment, the restaurant seemed a hollow dream. He missed Brooke. While they'd gotten past the worst of the septic debacle, a long-distance relationship was still hard.

A melodic sound up ahead slowed his strides. He'd all but forgotten about the spring along this stretch of the creek. Singing Springs. Scattered boulders invited him to sit for a spell. Like the paddle wheel at the Old Mill, the bubbling water played a song all its own. It was a soothing, joyful sound. The rhythm of life... rising, moving, welling up from the earth itself.

Kyle settled himself on a moss-covered stone and breathed in the elemental smell of snow, water and damp soil. For the first time in months, he let himself linger in the now. Little by little he became aware of his surroundings. The splotches of sunlight on the ground. The green pine boughs weighted down with snow. The mountain jay eyeing him from a branch. The red spears of snow flowers poking through the earth. The soughing of wind through the trees.

He'd been living beside Lost Lake and working near these woods at the Old Mill Restaurant, but this was the first time in a long while that he'd really seen it...paused to let the beauty of nature speak to his soul. Communing with God hadn't been on his to-do list.

The jay squawked and flew away in a burst of blue and white. Kyle rested his head in his hands, his fingers raking through his hair. His sin wasn't as obvious as polluting the creek would have been. Not that. But maybe just as deadly. It lay in not seeing the simple splendor on display all around him. God wanted to speak to him through the beauty of his creation, but he'd been both blind and deaf. Too busy to even notice. Too preoccupied to listen. What else had he missed?

Out at Lost Lake, a small celebration of sorts was in the works. The cabins, dusted in a few inches of powdery snow, looked like Christmas card cut outs. Bundled against the cold, Charlotte decorated a six-foot standing pine in the yard with a red tinsel garland and pinecones sprinkled with gold glitter. Interspersed, she hung bird treats made from hardened balls of peanut butter, covered in a mixture of millet, cracked corn, and black-striped sunflower seeds. A Stellar jay flew over to investigate.

Charlotte stepped back, letting the hood of her jacket fall away from her copper curls. Her pup, Bonfire, danced around in the snow, yapping in delight. She'd never had a Christmas like this one. A mountain Christmas. This time, the tree wasn't a dried-out pine, shedding needles—a sorry thing lugged home from the half-price closeout sale at a city tree lot. Instead, it was a live, fresh and fragrant fir growing in her own front yard. Against the backdrop of Lost Lake, it was especially beautiful.

In the year since she'd come to live with Rowdy, she'd become familiar with this place— the stillness and raw beauty of it, the glistening pewter surface of the lake, the animal tracks in the yard.

Tomorrow, on Christmas Day, she and Pa would go to Wyatt and Amy's cabin for brunch. But today they were sticking close to home.

She looked up as Kyle's truck pulled into the clearing. He parked beside his cabin and gave her a friendly wave.

"Hey, Kyle..."

"Hi, Charlotte. Nice tree you have there."

"Come see."

Kyle walked over and admired the glittery pinecones and bird-friendly treat balls. Already, a few nuthatches and a jay had found the seeded ornaments. "You made these?" he asked, fingering one dangling from a string.

"Yep."

"Nice." Kyle looked out at the lake. He'd forgotten how pretty it was—all shining water and verdant pine-edged shore. "I was admiring your paintings at the Old Mill today," he said. "They fit right in." He saw how her paintings reflected her love of this place, the quiet and the serenity of it.

"I'm glad." It was a thrill to have her artwork on display. "Come on up to the cabin. We're about to have some hot chocolate and sugar cookies. Join us."

Kyle might have declined on another day, wary of intruding on their father/daughter time. But after his visit to the springs, he was hungry for family. And family, he was learning, was where you found it.

After all, he and Rowdy had become friends working on their restaurant. And Charlotte had fit right in with the soda fountain, coming up with all kinds of new ice cream concoctions.

"Thanks." He followed her to the porch. It was a mild day, so he sat in one of the Adirondack chairs while Charlotte went inside to heat the hot chocolate.

Rowdy joined him, stretching out his long legs and booted feet. "Howdy, Kyle. Nice you could join us."

Kyle nodded. He'd grown to appreciate Rowdy's steadiness and his down-to-earth style, an asset he was passing on to his daughter. "I like Charlotte's tree."

"Me, too." Rowdy lifted his hat and resettled it. "And to think I almost missed gettin' to know her."

Charlotte came out, carrying a tray of mugs filled with steaming hot cocoa topped with mini-marshmallows. A plate of homemade frosted sugar cookies sat at the center. They were slightly burnt on the edges… Just the way Kyle liked them.

Sweet Apple Farm nestled into the snow. A tendril of smoke rose from the chimney, promising firelight and warmth inside. Christmas Eve supper was a simple affair. Hot minestrone soup served with warm, buttered biscuits. Tonight, would be just their small, but exuberant, family—Gabe, Lizzy and their three children. Bonded by love, if not by blood.

They sat around the kitchen table, little River propped up in a baby seat next to Lizzy. Gabe prayed a heartfelt blessing:

"Lord, we are so thankful for our family. For allowing Lizzy and me to share the blessing of our three wonderful children, Max, Chloe and baby River Grace. We thank you that you sent your son, Jesus to earth at Christmas so long ago to guide us to heaven. Help us to love each other as you first loved us. Amen."

Max reached for a biscuit. "Why did Jesus come at Christmas?"

The Old Mill

"It was the other way around," said Gabe. "Jesus came to earth from heaven, and later folks began to celebrate Christmas each year to remember how special that was."

"Like when I got 'dopted?" Max slapped butter on his roll.

Gabe looked at Lizzy. "A lot like that. Jesus adopts us into his family...the family of God."

"You mean I belong to the family of God?"

Lizzy smiled. "If you ask him into your heart, you do."

"Like I did at Sunday school?"

"Yes." Lizzy finished ladling up the soup. "Just like that." Some of her favorite times were Sunday mornings, worshipping in church, her husband and children beside her in the pew at Good Shepherd Chapel.

"I asked Jesus into my heart, too," threw out Chloe. "I closed my eyes and meant every word."

"Oh, how Jesus loves the little children," said Gabe, with a wink for Lizzy.

Max was so eager on Christmas morning that he got up way before the old rooster had half a mind to crow. He dressed quickly, and snuck down the stairs. He was out in the barn before Gypsy was even half awake. His breath frosted in the cold air, and he rubbed his mittened hands together to get some warm into them. If he hurried, he could get all the stalls mucked out and the livestock fed before anyone else got up. He knew he didn't deserve all the presents tagged with his name under the tree, especially since he'd already gotten all those shiny new tools at his adoption party.

He planned on working extra hard today to show his folks he was halfway worth his keep. Bringing in more firewood. Washing up the dishes. Running errands. Making sure everybody's glass was filled with eggnog during the big party later. Fetching things needed for baby River.

A big hand clapped onto his shoulder, making him jump. "Son," said Gabe. "Why are you out here so early? We haven't even had Christmas breakfast yet."

"Thought I'd best get some work done," he said. "Afore it gets busy 'round the place."

"Come here, Max." Gabe sat on a hay bale and patted the space beside him. When the boy sat, he gave Max's shoulder an affectionate squeeze. "There's something you need to know about family," he said. "You don't need to earn your way in."

"What d'ya mean?"

"Love makes a family." Gabe faced him. "Love lets you in. And love keeps you there."

"But, what if I mess up?"

"No matter," said Gabe. "We all mess up sometimes. But we're still family."

"No matter what?"

"Always... No matter what." Gabe stood and ruffled Max's hair. "Now come inside and have some Christmas pancakes."

"Dad," Max called out—the new name, feeling good on his tongue.

Gabe turned, his eyes bright. "Yes, Son."

"Thanks." Max threw his arms around Gabe's knees in a big hug. The hug lasted long enough for the barn cat to trail his fluffy tail across their ankles. Together, Max and his dad walked through the snow, back to the farmhouse.

Max wasn't sure what to expect on Christmas with his new family. Gabe read the Christmas Story about baby Jesus being born and they opened their gifts. Lizzy cooked a big breakfast of

THE OLD MILL

bacon and eggs, and made pancakes shaped like snowmen, with raisins for eyes.

Afterwards, Gabe took Max and Chloe outside to make a real snowman. He helped them roll three fluffy balls and stack them in a pile, littlest one up top. Max found some sticks for arms and Chloe used black walnuts for eyes and a smiling mouth. Lizzy brought out a carrot for a nose and a red scarf for wearing around its neck. They put an old cowboy hat on the snowman and took a lot of pictures together, laughing. *Guess that's what a family does.*

By nightfall, the house was full of folks. Harley and Doris. Aunt Wilma. Sheriff Buck. Rowdy and Charlotte and her brother Wyatt and his wife, Amy, the town vet. Kyle brought his new friend, Brooke. Even Lucille from the mercantile showed up. They sat here and there and spilled out onto the porch. There was so much food that the table was stuffed full, just like his belly after he snatched that second piece of pecan pie.

As Max wandered around, he found himself alone in the kitchen with Lizzy. She was making more coffee in that big old urn and filling mugs for a tray. "Looks like half the town's here," he said.

"It's a crowd, all right. Aunt Daffy was the one who started this Christmas get-together for friends and family." She poured another cup of coffee from the spout. "Everybody loved Daffodil and I feel close to her by carrying on the tradition."

"Guess I'm family now," he said. "And part of Aunt Daffy's family, too."

She nodded. "Yes. You surely are…"

"Mom," he said, the word fresh between them. "I love you."

She knelt to enfold him. "I love you, too."

As the evening wore on, Max watched the women pass around baby River like she was a prized baby lamb. His littlest sister had already won his loyalty the minute she wrapped her baby fingers around his and gave him a gummy smile.

Folks told Chloe how pretty she looked in her red Christmas dress, which made her grin. And he was glad for it. He was learning there was plenty of love here at Sweet Apple Farm— both to give and to get. Love that let you in...like the words his dad had carved in the fireplace mantle—*Live Simply, Love Deeply.*

Max slurped down some hot chocolate and ate another sugar cookie shaped like a reindeer. The deep well of love sloshing around in his chest had him nigh onto busting out in a little dance or something. So, he ran out to the barn for a spell and fed Gypsy a carrot left over from the snowman making. He patted her velvety nose and let her snuff his hand. He hugged her around her neck and headed back to the farmhouse, his breath a silver cloud in the chilly air.

He found his Aunt Wilma in the parlor, chatting with Lucille. He gave her the little wooden frog he'd carved from a piece of river driftwood. "To remind you of me..."

Wilma pulled him close. "It's beautiful. Thank you. But I don't need a reminder of you, Max." She pointed to her heart. "You'll always be right here."

Through the window, Max saw Sheriff Buck standing all by himself out on the front porch. He looked kind of sad as he bent over and leaned his elbows on the railing. Max went out and stood beside him. "Hey, Sheriff..."

"Hi, Max."

"Where's Gloria?"

"Don't really know..."

"That why you're so sad?"

"Guess so." Buck looked down at the little boy who'd been through so much and still found a way to trust. The lad was the only one who'd asked about Gloria. The only one aware of the ache in Buck's heart.

Max took Buck's big hand in his small warm one. "It's gonna be all right... I just know it." He tugged the sheriff inside. "Come in and have some hot chocolate. I'll put some marshmallows on top."

It began to snow, the flakes falling light and feathery against the windows. Amid the joys and the sorrows and sweet insistent love of the season, Christmas came softly to Sweet Apple Farm.

Chapter 23

Grace

*My grace is all you need.
For my power is perfected in weakness.*
2 Corinthians 12:9

Rowdy faced a quandary. What on earth was he supposed to do about Charlotte's rag-tag collection of friends? He wanted to keep her away from their bad influence. Keep her safe with him out at the lake. But that'd be like trying to halter tie a green-broke filly—bound for a bad end.

Somehow Charlotte had talked him into letting four of her friends come out to the lake today to kayak. He'd tried to tell her it was too cold to be out on the water, but these were mountain kids. Who was he fooling with such a flimsy excuse? So here they were… At least where he could keep an eye on them.

He stared out at the shining surface of Lost Lake and bend his heart toward prayer.

"Tell me about your friends," he'd asked Charlotte last night.
"What's to tell…?"

"They have names, don't they?"

She rolled her eyes. "You already know my best friend, Jade. She's in my art class."

He nodded. Jade was hard to miss with her short purple hair and showy sleeve tattoo. She and Charlotte had bonded while sketching down by the lake and, he suspected, with cigarettes smoked behind the lodge. Hard to get a read on a gal who didn't say much. Jade's eyes sparked with life, but his attention got waylaid by the thin silver circlet piercing her right nostril—like a ring in a bull's snout.

"The two guys are Brian and Scott," Charlotte added. "Brian's a math whiz and good at coding. You'll recognize him by his black-framed glasses. His folks fight a lot. His dad's pretty angry and a mean drunk, so Brian mostly stays away from home."

"Oh..." Rowdy had no idea what coding was. A drunk dad he understood.

"Scott's a redhead," said Charlotte. "Freckles, pale skin...the whole bit. He and Brian are computer geeks and spend a lot of time gaming."

"Okay." He hoped to keep the information flowing, so didn't say much.

"The last one's Peggy. She loves books and keeps one with her at all times." Charlotte brushed her hair aside. "She also loves to eat...a lot. So, she's a loner, which is the reason for the books... romances mostly. Gives her something to look busy, instead of just pathetic."

Rowdy studied his daughter. She saw more than he'd given her credit for. And had a kind heart to befriend kids in such pain.

"I'm proud of you, Charlotte," he said. "You're a good friend."

"Sometimes..." She shook her head. "But sometimes I'd just like an invite to the popular table."

GRACE

Rowdy looked toward the dock where his daughter's friends were scrambling into three of the resort's kayaks. After last night's conversation with Charlotte, his heart had softened toward them.

Their chatter livened the lakeshore.

He could tell Jade had kayaked before by the way she steadied the craft as Scott edged one foot into their unsteady tandem craft. "Plant your left foot in the middle and sit down quickly," she instructed. Scott was a ginger, all right—his carrot-top hair far too long, hiding much of his face. He somehow managed to ease his lanky frame into the boat without tipping them both in.

The second kayak, a red Wilderness tandem, held the chubby girl, Peggy, who clutched a book under her right arm. Brian, wearing glasses and a grin, clambered into the front canvas seat. He adeptly handed a paddle to Peggy and pushed the drip guards down on his own oar. She set the book, wrapped in plastic, between her feet and dipped one end of her paddle in the water. Who took a book out on the lake?

Charlotte settled into her favorite yellow Ocean kayak—a sit on top—and braced the paddle across her knees, ready to lead the group out.

Rowdy hurried over. "Got your life-vests on?" He sounded like a typical overbearing parent.

"Really, Dad?" Charlotte groused. "We're not babies."

He checked anyway. Their life-jackets were on...if not buckled. "Which way you headed?"

"Goose Island." Charlotte pushed off from the dock with her blade. "We'll be back by noon."

"Good." Rowdy shaded his eyes from the morning sun. "We can eat lunch then." They paddled away quickly, across the glassy water, laughter following in their wake. He watched until they became just three small dots, far across the lake.

At lunchtime, Rowdy studied the kids as he grilled burgers. Scott and Brian played some game on their cell phones, intent on their screens. Scott's cheeks, partially hidden by longish red hair, were florid with freckles and acne. Brian had a nervous habit of pushing his glasses up on his nose, and a weird snort for a laugh.

The three girls giggled over some Facebook posts. Peggy cradled her book on her lap and chewed absently on a fingernail. "I'm starved," Peggy said, to no one in particular. Jade, smelling faintly of cigarette smoke, fingered a row of jeweled studs punched into her right ear. He noticed the nervous jiggle to her leg.

Not exactly the popular crowd. But…who was he to judge? As a 4-H kid and wanna-be rodeo cowboy, he'd been on the social fringes during high school, too.

Short of demanding that they all put down their cell phones, Rowdy had no idea of how to interact with Charlotte's misfit crew — two computer nerds, a tattooed artist, and a hungry book lover.

"Burgers are done." He dished the meat onto a platter and set out buns, a pot of hot chili beans, chips and some sodas. The kids filled their plates and dug in. Rowdy took a bite of his burger and studied Brian out of the corner of his eye. The kid had a bruise on his chin and he noticed that the corner of his black-framed glasses was broken, held together with a paper clip. Rowdy clenched his hand into a fist. The poor kid deserved better than a dad who beat him. So why would Brian choose a brutal video game over the quiet of the lake? Or was he just a typical teenaged boy?

Peggy helped herself to a second burger. She gulped it down as if she was starving, then reached into the bag of chips.

Rowdy winged up a silent prayer of sorts. A plea for guidance. "I need your help here, God. These kids are drownin' and I've no idea at all how to help 'em."

His mind drifted to his latest restaurant worries. The idea of setting up schedules for waiters and kitchen staff and managing inventory lists terrified him. Rowdy didn't know a thing about computers. And Kyle, always on the phone with Brooke, wasn't much help. Rowdy mentally chewed on his worries, like a dog with a bone.

A stray thought came to him. "Hey, Brian," Rowdy said, gesturing with his half-eaten burger. "You and Scott know anythin' about a computer program to keep track of inventory or staff schedules at my restaurant? I need help gettin' somethin' set up, but I don't even know where to start."

Brian adjusted his glasses and looked up. "Should be pretty basic. I'll bet I can find something online that would work. If not, I can create one."

His buddy, Scott, tugged a strand of hair back from his face. "I did an inventory sheet for my mom's flower business."

"Really?" Rowdy's expression brightened. "Think you two could help me with it?"

"Piece of cake," said Brian. "You got a computer?"

"At the restaurant," he said. "But Charlotte's got a laptop in the cabin."

Charlotte glanced up from her phone. "What's up?"

"Can we use your laptop?" Rowdy looked at the boys. "These guys are an answer to my prayer."

The three girls darted him a look. Too late he realized he'd said exactly the wrong thing, pitting boys against girls. What an idiot. He fingered the rounded pebble he'd put in his pocket this morning at the lake, and asked for God's help with the mess he'd just made.

It came to him then. Each of them needed purpose, encouragement...love. Maybe even a reason to look up from their phones.

"Thing is..." he said. "With the openin' of the restaurant just 'round the corner, I could use help from all of you. A lot of help." He looked around the table at his misfit crew. "Listen up..."

By the time he'd laid out his ideas, the cell phones had been abandoned. Soon, the kitchen table was covered with printouts, excited chatter filling the cabin. By mid-afternoon, the guys and gals were trying on Old Mill aprons and caps, preening for their new jobs as computer programmers, schedule makers, food preppers, soda fountain jerks, wait-staff, and busboys.

"This staff schedule should work out great," beamed Brian, clicking on the keyboard of Charlotte's laptop. "Just fill in the names for each worker's time slots. I can always tweak it if you want."

Scott stapled some printed sheets. "And as soon as I can plug in the specific inventory items you want, we can schedule weekly orders."

"Can't wait to scoop up some ice cream," said Peggy, her book forgotten. "Charlotte's been filling me in on the basics for weeks already. How does this cap look?"

Jade held a stack of laminated menu covers, pulled from a box delivered last week. She slipped a fresh menu printout inside. "I'm pretty good with InDesign," she said. "See how you like this dummy of your menu inserts." She handed the sample over.

"This is great," Rowdy scanned the new menu dummy. "I'll pay you for the design work—like the professional you are."

"I'm not a professional yet," she said. "But I could sure use the money for my art college fund." Jade smoothed a menu sheet. And if you'd train me as a hostess..." She grinned. "I would even lose the nose ring."

"Not necessary," he said. The ring was definitely growing on him.

With the grand opening less than a week away, things shifted into high gear at the Old Mill Restaurant. The first days of January sped by in a flurry of last-minute supply orders, staff training sessions, and finishing up the final touches on the building.

For the first time, Rowdy didn't feel like he was alone with the staffing and inventory worries. With Charlotte's friends on board, he'd gained a young crew, eager and ready to work. They seemed excited that they had a foot in the door as workers at the newest business in town. Status they'd never had before.

Wilma had moved into a small rented cottage at the edge of town. As head waitress, she'd been called in to train the new wait-staff. Rowdy paused in the kitchen doorway to eavesdrop on her session in the main dining area. She was practical, yet lighthearted, in her approach.

"Folks come to a restaurant to be pampered," she said. "Maybe the wife's put out three meals a day for months. She's sick of frying eggs, making spaghetti and washing up dishes. She's finally talked her hubby into a night out and a chance to eat someone else's cooking. A time to get away from the ol' *what's for dinner?* grind..."

She eyed her crew. "Your job is to make the evening memorable...make her feel special."

Wilma scooped up an armful of menus. "It starts at the door," she said. "Whatever you do, don't leave the family standing there like bumps on a log, hoping to get noticed. Start the visit off right with a smile and a warm greeting. Use their names if you know 'em."

Rowdy watched from his kitchen hideaway as Wilma came to life at the front door, smiling at imaginary customers. "Jim... Thelma... how nice to see you. Would you like a nice quiet table by the window?" She gestured them in. "Please come right this way." Wilma led her pretend couple to a nice window table and pulled out the chair for the missus. "I'll be right back with some water." She carefully set the menus in front of each patron, like a genteel lady serving tea. "Anything I can get you while you look over the menu?"

"Don't plop the menu down like a piece of trash," she cautioned. "Set it down gently, like the treasure it is."

"What do you mean?" asked Jade.

Wilma opened the menu, displaying the neat printout inside. The one Jade had painstakingly created with InDesign. "This is a wish list," she said. "It holds the key to a magical meal and memorable time here."

She ran a manicured fingernail down the list of lunch and dinner menu items. Then turned back to her crew. "Your homework assignment is to memorize this list. Learn all about each menu item and how it's made. You'll be given samples this week from the kitchen so you'll be familiar with each dish when they ask about it."

Brian licked his lips. "You mean we get to eat all this?"

"Just a sample of each, for starters," said Wilma. "Remember that you are salespeople for these meals. Speak as highly of the food as you would your own children." She gave a wink to an older employee. "If there's an item you don't particularly like, never admit it. You can always say that it's very popular with the customers."

"Isn't that lying?" asked Peggy.

"Honey, with this great menu, everything on it will be someone's favorite. Maybe, just not yours."

Peggy smiled. "Got it."

"Notice anything?" Wilma stood tall, looming over the table.

"You're taller than I thought." Scott peered out from beneath his red hair.

"That's the thing," said Wilma. "As a server, you're standing... They're sitting down. You don't want to intimidate 'em. So, what can you do?"

"Hunch over?" suggested Scott.

"No. Never slouch," Wilma commanded. "You are proud to work here."

"Then what?" asked Peggy.

Wilma squatted down to the girl's level and touched her on the shoulder. "And what can I get for you today, miss?" She straightened. "How'd that feel?"

"Nice," Peggy chewed her lip. "Like we were friends or something."

"A little insider tip," revealed Wilma. "You'll get a bigger tip if you touch the customer...nothing out of line, just a little pat on the arm or a touch on the shoulder. People like the friendly feel."

In the doorway, Rowdy grinned. He'd made a good choice in asking Wilma to head his wait-staff. He could tell she had the experience and the no-nonsense personality to do the job.

When the training session was over, Brian tagged after Rowdy, helping him move boxes into the storage room...sweeping up. He'd been dogging Rowdy's heels, like a puppy, since that day at the lake.

Rowdy understood. The boy needed a role model who didn't lead with his fists. Rowdy pulled out the eyeglass repair kit he'd picked up in town. He held it up. "Mind if we fix those glasses?" Rowdy reached out his hand. "Take 'em off. Let's see if we can fix that hinge...and maybe add a nose support that'll help 'em stay where they belong."

Brian flushed, but handed over his glasses. "Busted 'em p-playing basketball," he stammered.

Rowdy nodded. "Let's find a screw the right size and see what we can do."

Together, they removed the paper clip and added the new attachment. The nose support went on next. Rowdy rinsed the smudged glasses off under the faucet and handed them back to Brian, who put them on.

Gesturing to the storeroom, Rowdy tipped his hat. "Nice work. Looks neat as a curry-combed filly. I appreciate your help today, Brian. I think you'll be a real asset around here."

"I hope I don't mess up," said Brian. "Never worked in a restaurant before."

"You'll do just fine," said Rowdy, clapping him on the back. "One word of advice from an old cowboy..."

Brian pushed at his glasses, even though they'd stayed in place. "What's that?"

"Don't look back. You're not headed that way anymore."

Next day, Gloria walked the strand in Morro Bay. The sun was setting, gilding the bay in shimmering reds and golds—more beautiful than any artificial Christmas decoration. God was real. Christ had come. Her heart was full.

A phone text pinged. Still aglow from the tenderness of finding her way back to God, she wasn't surprised to see Buck's name pop up on her screen. He'd been heavy on her mind. *"Forgive me,"* his text read. *"Please come home."*

She didn't reply. How would Buck react to her newfound faith? She couldn't imagine the big, tough sheriff ever bowing the knee. And she couldn't bear it if he made light of what had just happened to her.

Gloria stayed at the beach over Christmas and part way to the New Year. She had some things to figure out. Things that didn't involve Buck. Deep inside, pride, self-sufficiency and a backlog of unforgiveness still warred with the newly found joy of being washed clean.

Things would have to be different now…because she was different.

Kyle had been extra busy getting ready for the restaurant opening. But today, midmorning, he'd arranged to meet Brooke at the trailhead to Singing Springs. He needed some time away from the stress of his job and they'd both enjoy a short hike.

While he'd tried to put the septic incident behind him, their relationship still felt a bit rocky. He liked Brooke. Really liked her…but he didn't quite understand her. Not the way he wanted to. Some piece of the puzzle was still missing. But what?

Her car pulled into the turnout and Brook got out. Seeing her did the usual quivery things to his insides. She wore her long chestnut hair up in a ponytail that swung across her back as she moved, her body feminine and athletic. Her smile was sunny…her eyes green as the pines. She tucked her hand in his as they started their hike, chatting about her week…catching up.

At the springs, the musical call of the water was as tranquil as ever, soothing the senses and bringing a feeling of calm. They settled on the boulder grouping, content to sit quietly together. A blue-jay squawked from a branch above them.

Her expression sobered. Brooke leaned forward, her hands resting on her knees. "Kyle, there's something you need to know about me."

Kyle could feel his heart pounding in his chest. "Okay. What is it?"

"It wasn't just a bad breakup that messed me up." Little frown lines furrowed her brow. "It was the worst kind of betrayal."

"What happened?" Kyle's mouth ran dry. He wondered what had brought such a look of pain to Brooke's eyes.

"It was my wedding day." She fidgeted with her bracelet. "My sister was my maid of honor. We'd always been close, just two years apart. Me, the eldest. She'd helped pull all the nuptial details together, invitations, flowers, cake..." Brooke twisted her fingers together as if trying to scrub the memory away.

"I was already dressed in my wedding gown and went in search of her for help with pinning my veil. I opened the door to a church ante room and came upon a couple caught up in a passionate embrace. I was about to slip away and give them some privacy when he looked up and I recognized the face of my groom—the man I was about to marry. I was already in shock, when I spied a beribboned flower bouquet on the floor that had tumbled from the woman's hand. The spray of fern and pink roses belonged to my maid of honor...to my sister."

"Good Lord..." Kyle drew her into his arms. No wonder she'd lost the ability to trust.

Brooke burst into tears, burying her head in his chest. "They eloped a week later."

"The guy's your brother-in-law, now?!"

"Afraid so." She pulled back, wiping her eyes with a tissue. "I lost both my fiancé and my sister that day."

"That's terrible. What about your parents? What did they say?"

"They've decided to accept what happened. Including their new son-in-law...just with a different sister."

"Can this get any crazier?" Kyle smoothed a strand of hair from her wet face.

"Only on holidays."

No wonder she'd been so eager to join him at Gabe and Lizzy's on Christmas...rather than be with her own family.

"Oh, Brooke. I'm so sorry." He wiped away a tear on her cheek. Kyle pulled her closer, wishing he could shield her from the cruelties of life.

"It's amazing you're still breathing." He dropped a tender kiss on her trembling lips.

She reached for his hand. "Now you understand why I have issues with trust. I wanted you to know... So you don't think I'm crazy."

"You're not crazy," said Kyle. "Just human."

"You must find me pretty pathetic...getting played like that."

"No. I think you're strong. Resilient. Vulnerable." Kyle squeezed her hand. "Being with me. Risking your heart again."

"Not...not without some fear and trembling." Brooke looked down.

Kyle understood now. The deep well of pain and the anger. He tilted her chin up, her eyes meeting his. "I'm not him," he said. "I'm all in."

"I'm trusting in that." Brooke closed her eyes and leaned back into his embrace.

As they held each other, the waters of Singing Springs played a sweet and simple melody—a hymn of grace.

Chapter 24

Open Delight

*Delight yourself in the Lord
and he will give you
the desires of your heart.
Psalm 37:4*

Gloria returned to Buttermilk Falls just before the new year. She'd promised Rowdy that she'd be back to hostess the soft opening of the Old Mill Restaurant. Kyle had insisted that she come over tonight, the night before the opening, to see the place lit up and ready to go. He wanted her to wait until then to set up the table centerpieces and see if the site needed any final tweaks to the decor. She pulled up just as it grew dark. The place looked gorgeous—light spilling from the windows, the deck strung with twinkle lights. A fire blazed in the outside fire pit, offsetting the cold.

She carried in some boxes holding succulents and potted flowers. Kyle met her at the door. "Thanks for coming, Gloria." He ushered her inside. "So…what do you think?"

"It's beautiful…even better than I imagined."

Gloria unboxed the greenery. They'd decided to use small ceramic containers of succulents for table centerpieces. The glazed pots had been hand-thrown by students in the high school pottery class. Far better than the usual cheap vase of cut flowers, too tall to see over. Set on each table, the small potted gardens leant just the right touch to the polished wood of the tables. She placed some larger succulent displays at the hostess and serving stations.

"Nice," said Kyle. He eyed a box she'd brought. "What's with those extra potted flowers?"

She pulled out some gloves and a small hand trowel. "I wanted to add some last-minute color to the planter barrels outside."

"Great idea," he said, carrying the box out to the deck for her. "You always know what little touches the place needs. I really appreciate it."

"My pleasure." She knelt beside the nearest wooden barrel, flanking the door.

"I'll leave you to it then," Kyle said, heading back inside. "I've a million and one last minute things to do."

Soft music lilted from the outside speakers. *Nice touch*, thought Gloria, tucking a strand of hair behind her ear as she bent to her work.

She didn't pay much attention to the flash of car lights turning into the back parking lot. Likely another worker.

But soon, she became aware of someone behind her. She turned to see Buck standing there. Gloria did a double take. She'd never seen him so dressed up. Slacks, dress shirt, tie and a sports jacket covering his broad shoulders. She stood and smoothed some wrinkles from her dirt-stained sweatshirt, nervously fingering the requisite sparkling rhinestones at the neckline.

"Buck? What are you doing here?"

"You're back." he said. "Wild horses couldn't keep me away."

Kind of poetic...coming from Buck.

"You look beautiful." He pulled her into a bear hug.

She'd forgotten how big and strong, male and downright overwhelming he was. Gloria pushed away to get her wits about her. "And you look...different. What's up?"

It was chilly outside. Buck took off his sport coat and draped it around Gloria's shoulders. He moved them closer to the firepit and motioned her to one of the Adirondack chairs. He sat in the other. Flames danced into the night air, creating a warm glow.

He braced his muscled forearms on his thighs, threaded his fingers together and leaned forward. "Well... for starters, I want to apologize."

"Have pigs learned to fly?" she joked. "You never apologize."

"Then it's past time I did. I'm sorry for treating you so casually, Gloria. You deserved better."

"Got that right."

His eyes locked on hers. "It wasn't right to leave you hanging at Christmas. I aim to do better." He took her hand in his. "I really care about you, Gloria."

The firelight played on his earnest face, making it even more ruggedly handsome.

She tugged her hand loose. "Before you get too carried away... Something big happened to me while I was gone."

Buck blinked. "Oh... What?"

Gloria leaned forward, let go of her pride and opened up. "We had this nativity set when I was a kid," she began. "I lost it somewhere after my mother died. Lost my faith, as well." Tears glistened in her eyes. "Thing is... Baby Jesus reached out to me from a manger in front of a little church down in Morro Bay."

The old Buck might have laughed. This new Buck drew her close. "Tell me..." he said.

And she did.

Buck was silent for a while, sitting quietly while the fire crackled and sparks shot into the dark night sky. He stared into the flames, taking her hand in his. "Guess God has a wicked sense of humor?"

"What do you mean?" she asked. "You making fun of what happened to me?"

"Never," he said. "I had my own spiritual encounter."

"Are the hounds of hell after you, or something?"

Buck gave a whoop. "Not exactly." He toyed with her fingers. "Let's just say…heaven reached out to me, too."

"You and heaven…that's an unlikely combination." She spread her hands toward the warmth of the fire.

"I thought so, too," admitted Buck. "Until a few days ago."

"Wait… Are you saying God tugged you in, too?"

"Exactly right," he said, with a completely straight face.

"How in the world did that happen?"

Buck grinned. "Well, it took an explosion, a demon, and missing you like hell."

"You're kidding?"

"Dead serious."

She smiled at that. "Tell me."

So, he did.

Kyle poked his head out the door, so he could glimpse Sheriff Buck and Gloria out by the firepit. Looked like all was going well. So far, so good.

He still wondered how Gabe had pulled him into this crazy plot to get the two reluctant lovebirds back together. Seems that Max told his dad about Sheriff Buck's lonesome Christmas, and asked what they could do to help. And before you could blink, a scheme was hatched. It had been easy enough to lure Gloria here with a legitimate request to finalize the décor. And Kyle felt a little smug for suggesting, to a surprisingly compliant Buck, that he have his reunion with Gloria tonight right here at the Old Mill. The man muttered something about divine providence.

Kyle had to admit it was a pretty romantic setting. The twinkle lights. The warm fire. The soft music. The red paddle wheel, lit by a spotlight, splashing a soothing rhythm as it churned the cold water below. A guy like Buck needed all the help he could get. And Kyle was rooting for him. Buck and Gloria would make a perfect couple…if they didn't kill each other first.

"That's some story, Buck." Gloria squeezed his hand. "Guess we both managed to ignore God most of our lives. So… What happens now?"

He held her gaze and raised an eyebrow.

"What?" Gloria questioned.

"You might be surprised." Buck took her fingers in his. "I love you, Gloria. Maybe from the first time I saw you. I've just been too bull-headed to admit it." He brought her hand to his lips and kissed her knuckles. "I want us to have a life together. I want you for my wife."

She pulled her hand free. "Are you nuts?"

"No. Trust me… This is the sanest I've ever been."

Gloria felt her bottom lip begin to quiver. "You can't just waltz in here and say you love me."

"Why not? It's true." He leaned closer. "I should've told you sooner."

"Wait just a minute, buster." She gave his shoulder an ineffective shove, trying to put a little distance between them. "Didn't we agree that neither of us is the marrying type? That we're best in a casual relationship, coming and going as we please?"

Buck lowered his head. "I was wrong. Dead wrong. That's the way I treated God, too. Just wanted him around when it was convenient...for me." He gave her a shy smile. "Thing is...I found out that even when I didn't really believe in God, he still believed in me."

Good, Lord...The man was serious. Gloria leaned back in the Adirondack chair. "I don't know what to say."

"We'll go with that, then." Buck got down on one knee in front of her.

Kyle leaned farther out the doorway. This was getting good. He didn't know Buck had it in him.

Rowdy brushed past Kyle's shoulder, peering out from behind him at the unfolding scene by the firepit. "Great balls o' fire," said Rowdy. "Is Buck really proposin'?" He leaned out. "Turn down the music. I've got to hear this."

Charlotte joined the queue by the doorway. "Isn't it romantic?" she gushed.

"Have some sensitivity, will you?" Kyle turned the music up a tad to ensure the couple some privacy and backed the gawkers away from the door.

Buck, down on one knee, only had eyes for his girl. "Gloria, I really and truly love you. I want us to be together. As husband and wife." He reached into his pocket and pulled out a ring. "Will you marry me?"

Gloria swallowed. *Was this for real?* She studied the ring. A gorgeous vintage diamond ring. *Not paste. Genuine.*

"It's time we gave love a chance." Buck's piercing gray eyes looked up into hers. "I'm pledging my grandma's ring and my sacred honor that you're the one for me. You always have been. I was just too blind to see it."

Tears sprang to Gloria's eyes. Tears of delight. Tears of trepidation. She'd worked hard to become her own woman. Learning to stand on her own two feet. Could she give all that up? What would Buck expect of her? She placed a stubborn hand on her hip. "I suppose you'd want me to give up my business. Become a dutiful little housewife…"

"No. Don't change a thing." He grinned. "Just be who you are. That's all I can handle."

"Are you messing with me?"

"No. I'm asking you to be my wife." He held the ring steady in his fingers.

"Things are moving kind of fast," she said, stalling. "We've both just come back to faith... Shouldn't we give it some time to settle in?"

"We've wasted enough time already, don't you think?"

Gloria battled a wave of uncertainty…and fear. "What do we even know about love?"

If Buck's knee was aching after pressing so long into the hard deck, he didn't show it. He grasped her hand and spoke aloud, "I know this…" he said. "Love never gives up. And I'm not giving up on you, Gloria. Not now. Not ever."

Gloria blinked. "You'd love me like that?"

"Yes. I would."

Her heart filled, aching with longing. Buck was a man of his word. At that moment, Gloria fiercely wanted to be a woman worthy of him. "Then…I'll… I'll try," she said.

"Is that a *Yes*?"

Gloria discarded the snarky answer that came to mind. She pulled him to her instead.

Sheriff Buck Buchanan—her strong, smart, hunky, thoroughly exasperating man.

"Yes...Yes...Yes!" She showered his face with kisses. "I'm not getting any younger."

He slipped the engagement ring on her finger. "Just more beautiful each day," he said with a grin.

In the doorway, a smattering of applause broke out.

"Bravo!" shouted Kyle.

Charlotte burst into happy tears.

Rowdy beamed. "Congratulations, you two. Our first proposal at the Old Mill."

Kyle untied his apron. "The Buttermilk Falls grapevine will be off and running by first light."

"At a full gallop," threw in Rowdy.

A silly smile lit Buck's face. "I'm counting on it." He kissed Gloria soundly on the lips in front of God and everyone.

Gloria snuggled into his side, feeling whole...feeling loved.

The soft opening of the Old Mill Restaurant was upon them at last. Kyle donned his official work attire for the first time. He lifted a custom flour-sack apron from its shipping box. Unfolding it, Kyle ran a hand across the striking red and gold Old Mill logo printed on the front. This dream had been a long time coming. He slipped the apron on over his white shirt and black dress pants—his black athletic shoes the only nod to the grueling hours-on-his-feet evening ahead. The same restaurant logo was emblazoned on the requisite black baseball cap he settled on his head. All of the workers would be dressed in like fashion, giving unity and a touch of class to the establishment, and setting them apart from their guests.

Guests. The word rolled around in his head. For a long while, the restaurant had been all about him. What *he* envisioned. What *he* wanted it to look like. What menu items *he* fancied. His ego trip as the proud owner, making it all happen. But this night, he felt differently. Tonight, especially, it wasn't about him. It was all about true hospitality—all about the guests.

Tonight, for this special soft opening, they'd invited friends and family to a small, intimate gathering to celebrate.

The next day—just a few days past the New Year—would be the official grand opening for the public. Kyle sure hoped folks would show up. His dreams and his bank account depended on it. Hopefully, by then, they'd work out any last-minute kinks.

But this evening was more of a pre-opening party. A party for those he'd grown to love in this town. His stomach knotted in anticipation. Kyle ran a damp cloth over the spotless counter, waiting for the first of the invited guests to arrive.

He and Rowdy had worked months for this moment. His thoughts drifted back to the first day he'd come to Buttermilk Falls...running away. Back then, he'd wanted a place to hide. A place to lick his wounds. What he'd found instead was a place to belong.

Now he wanted to create that for others. A space to sit and chat. A spot to relax with good food and honest conversation. A mellow place to cheer folks up. Kyle swallowed. He was asking a lot of an old mill.

The main door swung open. Show time.

Gloria, the honorary hostess for the evening, greeted Gabe and Lizzy and their kids at the door. "Right this way," she said, ushering them to a family table. If Gloria's diamond engagement ring flashed in the candlelight, it wasn't her fault.

Lizzy gave her a side hug and a few words of congratulations. "All the best to both of you," she said. "It took a really special women to bring Buck to his knees."

Gloria could only laugh, a slight blush creeping up her cheeks.

Wilma hustled over with some menus. "Hi, Lizzy... Gabe." She grinned at Max and Chloe and dropped a kiss atop baby Grace's head. "The Timber Burger's the early bird special tonight." She winked at Max. "With sweet-potato fries." She filled their water glasses. "Chef's choice tonight is the glazed pork chops with a cranberry/orange sauce, steamed asparagus, and roasted rice pilaf with scallions."

"What's *pill-off*?" asked Max.

Wilma grinned. "Think of it as rice that gets all gussied up by putting on a nice dress and earrings. You'd like it."

"Think I'll stick with them sweet tater fries."

"Can I have some *pill-off* with my burger?" asked Chloe. "I like to dress up." Her gaze wandered to the lights of the soda fountain. "And a big bowl of ice cream...covered in chocolate sauce with three cherries on top."

"I'll leave that to your folks to decide," Wilma said, diplomatically.

The place was quickly filling up. Kyle noted each new arrival. Rowdy's son Wyatt and daughter-in-law Amy. Doris and Harley from the farm. Sheriff Buck, who couldn't stop smiling after nuzzling Gloria's neck on the way in.

Lucille, the mercantile manager, bustled inside—her bright eyes darting about, eager as a country mouse to take in all of the details. Fresh fodder to be dispensed over the counter free of charge and most likely free of any self-editing before spilling out to her hapless customers. No doubt Lucille relished her front row seat to the juiciest town gossip since Doc Amy accidentally dyed Jeb's prized Suffolk lambs pink.

Kyle drew in a breath as the front door banged open. *Oh Oh. Here she comes.* Maggie, owner of the local diner strode in. She'd been invited in hopes of taking some of the sting out of the fact that the Old Mill was her newest competition. The woman barreled inside, head high, wearing one of her usual flowered dresses...and a frown.

Rowdy ushered Maggie to a table in the center of the room, seating her next to Lucille. "Don't fret," he reassured. "We're not even open for breakfast." He pulled out her chair, waiting while she was seated. "Besides, nobody can top your delicious smoked bacon and buttermilk pancakes smothered in real maple syrup." Rowdy filled her water glass. "Together, maybe we can get local folks eatin' out more often."

"Harumph!" Maggie snorted. "Don't bother sugar coating things. Folks are always a sucker for anything new."

Lucille scooted her chair closer and touched Maggie's arm. "Just relax and enjoy it. Think of it as a chance to eat someone else's cookin' for a night. Have someone wait on you for a change."

"Easy for you to say," Maggie retorted. "They're not coming after your business."

"Don't be ridiculous, Maggie," said Lucille. "Folks'll still come to the diner. The breakfast crowd. Folks stoppin' in after church. The Bubbas comin' every day for sweet rolls and mid-mornin' coffee..."

"That bunch of old geezers..." snorted Maggie. "They take up the corner booth for two hours and leave me with a measly pile of ones and coffee rings on the table top."

"And you love every minute of it," Lucille reminded. "The best part of your day, just before the lunch rush on reuben sandwiches and apple pie. And the kids love your mac and cheese."

Maggie scanned the menu. "Don't even see any mac and cheese on here."

"My point exactly. Different strokes for different folks."

"Don't you dare bring up the Bubba's at the mercantile, Lucille," Maggie warned. "They're my old geezers and I won't have you badmouthing 'em."

Lucille leaned back and laughed. "As if I'd ever..."

Kyle hustled between the kitchen and the tables. The back of the house was running smoothly, for the most part. Rowdy had only burned a few burgers trying to manage a large order while grilling onions for on top. And his cowboy chili was getting rave reviews. Maybe Rowdy's chuckwagon experience was more extensive than he'd let on.

The new chef, William, was a marvel. He managed flaming pans and steaming pots with ease, adding garnishes of parsley and lemon to the beautifully plated meals, like a maestro leading an orchestra. Kyle had lured him away from the Culinary Institute with photos of Lost Lake and the promise of a splashy photo spread in the Edibles of Plumas County magazine. In Buttermilk Falls, William could be a big fish in a little pond, bringing a professional cache to a historical site. Anyway, that's what Kyle told him...and the magazine. Kyle figured the warmth of the community would make up for any false expectations. Fingers crossed.

All the slicing and dicing prep of the early afternoon by the teens was paying off. Meals were coming out in about fifteen minutes. Burgers sooner than the pork chops.

He wiped the sweat from his brow and carried a tray of drinks to the front of the house. A pleasant buzz of conversation rose above the background music. The lighting from lamps, candles and the hanging crystal chandeliers created a soft glow. The artwork, plants and wall art, including the giant saw blade, gave a cozy feel to the space. It was just as he imagined. Couples in quiet corners, families gathered at the larger tables, kids dipping French fries in ketchup, adults sipping wine.

In a town where everybody knew everybody, there was a warm camaraderie as greetings were exchanged and folks stopped by each other's tables or pulled up a chair. Laughter spiced the air like cinnamon sticks in cider.

Even though evening wasn't prime time for the soda fountain, Kyle noticed that Charlotte had attracted a group of teens and a smattering of youngsters who perched on the red-leather stools, watching in fascination as she took a mini-blowtorch to one of her trademark S'more Sundaes. Her bright eyes and mane of red hair were a beacon of light, as she spilled merriment and ice cream confections from behind the counter.

Max sat on a swiveling stool at the soda fountain and swung his legs, spinning himself around in a lazy circle. Then he settled, watching the yellow flame of Charlotte's little blow-torch melt a mound of marshmallows into toasted goo, atop a bowl of ice cream and graham crackers. She handed it to a customer. Max licked his lips. This place was amazing.

He'd never seen the likes of the lit *Soda Fountain* sign behind the counter, or so many kinds of ice cream and toppings to choose from…the fixings sitting there right in front of him. Heck, now he wished he'd skipped the Timber Burger and sweet tater fries. Beside him, Chloe was already digging into her ice cream sundae, chocolate sauce dripping down her chin. Since ice cream was her idea, he'd let her order first.

"And what will you have, Max?" Charlotte turned toward him. "Your folks said to put it on their tab... So, choose anything you'd like."

Had he died and gone to heaven? In the soft lighting of the soda fountain, Max studied his reflection in the mirror—blond hair neatly combed, freckles dotted across his nose. He'd grown tall enough that his image showed over the glasses and pewter bowls stacked below. His big smile bounced right back at him. Max looked away and studied the menu board on the wall. So many choices... "What should I get?"

"How about a banana split?" Charlotte suggested. "With two scoops of ice cream...maybe chocolate and vanilla?"

"You got any strawberry?" Max asked. Strawberry was his favorite.

"Sure do." Charlotte pulled out a long silver bowl and peeled a banana. "So...one scoop strawberry, one scoop vanilla?"

"Yep. Does it come with whipped cream?"

"Of course." She scooped ice cream on top of the sliced banana and reached for a ladle. "And chocolate sauce with chopped nuts and a cherry on top...if you want."

Max's eyes widened. "All that doesn't cost too much?"

Charlotte glanced over at Gabe and Lizzy's table. She pointed to Max and the banana split and gave a questioning thumbs up.

Lizzy was tending to the baby, but Gabe responded with a wink and a double thumbs up.

"He says it's okay," said Charlotte. "After all...he's your dad, and this is a special night."

Warmth filled Max's chest. He nodded and took in a breath. This new feeling had something to do with Gabe's strength and the kindness underneath. Something to do with the quick smile Lizzy sent his way as she wiped baby food from little Grace's chin. Something about Aunt Wilma patting him on the shoulder as she passed by with a tray of food. With family all around, Max didn't have to worry about any haints tailing him here.

Charlotte squirted whipped cream over the chocolate sauce on his huge banana split. Max noticed the nod and smile she gave her own pa, Rowdy, as she put an extra cherry on top and handed it over.

"Thanks." Max grinned, digging into the treat. Turned out he wasn't as full up as he'd thought.

Looking around, Kyle noted all the people who'd come alongside him to help make this restaurant happen. Charlotte's friends, who he'd hired at Rowdy's insistence, were sprinkled around the place like chopped nuts on whipped cream—fiddling with the computers, bussing tables, prepping salads, washing dishes in the back. Their high spirits were contagious.

Rowdy, flipping burgers on the grill. William, the chef they'd stolen away from the Culinary Institute, hefting a flaming pan in the kitchen. Gabe, booted feet resting on the floors he'd helped reclaim—Kyle's mentor for all things construction. Lizzy, who'd welcomed him to their supper table more times than he could count, now eating at *his* table. He was surrounded by townsfolks and friends. Family.

If only Brooke was here.

Unfortunately, she'd been called to Sacramento for a big project and wasn't due back until the end of the week.

Since their heart-to-heart at Singing Springs, he'd been calling her every day.

More compliments came in as the evening wore on. *Can't believe what you've done to the old place. Lovely. Inviting. Splendid food. Love the chandeliers. Can't wait to come back.*

It was all heady stuff. Exhaustion and triumph warred in Kyle's body and floated in his head.

Kyle was carrying a stack of dirty dishes to the kitchen when he saw her. Brooke sat on a stool at the soda fountain. She wore black skinny jeans tucked into knee high boots and her long chestnut hair cascaded down her back. When she turned toward him, the eyes that met his were as green as the emerald sweater she wore.

Had he conjured her from his earlier vision of the girl of his dreams walking into his restaurant…sitting at this very soda fountain? Falling madly and hopelessly in love at the sight of her? She smiled up at him. She was real, after all.

He hurried over. "How did you get away?" He took her hand.

"Claimed a family emergency," she said. "This was far too important to miss."

"Thank you." He kissed her on the cheek. "I needed you here."

"And I needed to be here." She looked around the cozy restaurant, full of family and friends. "Is it everything you imagined?"

"More," said Kyle, drinking in the sight of her. "More than I deserve."

Charlotte came over to their end of the fountain bar. "Would you two like to share a sundae?" She was always on alert for romance.

"Not right now. But thanks." Kyle tugged Brooke along with him, out the open French doors, to the deck. They settled into the Adirondack chairs by the firepit, the blaze warm and inviting. Music played, as soft and soothing as the murmur of Coyote Creek below.

"Heard the sheriff just got engaged…" Brooke murmured. "…to Gloria."

"Yep. Right here by this firepit."

"And you did some matchmaking?"

"I did what I could. But Buck was already smitten, pure and simple."

"Nice." Brooke leaned against him.

And it was... Very nice.

Just over a year ago, Kyle had landed here...almost by accident. Wanting only to get away from all he'd become. The year had changed him. Living in the woods. Working with his hands. Following his dreams.

Kyle held Brooke's hand and looked toward the warm, welcoming light escaping from the lit windows of the Old Mill Restaurant—his restaurant. Laughter and high spirits spilled out the open door. It had only been missing the people to bring it to life. The good people of Buttermilk Falls.

Out of the shadows, Rascal scampered across the deck and put a paw on Kyle's knee. Kyle slipped the raccoon a bit of kibble.

"Thanks, Rascal," said Brooke. "...for setting me straight." She ran a hand along his furry back as he scuttled away.

The waning gibbous moon climbed above Lonesome Mountain, painting the surrounding pines with strokes of silver. Kyle held Brooke close and she rested her head on his shoulder. He breathed in the flowery scent of her. Kyle intertwined her small fingers with his, peace filling his heart. Here in the high country of Buttermilk Falls, at the Old Mill—with Brooke—he'd found his home at last.

A log settled into the fire, shooting colorful sparks into the dark night sky. The flickering flames softened the couple's features and lulled them into wistfulness. Behind them, the red paddle wheel turned, churning the deep waters in an ageless song of life. An eternal song of love and longing.

Acknowledgements

Many thanks to my writer's group, the Ojai Scribes: LaNette Donoghue was quick to give a word of encouragement and a keen observation to sharpen my prose. Anne Boydston reminded me to keep my descriptions short and delighted to assign two hearts to a worthy section. Patric Peake helped me keep my men's voices manly, my plot on point, and my spirits up. I miss you every day. You have all been such a blessing to me.